Lyons and Tigers and Bears

Also by Dermot Meagher
Judge Sentences: Tales from the Bench

With Robert Coles, M.D. and Joseph Brenner, M.D.
Drugs and Youth

Lyons and Tigers and Bears

A Judge Joe Lyons Mystery

Dermot Meagher

*For George Gillow,
The nicest man in town —
whatever town he is in —
+Dermot M.*

No part of this publication may be reproduced, stored in
a retrieval system, or transmitted in any form or by any means,
electronic, mechanical, photocopying, recording or otherwise,
without the prior written permission of the author.

Book and cover designed by Charles L. Ross
Cover photography by Charles L. Ross

Copyright © 2012 by Dermot Meagher

All rights reserved.

ISBN: 10-0-615-55911-5
ISBN-13: 978-0-615-55911-7

To
Renato Cellucci

CONTENTS

Joe Lyons' Righteous Indignation 11

The Tie Up 18

The Early Education of Joe Lyons 26

Reality Sets in for Joe 37

A Fat Plot Thickens 47

Joe's University Education 53

Confrontation in the Cathedral Crypt 61

Joe Crashes His Coming Out Party 72

Good Advice Well Taken 82

Joe Cannot Hide in Ireland 98

Joe Never Could Hide in Ireland 106

Surprises at the Ancestral Home 114

Young Joe Falls in Love 125

The Endurance and Changeability of Love 129

More Mystery in the Homeland 136

Down Mystery Lane 154

Venice and Veronese 171

- 179 A View of San Giorgio
- 190 A Dog Barks in Church
- 205 Joe Returns to Court
- 213 Joe's Ethical Dilemma
- 220 Joe Goes to Provincetown
- 232 A Surprise Family Reunion
- 247 An Angel at the Meat Rack
- 269 Passion at the Dick Dock
- 291 Return to Boston
- 297 Revelations at the Dolmen
- 307 Sergeant Detective Shaughnessy Does Extra Duty
- 315 Return to Ireland
- 326 Meanwhile, on Madison Avenue
- 333 Escape from Ireland
- 342 An Impromptu Vestry
- 353 Bumpy Business at Saint Patrick's

Principal Characters
more or less in order of appearance

Sergeant Detective Shaughnessy of the Boston Police Department

Joe Lyons, the Honorable Joseph Lavin Lyons, Massachusetts Appeals Court

Dino Randozza of Charter Street in the North End, Boston

Maureen Randozza, Dino and Rocco's niece,
 also daughter of Tim Ronayne's sister

Tom Murphy, a lawyer in a big firm, an old friend and advisor to Joe Lyons

Monsignor Rocco Randozza, later Bishop Rocco Randozza of Hartford

Tim Ronayne of Dundalk, County Louth, Ireland

Josie Lavin of Providence, Rhode Island, the aunt of Joe Lyons

Giuseppina Randozza, mother of Dino, Rocco, Aldo and
 the late Vito Randozza, grandmother of Maureen and Lorenzo Randozza

Lorenzo Randozza, the son of Aldo Randozza, nephew of Dino and Rocco

Nora Lavin, Joe Lyons' cousin by marriage of Ballyfirglin, County Louth

Grainne Lavin, a nurse, Joe Lyon's cousin from Ballyfirglin and Paris

Maeve Sand, a painter, Grainne Lavin's lover, also from Ballyfirglin and Paris

Professor 'Paddo' Barmesian, an Irish scholar

Peter Lavin, Joe Lyon's cousin and handsome grandson of Nora Lavin

James Ronayne Ferrick, the 19-year-old redheaded nephew of Tim Ronayne

Donal Callahan, a colorful and helpful professor in New York

Joe Lyon's Righteous Indignation 1

"And where did you meet him?" Sergeant Detective Shaughnessy asked.

"We met…we met on the…on the…on the computer," Joe replied.

"What do you mean?"

"There's a Web site for older men and their admirers, for people who like them, gerontophiles they're called. That's where we met." Joe was getting irritated. *Why do I have to go through this,* he thought? *I'm the one who was robbed. Why do I have to explain myself to this baby faced gumshoe?*

Joe thought again, from the more judicious side of his personality. *You're explaining yourself because you were robbed, jerk. You took a guy home who tied you up with your own neckties, while you were naked and tumescent, before the Viagra wore off. He took photos of you with your own digital camera and then ripped off the camera. He stole your memory box—an antique mahogany box, with your initials on top, JLL, lined in green velvet containing your sentimental belongings and some valuable ones too: your father's gold cuff links; your great grandfather's Civil War medals; two of Arthur Bruce's sable paint brushes that he'd left at your* house just before you broke up; holy cards for dead relatives, friends and lovers; some dried flowers wrapped in fancy handkerchiefs; an ascot you wore in a period of extreme pretension; pictures of yourself (in the third grade, and naked in a field in the lotus position much later); pieces of old china found in the Boston Public Garden; a piece of slate from the wall outside the kitchen door of your mother's house in Newport; rings and other love presents from old romances, including a souvenir from Trinity College in Dublin which looked like a fragment of a page of* The Book of Kells.[1]

The bastard threw the box into a beautiful leather bag that you had bought at Papini's in Florence by the banks of the Arno. That's why! Now stop whining and answer the aging Irish boy detective.

"Tell me about this Web site," said the detective.

Christ, now he's sounding like a shrink, thought Joe.

"It's called *The Gray & Gay Network*." *That name is just too cute*, Joe decided all of a sudden. "You get it up on the computer and tell it what you're looking for. I told it that I am 65, 6′3″, 220 lbs., green eyes, white hair all over, in great shape, looking for anyone 30 to 50 in Massachusetts. I wanted to pick from that select bunch."

"You don't look 65," the detective said.

"I'm not, but on this site people are looking for older guys. I'm not 6′3″ either and I weigh more like 240, but you have to start somewhere. Five ads popped up. Three had photos that didn't interest me. His photo did."

The detective did not ask the obvious question, which was "Why?" Instead he said, "What did they say?"

"I'm not sure."

"The photo was that good, huh?" the Detective said conspirato-

---

[1] *The Book of Kells* is the national treasure of Ireland. It was transcribed in the 9th century by Irish Monks at Iona, an island off the coast of Scotland. It is believed that *The Book of Kells* originally contained 370 folios (a piece of vellum folded in half to make four pages) and that each folio was 14 1/2 inches by 10 1/4 inches before being cut down in the 19th century. There are at least 30 folios missing. Most of the missing folios are from the front and the back of the book. They include some elaborate initial pages. There are also some duplicate pages.

rially, with a little smile.

That threw Joe off. *Could the detective be gay too, or just a computer geek?* Joe knew some Boston cops who were gay, but not all of them.

"I just didn't pay too much attention to the other information. They're usually lies anyway," Joe said. "Wait a minute! Wait a minute! In the ad he said that he was interested in the Middle Ages. Later he said that he knew about *The Book of Kells*."

"Why do you remember that?"

"Because it was a surprise to me that an Italian would be interested in *The Book of Kells*."

"Anything else? Did he give a name?"

Joe paused, and then said, "He said that his name was Felix and that he'd been in the seminary."

The Detective's eyes lit up. "What seminary? How old was he?"

"He said that he was 40, but he could have been lying down just like I lied up. Everyone under 45 looks the same to me."

Joe didn't say anything about *The Book of Kells* souvenir. If he did, he would have to say how he got it.

"He said that he studied at St. John's Seminary in Brighton and then went to the American College in Rome. Why are you so curious about the seminary?" Joe asked.

"Because I was there, at St. John's, and I'm 40. And I'm not lying—up or down," said Sergeant Detective Shaughnessy. "How did he tie you up? How did you get loose, Joe?"

"He tied my hands behind me and my feet at the ankles—with my neckties! He left the front door open a bit. The tie at my ankle was a little loose so I hobbled over to the door on my knees and opened it further with my nose. That's how I got this scratch," Joe said pointing to a mark on the left side of his nose. "Then I hopped to the elevator and pressed the button with my nose. When I got to the lobby I screamed. Larry, the doorman untied me without asking a word. I asked Larry a few questions. He said that he hadn't seen anyone leave carrying my Florentine leather bag. He seemed anxious to get back to his newspaper and radio."

"You're kidding," said Detective Shaughnessy, trying to restrain a laugh. "He sounds like a New York doorman. 'See no evil: Speak no evil: Hear no evil.'"

"Well, he's been at the building a long time. Larry minds his business, which most people appreciate, and he helps the old ladies with their packages," said Joe, wondering why he was defending the doorman. Could it be because Larry had turned a blind eye on some of Joe's visitors over the years?

"You didn't save the picture of this thief, this 'Felix,' on your computer, did you?" asked Sergeant Detective Shaughnessy, knowing full well that Joe would have.

Joe hesitated, then said, "The picture doesn't show his face, if you know what I mean. It's flashed out. It looks like he might have a moustache in the picture but you can't really see."

The detective nodded understandingly. "Is his original message with the photo on AOL? You can call it up from here."

Joe hesitated some more, and thought, *Oh fuck, why did I ever come here? Why did I ever report this? It's just getting worse. I can't tell if this guy is gay or just playing with me. Now he wants my jerkoff fantasy photos!*

"So, I'll just step outside and you call up the photo. I'll be back in a few minutes," Sergeant Detective Shaughnessy said. "We've got a color printer if we need it," he added proudly. Joe noticed that Shaughnessy wasn't bad looking himself, particularly after he took off his jacket. He had broad shoulders and a big chest like a swimmer. His hair, once blond, was going white and it was hard to tell where one color began and the other ended. He had good skin, probably never smoked, Joe thought, and wasn't a boozer. He wasn't Joe's usual type, but he must've been a looker in his day. He reminded Joe of somebody but, in all the excitement of the night, Joe couldn't put his finger on who it was.

Joe got into his email and his saved files. There was his assailant. The photo was a naked, almost-full body shot; the guy was coming out of the shower with a hard-on. In the photo his big chest was covered with silky black hair across the pectorals, which then grapevined down to his navel, expanded across his stomach like wings, then snaked down to and spread around the ample erection he was holding in his right hand. The photo produced a combination of fear and desire in Joe at the same time.

The man in the photo had a beautiful body, and the body really belonged to him, unlike a lot of other photos that Joe had seen on the computer. Joe discovered that much last night. They both got naked before Felix came back from the kitchen with a butcher knife and tied Joe up with the two Brooks Brothers and one Hermès tie. Joe had even kissed the guy and was willing and ready to do much more.

Joe wanted to leave the police station, but he was in too deep now. So he enlarged the photo on the screen, got up and walked around the room. *How did I get myself in this mess?* Joe thought. *I hadn't had sex with a man in three years. I was just killing time on the computer and this guy appeared. He looked good. So,....*

Just then Sergeant Detective Shaughnessy reappeared. He walked over to the computer, looked down at it, paused, more than 10 seconds, and then said softly, almost into the machine, "I know that man."

"How can you say that?" asked Joe. "You can't see his face."

The Detective turned, looked hard at Joe and said, "We had a pool at St. John's Seminary and a locker room. I swam every day and so did he."

"Oh," said Joe meekly. "But, how would you remember him?" Joe added after a thoughtful pause.

Sergeant Detective Shaughnessy smiled across the metal desk at Joe and said, "The body hair distribution. His name's not 'Felix.' That's Rocco Randozza of the Revere Randozzas, Point of Pines, to be specific. He was always showing off that chest hair. He'd either wear his shirt open three or more buttons or he'd pull a tuft up above his collar, his clerical collar. It's a little grayer now but still magnificent."

"Where's the gray?" Joe asked, taking Shaughnessy's observation of Felix' gray hair as a personal affront. Felix, or Rocco, or whoever he is, was supposed to be young after all. His ad on the *Gray & Gay* said he was 40.

"Up by the neck on the left, look," said Detective Shaughnessy. "There's a tuft of gray up there."

Joe leaned in and looked. "Jesus, you've got good eyes," he said. "Well, what are you going to do?"

"What do you do for a living, Joe?"

"What does that have to do with the fact that I was robbed?"

"We want to know how far you're willing to go with the prosecution of this. It won't be easy. And, for sure, it'll be public, if only in *The Beacon Hill News*. It may be that you can't afford, emotionally or otherwise, to go forward. We really can't force you to go forward either, although the D.A. would say otherwise. You could take a Dixie on the day of the trial. The D.A. could try to argue that this statement by you today, the morning after, is an 'excited utterance, a spontaneous exclamation,' but it isn't and unless we had a real dumb judge presiding, we couldn't get your statement today into evidence, the statement I haven't yet written down," and then Sergeant Detective Shaughnessy winked. "So, think about all this."

Sergeant Detective Shaughnessy paused to let 'this' sink in.

He then continued, "This is what *I* know, Joe. Rocco Randozza stayed in the seminary. I left. Concupiscence, you know. He's now the secretary to the Cardinal. His older brother, Vito, is in jail under the RICO statute and is doing time at various Federal institutions around the country. Aldo, another brother was killed a while ago. Most people think that the boys from Providence did it, but some people, including me and Dino, the youngest brother, also known as "The Tiger," who remains free and lives on Charter Street in the North End next to the cemetery, think that some of our Irish cousins killed Aldo. Dino has already caused to be seriously wounded three men from South Boston as a result of this belief. Dino was very devoted to Aldo, as he now is to his brother Rocco, the Monsignor. Dino could make your life miserable.

"Dino believes that Rocco adds a certain respectability to the family name. Similarly, their mother, Giuseppina, 'Pina' to her friends, who initially opposed Rocco's entering the seminary, has become fond of being included in the Cardinal's Annual Spring Garden Party. She enjoys wearing a big hat and being better dressed than those thick ankled, pink-faced Irish matrons with their blonde streaked hair in navy blue suits and flowered dresses. Pina imports a real Italian Count, albeit from Sicily, as an escort for these events. She also maintains him in an apartment on the Piazza Navona in Rome, to which she retires often to shop and to visit the Pope. You may have seen the annual photo of her with the Pope in *The Pilot*. Her mantillas are legendary. But, perhaps you don't read *The Pilot* anymore, Joe?"

Although the last question sounded like a question, it was also a declarative sentence. Sergeant Detective Shaughnessy knew a lot more about Joe than Joe realized. Joe hadn't thought of his exposure when he called the police. Now he may be in too deep to get out.

"Let me ask you again, Joe, what do you do for a living?"

2 The Tie Up

Three nights before his visit to the police station and his talk with Sergeant Detective Shaughnessy, Joe was sitting bored at his computer. He had rented the video of *The Great Gatsby*, but it did not have the allure that the book had had for him more than forty years before. Robert Redford, for all his talents, didn't cut it as Gatsby. It was hard to believe that he had ever gone to Princeton. Besides, Joe had always pictured Gatsby as someone darker and bigger, like the proctor of his college freshman dormitory, who imitated Gatsby and who, in fact, had gone to Princeton.

The month before, Joe's young friend Mike, a beautiful Gay League tag football player, also an insurance agent, who only liked older, short, stocky Italian men, preferably priests, after hearing Joe complain once again about his sorry love life, asked Joe, "Have you tried *The Gray & Gay Network* yet?'"

"The what?" asked Joe.

"*The Gray & Gay Network*. It's for older guys and their admirers."

"You're kidding," said Joe. "Does anybody get on it? What does it cost? Do I have to give my name? Can you call it up from any computer?"

"Yes, people use it, both old guys and young guys. I'm the September picture of the month—not my face, just my body, face down on the bed—nice bum, if I say so myself. It doesn't cost anything and you don't have to give your name or anything else. I'll show you how to get on. Just remember that these young guys like old guys. You don't have to lie about your age. If you do, just add years to it."

Mike came over to Joe's apartment and showed Joe how to get on *Gray & Gay*. He even put it on Joe's "favorite places" list just after the County Louth Historical Society. Joe called up *Gray & Gay* almost every night thereafter. He corresponded with a cowboy poet in Colorado and a Scottish soldier in Munich. Recently, they either changed the system or Joe got better at it and discovered there was a way to find somebody closer to home.

On a form at the beginning of the website you listed your age and location and then put in the ages and location of the men you were seeking. Joe gave his age as 65 and his location as Massachusetts and said he was seeking men from 30 to 50, also in Massachusetts. Five ads came up; three of them had photos. One of the ads without a photo said, "Good looking Italian, 40, 6′1″, 190lbs, works out, seeks big Irishman, blue or green eyes, gray or white hair, 60 and older. Hairy chest a plus."

After checking the ads with photos attached (two of which were torso shots of poor dears pushing out their chests, the third a full length, droopy-assed nude from behind) and finding none interesting, Joe replied to the "Good looking Italian."

"You've already got my statistics. I'm a big guy, 65, in good shape, green eyes, grey hair rapidly turning white. 100% Irish. You sound interesting. Send me a photo and I'll do the same. My name is Joe." Joe added that his chest was hairy. In the last ten years his back had become fuzzy too, but he skipped that part and hoped that it wouldn't queer the deal.

A photo with a starburst flashed out face, the body naked, tumescent, and coming out of the shower, arrived within the hour. The sender said his name was Felix. He had a chiseled chest perfectly covered with silky black hair, grapevining down to his navel where it spread symmetrically across his stomach like a pair of wings and then snaked down to his endowment.

Where have I seen that body before? Joe asked himself.

Joe sent back a picture of himself in khaki pants and a blue Oxford cloth, button-down shirt standing on the walkway of a beach. That's what Joe always wore in the warm weather. The photo was taken the year before. It was a little bleached, but it seemed honest to Joe. He thought, *I'd really like to meet this guy and I don't want to be embarrassed by not looking like my photo. I don't want him to walk away as soon as he meets me. Maybe he'll not see the other 20 pounds.* The idea that Felix might have liked him chunky never occurred to Joe.

Felix replied with a message that said, "You're hot. I really like you. Send another picture and I will too. I'll send a head shot."

Joe wanted to say, *Don't be ridiculous with the "hot" business.* Instead he sent a picture of himself wearing a brown leather coat standing in a boatyard on Cape Cod in the middle of winter. Joe thought that it was kind of masculine, standing outside in the winter and all. His face was a little clearer in this photo.

"Thanks for the sexy photo. You're *real* hot. You look familiar," Felix wrote. "I think we met before, a while ago. Don't worry. It was good. I'll tell you about it when we meet." Felix never did send the head shot but Joe didn't realize that until later, after the robbery.

Joe was hooked. He replied, "I have no idea where we might have met. I look forward to seeing you in person."

They made a date to meet in Panificio's, a coffee shop on Charles Street, the antiques store street at the foot of Boston's historic Beacon Hill, in three days, a Thursday, at five o'clock p.m.

◊ ◊ ◊

Joe arrived first, or at least he thought he had. He was there exactly on time. That was the way he was, even for less exciting events. He wasn't going to play the tardy ingénue. Joe ordered his tea at the counter and sat at a table in the far corner where he could keep his eye on the door.

While Joe was watching the door somebody slipped into the seat at the table next to him. Joe turned to look.

Actually there were two people at that table. He could see the back of a man's head, and the face of a red haired young woman. It was she who had just sat down. When she got up to go to the counter the man turned around and said, "Hello, Joe, I'm Felix. I'll only be a minute."

Felix was bigger than Joe had imagined. It didn't matter; he was beautiful. The redheaded woman came back before any more could be said. She and Felix talked a little more. The waiter brought her a cappuccino. She never drank any of it. She gathered up some papers that were on their table, tucked them into a red leather portfolio, put on her long black coat, and kissed Felix on both cheeks before she left. "I'll see you at home, Uncle Dee."

"*Ciao*, Maureen. *Va bene.*"

Felix moved over to Joe's table and extended his large right hand. "Nice to meet you at last. You're better looking in person," Felix growled softly.

Joe, whose knees were shaking at the sight of this beautiful man, took the hand and said, "So are you." How Felix could have been better looking when Joe had not seen his face before was a mystery, but Joe felt that he had to say something.

Felix said, "That was my niece. Her father's dead and I try to help her out with financial things. She's thinking of buying a condo in the North End. I'm not so sure she should; it's all changed."

"You don't have a moustache. I thought that I could see a moustache through the blur. It threw me off," Joe said.

"Oh, that was an old photo. I hope I'm not disappointing you," Felix said, smiling, knowing that Joe wasn't disappointed at all. "So, tell me about yourself. Do you come here often? Is this one of your haunts? What do you recommend? The coffee is awful."

"I drink tea." Joe said. "They have that 'infused' stuff. The 'Awake' is good if you're sleepy and the 'Relax' is good if you're jumpy. Would you like me to get you some? Would you like a pastry?"

"I don't eat pastry but get me some of the 'Relax,'" Felix smiled. "I'm a little excited right now."

Joe went to the counter and returned. Felix was looking through some papers which he quickly put back into the inside pocket of his dark green Armani jacket as Joe approached. Otherwise Felix was dressed in black: black slacks, and a black, cashmere, three-button sweater shirt with a collar. Tufts of black hair jumped over the opened collar of the shirt.

Joe wore a navy blue suit, always a good choice for a pink faced, silver haired Irishman, and a Ferragamo small patterned tie with beach umbrellas on it. Joe wore it to remind himself that, in most respects, his life was a day at the beach. One had to get close to see the pattern.

Joe put the tea, the little pot and the cup and saucer in front of Felix. "How long have you been here?" Joe asked.

"Nice tie." Felix said, "I arrived about half an hour ago. I was sitting up near the counter. I saw you come in and case the place."

Joe was embarrassed to have been spied on and blushed a little. It made him nervous, but not so nervous that he was going to walk out. Felix was much too attractive for that.

"I was looking for a moustache. I assumed that you had a moustache," Joe said.

"I haven't had one in ten years. My brother has a moustache. We look alike, but his moustache distinguishes us and he's older. When we both had them we used to get mistaken for each other all the time. It made for some interesting confrontations. Some of my friends would stop him in the street." The emphasis was on "friends." Felix smiled knowingly. Joe didn't know what to say, so he remained silent. Was Felix trying to say that his brother was embarrassed by being confronted by Felix' friends? Were Felix' "friends" really tricks?

Felix went on, "You know, you're a very handsome man. Have you ever been to Fort Lauderdale? There are a couple of bars there full of older men, but you're better looking than any of those guys. Have you been to Tropics? I thought that I might've met you there. There's also a nude beach halfway down to South Beach, Haulover Beach, where a lot of older guys go. Do you know it?"

"No, I don't," Joe said. "I haven't been to Florida in years and then I went to Key West. I have friends in South Beach, though."

"South Beach is OK for models and movie stars," Felix said, "but the older guys and their fans are all in Lauderdale. They call it 'Fort Viagra.'" Felix said.

They both laughed. And Joe loosened up. "Oh, I wouldn't know about that."

"That's good. Lucky you: your partners are lucky too." Felix said. Felix paused and then asked, "What do you want to do now?"

"I'd like to take you home and take all your clothes off," Joe said quietly, surprising even himself with his candor.

Felix smiled, stood up and buttoned his jacket.

They walked up the hill to Joe's apartment almost at the top of Beacon Street, almost to the State House.

◊ ◊ ◊

"That was quite a hike. You must have good legs," Felix said as soon as they got inside the door. The front hall was small but opened up onto a big living room looking over the Boston Common. There were lots of books and some good paintings, not all traditional. There was a well worn oriental on the floor, a rose-colored couch and two easy chairs; the one on the right had a reading lamp over it and piles of books and magazines beside it on both sides.

"The legs are willing, but the bladder is weak," Joe said as he headed to the bathroom to his right. "I have to go pee. I'll be right out. Sit down. I'll be out in a second."

When Joe returned to the living room, zipping up his fly, there was Felix, stark naked, tanned all over, looking better than his ad, walking towards Joe. He kissed Joe on the mouth. "I've got to take a shower," Felix whispered, licking Joe's ear. "Take your clothes off and lie down on the bed. I'll find you."

Joe did as he was told. He listened to the shower impatiently. *When will it stop?* Joe thought. *How lucky am I! I can't believe this.*

Finally the shower did stop. Felix came into to the bedroom with his hair slicked, drying himself off with a big pink towel. He had thick black hair across his chest perfectly covering his pectorals. It snaked down to his belly button, where it winged out, then narrowed in on its way to the bush surrounding his dick.

Felix dropped the towel to the floor and lay down next to Joe. They kissed, rubbing and patting each other as they explored each other's bodies. Joe reached down to Felix's crotch. Felix was hard as alabaster. Felix reached down for Joe. Joe was getting there.

"Where's some lotion? Have you got any lotion? I'll give you a massage," Felix said.

"There's some in the linen closet off the bathroom," Joe whispered.

"Turn over. I'll be right back," Felix said softly. Joe turned over onto his stomach.

The next thing Joe felt was Felix sitting on his bum and the lotion being squirted down his spine. Felix hadn't warmed up the lotion in his hands like a real masseur. Joe jumped at the coldness of it, but he really didn't mind. He would have accepted ice cubes he was so sex-starved. The lotion was spread across his back and down to the top of his bum, just before the crest of his ass where Felix was sitting.

Joe moaned, lowly and approvingly. *Now we're getting down to it*, he thought.

"You like that?" Felix said, "I want to please you. Put your hands behind your back. Reach for my cock behind you. Use both hands."

Joe did and may have even touched Felix' dick; big and hard as a rock is how he remembered it, resting in the cleavage of his ass. Then he felt Felix holding his hands together. The next thing Joe remembered was that Felix was tying Joe's hands together.

"Don't move. I've got a knife, a big knife, from your kitchen," Felix said lowering and hardening his voice at the same time. "It's the butcher knife with the black handle. I'm not going to hurt you. Just stay still. OK?"

After his wrists were bound Joe felt Felix tying his ankles together.

"What do you want?' Joe mumbled, his face in the pillow. *This is what I get for using the goddamn computer*, Joe thought.

"Just a few things. Just a few things. Things don't matter. They aren't worth getting hurt for. Are they? I'm going to take some stuff." Felix said, as if in a trance. "I know what I want."

"The stuff. The stuff, where did you hide it? It's supposed to be in the top drawer. Oh it's in with the boxer shorts. You look good in boxers, Joe. Real good."

Felix repeated, "Stuff, stuff, stuff," as he walked around the room, opening drawers and looking through the closets. "Don't move, Joe. Don't move," Felix added to the mantra, talking as if dazed. "I really do like you, Joe. You're very sexy. I like big, old, Irish guys. Pink and gray. Pink and gray. Polar bears, Polar bears. Furry and fuzzy. That's what I like, Joe. Maybe I'll come back and finish the rub. We can make love then, Joe. I'll be the boy. You'll be the Monsignor. Goodbye, Joe. Don't rush after me. Give me some time to get away," Felix added before he went out the door.

Joe waited until he heard the elevator arrive before he tested his restraints. They were not loose and he couldn't get them loose. Joe rolled off the bed and hopped to the door on his knees.

3 The Early Education of Joe Lyons

In September of 1958 Joseph Lyons came up from Newport to study at Harvard College. He was a sensitive young man of 17, very handsome, tall, slim, with a head of thick, curly black hair. His skin was creamy white and his eyes were very green. "Black Irish," they call his looks. Depending on which legend you believed, the Black Irish were descended from either the original Celts or the Spaniards wrecked off the West coast of Ireland during the ill-fated Armada.

Joe went to secondary school at St. George's on Purgatory Road above Second Beach in Middletown, and lived around the corner on Paradise Avenue in a house that overlooked the beach. The house had its own special Huckleberry Finn path through the marsh to the beach. There was also a path from the undeveloped land across Paradise Avenue from Joe's driveway up the hill to St. George's.

It was unusual for an Irish American boy from Newport to go to St. George's but Joe's father was the Latin and Greek teacher there. His grandfather, on his father's side, had been the groundskeeper, and his great grandmother, also on his father's side, had worked in the kitchen of the school's founder after coming from Ireland in

1854. St. George's was, other than its slender connection to Joe and his Irish Catholic family, a Waspy school, Episcopalian. Its Gothic towers evinced this inclination. They were embellished with gargoyles of young men holding various athletic appurtenances, bats, rackets and the like. From its hill you looked out over Second Beach and to Third Beach as well. It looked like an English landscape in a watercolor.

Usually, Irish Catholics in Newport who had money went to The Priory in nearby Portsmouth, run by the English Benedictines. Joe's father had studied there on a scholarship. That's where he developed his interest in Latin and Greek. And that is where he met his wife, who was the sister of his only friend at the Priory, that place being no less snobby than St. George's when it came to Irish Catholics without money.

Joe's mother was Ruah Lavin and she was the second daughter of a well known Rhode Island PFI (Pre Famine Irish) family. The Lavins came over before the Famine and not because they were starving. They were proud of this and didn't hesitate to let you know their provenance. Ruah's father and his brothers made a small fortune in the construction business during World War ll. Unfortunately, the fortune, which was in four parts because there were four brothers, had to be further divided ten ways when Ruah's father died because Ruah had six brothers and three sisters. Ruah went to school at Elmhurst, the local Madames of the Sacred Heart school, and then to Manhattanville.

Although originally from the Fifth Ward, the Irish enclave of Newport, the Lavins had moved out long ago and Ruah and her siblings grew up in a big house designed by Stanford White (for somebody else) on Red Cross Avenue.

Ruah inherited enough money for the pretty house on the marsh off Paradise Avenue, but not enough to send Joe to the Priory. However, faculty sons went to St. George's for free, so Joe walked up the hill to St. George's every schoolday morning from the eighth grade on. Most of the other kids on Paradise Avenue went to the public schools in Middletown.

Joe did not need all these factors to alienate him from his peers both on Paradise Avenue and at St. George's. He was a sensitive boy who preferred reading to sports—except for swimming. He was afraid of, or repelled by, most of the other kids on the street except for Jackie Crotty, the son of the doctor three houses up the street.

Jackie and Joe went to school together from Miss Fitzpatrick's Nursery School through the seventh grade. Together they explored the beach and the marshes as soon as they were old enough to escape from their mothers or babysitters. They dived off Elephant Rock and climbed dangerously down into Purgatory chasm. They watched hurricanes from Joe's house, then paddled out on surfboards to ride the waves at Second Beach once the storms passed. They fetched water from the well at the end of Paradise Road and explored the old one-room schoolhouse on the way to the well. They walked over to Sachuest Point, the old golf course, and to the World War II Army barracks, and before they were 10 they even rode their bicycles as far as Bishop Berkeley's house on the other side of Green End Avenue.

Harry Sayers met Joe on Joe's first day at St. George's. They each were 12. Harry was a boarder at the school. Harry came from Philadelphia. Harry's family was chaotic, although rich. Each of his parents had been married before and had children from that marriage and each had new spouses and more children. Harry liked to spend time at Joe's monogamous house, which seemed to him peaceful, stable, and polite.

The other boys at St. George's looked down their noses at Joe because he was a day student and a townie, because Joe's father was a teacher while theirs were heirs, stockbrokers or "Captains of Industry"; because he was Irish Catholic rather than Protestant, and mainly because they didn't know him and he was shy. His shyness manifested itself in the appearance of arrogance. He was sardonic, a trait inherited from his mother.

Joe was better looking than most of his classmates and he

dressed better than they did. One of his many cousins owned a men's clothing store up by the Casino on Bellevue Avenue called *The House of Lavin*. It was preppier, yachtier and clubbier than anything else in town. Both yacht clubs, the Ida Lewis and the Newport Yacht Club, ordered their emblazoned blazers from Joe's cousin's store. Joe worked in the store summers and before Christmas, when his schoolmates weren't around. One of the perks was a discount on clothes.

At first Harry Sayers and Joe were friends because they swam together. Harry was a diver and had won lots of prizes. Harry was shorter and more compact than Joe, who was lean and loose with broad shoulders. Joe came to excel at the Australian crawl. Harry was blond, white blond, like the Little Dutch Boy. Unlike pale Joe who burnt in the sun, Harry tanned honey colored.

Joe helped Harry with his schoolwork. They were having a Nineteenth Century British History exam in mid-November and Harry hadn't studied because he was perfecting his dives. Joe loved History and knew the course cold. He'd also learned Irish History, from his Aunt Josie Lavin, his mother's sister, who taught the sixth grade at a public school in Providence. She also sent money to the Irish Rrepublican Army. She was a good counterweight to St. George's and its Anglo pretenses.

Anyway, Joe managed to teach Harry the important events of 19th Century England, the names and dates of Victoria's prime ministers as well as what was happening in Ireland during their tenures. It was like Joe was Harry's Irish hedge school teacher because, of course, their British history teacher wasn't interested in what went on across the Irish Sea except as it affected "the Empire." Ireland was an intermittent thorn in the paw of the great lion, but not worth spending any time on. Ireland got a little attention when Gladstone proposed Home Rule but otherwise it was not relevant. The Great Famine of 1846-1848, which sent most of the Irish in Newport over to America, never came up.

Harry Sayer's grandfather on his mother's side, who had just died, was also Irish-American, of sorts. He was a Donohue from California, the son of one of the founders of the Bank of America. Mr. Donohue had been very kind to Harry during his parents' alcoholic divorces and remarriages. Harry attributed that kindness, rightly or wrongly, to the grandfather's Irishness. Mr. Donohue also left Harry a lot of money. Harry didn't appreciate that yet; the money was still complicated by trusts.

So Joe also taught Harry about Robert Emmet and the events of 1798, "The Union," Daniel O'Connell, the Famine, Thomas Francis Meagher and the Young Irelanders in and after 1848 in Ireland and later in Australia and America, as well as Parnell, the Parnell women, the Land League and Kitty O'Shea later in the century. These characters were much more interesting to Joe. You could hang your hat on their stories while decorating it with the prime ministers, press barons and other British ephemera of the 19th century.

Joe, and through him Harry, liked being subversive and knowing what was going on across the water while Disraeli served the Queen, but they kept it to themselves in order to pass the course.

Harry, for his part, taught Joe how to swim. Joe was a naturally strong swimmer when he arrived at St. George's, but he needed technique. Harry taught him how to breathe in the water, the same way that he taught the little rich kids at the Merion Cricket Club on the Main Line, where he volunteered summers—the same way Harry had learned to swim.

"Breathe in by turning your head and listening to the fishies. Breathe out by putting your face in the water and talking to the fishies." They both laughed at that, but Joe remembered the lesson.

Joe worked for his cousin at the Bellevue Avenue haberdashery, *The House of Lavin*, in the summer. The store's sign had a coat of arms of two lions rampant holding one sword while standing on crescent moons, which his cousin had borrowed from somewhere. Maybe the Marist Fathers had sent it to him. They had quite a little industry doing abbreviated genealogies and escutcheons for aspiring Irish Americans.

Joe finished work at 4:00 every day, bicycled home and then went for a long swim at Third Beach in Middletown where his family kept a cabana. The surf was calmer there and he could work on his technique.

In the summers Joe hung out with Jackie Crotty until the summer between their junior and senior years when Jackie had a girlfriend, from whom he became inseparable. That summer Joe dated girls a little, but really just so he and Jackie could doubledate and so he could be with Jackie. Joe really wasn't that interested in any of the girls, although some of them were after him. He was very goodlooking, all agreed. Sex between teenaged boys and girls was not as common as it is now, although it was talked about just as often. Joe's parents were not concerned about his lack of interest in girls. They welcomed it. Although they were much too Americanized to admit it, they more or less had inherited the Irish Catholic notion of sex as a terrible urge that had to be restrained.

Jackie Crotty had grown into a big lovable guy. He had long dark brown hair, blue eyes, a full chest and a fullback's physique. When he was 12 he was sent away to summer camp along with his brothers because his mother was having another baby. He came back well versed in sex and taught Joe how to masturbate.

Joe and Jackie continued to wank it together until after Jackie found the girlfriend. Joe knew enough not to appear too eager, that that would make the whole thing look queer, a word and concept Jackie had also taught him and taught him to avoid—the appearance of being queer. The sex never amounted to anything more than mutual masturbation, but it took up a lot of space in Joe's head, which even two miles a day in the cold water couldn't evict.

The same thing that scared Joe about sex excited him and he spent a lot of time plotting how to get Jackie alone. In May of their senior year Jackie told Joe, "Joey, I don't think that we ought to be doing this anymore." He didn't give the "this" a name and he didn't call Joe any names so Joe did not feel that he was being labeled by Jackie or even abandoned by him. He was a Catholic boy; he had known for years that they ought not be doing "this," but he was not going to tell Jackie that.

One door closes and another opens, they say. As fate would have it, that summer his St. George's swim pal Harry Sayers stayed in Jamestown at the house of Harry's most recent step-father from Philadelphia. For some reason earlier in the Twentieth Century a number of rich, social Philadelphia families had bypassed Newport and built shingle houses on the next island, Jamestown, in an area facing Newport called the Dumplings or out on the road to the Beavertail Lighthouse. You can still see the aristocratic Philadelphia names, Lippincott, Strawbridge, Wharton, and Biddle on the rural mailboxes by the side of the roads on Jamestown.

Although Harry and Joe were best friends throughout their school years, their friendship was chaste—initially. Joe showed Harry the Newport haunts that he and Jackie had explored when they were younger; Harry spent time at Joe's house; and Joe went to Philadelphia to stay at Harry's stepfather and mother's apartment in Rittenhouse Square over the Easter break. Neither Joe nor Harry had regular girlfriends and they were not interested in hearing about the heterosexual exploits of their classmates, particularly the football players.

In the spring of their senior year Joe was accepted at Harvard and Harry at Brown. They hoped to go to college together but Harry did not get into Harvard and Joe's parents were not too keen on Brown. It had been the school of their forebears' oppressors, after all. Harry and Joe vowed to remain friends, however. Providence was only 45 miles from Boston, they reassured each other. It was just an hour's train ride away.

Because they knew that they were going to be separated the next autumn, early in the summer Joe took the ferry across to stay with Harry in the Dumplings in Jamestown. Joe's parents thought that Harry was a good influence on Joe, that Harry got Joe out of himself. Harry encouraged Joe to swim and Harry took Joe away from his books.

Harry's mother and stepfather were happy that Harry had someone to hang around with. They were in the process of moving up from Philadelphia for the summer but they had seven-year-old twins who wouldn't get out of school until late June. The only people at Harry's stepfather's house were the housekeeper, Hilda Silva, and her nephew, Luiz, who was a gardener and jack of all trades. Hilda and Luiz came from Newport; they didn't stay over in Jamestown, which was kind of "the sticks" in their minds. There were times when Joe and Harry had the house to themselves.

Joe worked most weekends. That was when *The House of Lavin* was busiest. The weekenders came to Bellevue Avenue and wanted to take back a bit of Newport style. The natives and summer men were shopping for dinner jackets or blazers, ice cream colored linen pants and pretty shirts for yacht club dances and Bailey's Beach, to say nothing of parties in the mansions. Anticipating that the Fourth of July week was going to be extra busy, Joe's cousin let Joe take off the weekend before the Fourth.

On Friday night Joe caught the 5:30 ferry to Jamestown from the pier on Thames Street in Newport. Fifteen minutes later Harry met him at the dock in front of the Police Station at the foot of Union Street in Jamestown. Because there was no one at Harry's house they ate at the Bay View Hotel where Harry's mother had set up a charge account for Harry. Harry, just to see if he could get away with it, ordered gin and tonics for both of them.

Joe had never had a drink. Too many of his uncles and cousins sat around their houses in pajamas all day. His mother told him about the Irish propensity to alcoholism, with specific reference to various relatives. One of his uncles, his mother's brother Tom, was even in AA. Joe remembered Tom when he drank. He was a lot of fun up to the point when he would pass out. His wife would have to drive him home, and if she wasn't around, he would be put in the spare bedroom next to Joe where he often fell out of the bed in the middle of the night.

Harry had no such compunctions. He had been drinking with

his parents' consent since he turned fifteen. They always had drinks at lunch. Harry claimed that he really didn't care whether he drank or not, but this night at the Bay View it seemed like a challenge to get served. Besides, Harry had a plan.

The waitress did bring the gin and tonics. Actually they were served twice and Joe had a little buzz that persisted after the swordfish dinner. After a ride around Shoreby Heights, also known as Admiral's Hill, Harry drove out to the Beavertail Lighthouse in an old Plymouth station wagon with wooden sides. Harry parked the car by the side of the road just around the bend beyond the lighthouse. Harry and Joe walked down the rocks to the edge of the water.

"Let's dive in," Harry said.

Although Joe was a little buzzed, he knew his limitations. "No," he said, "The water is too rough here. Let's go down to that beach we passed. What did you call it? 'Concrete Beach?'"

"Mackerel Cove is its real name."

Harry drove back the way they had come and once at Mackerel Cove pulled the car up perpendicular to the water, away from the other teenagers necking in their parents' cars. There was only a crescent moon that night so it was dark. Harry and Joe took their clothes off in the car. Joe kept his boxer shorts on until Harry said, "No, let's go bollicky."

Joe was game; he tossed the boxers into the back seat. The sand was rough as they tiptoed into the water, which was calm and almost warm in this cove protected on both sides by long spits of land. It was like a rectangular notch in the island at its narrowest point.

Splash and then another *Splash*, and they were in, Harry first, then Joe. Somebody amongst the parkers beeped a horn and then the whole row turned their headlights on the water, and beeped in unison. Harry and Joe dove underwater and swam out underwater as far as they could. Harry came up first. Joe emerged 20 feet beyond him. They were laughing; the headlights had gone off. Joe swam in to Harry. Harry said, "Let's race to shore."

They did and Joe, the better swimmer (thanks to Harry's instruction) arrived on shore first. As Joe walked naked up the beach a single horn beeped weakly and one or two of the cars put on their lights briefly, but it was all dark when Harry got out of the water. Joe hovered near the passenger door trying to shake the water off. Harry reached in the back and grabbed an old beach towel. They were on the far side of the other cars shielded by Harry's car from complete exposure of their nakedness.

Harry wrapped Joe in the towel and rubbed him dry—from head to foot. "We have only one towel," Harry said and then he dried himself. They dressed wordlessly. Harry scooted over to the driver's side of the front seat and off they went, Harry flashing his lights and beeping the horn at the parkers in revenge. Harry took a right back to the Dumplings and they were home in two minutes, still laughing at their prank.

Harry immediately went to the pantry where the liquor was kept and made two more gin and tonics. He didn't even ask Joe if he wanted one. He went to the living room and just handed it to Joe. Joe drank it. Harry put some of his stepfather's jazz on the Hi-Fi, *Chet Baker with Strings*. Hi-Fis were new inventions. They had two more gin and tonics as they looked out at Newport's lights from two chintz-covered overstuffed chairs facing a big bay window.

Harry said, "I'm tired. I'm going to sleep in my parents' room. There are two beds. Why don't you sleep there too? There's a great view." Other times when Joe had visited, when Harry's parents were in residence, Joe slept in a little guest room down the hall from Harry. The parents' bedroom was right above the living room and had French doors out to a balcony which was over the bay window they were then looking out.

Joe said, "Yeah, sure."

Up they went to the master bedroom. The two double beds were side by side, about eight feet apart. Both faced the window looking across at Newport. From this height, from Harry's bed, his mother's bed usually, you could also see the House on the Rock Built without Nails, a local folly built by two architects years before.

"I never sleep in pajamas in the summer," Harry said in the dark room.

"Me neither," Joe lied.

"I like sleeping naked," Harry said.

"Me too," Joe lied again. He'd never slept naked in his life.

They each climbed into their respective beds and were silent for a while.

"Come over here and look at the House on the Rock."

Joe went over to Harry, grateful that the dark concealed his excitement.

"Climb in," Harry said.

Joe did.

Reality Sets in for Joe 4

Joe left Police Headquarters on Berkeley Street early in the morning as the sun was coming up and before the commuters and other office workers hit the streets. Boston becomes beautiful very quickly once spring finally arrives. The magnolias and the sickle pear trees were in bloom along Newbury Street and Commonwealth Avenue; cherry and crab apple trees burst out in the Public Garden. There was a particularly magnificent cherry right next to the Japanese lantern at the edge of the pond. The weeping willows were drooping chartreuse.

But Joe, as the Irish say, "wouldn't be looking at it." Joe was very confused. He could go forward with Sergeant Detective Shaughnessy or he could quit right here. If he could "handle the scandal, there would be no problem," Sergeant Detective Shaughnessy said. But Joe wasn't sure that he could handle the scandal.

It wasn't that he was closeted, but there is a difference between being gay in general and being gay in particular. "I don't care what you people do, just don't rub my nose in it," was the guideline. You couldn't tell them the specifics of what you did. Joe had been around long enough to know that.

He remembered when he and Arthur Bruce, then the love of his life, were in Nantucket at the summerhouse of a prominent straight couple who prided themselves on their liberalism. They asked him where he wanted to sleep. They were shocked when he said, "Anywhere, as long as it's in the same bed as Arthur."

"What would the children [15, 13 and 11] think?" they asked. "No, we couldn't do that. You have to be in different rooms."

On the other hand his parents in Middletown professed shock at his divorced cousin and her fiancé sleeping in the same bed. "Your mother is very upset that they sleep in the same bed," said his father. His mother said the same about his father. However, they said nothing about Joe and Arthur Bruce climbing up to the third floor to sleep in Joe's bachelor granduncle's carved mahogany bed. Denial works in strange ways.

What Joe really needed after his visit to the Police Station was to sleep. As soon as he arrived back to his apartment he fell into bed and slept until the middle of the afternoon.

He woke up to the mess of the night before. First he picked up the ties that Felix had pulled from the rack in the closet. Then he picked up the contents of his bureau that Felix had thrown on the floor. Finally he put things back into the drawers they came from. He'd be damned if he was going to let these scars stay exposed.

Apart from Sergeant Detective Shaughnessy, Joe had told no one about his disgrace. He hadn't had time for one thing, having gone to the police at midnight after getting out of the ties that bound him. For another, he was ashamed at having been so trusting and naive. He didn't want to lose the respect of his friends. Although he knew that at least two or three of them loved him no matter what, he also knew that they talked. This story would be in "*Queen Control*" in a minute. The lines would be buzzing.

Joe brooded with a cup of tea and finally decided to call his friend and law school classmate, Tom Murphy. Tom would be bound by the Attorney/Client Privilege. Tom would not be able to talk. He wasn't a criminal lawyer or even a trial lawyer, but he did give good advice and he could refer Joe to someone else if that proved to be necessary.

It was after five but Joe decided to call Tom at the office anyway. Tom was a partner in a big firm and there was someone on the switchboard all the time. The operator could get Tom in a few minutes if he wasn't there. One of Tom's stocks in trade was to call back always within the day.

Tom answered the call himself, "Hi Joe, What's up? Did you see me on television last night commenting on the Bishops latest diatribe against gay marriage? I told the reporter, 'Priests and nuns have been living together in same sex houses for centuries and they get to do it tax free.' Ha! Ha! Ha! That should get them at the Cardinal's Palace on Commonwealth Avenue. I already got four calls—three of them from priests congratulating me—and the *Herald* will probably do another editorial against me. It's a good thing that my name is Murphy and that I do such good charity work. It lets me blast the Church every once in a while."

Sometimes it was hard to get a word in with Tom Murphy, so energized was he by his own accomplishments, but once having got through he gave very good advice. For all the radical talk he was very sensible in other people's affairs. And he wasn't sentimental. Whether that was the result of having worked his way up in a very hierarchical big firm or being descended from subversive Irish farmers who knew how to tug a forelock when they had to Joe was not certain. Joe's tendencies were much more cavalier. That's why he always called Tommy Murphy when he was in a jam. Joe knew he'd get good advice even when it wasn't what he wanted to hear.

"Tommy, I'm in trouble. Can we talk on this line?"

"Would Swords, Healy and Fiske have insecure telephone lines? We're completely tap-proof. 'J. Edgar Hoover is a faggot.' That's what we used to say in the Sixties before we knew we were too. Ha! Ha! Ha! Talk to me."

Joe told Tom Murphy the whole story.

"Jesus, I know that Monsignor Randozza. Come to think of it, he's hot. He's stationed at Holy Cross, the Cathedral on Washington Street in the South End. According to my source, he's up for bishop and maybe for the Chancellor's job. Supposedly it's going to happen after the Cardinal's next trip to Rome. I get all the clerical gossip from Monsignor Pat Hurley at the Cambodian Church in Dorchester. He got sent there after he told his cousin who was a reporter at the *Herald* that the Church ought to think about ordaining women. He thought that it was just chat over the Thanksgiving turkey but the cousin saw it as a way to get a column. Meet me at the Victoria Diner on Mass. Ave in Roxbury at seven fifteen. We'll think of something. Don't panic! Will the detective blow the whistle on you?"

"No," Joe said, "Sergeant Detective Shaughnessy is not a mean guy. And thanks to the Supreme Court gay sex is no longer a crime. Soliciting for it isn't a crime either. If it were, I could invoke the Fifth Amendment. Shaughnessy may even be a sister. He's just a little too cute and knowledgeable and he was in the seminary with Randozza. My gaydar was buzzing after I calmed down a little. I'll be there at seven fifteen."

"If they're thinking of charging you with anything, we'll get Ellen back from California. She always confuses them. She's so beautiful and sexy, but only does gay cases. She's beaten the State Police so often at bush cases that they don't even make arrests for sexing at rest stops anymore. And she's straight besides. Furthermore, she used to be a nun. Now she has a surgeon husband and five kids."

"I know Ellen," said Joe.

"Oh yeah, of course you do. She does lots of appeals," added Tommy. "Seven fifteen at the Victoria then."

"Right," said Joe as he stared at something red in the Oriental rug, partially under the chair just beneath him. He bent over to investigate further. It was a small piece of fabric, like a sample of the color a bishop would wear, red but not scarlet like a Cardinal's robes, folded up into about a two inch square. It had been underneath the magazine that the night before Felix had started reading as Joe went in to pee. Joe unfolded it and there was a little piece of pasteboard attached. *Vestimenti Ecclesiatici, Fratri Fucini, Via dei Cestari, Piazza Rotonda, Roma*, the pasteboard card said in neat Roman script.

Joe folded the cloth and card up again and put it safely in his top drawer. Then he took off his clothes and went into the shower. He hadn't bathed since before going out to meet his admirer at the Charles Street café the night before.

There were black hairs on the bathtub floor. Joe picked one up and examined it. It was thick and long and very black. He thought of gathering them all up and making an amulet, which he would burn, like the *Santeria* ladies who used their ex-lovers' hairs to put curses on them—or to get them back.

En route to his meeting with Tom Murphy Joe couldn't resist driving by Holy Cross, the Catholic Cathedral. It was in the South End, which ironically had become an upscale gay neighborhood and was on the way to the diner. Once on Washington Street, he decided to drive around the Cathedral, which was newly lit and almost handsome in its Victorian imitation Gothic splendor.

"This church was built with the dimes and nickels of working out girls," his Aunt Josie had said to him on a rare trip to see him in Boston. She meant the hard won earnings of Irish domestics in Brahmin households in the late 19th Century. Joe always wondered what the men had done with their earnings, but was afraid to ask. His aunt would probably have said, "They drank it! Like some of your uncles, my brothers! The bastards!"

The Yankees would not permit the Catholic Cathedral in Boston to be built in a prominent place downtown. After it was built on then remote Washington Street they ran the Elevated Street Car in front of it so that the church shook whenever a train went by. The holy sacrifice of the Mass was interrupted by the loud, harsh roar and rattle of the train.

The Elevated, however, had recently come down and Washington Street was becoming gentrified. Construction was everywhere, some of it even sponsored by the Church. Washington Street was torn up and bumpy. As he rode down Union Park Street onto Harrison Avenue and the back of the Cathedral, Joe saw a number of cars parked in the lot between the rectory and the school. He even saw the car of a man he used to have sex with and he saw the one-time paramour get out of his car. *What's he doing here?* Joe wondered. *He still looks pretty good.* Then he remembered that the man told him that he went to an AA meeting in the Cathedral somewhere. Joe remembered thinking it was a peculiar place for an AA meeting.

Joe took a right onto Monsignor Reynolds Way, the Cathedral on his right and the public housing projects on his left, and came back around again. He pulled over to the right side of Harrison Avenue to scout out the scene a little more. More cars pulled into the schoolyard lot and more guys went behind the rectory, between it and the Cathedral. Joe got out of his car, pulled up his collar and walked ten feet behind an older chunky guy, who looked a lot like Joe ironically, and a young, handsome Chinese guy dressed in black Prada (if that's not redundant.) They walked down five stairs leading into the Cathedral directly opposite the back door of the rectory. At the bottom of the stairs the young Chinese guy held the red door open for Joe. Joe just walked on, trying to pretend that he was merely passing through. He walked around the Union Park Street side of the rectory and back to his car on Harrison Avenue.

It was just seven and he still had fifteen minutes before he had to meet Tommy, so he sat in his car. He wanted to go into the Cathedral. Maybe there would be a clue in there. Maybe he'd catch Felix/Rocco with the Cardinal and he could confront him with his infamy in front of the Cardinal. Then the pedestrian traffic into the Cathedral seemed to stop.

But soon another group of men started to assemble around the door of the school on his right. *What is this?* Joe thought as he looked for a familiar face. Some of these men he had seen over the years, in the bars and in the South End or at gay fund raisers, but there was no one he really knew until......wait a minute, there was the robbber!! Felix!! Rocco!! Whatever his real name was! It couldn't be!

Joe dared not look, but he had to. It really was Felix/Rocco. He was dressed down from the night before—just dark slacks and a dark brown leather jacket. *What's he doing with all these gay guys? And him about to be a bishop! Why is he meeting these guys in the shadow of the Cathedral? Could they all be priests? Is this some kind of gay priests group? (If that's not redundant.)*

What do I do now? Do I confront him? Not with all his friends around. Not after what Sergeant Detective Shaughnessy said. There was the new Station 4 up the street on the left a little. *Maybe I should go there and have them call Shaughnessy. What's the point of that? We already know who robbed me. I have to decide what I want to do. And that's why I called Tom Murphy. I'll wait until they go inside and then go to the diner.*

The gathered men didn't go inside in a hurry so Joe started the car without turning on the lights. He reached in the backseat and retrieved a Scally cap. He put it on and pulled it low on his brow and drove away.

Joe couldn't wait to tell Tom about this latest development. He gunned the car as soon as he was past the Cathedral School in front of Station 4. That was not a good idea. Somebody screamed at him. The shout came from a uniformed motorcycle cop coming out of the Station. Joe could see him in his mirror. Joe stopped his car and backed up slowly. The cop came over. Joe rolled down his window.

"What's your hurry, Mister?" said the cop as he approached the car window. He looked hot, was the first thing Joe thought. He was wearing jodphurs and boots. His healthy crotch was at eye level at the car window until he leaned down and laughed.

"Joe Lyons, you old devil! Do you think that I was going to let you pass me by. I recognized this shitbox. What's your hurry? How ya been?"

This vision was Padraic Lowell, the most recent openly gay cop in the Boston Police Department. He'd been a Marine, one of the few to be wounded in Desert Storm. He was given a medal, the Silver Star, and then became a weight training instructor before getting on the police force. Nobody bothered him because of his distinguished service record and his strength. He loved riding the motorcycle. He had a fan club in the South End. Joe had been one of his references for the Police Department and when called, Joe spoke highly of Paddy. As a result Joe could do no wrong in Paddy's book. Hopefully that included speeding on Harrison Avenue.

Joe said, "Can I call you later, Paddy? I'm in a jam. I have to go meet Tom Murphy to talk about it. Can I call you? I have some questions. I need some help."

"Of course, you can, Joe. Just don't ask me to do anything unethical. I love you, Joe, but I took an oath. And so did you, as a matter of fact. Tom's a good man. Tell him to take it easy on the Cardinal." Then Paddy laughed.

"Speaking of the Cardinal, what goes on over there at the Cathedral School tonight?" Joe asked.

"I don't know." Paddy looked over at the Cathedral School. A group of men were still huddled around the school door and it looked like they had expanded. "I'll go over and check it out."

"I really have to go now. I'll be late. I'll call you. Are you still with Owen? I have the number."

"No, we've been separated for a while. I'm seeing some guy on the force and Owen's going out with a Latino guy from Revere. It's OK now, but it was rough at first. I have your number. I'll call you. It's good to see you, ya bum. We'll get together."

Paddy was for real. He really meant it about the oaths and he called his friends "bums." That was usually accompanied by a jab to the shoulder or the stomach.

As Joe drove away Paddy swaggered over to the schoolhouse door as if he was still straddling a motorcycle or at least a big horse. Boy, were those guys going to get a thrill, thought Joe. And maybe that prick, Felix/ Rocco will get a scare.

At the diner Joe parked next to Tom's big Cadillac. For all his left wing politics Tom was still very much part of the establishment and he liked its accoutrements. Joe drove an eight-year-old Ford station wagon. He hated cars and apart from rare occasions like this he only used it to go to Newport to see his mother.

"He's in there," said Andros, the tawny, beautiful son and heir of the founder of the diner, as he pointed to the back room. Tommy was seated in the back booth of the back room. Tommy was wearing a suit. He always wore a suit, except when he was out of town. Tom looked up from his *New York Times* as Joe approached.

"The fucken Republicans in Washington..." Tom started. He ran his right hand through his straight black hair, which had been parted in the exact middle of his head since Joe first met Tom in law school. Tonight the hair appeared to be even a little darker than in those days, but Joe had never asked if Tom colored it. As they grew older together Joe and Tom excused and accepted each other's vanities.

Joe said, "Move to the other side of the table, please. I get claustrophobia if I face a wall."

"You just want to see Andros' ass when he comes in here to pick lint off the floor. Why does he always flash that ass at us?"

"Because he's a Mediterranean man, and they like attention from any source. He'll never put out, but he wants us to want him. And I really do get claustrophobia facing walls. Besides I want to see who comes in. It's my story that I may have to stop telling. You know that a lot of courthouse types come in here. There's just been a real strange update. You won't believe it, Tommy," Joe said all in a rush.

Joe told Tommy about his little reconnaissance mission and about Padraic Lowell.

"Ha! Ha! Ha! They'll love Paddy in his boots. They'll think that it's a *Tom of Finland* drawing come alive. You don't know what that group is? You won't need Paddy to do detective work there. That's the Sex and Love Addicts Anonymous group, SLAA. They're a twelve step group that meets on the top floor of the school." Tom loosened his tie and continued, leaning across the table into Joe, "They used to meet in the basement of the Cathedral. I went a couple of times with......I can't tell you who with. It's anonymous. He was afraid to go alone. You know me; I'm a sport. I'll go anywhere. It really helped him, however. I'm still doing research, as they like to say. Ha! Ha! Did I tell you about my last trip to Amsterdam? You have to go to the Argos bar, to the cellar. It's so hot. Ha, Ha, Ha, Ha! It's not like this prissy city these days."

Tom stopped to stab his eggs, "SLAA is really a good organization and it's helped a lot of people you and I both know. The guys going into the Cathedral basement are an AA group, but you probably know that. It seems like your man has a sex problem. He certainly is kinky, as you should know. Sorry." Tom didn't look sorry at all. He took another bite of the egg. "But why would he go to a meeting right next to the Cathedral? What's that old saying? 'Don't shit where you eat.' I never bring tricks into my law office. Ha! Ha! Ha! Well, maybe once, but nobody was there. It was late at night. Are you sure that it was him?"

"I think so. If it wasn't him, it's his brother," Joe said.

"Well, what do you want to do about it?" Tom said, looking Joe right in the eye.

"I don't know. Yes I do. I want to hurt him. I want to get my stuff back. I want to ruin his little game. I want to expose him."

"And you probably want to fuck him too, or *vice versa*. I never ask my friends' preferences. 'Every tinker has his own way of dancing,' my mother, God rest her soul, used to say." Tom then looked sadly at the now almost empty plate, like where did those eggs go, or was he thinking of his mother? "You can't confront him alone. It should be on your turf or in public. Maybe you can do it when he's all dolled up in his bishop's robes."

"I don't want to wait that long. I want to get him now and make sure he doesn't get the miter and crozier," Joe said.

5 A Fat Plot Thickens

Joe and Tom tried to think up ways to get to Felix/Rocco. One was to confront him at the SLAA meeting the next week. Another was to attend the ten o'clock Sunday Mass at the Cathedral, which was usually celebrated by the Cardinal himself, and slip the good Monsignor a blackmail note. Assumedly, Monsignor Rocco Randozza would be in the Cardinal's entourage and would also be on the altar. Joe and Tom agreed in principle, without specifics, on the latter plot and agreed to meet in Foodies, the market across the street from the Cathedral at 9:45 a.m. the next Sunday. They agreed to work out the details during the week.

This is the plan they devised. Thomas Aloysius Murphy, Esquire, would position himself at the end of Monsignor Randozza's communion line. After receiving the host, Tom would slip Monsignor Randozza a folded note containing a printout of Felix' photo from the "Gray &Gay" website. The note would say that the Monsignor had better return the goods that he took the previous Monday night, or the story, complete with photo, would be in the *Boston Herald* <u>and</u> the *Boston Globe* as well as the *Midtown Journal*.

Of course, Joe and Tom wouldn't go to the papers. Joe couldn't afford that, but they hoped that Monsignor Rocco Randozza didn't call their bluff.

Tom thought that Felix/Rocco's attendance at the SLAA meeting was a sign that he would be amenable to making amends. It was one of the Twelve Steps, Tom said. Felix/Rocco might even welcome the opportunity and interpret the note as the grace of God, an opportunity to make things right, Tom speculated.

The note, drafted by both of them over the rest of the week and typed on the word processor in Tom's toney law office, read:

"We know about your secret life. Return
last Monday's ill gotten goods. Leave
them in the Archbishop's Crypt in the
basement next Wednesday before
7:00 p.m. Do the right thing. Make amends
now. Otherwise you'll be reading about
your not so secret other life in the
HERALD and the GLOBE."

On the next Sunday, Tom and Joe did meet in Foodies market at 9:45 a.m. as planned. They both wore blue suits (Joe wore the same one he had met Felix/Rocco in) and nice ties; they looked like the good Irish Catholic burghers they weren't. By the frozen foods counter in the back of the market Joe showed Tom the picture of "Felix." Tom said, "Jesus, he's hot! No wonder you took him home. Look at that dick!!!" causing two men in their gym clothes 15 feet away up by the health bars to turn around and stare haughtily. Joe told Tom, "Just remember that picture. You'll recognize him."

Tom said, "How can I forget!?! Look at that fur on his chest!"

Once in the Cathedral before Mass started Tom walked down the center aisle while Joe stood in the vestibule watching. Tom took a seat in the middle of the church on the left.

Thank God that there was no processional from the vestibule down the center aisle. Joe would have been beside himself. The celebrants entered from the side of the sanctuary today. As it was,

Joe had to go outside two or three times just to get his breath. He couldn't make out his assailant on the altar. As befit a mass said by a Cardinal Archbishop, there were a lot of priests on the altar and twice as many acolytes. Joe could see the big, babyfaced, Irish lug who always accompanied the Cardinal. Joe wondered if he was really a priest or a bodyguard or both. The altar was about 50 yards away and it was dark. From Joe's vantage point there were a couple of priests who could have been the robber. One seemed to have the same silver and black hair as Felix/Rocco but he also seemed to have a grey moustache. Maybe not; it was hard to see. Joe trusted that Tom would get the right guy. Tom never forgot a hot man.

At Communion the two priests who looked most like Felix/Rocco went to opposite sides of the nave. Because the church was in a cruciform, in the shape of the cross, Joe couldn't see where they stood to distribute communion. He did see Tom get up and go to the end of the line on the left, the epistle side of the altar, and follow it down the now non- existent communion rail. But he lost Tom after Tom turned left. That was just as well. Joe couldn't have endured the excitement of watching Tom pass off the note.

About two minutes after Tom turned left he came back up the side aisle passing his pew in the middle of the church, and walked right back to Joe in the vestibule. He put his forefinger to his lips, in a shushing signal, then grabbed Joe's arm and marched him out of the church.

"Don't say a word, and don't turn around," Tom whispered as he led Joe across the torn up Washington Street, past the Greek church of St. John The Baptist on Union Park Street, across Shawmut Avenue, into the leafy elegant tranquility of Union Park itself and over to the Aquitaine Restaurant on the other side of Tremont Street, where they huddled in a booth in the back.

"Do you know who was in front of me in the Communion line?" whispered Tom.

"No, I could barely see the altar from where I was. Who was there?" Joe asked.

"Giuseppina Randozza," said Tom. "The mother! Monsignor Rocco Randozza's mother."

'Well, did you slip him the note?"

"She was wearing a long sable coat and a silver threaded mantilla. Didn't you see her? She knelt in front of him, closed her eyes and made him give the host to her in her mouth. That kneeling and mouth business went out with Vatican II, didn't it?"

"Did you slip him the note, Tom?" Joe said impatiently. He wasn't interested in a social commentary on the mother's observation of the liturgical changes wrought by Vatican II.

"She had two bodyguards. Didn't you see them? One was behind her and the other came down the side aisle. They were the guys with the broken noses dressed like undertakers. You didn't see them?"

"I only had eyes for you, Tom. Did you give him the note?"

"Of course, I gave him the note. I found an envelope in the pew for a collection for Discalced Carmelite nuns in the Amazon. I folded the note and the copy of the photo one more time and put them in the envelope. I wrote his name on the envelope and crossed out the business about the nuns. I handed it to him after he gave me communion—in my hand. I didn't want to receive the host like his mother. God knows what vipers exist in his mother's mouth. I stood up and took it like a man. Ha! Ha! Ha! I think he winked at me. Really, I think he did."

"I hope he doesn't send our little missive to the poor barefoot nuns in Brazil. That photo would really blow their sandals off." Joe said, relieved that this part of the enterprise was over. "We just have to wait until Wednesday, I guess. Now what's your brainstorm about that?"

"We'll walk into the basement after the AA meeting has started and we'll go back to the crypt, pick up your stuff and then we'll walk out the side door. They have to leave the doors unlocked from the inside. Remember the Coconut Grove fire?"

"No, I don't and neither do you. It's one of the few things we're too young to remember."

"My Aunt Louise was there and she said...."

"Oh please, Tommy. I thought everybody died in that fire. You had relatives at every important event in this city since the Famine."

"I come from a large family. She jumped out a window," Tom offered meekly.

"Anyway, that sounds like a good plan. Can we eat some breakfast now? You probably fasted before receiving Holy Communion," Joe said cynically.

"Of course, I did. Ha! Ha! Ha!" Tom replied.

The haughty, fashionably jaded, hungover waiter came over and said, "Can I get you gentlemen a mimosa or a bloody mary? They are complimentary with the brunch."

"No thanks, we'll just eat. Thank you," said Joe.

"No doubt," said the waiter.

"What do you mean by that? You skinny fop! Where's the manager? We don't need attitude from you this early in the morning," shouted Tommy. Joe cowered in the booth. If he could have fit under the table, he would have gone there.

The waiter rushed away with a toss of his head. Shortly thereafter a good looking redheaded young woman came over to the table. "Good morning gentlemen, can I help you?"

"Yes, teach that twerp something about service," said Tom, himself the descendant of Irish maids and stablemen.

"I'm very sorry about Rene. I certainly will talk to him. Could I get you something to eat?" said the redhead. "We apologize. I'll take care of you myself."

"I'd like the Eggs Halifax. Is the smoked salmon really from Nova Scotia?" Tom asked.

"Actually we import it from Ireland, from a town in Cork, Shanagarry, to be specific." She knew her audience and smiled accordingly.

"That's better. I'm impressed," said Tom smiling back, now

charmed.

"And you, sir?" she asked Joe.

"I'll have the ordinary Eggs Benedict. Are the eggs local? Joe inquired mockingly.

"They are from the chickens in my backyard," she smiled.

"And where do you live?" Joe asked.

"In the North End, with my uncle. So don't get fresh." She smiled again. "He'd probably like you," she added.

Joe's University Education 6

As they had promised, Joe and Harry did get together twice at swimming meets after they had begun their respective colleges, once in Cambridge at Harvard and the other at Brown in Providence.

In spite of all the freshman year initiation rites at Harvard which involved drinking—cocktails with the proctor, sherry hours, beer blasts, and "jolly ups" at Radcliffe—Joe was still not drinking. He hadn't had a drink since that night in Jamestown with Harry.

Harry, on the other hand, took to all the equivalent alcoholic rituals at Brown with glee. He pledged for a fraternity and ended up in the hospital as a result. At one fraternity house he fell out a second storey window naked. Fortunately he landed in a yew bush and was only scratched. The fraternity had a hard time explaining why Harry had no clothes on. All Harry remembered was the captain of the Hockey team inviting him upstairs for a drink.

The captain, who could have been Harry's older brother, a chunky white blond with unnaturally blue eyes, denied the whole thing. It was a mess. They searched the captain's room and of course, Harry's clothes were there. The captain said he had left his door open and that he was visiting a girl at Pembroke, the neighboring women's college, the sister school, at the time of Harry's fall. Three different girls at Pembroke vouched for his account. After a while the administration let it go with a warning to the fraternity about its pledging with alcohol.

So, when Harry came to Cambridge, as they were leaving the pool at the Indoor Athletic Building after the meet, Harry asked Joe where they could go for a drink. Joe took him to Cronin's, then on Holyoke Street. It was an ark of a place. They retreated into the booth of a waitress who Joe's friends called "Faith, Hope & Charity" because she wore a pin with the liturgical symbols of those virtues (a heart, an anchor and a cross) on her black and white uniform. Her real name was Mary Doogan. She was legendary among the freshmen because she never asked for IDs.

"What will it be boys?" she asked wearily, making no bones about the deceit. They weren't big tippers, the freshmen, but it was slow in the late afternoon. Something was better than nothing.

Harry ordered a large draft and Joe had a ginger ale.

"Do ya want a cherry in it?" she growled at Joe.

"Gee, Joe, you still don't drink?" said Harry.

"No, Harry, there are too many alcoholics in my family. You've met my uncles in pajamas. My mother says that alcoholism is hereditary."

"Oh, I'm sure it is," Harry said, "My family's full of alcoholics. We have a special suite at the Hartford Retreat, the Institute for Living, where they go to dry out. I don't let that stop me, however. I think that I've been drunk every weekend since college started." And Harry laughed.

This evening was no exception. Two hours later they left the bar. Joe helped Harry back to Joe's suite in Massachusetts Hall, also the building containing the President's offices. It was tough on the stairs to the third floor. Harry went limp. Joe put Harry in the bottom bunk bed and went off to the Union for supper. When he returned Harry was in the shower.

"Who uses the Bay Rum?" asked Harry from the bathroom. "Couldn't they be a little more imaginative?"

"It's my roommate Isaac's. He's away for the weekend, which is why you are able to stay in his bed. So don't criticize him and don't spill it all over the floor. Don't drink it either."

"Come in here, Joe. I want to show you something. Come in here," Harry said.

Joe went into the bathroom.

Harry dropped his towel to his knees, turned around and bent over. He had a shamrock tattooed on his right cheek. "Do you like it? I went down to Newport with my fraternity brothers and we all got tattoos at a sailor joint on Thames Street. This is in honor of my grandfather Donohoe. God bless him. They can kiss my royal Irish ass. We were bombed. Isn't it great! I showed them around town and then we all went skinny dipping at Second Beach. It was fun. We were loaded. You should get a tattoo; you're more Irish than I am. Show me your lily white ass, Joe. I'll draw one on you."

Although they wrote and talked on the phone a few times after that autumnal visit, they didn't see each other again until the spring, what with Thanksgiving, Christmas, reading period, and exams. Harry went to Philadelphia for Christmas and took his Spring Break skiing in Sun Valley. Joe went back to Newport for his vacations.

Before the end of his first term Joe had pretty much decided that he wanted to major in Medieval History. He enrolled in all the medieval courses he could and decided that he would ask the chair of the Medieval History department to be his tutor. Joe also joined the Schola, the Men's section of the choir at Saint Paul's Church at Bow and Arrow Streets in Harvard Square. The choir was famous; they had made a number of recordings. There was a school for the boy singers next to the church. There were a couple of other undergraduates in the men's choir. One, Ricardo Slade, had gone to Portsmouth Priory. He was a junior at Harvard and was already writing his senior honors thesis on monasteries in Catalonia in the twelfth century. Joe had met him at a party in Newport over the summer and was happy to see him when he went to Mass at St. Paul's the first time. Slade was very thin and tall. He looked like an ascetic, like a figure painted by El Greco, but he dressed like a lord. He always wore a suit and always had a white linen handkerchief in his coat pocket.

As a lark, Slade created an imaginary country in Eastern Europe where they spoke Latin and Slade wrote a constitution for this country, which was a monarchy, but a constitutional monarchy where the king had little power. Slade even drew pictures of the characters in the kingdom. The king looked suspiciously like Slade. The queen looked like Grace Kelly, but she came from Hapsburg and Savoyard royal lines.

Slade hung out with a group of similarly inclined people, all Catholics, mostly men and mostly Irish, although there were the Mullets, a brother and sister, whose grandfather on their mother's side had been the Duke of Norfolk, the highest ranking Catholic in England. They looked as well bred as afghan hounds, long narrow faces, slightly stooped, delicate hands, never a hair out of place. Slade's crew was very *Brideshead Revisited*. They called each other "M'dear" and talked about things being "too, too shymaking." Nobody had a teddy bear, at least not one they carried around. That would have been a little too much, even for Harvard Square with its Puritan past, in those pre-hippie days. Scuffed shoes and tweed jackets with patches were the height of fashion except for some Fancy Dans who had gone to Le Rosey in Switzerland, like the Aga Khan and the Marquess of Tavistock. The Marquess wore Duke of Windsor Glen Plaid suits with cowboy boots, as a nod to the former colonies, where he was now being educated, one assumes.

When Pope Pius XII died, Slade wore a black tie and tied a black silk kerchief on his sleeve. Shortly after, in October of 1958, when John XXIII was elected pope, after the white smoke went up from the Vatican chimney, Slade rushed into the Freshmen Union shouting, "*Habemus Papam! Habemus Papam!*" The dour ex-valedictorians from Dubuque and over-educated preppies from Exeter, eating their well-done roast beef, mashed potatoes and peas, had no idea what to do with this enthusiasm. So they assumed their usual look, which was disdain. The Green ladies behind the chafing tables, Irish women from Central and Porter Squares, smiled. They knew what he was saying. They had been waiting for this news as well.

Joe took all of Slade's enthusiasm for things Catholic with a grain of salt, but was fascinated nevertheless. He had never felt the rich culture of Catholicism before. He knew it existed but had never felt it. He knew that the Middle Ages were the last time, before the twentieth century, when Irish Culture shined. Irish monks preserved Civilization when the Briton barbarians were painted blue. Joe could own that and feel proud.

At St. George's he was made to feel second class as an Irish Catholic. The only others were the kitchen help, his father and the gardeners. The various shades of Protestants ran the school and were proud and rich dissenters.

At Harvard, besides the obligatory General Education courses, Joe took the introductory Fine Arts course, Fine Arts 13, aka *Darkness at Noon*, because it met at noon in the basement of the Fogg Museum. Most of the class consisted of lectures with slides of pieces of art in a darkened auditorium. The course began with the caves at Lascaux in France but soon progressed to the Irish manuscripts of the late 8th and early 9th century. When the *Chi Rho* page of Saint Matthew's Gospel from *The Book of Kells* flashed 15 feet high on the screen, Joe's heart jumped. And when the tweedy old Professor Deknatel called it, "The chief relic of the Western world," Joe believed that his Irish heritage had been validated at Harvard. As the class progressed through the religious art of the Middle Ages and into the Renaissance he reveled in the knowledge that he hailed from a tradition richer and worldlier than his haughty, washed out, WASPy classmates.

When Joe went home to Newport he spent a lot of time at the

Priory with Slade. Slade drove him down in his MG convertible. Slade was allowed to stay in the monastery. They walked around the school and talked about the reforms of Cluny, the relative merits of Roman vestments over Gothic ones, anticipated changes in the liturgy, and other Catholic stuff. They then attended Vespers and, after supper with the monks, they sang Compline in the chapel. They sat in the choir with the monks.

Joe became scholarly. He even wore rimless glasses and double-vented tweed jackets. Thank God for his cousin's store. Otherwise he shopped at Joe Keezers for old suits. There he bought a dinner jacket, white tie and tails, and a morning suit. His mother gave him her father's Chesterfield coat with the obligatory velvet collar.

In the spring, when Joe went down to Providence for a swim meet at Brown, the visit became a little problematic. For one thing, Harry had a single room and only one bed, albeit a double. Also, Harry was on the edge of being thrown off the swim team because of his excessive absences from practice. Third, Harry's fraternity was having a party on that Saturday night.

On Saturday afternoon Joe swam well, winning the butterfly and coming in second at the breaststroke. The relay team, of which he was a member, took first place.

He was exhausted, however, when he got to Harry's fraternity house. All he wanted to do was sleep. He took off most of his clothes, down to his boxers and climbed into the bed. It was about 5:00 p.m.

Harry arrived at the house about an hour later and had drinks downstairs before coming upstairs to change his clothes for the evening's festivity. Harry opened the door, saw Joe sleeping on his back in the bed, tiptoed into the room, took off all his clothes and slipped in next to Joe.

Soon Harry "accidentally" put his hand across Joe's chest. Joe didn't move. Slowly Harry's hand slipped down to Joe's boxers and then down Joe's stomach. Harry didn't move his hand and Joe didn't move either, except for his involuntary erection.

◊ ◊ ◊

When Joe was a junior at Harvard he still had not had sex with a woman. One Wednesday night Eliot Finn, a friend who had dropped out before his senior year and moved into Boston, invited Joe to go drinking at the Palace, a barn of a bar on Washington Street in the Combat Zone in Boston. The Palace was frequented by all types of people, sailors, hookers, blacks, Harvard clubbies, gays, lesbians and everybody else. It was before the busing crisis had divided the city so terribly.

It was a slow night at the Palace so Eliot Finn suggested that they go to his "little bohemian neighborhood bar" on the back of Beacon Hill, which was called Sporters. Joe had never been in a gay bar before but, after his eyes adjusted to the dark, he knew one when he saw it. All the women were on one side, dressed like lumber jacks and the men looked like Troy Donahue, the Hollywood heartthrob of the day. Joe recognized a man from Newport who now had dyed blond hair and wore eye makeup. Joe hoped that the man did not recognize him. But he did. He came over to Joe and Eliot Finn, while they were talking to a schoolteacher, whose nickname was "The Maw" because of her big mouth and large appetite. The Maw was with two other women, one a cute little thing named Debbie and the other larger and not so cute, named Ellen. They all lived on the Hill. Debbie was straight, but Ellen was not so sure. She was in the bar looking around to find out.

The blond from Newport tried to get a word in, but the Maw kept on saying, "Shut up Parkie, you're loaded. Nobody gives a shit if you know Finn's friend. He's probably straight anyway, although he is just a little too good looking."

Joe cringed and when little Debbie said, "Kiss me if you're straight," Joe did. Parkie exclaimed, "What a waste!" and fell into the booth that was mercifully nearby. The Maw said, "Ain't that sweet!" Finn disappeared with Ellen to do a two step to the Ruth Etting song that had just come on the jukebox. Joe was left with Debbie.

After she released his lips, Debbie whispered to Joe, "Let's get out of here." They did and she and Joe went up the backside of the hill to her apartment where he lost his virginity. After the deed, she said to him, "So, how long have you been a queen?"

He replied, "Excuse me?"

"How long you been a queen? You were with one of the biggest queens on Beacon Hill and you aren't a very good fuck. How long have you been queer?"

Joe got it finally and said, "I'm not a queen. I'm not queer." He proceeded to fuck her again, harder. In those days a goat would have turned him on, although it was the big, handsome Italian guy with the hairy chest, who had looked out of place standing in front of him at the bar at Sporters, who he thought of during the sex.

Joe slipped out of Debbie's apartment early in the morning and bought a coffee at Phillips, the all-night drug store at the corner of Charles and Cambridge Streets, which he sipped until he could return to Cambridge on the first train of the day. Although he was exhausted, he sat in the big chair in the living room of his suite until his roommate woke up.

"What are you doing up?"

"Oh, I just got home," Joe replied, not even lifting his eyes from last Sunday's *New York Herald Tribune*.

"Did you get lucky?"

"Don't be crass," Joe said. "A gentleman never talks," and he smiled. He wasn't going to get into details. They raised more questions than they answered. However after tasting the triumph of letting his roommate know that he was no longer a virgin, the evening's event had little worth. He certainly wasn't going to rush out to do it again, and certainly not with Debbie of North Anderson Street.

Now, as for the big, hairy chested Italian, that was another story, which every night Joe tried hard not to think about.

Confrontation in the Cathedral Crypt 7

On Wednesday at 6:30 p.m. Joe and Tom met in *Scrub a Dub, Dub*, the Laundromat across the street from the Cathedral, in preparation for the 7:00 p.m. AA meeting, their excuse for getting into the basement of the church. The SLAA group used to meet in the same space right after the AA group, until the SLAA guys claimed that the proximity of space and time of the two meetings interfered with their anonymity. SLAA then moved to the top floor of the school.

Tom had walked by the Archbishops' crypt when he went to the SLAA meetings in the Cathedral basement. It was *en route* to the bathroom. The crypt always gave him the creeps. Tom also knew that there was a side door to Union Park Street after the devotional altars to the right inside the lower church.

Tom said, "You'll go in early. I'll go in late. That way they won't know we're together. Be prepared for people to be very friendly. That's part of their thing and they are sincere. They won't ask more than your first name and if you have ever been there before. You know, it's anonymous. They're good guys as a rule. It won't matter if you appear nervous. They'll think that it's because you just stopped drinking."

"What if I recognize someone? I've known a lot of drunks in my day," said Joe.

"You probably will; you've been around. So you'll say 'Hello' and whatever else you want. I'll come in later and sit near the arch separating the little meeting room from the sacristy. At some point, maybe 6:50 p.m., I'll get up as if I'm heading to the bathroom which is just beyond the crypt. I'll wait for you in the hall just outside the sacristy and we'll go to the crypt together. We'll stay there until they've finished their meeting and if they shut off the lights, which they usually forget to do, I'll show you the way out the side door. I have a little flashlight here." Tom showed Joe the flashlight. It didn't look like it would do much good, but Joe wisely decided that this was not the time to say so.

"I parked the car on the side of the church near the door and if we aren't jammed in by one of the bruisers who work out at Mike's Gym up the street, we'll be out free. Don't worry. We can pull this off. What's the worst that can happen?"

Joe didn't answer that question because he didn't know. He was too nervous to think; he had to trust Tom. Tom didn't offer an answer either, as people usually do who say that. They then went next door to Foodies, the neighborhood supermarket, and bought bottles of Evian water to drink during the meeting.

"These AA guys always have to be drinking something. Usually it's coffee, but bottled water will do particularly for old farts like us who have to curb their caffeine intake. It's a good thing they don't let them smoke in meetings anymore."

Tom walked Joe over. They crossed Washington Street, went up Monsignor Reynolds Way, along the right side of the Cathedral with the housing projects on their right. Tom left Joe at an edge of the rear transept, just before the Cardinal's parking spot, where Tom retreated into the shadows.

Joe went down the stairs. There were four men there already. No one said anything to him, although they talked and laughed among themselves. One well-dressed guy, who looked Middle Eastern, "like a desert person," his Aunt Josie would say, handed out gold wrapped butterscotch candies while another thin, casually elegant man about Joe's age with white hair and striped socks that matched his shirt dutifully took the wrappers and stuffed them into a drawer on the side of the long table they all were gathered around. Somebody even passed a candy to Joe.

Maybe it's the sugar that helps them not drink, Joe thought. Should I eat it or not? Maybe it has drugs in it, like saltpeter for boozers. More people came. They all seemed to know each other. Joe recognized some faces. Finally, a very good looking man with a head of black and gray hair, a well-toned body and a long yellow silk scarf, like a Tibetan monk's, over a well-tailored blue silk suit sat next to him and said, "Hello, I'm Taylor. Have you ever been here before?"

"No," said Joe nervously.

"Well, you'll like it. It's a good meeting. Welcome," the sophisticate said.

Just then the thin, white-haired guy banged on the table with his book and began to read, "The Twelfth Step......." On they went each taking a paragraph. Joe got the long one summarizing each of the steps and then the one about "Most married folks," at which everyone laughed. Joe wasn't sure that he got the joke, but just as he finished Tom came in and sat in a chair under the arch to the sacristy. Tom looked around and nodded to the man with the candy who smiled back and sent a gold wrapped Werthers down to him. Shortly thereafter Tom got up and headed towards the priests' dressing cabinet built into the far wall. He went through the door on the left. A couple of men had gone that way before and returned. Joe waited for three more readers and then walked the same route.

Tom stopped Joe as he passed through the little hallway, "Shhh, I think the Latinos are having a wake in the lower church."

Indeed Joe could hear murmuring, in Spanish, like prayer.

Tom pulled Joe through the double doors, and then to a little chapel like room to the right, just before the sanctuary of the downstairs church. There were small prints of all the early archbishops on the wall facing them and two gaudy throne-like chairs against the back wall. They reminded him of Imelda Marcos.

"Sit here," said Tom, as he pushed Joe into one of the thrones. "They won't be able to see us. We have to decide how to get out of here. We can't just walk through carrying your memory box. If the people at the wake, one of whom might be a priest, don't stop us, they might follow us or recognize us later."

"I've no idea what to do," said Joe, which was both the truth and no surprise.

"We'll go get your stuff, carry it this far, and hope that the wake ends soon. If it doesn't, the meeting ends in a few minutes, at eight, and we can get out the door we came in. The only problem is that that door faces the back door of the rectory. The housekeeper might see us. We'll have to take our chances."

They got up and walked back into the narrow corridor which went behind the lower church's altars. There were various obstructions in the way, a big pine cross with no corpus, an empty votive candle rack and a pew or two, until they got to the entrance to the Archbishops' crypt to the left. On the wall before the door was a marble plaque listing the occupants, Archbishops Fenwick, Fitzpatrick and Williams. Their reigns went from 1825 to 1907. Directly in front of Tom and Joe, on another wall, was a big white crucifix, with a corpus about 3/4 life size, which was curious to Joe. Why didn't they go all the way and make it life size, he thought? The space was there. Would that have been too frightening? Nevertheless, the suffering miniaturized Jesus was foreboding enough.

At the crypt entrance, Tom, who was in front, turned on the light switch just under Jesus' left arm. In front of them as they turned into the crypt was an altar from the first Catholic Cathedral in Boston, which had long since been torn down and replaced by this edifice. Joe, ever the amateur historian, was all eyes. He tried to read the signs describing the altar's provenance in the dim light.

All of a sudden he heard Tom say, "Oh Christ!"

There was silence, and then a voice further into the room said, "No, just his humble servant. Now what's this all about?"

The voice came from the darkened end of the room where the episcopal cadavers had been placed in the wall. Joe couldn't make out the person in the half light.

At the same time Joe heard a noise behind him, the scuffing of feet perhaps. Joe looked back and in the portal they just passed through there was a big policeman, none other than Paddy Lowell.

"I'm Monsignor Randozza," the voice in the dark said. "What's going on here?" He stepped out of the shadows.

Joe was about to faint when Paddy Lowell said to him, "Jesus Christ—Sorry Monsignor—What are you doing here, Joe? How did you get mixed up with this? And you Tommy Murphy, what are you guys? Crazy?"

"I'm Monsignor Randozza, the Cardinal's secretary. Now, for the second time, what is this all about?" he repeated.

Tommy stepped forward, pushed his chest out and said, "Don't give me that clerical intimidation. You'd think that you guys learned a little humility from the last sex scandal with children. You know what this is about, and if you aren't careful, we're going to the *Globe*."

Tommy knew that the *Herald* would print anything. The *Globe*, being more respectable, would be feared more. "Now you're preying on old men. I am Attorney Thomas A. Murphy. I served on the Catholic Charities Board of Directors with you and I thought something was strange about you there, but I couldn't put my finger on it. You robbed my client, Joe Lyons, last week after answering an ad on the computer for...." Tommy searched for the word a second or two and came up with "companionship."

Tommy took a breath and went on, "I don't know what your game is but my client wants his property back, and now. I'm sure that you haven't explained your part in this to our friend, Officer

Lowell." Tom nodded to Paddy Lowell. "Don't think that you're going to bully us with your Roman collar. In spite of my charitable work, I am from a long line of anti-clerics, and now I know why. There never was a priesteen from our family." Tom had worked himself up thoroughly, and was now red in the face.

Joe stood dumbfounded. He felt like he did when he first went to the police and met Sergeant Detective Shaughnessy. *How did I get into this? I had no idea that I was Tommy Murphy's client. And what's this "preying on old men?" Am I really so old? And what is Paddy Lowell doing here? Are we going to be arrested?*

"I don't know what you're talking about," said Monsignor Randozza calmly. "I'm here in response to a cryptic note that was passed to me during last Sunday's mass. The Cardinal and I are aware and appreciative of your many good works, Mr. Murphy. Let's take this conversation into the rectory, Mr. Murphy, where we can clear it all up over an *expresso*."

Maybe it was the flattery, maybe the calmness in his voice, maybe it was the anticipation of *expresso*, or maybe Tom had come to his lawyerly senses. Tom said, "Fine, lead the way. This place is creepy. No offense, Monsignor."

"You're right about that one, Tommy Murphy," said Officer Padraic Lowell—the first one out the door of the crypt.

Monsignor Randozza followed and led them all to the right, down the hall, a right again past the sacristy, past the AA meeting alcove (now empty,) up the steps and into the back door of the rectory. Officer Lowell held the door and gave Joe a wink and a little pat on the bum as Joe passed before him.

"Bridie, would you prepare *expressos* for our guests, please." The Monsignor said as they passed the door to the kitchen of the Rectory.

"And what the hell would an '*expresso*' be, Monsignor?" said Bridie Cronin, the housekeeper who had been there since Cardinal O'Connell had moved out to the palace on Commonwealth Avenue in the forties. "If it's a cup of tea you want, we can do that. Perhaps the gentlemans would like something stronger."

"Tea will be fine, Bridie," said Monsignor Randozza. Tom had gone for his briefcase which was in his car parked next to the church. He had all Joe's documentation in there, including the photo of the assailant. They all sat in the dark panelled living room with the seriographed copy of a Raphael Madonna and Child on one wall and a large brass crucifix in the other. The chairs were stuffed dark green and maroon cut velvet; the rug a good, but dirty old oriental.

Tom returned with his briefcase and Monsignor Randozza shut the door.

Tom put his briefcase on a side table. It was embossed in gold letters "Swords, Healy and Fiske" and then one line down "T.A.M." Some fresh queens in Boston had been known to call Tom "Tammie" by reason of those initials, but never to his face. Tom opened the briefcase so that only he could see its contents, an old lawyer trick.

"Go ahead, Mr. Murphy?" said the Monsignor now seated as was everyone else except Paddy Lowell.

"Certainly, Monsignor. I'll get right to the point. My client was robbed last week by a man he had recently met in a coffee shop after conversations on the computer. The man had furnished my client with a photo of himself." Tim handed over the photo of the flashed out, faceless nude. "Reliable sources have identified the photo as being you. My client wants his property back."

Monsignor Randozza looked at the photo intently. Paddy Lowell peered over his shoulder. Just then the door burst open. Enter Bridie Cronin. Monsignor Randozza let the photo fall. The starburst faced nude landed face up on the stained Bokhara.

"Jeeezas, who is that child of God? Isn't that the bathroom upstairs? I should know; I've been cleaning it for fifty something years. What was he doing in there? Apart from the obvious, of course," and she laughed. "Well, God was certainly good to him. Wasn't he, Monsignor? At least we know that he's not Jewish. He could be your brother, or even you some while ago. Not that you're not a handsome man now, Monsignor, but you must have been a looker in your day. How did those Eyetalian girls in the North End let you go, Monsignor?"

Bridie put the tea down on the long table behind the chairs. "Now I hope that you don't want honey with your tea. We used to have some priests in the Sixties who only wanted honey for the tea. But they had long hair and wore bell bottoms too. Thank God, that business is over." Bridie added.

"I know who this is. It's not me," Monsignor Randozza said quietly after Bridie left the room muttering about "honey, Eyetalians, the Sixties, messy priests" and how hard it was to clean bathroom tile.

"Did the man who...." Now it was Monsignor Randozza's turn to search for the euphemism, "the man who 'encountered' your client have a moustache?" said Monsignor Randozza as he fingered his own.

Before anyone could answer Monsignor Randozza added, "The body is either that of my nephew, Lorenzo, who lived here last year while studying at the Kennedy School at Harvard, or of my brother Dino, who lives in the North End."

Joe jumped in and said, "I knew that it wasn't you. I knew that it wasn't you the minute I saw you in the light outside the crypt. You look like him but he's younger, not as gray. And he didn't have a moustache," Joe added.

"Well, why didn't you tell me," said Tommy Murphy, "before I made a fool of myself on your behalf?" as if Joe could've interrupted Tom once Tom got on one of his oratorical rolls. "What did he look like, the faceless body?" Tom asked.

"I can't say. I can't say. The body hair was like the guy in the photo."

"The photo would have been taken here. Bridie is correct, as Bridie is always correct. My nephew Lorenzo came over from Rome where he'd been living with his mother. He stayed here. He was going to be a priest, but he abandoned that. The Cardinal helped get him into the Kennedy School. Supposedly he's now in the fashion business, as a model. His father died when he was a boy. His mother took him to Rome when he was a teenager. My mother takes care of him when she's there as well. We have Roman connections. Lorenzo used to exercise across the street at Mike's Gym. He became so interested in body building that he neglected his studies and didn't complete the Kennedy School program. It was very sad…."

"And your brother Dino?" inquired Tom, who had sprung back to life and who knew a little about Dino. What adult in Boston didn't?

"My brother Dino lives in the North End. We look alike but he looks younger, which he is. Due to some unfortunate circumstances the responsibility for running the family businesses has fallen on him. He's stayed here from time to time, but not in a while." Monsignor Randozza rubbed his forehead as he made these explanations. It was obvious that all this was painful to him. But he had made a decision to try to get to the truth.

"I'll get your things back. Give me a week or two. I'll get them back. I promise. There's no need to go to the *Globe*, or the *Herald*. We'll all lose if that happens. You know that. I'll retrieve your belongings. I have to go to Rome on Friday, but I'll get your property back as soon as I can," Monsignor Randozza said. "This is very painful for me and it comes up at a very unpropitious time," he added softly.

Paddy Lowell, the policeman, had said nothing up to now. "Why did you think that the bad guy was Monsignor Rocco in the first place? Who are the 'reliable sources'?" Paddy asked.

"Your Sergeant Detective Shaughnessy," said Tom Murphy impatiently. "When Joe reported this to the police right after the…the event, Sergeant Detective Shaughnessy was on duty. He looked at the picture. He was in the Seminary with Monsignor Rocco Randozza and recognized the hair distribution on his body from their days in the pool and the locker room."

"Geez, I didn't know Sergeant Shaughnessy was gay," Paddy Lowell said. "Do they have 'hair distribution' experts nowadays?

I heard about fingerprint guys and they made us go to something about DNA but I never heard of hair distribution experts. What'll they think of next? It must be the FBI stuff. Too bad J. Edgar died before this came out. He would have enjoyed checking out everybody's body hair. 'Course he probably shaved his legs."

"I didn't say that Shaughnessy was gay, Paddy," Tom rushed to say.

Monsignor Randozza smiled, "I remember Shaughnessy. 'The Butterfly,' we called him. He swam the butterfly. He had the shoulders and the chest for it, big and hairless. He was a good man—and a good swimmer. I would like to see him again. It's been such a long time. He would have made a good priest. 'The Butterfly,'" he added wistfully.

"Jesus Christ," said Paddy Lowell. "Everybody's remembering everybody else's chests from twenty plus years ago. Maybe the *Globe* is right. Maybe those seminaries are hotbeds of homos. Sorry, Monsignor."

Monsignor Randozza ignored the outburst, and added, "We all have that body hair distribution. My grandfather, my father, and all my brothers have it. Most of the nephews do too. We have been called 'Bears' for generations, both here and in Italy. *Ursi* they call us in Italy. Mine is all white now." With that he stood up, took off his collar and opened the magenta cloth covered buttons of his cassock, showing his hirsute snowy chest against a very good tan.

"Where did you get the tan, Monsignor? Is it all over? Are you a Brownie from the L Street Beach in South Boston? " Paddy Lowell asked with a grin. Even in uniform, Paddy Lowell was always up for a good time, even in a rectory.

"Actually, I am, Officer Lowell, I swim all year round at L Street, but I also was in Capri recently." Wistfully, he added, "I swim down by the rocks, by the *Faraglioni*. The little restaurant there has the best Caprese salad in the world. You can swim and eat, sun and eat, sleep and eat. It's like heaven. I hope to be there soon again, after my business in Rome."

"And the assailant left this card," Joe said holding up the business card for *Vestimenti Ecclesiastici, Fratelli Fucini.*

"That's where I buy my cassocks. I hope to be there again next week. It is one of the best ecclesiastical stores in Rome. That magenta is the color for monsignori. I get samples like that from them all the time. I bet he took it from me. I'll get to the bottom of this."

8 Joe Crashes His Coming Out Party

In March of 1965, a few days before the 17th, Nick Moran, Joe Lyon's law school roommate said, "Why don't we go to the Saint Patrick's Day Parade in South Boston? It'll be a hoot."

It was their last year in Law School and they could spare the time. They took the subway to South Boston. In a crowded bar on Broadway, after a few beers, Joe became separated from Nick Moran. Joe didn't see any of the parade but he found himself in the big barroom standing next to a good looking girl with a "Kiss Me, I'm Irish" pin on her raincoat. He did and she smiled. He bought her a beer and they sat down at a booth but were soon crowded out by some rowdies falling on the table.

She suggested that they go into town to an Irish Bar named McNiff's on Boylston Street near Massachusetts Avenue. They were sitting across from each other on their fifteenth beer or so when she slurred out of nowhere, "And you're a jerk." Joe stood up and left.

Joe knew that his friend Eliot Finn lived nearby and Joe had a vague memory that Finn gave a party on St. Patrick's Day. So, Joe toddled off around the corner to Finn's apartment on Beacon

Street at Massachusetts Avenue next door to the old Harvard Club.

Now, Joe also knew that Finn was gay but Finn didn't interest Joe as a sex object, so in that sense it didn't matter to Joe what Finn did in bed. With all the beers it seemed to Joe that Fate had sent Joe to Finn's door.

Finn had a great big floor-through apartment with lots of old maroon velvet and brown wood furniture. Finn's roommate, an Emerson College acting student, answered the door. The roommate called for Finn, who was in the parlor. Even though Joe was very drunk, Finn greeted Joe cordially. Seated in the parlor, and parlor it was with its old fashioned stiff, plush, dark furniture—it looked like a funeral home from the Forties—were a nice looking, refined man about Joe's age and two women with short hair, both of whom were gym teachers in the suburbs. Joe asked if he could take a little nap and was directed to the roommate's room where he promptly passed out on the narrow bed. About a half hour later he was awakened by coats being dropped on him. He got up to see what was going on. Peggy Lee was singing *Is That All There Is?* over the noise of a crowd.

Joe still had a buzz on. He later learned that the roommate had been telling everyone that, "Finn's straight Harvard chum" was passed out in the bedroom. People came in to look at Joe, like a monkey in the zoo. It was nice of Finn to tell people that Joe was straight, to protect his reputation, but Joe knew that Finn hoped otherwise. Joe didn't know if Finn wanted him for himself or if he was just trying to make Joe's opening of the closet door easier. Finn was capable of such kindness. Maybe it was both. Anyway, in those days Joe certainly hoped that he was straight. He had better be straight. He could be straight when he had to, like he had been on two or three occasions—two to be precise.

There had been those times, however, with Jackie Crotty and Harry Sayers, which were a little too frequent and which had gone well past adolescence to pass as "boyhood sexual experimentation." Joe had also made some forays down to the Magic Mile by the Public Garden or to the riverbank at Harvard. But, most of the time in Joe's mind, they didn't count. Most of them had been awful and filled him with guilt. He usually met men who talked in drag, calling everyone "she." These incidents were very confusing and not very satisfying. They sent Joe back into the closet for long stretches.

However, one exception had been that handsome Harvard student on the riverbank one crispy fall weekend night who wouldn't take Joe back to his room. Crazed with passion, they did it right there on the riverbank in front of the Harvard Business School with the traffic whizzing by on Storrow Drive. That was great. But mostly Joe's desire for men lived in his head, and he hoped he could keep it down, as it were.

So Joe wandered around the edges of the party. He talked to the refined guy who was there when he arrived. He was a French teacher at a Catholic Prep school on the North Shore and he had written some short stories which were going to be published soon. Joe was both impressed and jealous.

Joe was near the door when a handsome man came in at the side of a woman with a Cleopatra hairdo, who was wearing a skirt, which was unusual for the women at this party. Elizabeth Taylor had just made the Cleopatra movie and immortalized the hairdo.

Joe heard someone greet the man as "Michael," and he looked over curiously at the the couple. Michael was the "Harvard student" Joe had met on the Riverbank two years before! Joe couldn't believe it. Michael looked hard at Joe, a little smile appearing before he looked away. Joe was sure that Michael recognized him, but not sure enough that he dared approach Michael. However, Joe did not let Michael out of his sight and he followed Michael, at what he thought was a discreet distance, all around the party.

Finally Michael turned around and said, with a big grin, "And what's your name?"

Joe told Michael his name.

He said, "Well, I'm Michael Ferrara and I'm very, very glad to see you...again."

Joe blushed which made Michael smile more lasciviously. He had this mock challenging way of talking which scared Joe.

Michael added, "I hoped that I'd run into you some day. I asked around but nobody seemed to know you—not even Larry. Do you remember Larry? He's the guy on the Riverbank who wanted to take us to his house; he gets around everywhere, but he didn't know you. Where do you hide? So, you're a friend of "the Finn." I should've known. You look cute in that tweed jacket, by the way." He leaned in and straightened Joe's green and white striped tie, Joe's nod to St. Patrick.

Joe was speechless. All Joe could say was, "I went to college with Finn. I didn't know there was a party going on. I go to law school now."

"That's a song."

"Excuse me?"

"That's a song, *I didn't know there was a party going on.*' Don't you know it? Anyway, how lucky for you—and for me, m'dear—that we should both be here."

Joe didn't know how to respond. His previous encounters with men hadn't involved much chat and certainly not this coquetry. He hadn't a clue how to flirt with a man. All this "m'dear" business was very bizarre. Michael wasn't a sissy. He looked like an Italian football player. He stood very straight and pushed out both his jaw and his hairy chest. He talked tough but the toughness was banter. He wasn't being mean but he was making sport with Joe.

"I have to move around for a while but you hang on. I want to take you home with me," Michael said straightening Joe's
tie again.

Michael didn't give Joe a chance to respond. He turned and went into the living room and started to talk to Cleopatra. Joe heard her say, "Straight, my ass!"

The only other woman in a dress approached Joe, and at first Joe thought, "Oh good, if she is talking to me, they won't think I'm queer."

She had lots of red hair and wore a green silk dress. She said, "I'm Sheila Sullivan. And you look like the pick of the parish. Who brought you? I saw you with 'The Michael.' He's a good guy."

Christ, she's on to me, Joe thought. There are 70 people at this party and she has me pegged. Well, nobody there was 100% straight, but Joe didn't know that. He had never been to a gay party before. He didn't know such things existed. She said that she was waiting for her lover to get off duty at the Mass. General Hospital.

"Oh, is he a doctor?"

"No, but she is."

"What time will she be here?"

"She gets off at 11."

"It's almost that now."

"Yes, I can hardly wait," she said with a smile. "You take care of yourself. Michael is a good man but he hasn't found himself yet. Maybe you can help him." All Joe cared was that Michael find him. Now Michael was in the front hall talking to a big woman in blue jeans and a man's white shirt with hair half dyed blonde pulled back in a pony tail like Grace Metalious, the author of *Peyton Place*.

In his drunken state Joe decided to go over and be charming.

"And who's this pretty?" the woman said as Joe approached. "Is this one of your tricks, Michael? Where did you meet him? He looks a little more respectable than your usual?"

"Hello, I'm Joe Lyons. I'm glad to meet you."

"Well, at least he's Irish, probably Catholic, and he's polite. That's an improvement over the rude pagans you usually drag home, Michael. Your Irish mother would be proud. Ha!"

She didn't acknowledge Joe's introduction, although she held Joe's extended hand firmly. She said nothing to him. She talked about Joe to Michael like Joe was an object elsewhere.

Michael said, "Let's get out here, Joe. Good night, Alice."

Alice said, "Be nice to this one, Michael. He looks like quality."

They went to the back bedroom to find their coats. There was a couple in there in a clinch, two women. They straightened up as Michael and Joe entered.

Michael said, "Don't let us disturb you m'dears. We're just looking for our coats."

Once outside Joe said, "Where's the nearest subway station? Are we going to take the subway?"

"M'dear, you're much too good for the subway. We're going to take a cab."

Joe hoped that they weren't going far because he had very little money left. The notion that Michael would pay hadn't occurred to Joe.

They didn't go far. They went about a half mile to St. Mary's Station, just over the Brookline border, to the apartment of one of Michael's friends where Michael had a room. The friend was still at the party and was going to stay at her girlfriend's house. Michael gave Joe a beer and put on a Billie Holiday record. Joe followed Michael like a puppy as he did these chores. They sat on the couch awkwardly for a minute and then Michael leaned over and kissed Joe right on the mouth. He even tongued Joe.

With men, Joe had been one of those "no face stuff" guys, up to now. So he wasn't entirely comfortable with the kiss, but when Michael's hand went to Joe's crotch it didn't matter what else they were doing. Joe was so ready. Joe reciprocated. Michael was hard too. Michael began to undo Joe's belt buckle and Joe leaned back to let him. Michael opened Joe's pants and then Joe's shirt.

The music changed to Nina Simone as they entered Michael's little side bed room.

Joe had never had sex that good, at least not since they had met the first time. But here they didn't have to worry about spectators, or the cops, or falling in the river. Joe didn't believe it himself. They did things Joe hadn't even read about. Michael's body was beautiful. He was solid and had a beautiful hairy chest. The hair spiraled down to his navel, then across his stomach and down to his cock. He was like those boy athletes Joe had disdained, but really lusted for. Joe couldn't believe his good fortune. They did it three times before the sun came up. After each, post-coitally, Michael told Joe more about himself.

Michael was born in Somerville but his father made some money and the family moved to Winchester, "with all the other rich Dagoes," Michael said. Michael knew that he liked men and had been cruising in town since he was 15. He went to Boston College High School, the best Catholic High School in Boston. There was a cafeteria on Charles Street called *Sharaf's* where gay kids hung out. Michael fell in love with a classmate in his senior year and sent him a love letter which the loved one's mother intercepted and read over the phone to Michael's Irish mother.

She told his father. He threw Michael out. Michael went to live with Alice, the woman who they had just left at the party. Eventually Michael got back with his parents and finished high school. He went to college for a couple of years but flunked out in his sophomore year. Michael wasn't clear about how he supported himself; he wasn't forthcoming on that subject. That didn't matter to Joe. The whole thing was so romantic and rebellious. This was 1965; "The Sixties" as a cultural phenomenon were just beginning.

Michael told Joe about all the people at the party. Both of the women they'd interrupted while getting their coats had long term lovers, and one of them had two kids as well. Finn's roommate was a drag queen, and hung around rest rooms in the Common in a dress. Sheila, the redheaded woman Joe had been talking to was divorced from her first husband and was sleeping with the woman doctor she mentioned, but she'd also persuaded a priest to leave the priesthood; the priest thought Sheila was going to marry him. Joe's "college chum," Finn, probably had designs on Joe but could be deterred with a "No." It was not a good idea to get on his wrong side, however, because he could be vicious. Did Joe know that half the English Department at Harvard could be found dancing at the *Punch Bowl*, Boston's most famous gay bar, on any Saturday night? And Larry, the man who had offered to take them home when they had met on the riverbank two years before, was the president of a big Boston bank.

Joe really fell for Michael. It was his body, the sex, the story, the music, the rebellion. It was everything Joe had been waiting for. Joe had been playing it safe too long. After three dreary years in Law School Joe was ready for all this.

They slept for about an hour and when they woke up they had sex again. Michael put on a bathrobe, gave Joe a robe and then made bacon and eggs. In those days Joe usually had a cup of coffee and a Chesterfield for breakfast. Joe had to get to his Evidence class. The professor took attendance and although it was the last semester, Joe wasn't out of Law School yet.

Joe said he'd call Michael later. Michael said, "Make it after noon. I'm going back to bed."

Joe was hooked. He was out.

There was a song, an instrumental, which was popular that year. It was called, *Cast Your Fate to The Wind*.

Joe had.

◊ ◊ ◊

In the middle of the brutal winter of 1966, Joe got the best tan of his life. He'd gone to Palm Beach. The man he thought that he was in love with, not Michael anymore, someone named Gerry, ditched him as soon as he arrived. So he spent every day lying in the sun alone and every night hanging around a shabby gay bar called *The Isle of Capri*.

When Joe returned he found a notice waiting for him at his parent's house in Newport from the Draft Board. Joe was to report for a physical examination. Joe went to Providence for the physical on a bus that left from Eisenhower Park in Newport, next to the YMCA, at 5:00 a.m. Joe's cousin, Brian, was also on the bus. The cousin had almost cut off his hand with a power saw years before and was never going to be drafted, but every time they lowered the standards of eligibility they called Brian back. Joe and Brian commiserated and listed all their crazy relatives in order to give their names to the doctors, should they get in to see one.

Joe had a letter from a doctor who had treated him for a broken foot a few months before. That was enough to get him into the Draft Board doctor along with all the other wimpy boys who had letters about physical ailments. Joe had also checked off the boxes on the form for depression and nervousness. After a chat with the doctor, a dermatologist, who found it surprising that anyone would say such things about oneself and who examined his foot and found it serviceable, the doctor sent Joe to a psychiatrist. The appointment was two weeks later, also in Providence.

The psychiatrist was older than Freud and came on tough until Joe said, "Look, the doctor at my physical, a dermatologist, sent me to you. I'm about to be a lawyer, I hope. I'm waiting for the results of the Bar examination. I'm aware that anything I tell you can be revealed to the Draft Board. A cousin of mine is on it. My family is well known in Newport. I may want to run for office some day. I'm not malingering, but I am going to give myself the benefit of the doubt. I'm telling you the truth. If you think that I am eligible, so be it."

"I understand your hesitation. I understand the political ramifications of this. Is there anything else you want to tell me?" the psychiatrist responded a little more meekly. The worm had turned.

"There is more that I can tell you but, as I just said, I know that nothing is confidential...."

The psychiatrist interrupted, "You don't have to worry about confidentiality with me."

"Allright, I'm homosexual." People weren't saying "Gay" outside of gay circles yet.

"How long have you been 'homo'?" the psychiatrist asked in all seriousness.

Joe immediately regretted telling the old fart anything, but instead of blasting the doctor for his crassness, he blamed himself for his misjudgement. This was 1966 after all.

Joe replied, "I've been out for about a year." He wasn't sure that the doctor would understand the concept of "being out" but now he didn't care enough to explain.

"Are you active or passive?" the doctor asked.

Now Joe didn't understand that concept. But he knew that he'd been actively having sex with men ever since that fateful St. Patrick's Day the year before when he remet Michael. So, he replied, "Active."

The doctor said, "You hate your father. I'll write a vague letter that will keep you out of the draft. However, it will say that you are emotionally unstable. You'll be found to be 4F, which disqualifies you from the draft."

Joe left the Doctor's office, got on the bus to Boston and headed to Lundin's Turkish Baths in Park Square. He sang to himself, "I'm not going to Vietnam/ I'm emotionally unstable/ I hate my father/ I'm not going to Vietnam."

9
Good Advice Well Taken

Tom Murphy and Joe left the rectory more confused than before. Although it appeared that Tom had made a comeback while in the rectory, Tom rightfully still gave Joe hell for letting him go on before telling him that they had the wrong guy in Monsignor Randozza. Joe took it like a man and then said, "What do we do now?"

Tom replied, "I don't want to fool around with the brother in the North End. He's tough in a way we could never be. You know that they call him "The Tiger?" Are you sure that you saw him over here, outside the school, on a Wednesday night?

"I'm sure, Tommy. Not to make excuses, and I'm sorry I let you go on in there—you were great by the way—but remember that I wasn't the one who identified the Monsignor. That was Sergeant Detective Shaughnessy. He picked up on the body hair. I'm sure that the man I saw outside of the school was the guy who robbed me. I was only 15 or 20 feet away, parked on Harrison Avenue. I agree about not going after the North End brother. We could get hurt."

"Well, it looks like I have to go to SLAA and snoop for your robber. The gay guys call this meeting "Dirty Girls." I'm sure I qualify.

It wouldn't hurt. Ha! Ha! Ha! I could go up there right now. The meeting's just ending. I have to ring a bell and they'll let me in. I don't know what to do. You go home. I'll call you later."

Joe walked to Tremont Street, stopped in the Garden of Eden and had the Appleton Sandwich, chicken salad to the rest of the world. While there he saw a couple of the men from the AA meeting. The guy who was passing out the candy, "the desert person," came over to talk to him.

"How are you doing? I'm Allen. Did you like the meeting? If you need to talk, here's my number."

"Thanks a lot. I enjoyed the meeting. It was very interesting. Thanks for the number," Joe said.

Allen paused and began to walk away. Then he turned and said, "Don't I know you from the Napoleon Club? I used to be standing by the piano singing, except when I fell down—but I'd come up singing and I never spilt a drink," and Allen laughed. "Marie would play *If I was a Rich Man* whenever I came in the bar.

"I don't remember you, but I don't go out much. I mostly stay at home," Joe said.

"Ooh, a 'solitary drunk!' I drank at home too. I couldn't get out of the house the last couple of years. I was lucky to get to work, and luckier that my father owned the business." Allen laughed again. "I'll see you around and if you ever want to talk, that's my number."

Joe finished his sandwich, flagged a cab and went home. He skipped the elevator and climbed the stairs to his apartment.

Sitting on the floor up against his apartment door there was a teddy bear with its head torn almost off. He picked it up and went inside. He thought that maybe a kid from one of the two floors above had dropped it. He put the teddy bear on the table in the hall along with his keys. He'd check tomorrow to see who owned it.

There were two messages on his machine. The call recorder indicated that one was private and the other was from Rhode Island, but the numbers were not immediately familiar to Joe. Joe pressed the button to hear his messages.

"Stop fucking around. Give it up. Take it like a man. You almost did last week. Ha! And you might get a second chance. Otherwise, you might get hurt. Love, Teddy Bear."

The voice was not familiar. It didn't sound like the robber. It was much rougher and cruder—more guttural, like some man trying to imitate a gangster. Joe sat down for the second call.

"Hello darling, this is your mother. I'm at your Aunt Josie's. We were thinking of you and wanted to say we loved you. I'll call you tomorrow when I'm back home."

Those were certainly two different love messages. Joe paced as he waited for Tommy's call. He thought of leaving, but where could he go?

He called his mother back at the number on his call recorder. His aunt Josie, his mother's immediately older sister, answered, "Joseph darling! No, you didn't wake me up. I'm watching the baseball game. The Red Sox are losing. What else is new! And how are you, my darling? Do you want to take me to Ireland? I won the prize at the Newport Irish Society raffle at Saint Augustine's, the church in the old Ward 5. Some handsome professor from Washington was speaking. He was marvelous. They're all studying the American Irish now, you know. It's grand. I could tell them a thing or two. Just remember, we were proud of being Irish before Jack Kennedy became President. Sooooo, I have the two tickets. Would you like to go? We can visit the cousins in Louth. They still have the farm. You need a rest. They work you too hard. All that thinking and writing, sitting and…pondering. Let me know. I have to go. We just hit a home run. Bye, bye." She hung up without letting Joe say a word.

Ireland sounded like a good idea. Joe would have left right then, but he had to wait for Tommy's call.

Just then the phone rang. Tommy shouted, "For Christ's sake, you have to get call waiting. The millennium has passed! Get with it! I've been calling for twenty minutes. I'll be right over."

Joe said, "No, I'll meet you at your place. I can't stay here tonight. I'll tell you about it. They're on to us."

"Okay, Okay, Come right over. You can take my son's bed. I knew there was a reason I kept this big house. Hurry up, though. I have to go to sleep. I'm usually in bed by 8:30, unless I'm in Las Vegas or Amsterdam. Ha, Ha, Ha!"

Joe packed a large carry-on bag and put two suits into a suit bag. He even threw in his passport. He knew that this exile wasn't going to be a one nighter.

Years before, after he was robbed in his house in the South End, Joe had camped out at Tommy's. They could live together without killing each other, he thought, at least for a couple of nights. Why did he think that being with Tommy was any safer? Well, he wouldn't be alone for one thing.

He told Tommy about the teddy bear and the call. He even called his message and let Tommy listen to the scary one.

"Well, it's your boyfriend or one of his pals. It sounds like he still wants you. That's something. Two months ago you were full of self pity, thinking that nobody would ever love you again. Now somebody seems to know your every move, our every move. Maybe you ought to get out of town for a while. Where can you go? Can you get the time off? Oh, of course, in your job they never know where you are."

"So long as I come in twice a month and keep the work coming, you're right. But in this instance I ought to get permission," Joe said.

"Well get the permission and get out of here!! You can work wherever you go. Where will you go?"

"My aunt wants me to go to Ireland with her. She won two tickets in a raffle in Newport. Otherwise, I could go to Vieques. I know that place."

"Oh yeah, that's the island off Puerto Rico where you went after you flipped over Arthur Bruce leaving, right?"

"Yes, it was very healing," Joe said wistfully.

"Healing? Healing? Yeah, Yeah, but you need to be alert and on the move. Besides after a tan those Italians look like Puerto Ricans. You want to be able to spot the bastards if they're tailing you." Tommy liked to sound like a tough guy. "You'd better go to Mother Ireland with your auntie. They'll think you're a priest. Whoops! We better stay away from that subject.Ha! Ha! Ha!"

"But I don't want to go to Ireland with my Aunt Josie. She's old and difficult. She eats supper at 5:30, for Christ's sake. She goes to bed at nine. How can I do that?"

"Well, you can park her with the cousins. Put her in the Carmel Quinn motel in Clare. Ha! Ha! Ha! Where are your people from? Louth, did you say? You must be gentry. The rest of us around here are from the West, Galway, Roscommon or 'Mayo, God help us.' The aunt can go search the graveyards looking for dead heroes and you can hang around the docks looking for dusky sailors. How the fuck do I know what you ought to do!?! All I know is that you have a homicidal nutcase chasing you around. We don't know if he wants to kill you or fuck you or both, possibly in that order." Tom was on a roll. "What I do know is that you have to get out of town. In Ireland you'll know the language, if you can understand those people. Stay out of Kerry. They talk Greek there. And stay away from the sheepshaggers in Tipperary. They may be looking for a little variety. Baaaaaah! Ha! Ha! Ha!"

"That's where my father's family is from," Joe said.

"Well, good luck to you. Maybe that's where they come from, your 'predilections.'"

Joe ignored Tommy's dig and said, "When should I leave? I'd better call Aunt Josie and tell her I'll go with her. I'll call Bernie at his travel agency and have him make the arrangements. We'll need a couple of nights in Dublin, a car, a place north of Dundalk, and other places. Maybe I shouldn't create an itinerary in advance. If the robber finds it, I'm fucked."

"Well, that may be so. Call Bernie. He makes all the travel arrangements for the Archdiocese. That's why he's so afraid of being out. If the Cardinal knew he's gay, he'd drop Bernie in a minute. Some of the priests do know. Bernie knows all the hotspots in Rome and he's discreet," Tom added. "You could do a 'Triple I' tour, like the New York politicians, Ireland, Italy and Israel. You'd like those Israelis. I met a soldier in a park in Tel Aviv one night. He came back to my hotel with the machine gun. It was hot. The next night I met a Palestinian. He was hot too."

"Oh Tom, you're too cosmopolitan," Joe muttered as he headed to bed.

The next morning Joe returned to his apartment after calling Josie from Tommy's house to tell her he would go with her to Ireland. He'd called Bernie first, who booked them at the Shelburne Hotel for three nights and rented them a small Mercedes. Bernie wasn't too happy about the absence of a commission on Josie's raffle prize ticket, but Joe's requests for fancy ground accommodations softened the blow. He'd get the commission for those. In addition, Joe upgraded the tickets to first class. Bernie was okay, but could be a pain in the ass if he thought he wasn't making enough money. Tom often told Bernie that he still had his First Communion money. Bernie was neither insulted nor amused. He just went on about how he could be using the time to send 50 Pioneer of the Telephone Company retirees to Cancun and make a bigger profit.

"But they'll be dead in ten years and I'll still be calling you," Joe replied.

Joe went to his own place. He wasn't afraid to be in his apartment in the daytime, but he couldn't stay long this night. So after he packed a bag and his laptop he left for his mother's in Rhode Island. He and Josie were scheduled to leave in two days out of Green Airport in Providence. As soon as Joe got over the border into Rhode Island, he felt better. Somehow he thought that the long arm of his "admirer" couldn't reach him there. It was like his assistant district attorney days. If he'd had too much to drink in Boston, he felt at ease once he got over the county line into Quincy. Theoretically, as an assistant district attorney he could *nul prosse* his own case. He could wipe it out. That is, if he could find the book that the forms were kept in. The book was under lock and key in the top drawer of the District Attorney himself.

Anyway, as irrational as it seems, Joe felt safe in Rhode Island and safer yet once he got on Aquidneck, the island that contains Newport, Portsmouth and Middletown. He passed Jackie Crotty's house and felt a twinge, even though Jackie had long since hopped on a motorcycle heading for California, with his girlfriend sitting behind him. Second Beach never looked so good. The same for St. George's up on the hill.

Joe appreciated the comfort and safety of his childhood and adolescence, as confused as they may have been for him sexually. Of course, he had just denied his longings then, swam them away, put them in a drawer somewhere, to be activated only when someone else, like Jackie or Harry opened it. He'd tried to be sexless in those days. He gave that up as he got older. In his late thirties and early forties, the later seventies and early eighties, he joined in the revelry. Then AIDS hit and that cooled him, and a lot of other men, down.

His mother was waiting for him. She made him some tea. They sat in the living room overlooking the marsh and the beach beyond. The sun was going down. It was beautiful and peaceful.

As soon as they were seated she asked, "What made you decide to go with Josie? You seem distracted recently. Is there something going on, something that you can talk about, that I would understand?" She leaned over the low table to pour the tea, then added, "I know that you deal with very serious matters at your work. Can I help you in some way?"

She got up and went to the kitchen as soon as she said all of this. Experience had taught her that she wouldn't get a true answer, but all the mother books as well as "Dear Abby" had taught her that she should ask nevertheless. She suspected that it was something romantic but she and Joe never discussed anything like that. They wouldn't have, even if Joe was straight. It just wasn't the way she had been raised. Was it an Irish trait, or a Catholic one? One shouldn't talk about anything that might lead to a discussion of sex. Was it avoiding an occasion of sin?

Joe told his mother something about Arthur Bruce years before. He told her that Arthur left because he could be more successful as an artist in New York. She heard him mention that he had seen Arthur from time to time since. She detected Joe's affection for Arthur from the tone of Joe's voice. She didn't want to be a prying mother but, of course, she put together what she was told into some kind of a story that had a few contact points with the truth, the ones he gave her and those she read in newspapers or saw on television.

While home in Rhode Island, Joe slept a lot and walked the beach. Like he used to do in the old days, Joe came back with treasures from these walks, pieces of battered, painted wood, beach glass, seashells and well-worn rocks from the end of the beach closest to their house, where the surfers vainly surfed, hoping that a California wave would get lost, defy geography, and crash on the East Coast.

On the second night they went out to dinner in Newport, to *Juventuti's*, the name of which always amused Joe. Did it mean "the youth?" or had Joe forgotten his Latin? The food was always good there. The owner was at the door. Although younger than Joe, he knew Joe's mother and sat them at a table for four upstairs in a quiet corner. Joe's very talented woodworker cousin, Lizzie, had designed and built the bar and the tables in the restaurant.

As a matter of fact, Lizzie was eating in the opposite corner of the upstairs room with her partner, Joanna, when they arrived. Although she wasn't officially "out" to Joe's family, everyone knew that Lizzie and Joanna were inseparable. Lizzie rushed over to see Joe and his mother. She kissed them both. Lizzie was tall and thin. She was the only one of Joe's many Irish cousins to have red hair. It was thick and wavy and always looked like it needed to be tamed. Tonight it was; it was pulled back and tied with a black velvet knot.

"How are you?" Lizzie said to Joe. "What are you doing down

here? I hear that you're going to Ireland with Josie. She'll run you around. When do you leave? And you're staying at the Shelburne in Dublin! Aren't you the one! I wish that I could join you. If Joanna didn't have her doctoral exams, we'd go too."

"I wish that you would. We're going up to Louth to the farm on the Marsh. Josie has been corresponding with Nora Lavin, our cousin over there, the wife of a cousin actually. Her husband's grandfather was our great grandfather's brother. He got the farm when our great grandfather left. You probably know all this," Joe inquired solicitously. "Josie has pictures of both of them and of their parents as well. Apparently our grandfather, Mom's father," Joe said with a nod to his mother, "went back in the early 1900s with his father. Josie has the whole reunion all planned. We're going to stay in the old Big House, which is now a hotel for golfers. Josie wasn't sure she wanted to stay there until she found out that the Protestants didn't own it anymore. Now she wants to sleep in the Presidential Suite."

Joe always loved his cousin Lizzie. She was warm and kind and smart. When he found out that she was gay too he was glad he had an ally. Lizzie kept in touch with everyone in the family. Her father was Joe's mother's youngest brother. All the family loved her. Maybe they'd love him too, if he told them the truth, he sometimes thought. Not yet, it was too much effort. Besides, they probably already knew. And it was her personality they loved; her gayness had little to do with it.

Joe was happy that Joanna made Lizzie happy after Lizzie's years alone. Lizzie had degrees from both Yale and the Rhode Island School of Design. She'd spent six months hitchhiking around Ireland in the seventies and another six months apprenticing as a carpenter before going to design school. For a long time thereafter all Lizzie did was work.

Josie and Joe had a suite on the fifth floor of the Shelburne Hotel facing the park, which is called Stephen's Green. Joe wanted to nap after the flight, but Josie was out in the park the first thing after her bath.

"We've forgotten about tubs, Joe. We in America have forgotten about bathtubs, and it's a shame, Joe," she said solemnly after she returned. "Now a shower may be faster but speed isn't everything. What's the rush? Where are we going, Joe? Why are we in such a hurry? We've forgotten about tubs, and we've forgotten about tea, Joe. Now this is a cup of tea. Not that dishwater we get at home. And this brown bread is delicious, as is the raspberry jam. I do make good raspberry jam myself, but this is delicious. And isn't it nice to have real butter? We're a Northern people, Joe. We like our dairy products. It's too bad they're killing us. It doesn't seem fair." Josie paused for a second, but only to allow reflection on what she had just said. She continued, "Why should the Italians have olive oil, beautiful skin, and good health? Who invented this cholesterol anyway? You never heard about it when I was growing up. Of course, all the men were dying in their fifties. 'Portly' they were. That's what we said then. You're getting a little big yourself, Joe. It's all that sitting you have to do at work. Can't you get up and walk around every once in a while? It must be the sitting. Is it a conspiracy, Joe?"

Of course Joe was not expected to answer all of these questions. It would have been unbearable if he had to respond. Who could? It was enough to nod knowingly and let her go on. "Sacred Listening," was what one of Joe's colleagues called it. Joe had learned it years ago at Josie's knee. He couldn't do otherwise.

"Let's go out to the park, Joe. You've had your rest. Now let's go. I'll give you a tour."

They walked across Lower Baggot Street at Kildare Street and entered Stephen's Green at the corner near Grafton Street, now a pedestrian mall and not a bad one at that. They walked by "the cottage," the toilets, where a few poor souls were lounging about, smoking cigarettes and looking furtive. Later one of Joe's pals told him that there was a camera in there. Josie headed directly for a statue, the head of a beautiful man with wavy hair on a plinth.

"This is James Clarence Mangan, a nineteenth-century Irish poet. He was beautiful, no? James Joyce praised him. I've never read anything except a little piece called 'Dark Rosaleen.' It's lovely in that nineteenth century flowery way but it did nothing for me. He was also an alcoholic, and a drug addict, and as a result he died too young. So let that be a lesson to you. It's not enough to be handsome and a poet. Now come over here. This is O'Donovan Rossa, a leader of the Fenians in the late nineteenth century. He may have known your great grandfather, the one who fought in the Irish Brigade under Thomas Francis Meagher. Thomas Francis Meagher is another story but there's no statue in this park—maybe because he was a bit of a ladies man—so I'll save the story," Josie said mercifully. "O'Donovan Rossa went to New York after getting out of the British prison. He owned a hotel in New York. He ran the 'Dynamite Brigade.' They were going to blow up everything. His body was returned to Ireland after he died."

Josie then looked directly at Joe and said, "You know that the people of Dublin were not too keen on the 1916 Uprising at first and that they booed the rebels. The worm that is 'the populace' turned, especially after the Brits executed the captured rebels." Josie waited for Joe to acknowledge that indeed he did know. Joe nodded.

"Over on the other side of the park is a statue of another Irish rebel, Oscar Wilde. He's lounging by the side of the road in a very languorous state. They like him here for his wit, but also because his mother Speranza was a rebel herself, albeit Protestant, and because the English persecuted him. And, of course, he converted on his deathbed, probably just after he commented on the wallpaper saying, 'This wallpaper is very ugly. One of us has to go.' He left Ireland as soon as he could, but he was an outsider in England just as we are over there to the West. It gives us perspective to be strangers. You know that? They haven't assimilated you, have they? Even with all that Harvard business you're still an Irishman, I hope. I've worked hard to make sure you don't fit in with those people."

Josie was developing a brogue after less than six hours in Ireland even though she was a very proud Pre-Famine Irish-American woman in Rhode Island. It was like she had waited all her life to be restored to her roots. When she talked to a native she tended to lecture and couldn't understand why they weren't as enthusiastic about Ireland as she was. She didn't understand that they usually just wanted to be left alone to make a living, like people anywhere.

Josie and Joe walked around the ponds and then returned to the hotel. As they entered, one of the bellboys ran through the lobby shouting, "The Honorable Joseph Lavin Lyons, The Honorable Joseph Lavin Lyons, telephone. Telephone for the Honorable Joseph Lavin Lyons!"

Joe went to the front desk, told the man who he was, and was directed to a small cubicle in a hall on the way into the grille.

"Hello, Hello, this is Joe Lyons."

"Hello, Joe. Are you enjoying yourself? Call your lawyer friend, Murphy, off. I'm waiting for you. I want you, Joe, but don't make life hard for me and I won't make it hard for you. I'll be hard for you, however, whenever you want. I know that's what you want. Just call the dog off. "

The voice was the same as the last caller's back in Boston, but again didn't seem to be the voice of his original assailant. Perhaps the voice was disguised, but it sounded like someone else, someone rougher and more dangerous. Understandably, Joe was shaken. He must have been referring to Tommy as "the dog." What was Tommy doing now? Or was it Monsignor Randozza who was causing the stir? Joe had to call Boston. He'd call Tom tomorrow. The guy said he was waiting for Joe, so it seemed that he wasn't in Dublin or so Joe hoped. What would he tell Josie? He'd tell her nothing, he decided before arriving back at the lobby. There was no point in alarming her. He could handle this himself.

When Joe returned to the lobby of the Shelburne Josie was seated in a big chair regaling a couple from Cleveland with her Irish lore.

"And what was your maiden name, dear?" she said to the wife.

"Brown? Brown? That could be Irish, dear. Kozlowski would never make it but, don't despair. Do you know about the Countess de Markiewicz? She led the Irish boy scouts, the Fianna, named after the liegemen of Finn MacCool. Although she was Anglo-Irish and married to a Pole, she was more patriotic than many of the Catholics. We Catholics have to remember that, that many of the patriots over the centuries were Protestants, Robert Emmet, Wolfe Tone, Roger Casement."

The bewildered couple had no idea what she was talking about. He was here to play golf and she wanted to shop. He'd made some money with a string of bowling alleys and she'd been able to stay home in Shaker Heights for the last 10 years. The kids were gone and so they traveled. But Josie could care less. It was her duty to educate. That was what she had spent the past 45 years doing, teaching seventh graders. These adults were much easier and how could they not care? Why else would they have come here but to learn about Ireland?

"And here is my nephew now. He just was paged in the lobby as we were coming in. God help you if you're trying to hide out in this town. Those bellboys are better than beagles for tracking you down. And then everybody is related here so if you don't respond, one of your cousins will tell the caller that you were seen down the street in Bewleys an hour ago having a cup of tea. It's terrible the way they all know each other's business in this country, but it's lovely too. It's what a country should be about. Don't you agree? Of course, of course," Josie nodded in agreement with herself.

"Now, what was the call, Joseph?" she only called him Joseph in front of other people. "Was it your office? Do they need you desperately? Can't they give you a little peace? It's bad enough that you have to carry it all around inside your head. Churning, churning all the time. I wish they would leave you alone, darling."

So Joe didn't have to invent anything. Josie had done it all by herself. He just had to worry about his back.

As they returned to their rooms, Joe could see something on

the carpet outside their door. As he got closer he saw that it was a teddy bear, its left leg dangling, half torn off.

Joe rushed forward and picked it up before Josie could see it, or so he hoped.

As Joe was bending down to pick it up, Josie said "Why that's the second maimed teddy bear I've seen in this hall today. There was another one two doors down when I came back from my walk. There must be some forgetful children on this floor, and rough ones too. Just leave it on the windowsill, Joe. That's what I did with the other one. Its arm was broken. The parents will come by and pick it up. I hope their mother can sew."

Just then a very well-dressed older woman came out of the door two doors down, just where Josie said that she had seen the first teddy bear. She was Italian, tall and stately, in a dark aubergine suit. Her hair was in a bun and she carried an enormous Gucci bag. A mantilla hung out of it, as if it had been hastily tucked in.

Joe froze. It was Giuseppina Randozza. Behind her came a thin elegant man, in his seventies at least. He was smoking a cigarette. He wore a bespoke, soft grey, double breasted, pin striped suit with a white handkerchief nonchalantly tucked in the breast pocket, a very English suit, although he clearly was something more exotic. They spoke in Italian.

"*Chiude la porta, Virgilio, per favore,*" she said.

"*Si, Cara mia, si, si,*" he replied, as if he were used to her orders.

They walked in the direction from which Joe and Josie had come, toward the elevators.

When they got in their room Josie said, "What an elegant couple! They looked like Papal nobility. Did you see that mantilla? Rose Kennedy never had a mantilla that fine."

"She's from Boston," Joe said quietly. He didn't know why. He certainly didn't intend to get into the whole story with Josie.

"What!" said Josie. "I know Rose Kennedy is from Boston. Everybody knows that. Don't be foolish, Joe."

"She's from Boston," Joe repeated. "The woman we just saw is from Boston."

"She can't be from Boston. There is nobody that elegant in Boston. The women in Providence dress better than the women in Boston."

"Actually, she's from Revere," Joe said.

"Revere? Isn't that where the beach is? Where they used to have the amusement park?" Josie asked.

"You got it," said Joe.

"Tell me everything," Josie said. "You know much more than you're telling. What's the story? And who is the man? Don't tell me that he is from Revere too. Maybe he's from Chelsea," and she laughed. "Ooh, I get it now. You know them from your work. You can't talk about it. I understand."

Joe said nothing more on that subject. "Where would you like to eat, Auntie?" Joe asked. "I have tickets for us to see *The Plough and the Stars*, right down the street at the Gate Theater. It starts at eight. We won't have a lot of time," Joe said.

"Why don't we get a sandwich at Bewley's? It's just around the corner. We can eat there quickly. I discovered it earlier on my walk, while you were napping," Josie added, to remind Joe that she was more adventuresome than he.

The play was marvelous, but better than the play was the audience. There were a bunch of schoolboys, 14 or 15 years old, in the first balcony and they were having a grand time rubbernecking and throwing spitballs. Once the play began they hushed and followed every word. The other faces were like high mass at Saint Mary's in Newport, lots of red cheeks, blue eyes and white hair.

Joe had a hard time with the political nuances in the play. He didn't know who was a socialist and who wasn't, or why it mattered, but Josie set him straight. He knew that the poor son was sick and an informer, but was he sick because he was an informer or an informer because he was sick? Michael Gambon was brilliant as the father, hiding the bottles, and the mother was good too. It stirred Joe's Irish soul and gave him courage in his own battle with the hydra-headed forces of evil, which seemed to have followed him even here to Dublin.

10
Joe Cannot Hide in Ireland

The next day the first thing that Josie wanted to see was *The Book of Kells* at Trinity College. Joe remembered his souvenir fragment bookmark from his first visit to Dublin. And he remembered that it had been stolen. That made him angry all over again.

Each day they show a different page of *The Book of Kells* in the Trinity Library. That Saturday the exhibited page was the lion, the symbol of Saint Mark, one of the four evangelists. Josie was touched because the same page had been showing when she was last in Dublin in 1962. Joe had also seen that page on his first visit. He wondered what Mark, the patron of Venice, was trying to tell them. Was the lion talking to Joseph Lyons? His souvenir had drawings of cats, striped cats, tigers maybe if they knew anything about tigers in Ireland in the 9th century.

The viewing room in the library at Trinity was considerably dolled up since Josie's previous visit. "German money," the guard muttered when they inquired about the renovations as they left the room. He meant European Economic Community (EEC) money. It had transformed Ireland's infrastructure and the sites of its artifacts.

Joe and Josie's plan was to go down to County Cork after early Mass the next day to stay at the Ballymalloe House overnight for a round of meals, and then drive back north to Athlone to see the ruins there on the way further north to Ballyfirglin in Louth, near the border with Ulster, where his Lavin cousins lived. Although they were known only by infrequent correspondence, the connection across the water had been maintained for over 150 years. Joe realized that their route wasn't the most efficient, but Joe didn't mind. He was killing time, if you will.

Ballymalloe House was magnificent. It looked like a Southern plantation mansion. It was reputed to serve the best food in Ireland and had a renowned cooking school. A pal of Joe's in Boston, "The Commissioner" Walsh, had been a student there and insisted that Joe visit.

They arrived late in the afternoon on Sunday and were shown to adjacent rooms on the second floor. Joe changed into a suit for dinner and Josie wore her navy blue linen suit—the summer wedding and funeral suit. They met in the cocktail room downstairs where Joe had commandeered a sofa in front of the *hors d'oeuvres*. Joe was sipping mineral water when Josie appeared smiling and looking magnificent, like Queen Mary with a sense of humor. He stood up when he saw her coming. She kissed his cheek and sat to his left in a big stuffed chair.

After she ordered an "American martini with Irish gin," a fitting metaphor for her patriotisms, Josie surveyed the room. Next to them were two beautiful young Irish women, one still in riding clothes, the other in a big flowery soft dress.

When Joe started to ask Josie if she liked her drink Josie put her finger to her lips, whispered, "Shhhh," and nodded towards the women. She was eavesdropping and she didn't want to miss a word. Once, years before, when she and Joe's mother were sitting in a booth invisible to the conversers behind her, Josie had loudly told Joe's mother to keep quiet because she couldn't hear whose wife was cheating with whom. She thought that because the men in the next booth couldn't see her they wouldn't hear her either even though she had been listening to them. As you would expect, dead silence ensued.

The fashionable women at Ballymalloe were talking about banking—of all things. Joe couldn't get over it. To him it was incongruous. Brogues so sweet shouldn't be talking about money, he thought. He said so quietly to Josie.

"Welcome to the new Ireland, 'The Celtic Tiger!'" she said. "I didn't know that you were so romantic—or so sexist. Does it bother you to hear women talking business, or is it just here? The President of Ireland is a woman and so was the one before her. That's better than we're doing, with all our Betty Friedan and Hillary Clinton stuff. Get with it, you old fuddy duddy!"

She continued looking around, occasionally sipping the martini. At one point she even craned over Joe's head and stopped in that awkward position to look more closely at the people two couches away to their right.

She said, "Joe darling, don't look now, but isn't that the fashionable, old Italian couple we saw in the Shelburne, the Countess from Revere and her boyfriend?"

Joe froze but couldn't let Josie see his fear. This was more than a coincidence, he was sure.

Joe excused himself and headed to the loo, which was just outside the double door. Without moving his head he looked to the right. Indeed it was Giuseppina and her boyfriend. She was again dressed in a well-made suit, this time it was a soft yellow green, just a shade darker than the wallpaper and coordinated drapes. Giuseppina never looked at Joe, and, apart from assuring himself who was there, Joe did not look long at her. He went into the tiny loo, threw cold water on his face, peed, washed his hands, combed his hair, took three deep breaths and walked out.

The Count was outside the loo door waiting to go in. Joe stepped to one side to give him way. The Count bowed a little, said, "Thank you," with an Italian accent and Joe returned to the drawing room.

He couldn't see Josie in her chair. He felt a moment of panic. He looked around the room for her.

There was Josie in a pretty little side chair, waving her martini glass around, seated right next to Giuseppina on the couch. They both were laughing like old friends. Joe stopped dead in his tracks.

"Joe, Joe darling, come over here," Josie said loudly, waving at Joe across the room as all eyes turned.

Joe knew he had no choice. So, like the moth to a flame over he went.

"Since we're all from New England I thought that we ought to meet each other instead of passing like ships in the night," Josie began. "Giuseppina Randozza, this is my nephew, Joseph Lyons, who is escorting me on this trip. Giuseppina is traveling with the Count of Trapani. They came over for the Horse Show in Dublin. Otherwise, they spend a lot of time in Rome." Obviously Josie had lost no time obtaining information.

Joe hoped that it wasn't the martini talking and that the warmth Josie assumed was coming from Giuseppina was real.

"It's a pleasure to meet you, Judge Lyons," Giuseppina said. "Virgilio, my friend, studied law in Rome. He'll be interested in talking to you. Here he comes now."

Joe remained standing as the courtly man who was waiting outside the bathroom door arrived. "A pleasure to meet you," Joe said, trying not to sound stiff or scared.

Giuseppina spoke to the Count in Italian and then said in English, "Judge Joseph Lyons, this is Virgilio Scola, the Count of Trapani."

The Count spoke hesitantly, with a heavy accent, "I am very pleased to meet you."

Joe returned the compliment.

"I studied law years ago but I never practiced. The War came and I joined the Italian Resistance. After the War I returned to my family's farm and rebuilt it. I studied the Common Law. It's an admirable system that you have, particularly the Separation of Powers. Isn't that what you call it? I seem to remember that's what it's called. In Italy the judge and the prosecutor are all rolled into one, like *braciole*, no Giuseppina?

"I wouldn't know," Giuseppina said. "I try never to involve myself in the Law, either in America or in Italy. I do know *braciole*, however. Judge Lyons, you should taste my *braciole*. When you and your lovely aunt come to Rome I will cook for you."

"I'd like that, "Joe said lying through his teeth. He was sure the meat would be poisoned.

"I heard that the food here at Ballymaloe is wonderful. I'm looking forward to it. Irish food has an undeservedly bad reputation. It's been very good so far. I grew up with the Irish, you know. I'm originally from Dorchester. It's lovely to see their country at last. They suffered so. I'd read about the Famine before coming over. What a tragedy. Yet it explains so much about Boston," Giuseppina said. "They seem to have gotten over it here, however," she added.

Joe, astonished by the breadth of Giuseppina's interests, forgot that this was the mother of the man who'd tied him up and robbed him.

Joe got right into the discussion. "They're only now thinking about the Famine. There was a lot of shame involved. Not all people behaved well. The survivors had guilt and so do their children. It was so devastating. Our cousins said that they gave up land for the poor. I think what they mean is that they stopped collecting rents because nobody could pay. I think that they were deposed Catholic Irish nobility who became land agents for the absentee British landlords once their land was taken. They only recently got their 30 acres back and that makes them proud. Wealth is measured in land here, land and cows. It hasn't changed a lot, the EEC notwithstanding."

"Just give me the land; it's so beautiful," Josie said. "I've never been fond of cows, except for a good steak."

"Speaking of food, I believe the hostess is looking for us, Josie, to go in and eat. It's been a pleasure to meet you both."

And into the dining room they went to the most wonderful

meal of their trip, beef and lamb and salmon, fresh vegetables of all sorts, even turnips and parsnips, which Joe usually claimed he hated, and beautiful cakes, sorbets and fresh berries. Joe couldn't help thinking that this was a far cry from the Famine that sent his ancestors across the sea.

Giuseppina and the Count came into the dining room shortly thereafter and were seated on the far side of the room.

"Should I go ask them to sit with us, Joe?" Josie whispered loudly, the only way she could whisper. "They seem very nice and you can talk Law to the Count. I bet he was very handsome in his day. He still is, of course, but she has him under lock and key. Isn't he romantic? I wonder where she found him. Certainly not in Revere, although I'm sure there are some very handsome men there too, but not many counts. 'The Italians are God's gift to the Irish,' or so they say. Handsome as the men are, they're usually very difficult for Irish women because their mothers spoiled them so. Talk about 'Get up and let your brother sit down.' They've perfected it. The girls are lucky if they get to eat at all. The Irish women are too independent for them. They like our fair skin and light eyes but we have wicked tongues. Furthermore, we can't cook like their mothers. Food is very important to the Italians, you know, just like the Chinese, Joe. Now, the other way around, the marriage of an Irish man and an Italian woman works very well. Everybody eats well and the children are beautiful."

She would have gone on with this wisdom accumulated over her many years but Joe interrupted, "I think they're very happy where they are, Josie, and so are we. But let me ask you a question. Did you tell Mrs. Randozza that I'm a judge?"

Josie paused and thought a bit. "No, I didn't. I'm sure I didn't. I simply told her that I'm traveling with my nephew and that he had gone to the loo. I love that word 'loo.' It's so much nicer than our words. Your mother says 'biffy' and that's nice too. No, I never told her that you're a judge. Of course, I'm proud that you're a judge but I remember that once you told me never to call you 'Judge' in public because you never know who's going to be around. You deal with some pretty shady characters. I don't know how you do it, Joe. But she seemed like a pretty smart woman. She may be like us, knowing 'who's who and what's what.' She did say that she grew up in an Irish neighborhood and she may have learned those skills from her Irish neighbors. Besides, you were in the *Boston Herald* three years ago for that lesbian child support case. People don't forget and you're very good looking. Once somebody saw your face how could she forget it? It was a very nice photo in the *Herald*. I'll say that for it. The article savaged you but the picture was very nice. Who did that photo, Joe? Was it Fabian Bachrach?"

"Well, it's strange," Joe said. "People usually know the trial judges, especially the local ones and the judges who have celebrity cases. And most lawyers know the names of the seven justices of the Supreme Judicial Court. But there are 25 of us on the Appeals Court and we're pretty anonymous as a rule. Some people call us 'The Anonymous Court.' It can be a good thing sometimes. Some poor trial judges were followed for days by the TV people a few years ago, just to make sure they were working the full day."

"Well, you shouldn't be anonymous, Joe. You're just as smart as those other people. Weren't you at the top of your class in Law School? I tell everyone you were. And you were a very good Assistant District Attorney. Madge Mullin sat in on one of your cases and she told me you were brilliant, absolutely brilliant, and you know that she's not one to shower praise on anyone. She doesn't even like Jesus' haircut. The only person more critical than Madge is Tammy Walsh. She only likes her husband and her dog, and not necessarily in that order. I don't know which she'd rescue first in a fire," Josie replied, going just a little farther afield.

Joe said, "You're a peach, Josie." He wanted to add, *but sometimes you get carried away and it's usually after two martinis*, but he didn't. Josie worried about alcoholism, having seen the devastation it had brought on her family. One time she said, "I would drink more than two drinks, but I'm afraid that I'd never stop."

They finished the meal with three kinds of cake, raspberries and blackberries and decaffeinated coffee, then went up to bed to rest for their ride North the next day. Josie wanted to go everywhere, Clonmacnois, Galway, the Aran Islands, and then to Faughart in Louth, the ancestral graveyard with the Saint Brigid's well. Joe wasn't so sure that he wanted to make quite this trek but he was humoring Josie while hiding out.

11 Joe Never Could Hide in Ireland

In 1961, his junior year at Harvard, Joe enrolled in a course in Irish literature. It was the only Irish course offered at Harvard that spring and you could only take it in the spring because the same one professor taught the course in Irish history in the fall. God forbid that Harvard should hire two professors to teach things Irish. The professor was a prematurely white-haired man with frightened blue eyes and a beautiful brogue. Joe's friend Slade called him a "spoiled priest," but that may have been because Slade liked the combination of the words and the notion. The professor was actually from Lowell; he got the brogue on the G.I. Bill when he studied in Ireland after World War II. He also had a stammer but that vanished when he read, and he read beautifully. The course reading included the Twentieth Century "O"s—Liam O'Flaherty, Sean O'Casey, Frank O'Connor, Sean O'Faolain as well as James Joyce in *The Portrait of the Artist as a Young Man*, *The Dubliners* and selected bits from Ulysses. They also read Somerville and Ross, other 19th-century Protestants, and Synge and Yeats, of course.

In spite of the Irish literature class it was not a good semester for Joe; he slept through most of it. These days they'd say he was depressed, but it was probably just being in the closet without a clue how to get out. And there was nobody there to help him, unless you counted some lecherous English tutors. The course was a bright light in an otherwise gray time. Joe's previous exposure to Irish books was limited to Maurice Walsh, a favorite of his father. Walsh wrote rural romances about Irish country life among the middle classes.

It was good for Joe to know that he came from a culture that was still alive. Of course, he knew about *The Book of Kells* and that Ireland had been an intellectual stronghold while the Britons were still painted blue, but Irish culture hadn't been updated to the Twentieth Century for him and it hadn't been presented all in one package. The course gave him pride.

Joe had nurtured the dream of going to Ireland for a long time. But law school, a career, the pleasures of gay life and being the "Numero of 1965," as well as short money got in the way until 1969 when he just decided to go. The wife of a friend told him about the Aran Islands, remote bastions of the Irish language off the coast from Galway. She even gave him the name of a woman who ran a bed and breakfast in Kilmurvey on Inishmore, the largest of the three Aran Islands. An older gay friend, a professor at Harvard, told him about Bartley Dunnes, the one gay bar in Dublin at that time. So, armed with this spiritual and carnal knowledge, off he went in the late summer of 1969 on *Aer Lingus* from Boston.

He arrived at the Harcourt Hotel, a small, second class hotel on Harcourt Street near Stephens Green in Dublin in the late afternoon and took a nap. After the nap he ate in the hotel dining room where they had a special fork for potatoes, which he found comic. The country girl dressed up in her black and white waitress outfit didn't find it so amusing and asked, "And what do you Yanks do with potatoes? Eat them with your hands?" She asked him where "his people" were from and he told her as best he knew.

The very respectable maiden ladies at the next table, who were also hotel guests but hadn't known each other before, played Irish genealogy up one coast and down the other until they realized that although from different parts of Ireland altogether, they were third cousins and both related to the Bishop, Catholic of course, of Limerick. It reminded him of his Aunt Josie who could tell you who was related to whom in Rhode Island and go back generations.

The ladies were about to set on Joe just as the busboy cleared away his plate. Joe excused himself and walked down to Stephen's Green and thence to Bartley Dunne's, the "theatrical" pub he had been told about. It was then about ten o'clock in the evening and there was a small crowd. More women than he expected. He talked to a handsome, moody young man with pale skin and dark hair, named Aidan, who said he was a journalist for the *Irish Times*. Aidan drank like a reporter. They talked for a long time, until Aidan got too drunk and a little nasty. Aidan gave Joe his number at the newspaper (he didn't have one at home) and they agreed to meet the next day, when Aidan would take Joe around Dublin.

Joe went to the Men's room. In the loo a giant of a man, blond, frizzy haired, pink cheeked and also drunk grabbed Joe and began to tell Joe his life story. He was a farmer from Tipperary in town for the weekend who said he would like to take Joe back to Joe's hotel and show him the real Ireland. He himself was staying with a cousin in North Dublin. He was unzipping his fly when Joe slipped out from under his big arm. Joe came back to the bar to find Aidan, the reporter, passed out.

Joe needed some sleep and decided that this was enough adventure for one night, so he left. Just behind him at the door and then beside him on the wide sidewalk was an angelic, sturdy, young redhead who kept pace with Joe as Joe walked back to his hotel. When Joe slowed down, he did too; when Joe speeded up, so did his sidekick. However, the young man never looked over at Joe. He pulled a magazine out of his back pocket and appeared to be reading it by streetlight as they headed towards Stephens Green. At the corner of Stephens Green and Grafton Street Joe took a right. The angel did too. He had something in his mouth like a whistle but smaller. Joe saw that the magazine was *Newsweek*. Joe finally overcame his timidity and asked, "What's that in your mouth?"

"It's a football pin, to blow up a football. I've just been to practice. I play football, Irish football."

"Why are you reading *Newsweek*? Is there an Irish edition?"

"It's an American magazine. It is." He said proudly. "I love the States. Where are you from?"

"Boston, Boston in Massachusetts," said Joe, as if there might be another.

"A lovely place. A lovely place, I've heard. The Kennedys are from there?"

"They are. They are." Now Joe was talking like him, repeating everything, like he was talking to an old man with a hearing problem.

"Do you know them now?" the football playing angel asked.

Joe was caught unawares. What to say to capture this prize? Tell the truth, deny them or embellish? "I met the President once and Teddy, the Senator, a couple of times." That was the truth.

"They're lovely men. Lovely men. Where are you walking now?"

"I'm going to my hotel; it's up on the right on Harcourt Street. I'd invite you in, but it's a small hotel and I suspect they're very nosy."

"Walk a little further up the street with me. There's a little green up there. I'll show you."

They walked past Joe's hotel, which was two row houses joined together, and continued up Harcourt Street another fifty yards or so. Just before the next corner, Montague Street, there was a rickety wooden fence to the right. Joe's companion pushed two boards aside and held them back for Joe. It may have been a green once. There were a couple of trees and there was grass on the ground amidst the weeds. Otherwise, it was a dump. There was an old car chassis and other debris. The football player walked into the wood about ten feet near a tree. Joe followed. The angel reached up on tiptoes and kissed Joe. Then he took off all his clothes and began to unbutton Joe's shirt. He had a beautiful, sturdy, pale body and lots of red hair on his chest and stomach and bush. He glowed in the dark like a birch log on fire. Joe let him take off his shirt; Joe loosened his own pants at the same time.

As he stood there with his pants around his ankles Joe whispered, a little bit late it might seem, "Is it safe here?"

"Safe as church," the angel said as he went down on Joe, rubbing Joe's ass with both hands as his mouth worked Joe's cock. Joe came quickly, partially from excitement, but also partly out of fright. Joe tried to jerk the angel off, but the angel pushed his hand away and said, "It's not necessary. Thanks, Yank."

Joe pulled up his pants and the angel put his clothes back on. They left the green through the boards of the fence. The angel said, "I'll walk you back to your hotel. I've got something for you."

"The football pin, the new *Newsweek*?" asked Joe.

"No, you foolish lad! Here take this. It's the real thing. It'll be safer in America. Don't open it 'til you get back home to Boston."

Joe looked at the small 4″x 6″ flat packet. Whatever it was, it was wrapped in a newspaper that looked like *The Irish Times*, not the paper a Catholic boy would be reading.

Joe wanted to give the angel a memento as well. He had a small silk scarf, an Indian pocket square, red and orange and purple, in his jacket pocket. It had been given to Joe by a friend, who said that he had gotten it from Errol Flynn's son, Sean, in Paris. Sean Flynn had later been killed in Vietnam where he was a war correspondent. Joe didn't tell all this to the angel. He just said, "Take this. Its first owner was an Irishman. And he was very beautiful, like you. What's your name?"

"My name is Tim, and you're Joe. We're almost at your door."

When Joe got to the top step, at the door to the hotel, the angel said from the street loudly, "Thanks, Yank! Thanks! Good night and God bless you! God bless you! Don't let the tigers get you!"

Now how did he know my name? Joe wondered as he watched the angel vanish into the night, as angels do.

Of course, Joe opened the package immediately once inside his room. The outer wrapping was newspaper, but inside was a letter. Then there was another layer of tissue paper.

The letter said:

> *This is a piece of a page of The Book of Kells.*
> *During the Famine my great grandfather and seven*
>   *other men*
> *retrieved the page from their landlord before*
> *setting his house on fire after he let his tenants starve*
> *He'd turned his fields to grazing lands*
> *and sold what crops remained to England.*
> *My great grandfather and the others were called Fireboys.*
> *The mother of one of the eight men*
> *was a maid in the house and had seen the*
> *landlord show the Page to his son. She also*
> *heard him describe it. She saw him hide it*
> *in his library in a secret drawer beneath his desk.*
> *Before torching the house the eight men cut the page*
> *into eight parts and divided it amongst themselves.*
> *The men took an oath that the Page would not be reunited*
> *until all Ireland was free from British rule,*
> *and the snakes once again driven out of Ireland.*

Joe then opened the tissue paper and saw a piece of thick vellum with ancient Insular majuscule script on it. It read on one side:

> *misertusest sup*
> *oves nonhabentes p*
> *cere illosmulta et*
> *fieret accesserunt d*

And on the other side:

> *acceptis quinque pa*
> *us intuens in caelum*
> *anes et dedit discipu*
> *nteeos etduospisces*

Before the "m" in *misertusest* and three lines down at *et* small drawings of striped cats, almost like tigers, appeared. Joe knew that, of course, there had never been tigers in Ireland in the ninth century.

Joe recognized certain words—*oves, illos, multa, quinque, caelum, pisces*. He also remembered learning that early scriveners sometimes ran three words together like "*etduospisces*," which translates as "and two fish." Joe sensed that perhaps the full text was one of the narrations that each of the Evangelists made of *The Miracle of the Loaves and Fishes*.

However, Joe was skeptical that what he was looking at was authentic. He had just had sex with an over imaginative young Irishman, who indulged in fantasy about Americans, football, *The Book of Kells* and the Irish Struggle. To the recently academic Joe it seemed unthinkable that anyone would dare to cut up a page of Ireland's most sacred national treasure, a lavishly illustrated 9th-century rendering of the Four Gospels. Joe knew its importance in contemporary Irish culture; he'd learned that at Harvard College, of all ungodly places. He also knew that *The Book of Kells* was just up the street from his hotel at Trinity College, where it was enshrined in a special part of the Library, open to view by the public under controlled conditions. He knew that a different page was opened every day and that The Book was kept in a glass case. He had read all this in at least one tourist guide. It was a "must-see" in Ireland, said the guide.

Besides, if the fragment was real, Joe didn't know what to do with the responsibility it would entail. He was too tired; it had been a long day. It was more convenient to think that what he was looking at was probably just a souvenir bookmark that was sold at the Trinity College giftshop, accompanied by a bit of the angel's blarney about his revolutionary ancestry, creating eight men who retrieved "the Page" and burnt down their landlord's house. This kid was adorable, but not believable. Joe could hardly believe any part of their encounter was real. For one thing, the angel was so sweet, not like the smart sophisticates Joe was then cavorting with back home in Boston and New York. It was like all of Joe's fantasies about Ireland, and a lot of other matters, were packaged in the angel and offered to him in one bundle. Joe went to the window to see if he could find his lovemate so he could clarify this rationalization, but the street was empty. Was any of this real?

Soon Joe was so tired from the trip and his day's adventures that he fell sound asleep. Before nodding off he determined to visit *The Book of Kells* at Trinity College the very next day and he did.

12 Surprises at the Ancestral Home

Joe and Josie decided to go directly to the ancestral home, to Ballyfirglin on the Marsh, up North, in Louth near the border with Ulster and on the Irish Sea, facing England and Scotland.

Although there were cousins younger than Joe, Nora, the matriarch, was the widow of the last of the Lavins on the farm. Somehow she and Josie had kept up a correspondence throughout the years. And even though Nora was only a Lavin by marriage, she knew and maintained all the lore of the family. Being an outsider she had a greater respect for it than most of the insiders. Her marriage to the landowning Peter Lavin had been a step up for her. She was better than a blood relative for Josie's purposes, which was to gather information that would bolster her lofty ideas about the Lavins of Ballyfirglin. Surely, they were as worthy as the O'Neills who had been the Kings of Tara and All Ireland and the O'Neill who, in order to gain the kingdom, chopped off his hand and threw it onto the Irish shore.

They arrived about midday at Dundalk. They knew well enough not to arrive at Ballyfirglin on the Marsh emptyhanded. So they stopped in Dundalk for lunch and to buy some presents for Nora. On the way Josie whispered to Joe that Dundalk was a hotbed of rebellion, full of Nationalists. Joe looked for IRA men everywhere to no avail. There were almost no men at all on the street. He thought they must be holed up in a pub somewhere conspiring, just like in the movies. At one o'clock in the afternoon the town did not appear very conspiratorial, but, just in case, Joe wanted to avoid eating in a pub. His court had upheld the sentence of IRA gun runners from Charlestown. He didn't write the decision but he had been on the panel that issued it. All these Rebels knew each other. They even conspired back home in Charlestown and South Boston.

There was a pizza joint with a Victorian exterior on the main drag of Dundalk patronized mainly by pink-cheeked, uniformed school kids and young mothers pushing baby carriages while holding on to one or more other kids. *Maybe the men stay in all day to conspire and breed all night*, Joe thought. Joe hadn't seen so many kids in one place since his trip to Mexico in 1965.

Joe ordered ham sandwiches for both of them and some kind of Orange Crush drink. Joe and Josie tried not to stand out but their clothes gave them away. Josie looked like she had just come from Benediction in 1957, in her trusty navy blue suit and sturdy navy pumps with low heels; Joe was wearing a gray suit and a tie. The men they did see all wore American blue jeans.

Josie and Joe faked a very self conscious conversation, certain that they were being listened to, although most of the women were busy enough trying to keep their kids in line.

"It's a pretty town, isn't it, Joseph?" said Josie.

"Ooh yes," Joe lied, looking around cautiously.

"Did you know that when your grandfather James brought your great grandfather Henry back here in 1905 they all recognized him even though he had been away 50 years? 'Hello Henry, nice to see you home,' they said as he drove a wagon down this very street. It's all in James' memoir of the trip. How lucky we are to have that. And the photos from that trip! Your father's family has no idea about its past."

Josie didn't understand a family like Joe's father's that had no interest in its roots. She loved Joe's father, although she didn't understand him any more than anyone else did. He had made her younger sister happy and had given them, and her, this wonderful boy, the now white-haired old Joe. But how could Joe's father spend so much time with the ancient Greeks and Romans and care little about his Celtic past? Oh well, it wasn't worth worrying about. What was important today was what presents to bring Nora on the farm.

The market was one street back, almost like a mall, farming supply store and supermarket all under one roof. Josie bought some good tea and some French cheeses. "Thank God for the E.E.C.," she whispered to herself. Joe wandered off and bought a bottle of Wild Turkey bourbon, thinking that they probably had never tasted that on the Marsh. On the way back to Josie he saw some daffodil bulbs from Holland and bought two dozen. Maybe they could plant them at the farm as a memorial to their visit.

Josie clutched Nora's letter with the directions in her hand as they drove on the main road to the Marsh. Another cousin had also given her the landmarks. The "new" (1850) manor house, now a fancy hotel for golfers, was on the left and then you took a right onto a dirt road after a little clump of houses. The cousin Lizzie had gone two summers before. She said it was a shock "to see all these kids playing in the dirt road who looked just like us." Nora had divided some of the property along the road into house lots for her six children. She kept the old house at the end of the road for herself. Joe had seen photographs of this house taken in 1905 by Josie's grandfather. Apart from new windows it looked just the same—two stories with a front door on one side in a little arched porch and a similar door in a similar but larger arched porch in a larger house with quoins and symmetrical windows on the other side near the field. A two storey house indicated gentry, his cousin Lizzie had told him.

They had also seen the cousin Lizzie's photos of her recent trip, so they knew what Nora looked like. They parked a little beyond the house in front of a couple of barns. A dog barked at them as they approached the door. A woman's voice from the door shooed it away. It was Nora. She was a small woman in her eighties, although she looked younger. She had just been to the hairdresser and she was wearing a churchgoing dress. With her was one of her daughters, one of their cousins, dressed in slacks and a sweatshirt. The cousin, maybe in her early forties, was sipping a Diet Coke out of a can.

Nora thanked them for coming and put the gifts unopened on the kitchen counter. The kitchen was the room they had gone into. It was all modernized. Nora's son-in-law had done it. He was a contractor. It looked like America, almost, but there was the obligatory Sacred Heart, with a red light in front of Him, high up on the wall.

The meeting was stiff for a while. The daughter looked at them suspiciously. Maybe she thought that they had come for their inheritance, to take the land back. Nora finally said, "We've never had a judge here before."

"I'm harmless. I can't evict you," Joe said. They all laughed.

Josie had a list of questions and Nora knew the answers to some of them, but she had only been out on the Marsh since the Forties. So she had only second-hand information, mostly from her husband's uncle Peter, who had lived with them and from whom she and her husband inherited the farm after taking care of him for the last ten years of his life.

The Lavins had fished the river from time immemorial by stretching a net across it. Peter made and mended the net in the winter. The fish gave them a little bit of extra money to get by. Then the Englishman, Ryder, put in a slaughterhouse up stream and all the fish died from the cow's blood that poured into the river. Her husband sued Ryder, the slaughterhouse owner, but lost and so that ancient practice stopped. Joe wasn't too sure when all this happened but presumed that it was while Nora was resident there. He didn't want to interrupt the flow of Nora's narrative by asking.

It was possible to walk across the marsh to Dundalk and Peter used to do it to visit his friend Padric Ronayne in Dundalk until Peter became too old. They now had sixty acres again, just like they had before the Famine when they gave away some of the land to the tenants. They bought the last parcel in the early Nineteen Seventies from the estate of the last of the McDaid sisters, who had moved to Scotland, and they paid dear for it. There were still some cattle and would they like to go see them in the field by the marsh. Nora couldn't come with them because she "couldn't walk too well. But just go out the door to the left and walk around the other side of the house to the gate."

Josie, who wasn't much younger than Nora, marched out determinedly until the ground became a little spongey and the cow pats became difficult to navigate. Josie was still wearing her low navy blue pumps. She delicately navigated her way to the gate. Joe followed. He opened the gate until a big horned beast approached them slowly but steadily. They hurriedly left through the gate and retreated back towards the house. Before they got there they saw two barns side by side with a little shed behind them. The doors of one of the barns were open.

These very same barns and shed were in the 1905 photos taken by Joe's grandfather, enlarged copies of which Joe had brought with him, particularly one photo that had five or six children lined up between two barns. In the photo the younger kids had bare feet; all the girls wore aprons and they were looking at the youngest boy who was standing on the left, a little away from the girls, barefoot with a cap on. Two adult men seemed to be escaping from the right side of the photo in the foreground, one of them ducking down. Perhaps he was arthritic, the way he was doubled over. In the back of the lineup of the children was a man with a fedora in a little alley between the barns looking into the high window of one of them, the one that now had its doors open. A handsome boy, about fourteen, who looked like Joe at the same age, flanked the girls but was looking back at the man peering into the window. Joe had always been curious about the photo. There was so much going on it.

First of all, who were these people? Were they relatives? They looked like they could be. The girls were thin with great heads of hair. The men looked like various Lavin uncles. He was most curious about what the man in the back had been looking at through the window. And who took the photo? Was it Joe's grandfather, rich from America?

So while Josie took photos of her own over the fields to the marsh beyond, Joe walked into the barn almost one hundred years later to see if he could solve the mystery.

On the left side of the inside of the barn, which was lit up by the afternoon sun from windows on the right and from the open doors, there was painted a giant striped cat, almost like a tiger, like one of the cats which was on Joe's manuscript fragment, except this cat was standing rampant and appeared to have an erection. Joe turned white. He may even have blacked out a bit. He was brought back by Josie's voice behind him.

"My, what have we here? That's pretty racy for 'Holy Ireland.' But, Joe, you remember seeing the 'I' initial letter made of a striped cat in the copy of *The Book of Kells* that I keep on the coffee table at home. That book was the rage in the seventies. Every good Irish house had one. I bought one for your father, hoping to direct his scholarship to his own kind, but he wouldn't be looking at it, of course. Myself, I'd recognize almost every image in that book. This cat looks like the one that makes up the 'I,' but I don't recall ever seeing a cat rampant in *The Book of Kells*. Maybe some modern, artistic boy borrowed the image and put his monogram up here. Do they do 'tagging' in Ireland like my high school city boys back home? I hope not. This country doesn't need graffiti." Then she lapsed off, "God only knows what boys do in barns anyway."

Joe also had to find out what this image was about for reasons far beyond satisfying Josie's passing curiosity, but he couldn't give too much away either to Josie or Nora. Nora must know that the erect rampant cat was in the barn and she also must know what its artistic antecedent is. But how do you bring up a striped cat with a hard-on to an 83-year-old Irish matron? Josie would be OK, as she had just demonstrated, but Joe wasn't comfortable referring to anything sexual with her either.

When they returned to the kitchen Nora and her daughter had laid out a large tea on the table. There were ham and chicken sandwiches, two cakes, other pastry and the tea. There were none of the things that Josie and Joe had brought —perhaps to show the visitors from America that Nora and her family could provide without help from America. Thank you very much. Joe knew that there was a lot of prideful resentment, usually unexpressed, in Ireland at patronizing Yanks, especially Yank relatives. Josie and Joe's presents still sat on the counter.

They all sat down. Nora and the daughter seemed more relaxed now that the food was out. Maybe they had found that Joe and Josie were not so formidable. Whatever the reason, after Joe finished the first half sandwich, Nora asked Joe, "Did you watch the Nanny trial?"

"Well, I didn't," Joe said in surprise. "I saw clips of it on the News. I know the judge."

"Do you now? We liked him, especially when he reversed the jury. It was on British television and we can pick it up here. I watched it every day. Fascinating! Of course they shouldn't have prosecuted the poor thing in the first place. They'd never do it here."

The daughter agreed, "That prosecutor, the blonde, was a witch."

Joe couldn't believe that they were talking about this Massachusetts trial of more than a few years before and in this impassioned way. He'd already been shocked when Nora told him she was very disappointed in the Church after the Irish Christian Brothers' scandals. He expected total loyalty to the Catholic Church in Ireland and thought they would be similarly supportive of the Irish across the sea, one of whom was the "witch," the blonde prosecutor in the Nanny trial, with an Irish last name. The incongruity of their response knocked him off the script he had prepared, and made it harder for him to find a way to change the subject to the cat in the barn.

Joe said assertively, as assertively as he could without being impolite to his cousins in their own house, "Well, my cousin, your cousin, Andy Lavin, used to date the prosecutor. He almost married her. She's very nice. She's Irish American, you know. It's funny that you should like the judge. Most people, particularly lawyers, find him difficult. Somebody said that the prosecution was an Irish plot against the British."

Joe didn't add that the judge was an Anglophile and had all sorts of British affectations, like the nosegay on the bench. Joe wasn't liking the way this conversation was going.

"That's nonsense," said Nora "and we don't care if she has an Irish name. It was a terrible thing to do to a young girl. I'd never leave my baby with a girl so young. It's the mother's fault, the doctor mother. And I'm glad your cousin, whoever he is, didn't marry her. She's a hard one."

"Nor would I leave my child with a girl so young," the daughter added, emboldened by her mother.

"I'm surprised that they broadcast the whole trial over here," Joe offered. Did you listen to the judge's instructions on the law? That part wasn't televised over there, in America, and of course, that's the most important part as far as I'm concerned."

"No, we didn't see that part and the first part wasn't broadcast over here either. Wasn't that little lawyer magnificent in his argument to the jury!?" Nora said.

Now Joe understood. They hadn't seen the prosecution's case—just the defense. No wonder they thought like they did. He decided to keep that opinion to himself, but this realization gave him courage to change the subject.

Josie whispered in Nora's ear. Nora nodded to the daughter and the daughter stood up and took Josie through a door on the right.

Before Josie returned Joe asked, "What's the significance of the painted cat on the wall in the barn?"

Nora blushed and looked up at the daughter who came back just as Joe asked the question. The daughter smiled.

Nora said, "It's always been there. From time to time it gets repainted. These days we call it 'The Celtic Tiger.' Of course, we aren't even supposed to know that it's there. That's the bull's barn and women aren't supposed to go in there. We no longer keep a bull. And of course, the first thing I did after the men went away for the day when I first came to the Marsh was to go in the bull's barn. My husband wouldn't talk about it, but Uncle Peter had the same symbol, the rampant cat, tattooed on his shoulder. One night Peter told me that it was a Fenian symbol and that before 1916 the Fenians and before them the Whiteboys used to meet there. His friend in Dundalk, Padric Ronayne, had the same tattoo. One day I saw them fishing with their shirts off. At first Peter wouldn't tell me what it meant. He said that I shouldn't worry myself about it. I hadn't worried myself about it up until then, but after hearing him, I began to change my mind. That and the fact that Dan, my husband, wouldn't talk about it. That gave me curiosity.

"Somebody used to come from Dundalk to repaint it every once in a while. Actually a man came last month—Tim Ronayne, the Red. I think that he is the grandnephew of Peter's friend, Padric Ronayne, the Black. Tim the Red once was sweet on one of my daughters, I don't remember which one, but nothing came of it."

"What's he like? What does he look like? Where does he live now? How old is he?" Joe asked, all in a rush. He hadn't meant to be so obviously curious but he couldn't help himself.

Nora didn't seem to mind. "He's a shorter man, maybe fifty. His hair used to be very red, unlike his grand uncle who had jet black hair. Now it's mostly white as happens to redheads. He used to be quite the football hero here. He is still quite athletic, I hear. He left for America for a while. He always loved America. He returned after about ten years. He used to talk about America all the time, even when he was a kid."

"He's been back more like twenty years, Mother," said the daughter.

"There was a rumor that he'd gone to jail for running guns to the IRA, but we stay away from all that so I wouldn't know. God knows there's always been a lot of madness going around, especially when there's not enough for the men to do here. Peter had been in the IRA, but not my husband. His mother wouldn't let Peter talk about it in front of my Dan. Dan's father died early and I always suspected that it had something to do with 'The Struggle.' I don't even think that Dan knew what happened. He just remembered his father taking him on a boat ride up North. Dan's father was very handsome, dark haired and handsome. I have a picture in the parlor and a picture of Dan as well. Would you like to see them?"

Josie returned. Joe wanted to know more about Tim Ronayne, the Red. He didn't want to be too curious in front of Josie, however. He had a hunch about him—that maybe they'd met. Where did he live? More to the point, where was he right now? Joe realized that he had to be patient. More would be revealed. Just calm down and indulge Nora with her photos. She's an old lady and there's probably not a lot left but the memories. That also applied to him more and more each day, he thought ruefully.

He wondered if there was anything else to this house other than the kitchen. He saw lots of doors but had no indication where they went. From the outside the house was very large. It was almost an Irish cliché to spend all the time in the kitchen. He was happy to see some more of the house.

The parlor was very formal and neat but low ceilinged. The stuffed chairs had old slipcovers but looked never sat in and they weren't asked to sit in them now. Nora went over to a small end table which had three or four framed photos on it. First she showed them Dan, her dead husband and Joe and Josie's blood cousin.

Josie burst out, "He looks just like my brother Michael. I can't believe it! They could be twins!!"

Nora looked a little pained. "Is Michael still alive?" she asked.

Dan had died two years before.

Josie was sensitive to Nora's discomfort. "Yes, he is," she said quietly while putting an arm around Nora.

Nora picked up a second picture. "And this is Uncle Peter. Isn't he handsome?" She handed it to Josie. "And this is Peter and Padric Ronayne," Nora said as she picked up another photo and handed it to Joe. In the photo Padric and Peter had their arms around each other's shoulders and they were laughing. They wore suits and ties. Curiously, the Piazza San Marco in Venice was in the background. They were standing next to one of the lions.

Could that have been a photographer's studio backdrop? Joe wondered. Or were they really in Venice? There wasn't a lot of money to travel in those days.

It looked like the thirties but could have been earlier. Padric Ronayne had a moustache and wore rimless glasses. He was tall and his eyebrows were dark. They met between his eyes. His chest appeared to be bursting through his suit.

Probably hairy, Joe thought. He almost looks Italian. *I bet he had beautiful chest hair,* Joe mused as he held the sepia photo in his hand for too long.

"That was taken on a trip to Italy, sometime in the early Thirties, before I arrived here. I've always loved it. Peter was not often happy, particularly after Padric died."

"Padric looks like your old friend, Joe. What was his name again?"

"Arthur, Arthur," Joe said softly.

"Of course, Arthur, Arthur Bruce," Josie replied.

13 Young Joe Falls in Love

At the end of the Sixties, which means in 1974, Joe met a sexy, tall, broad-shouldered handsome man, with white skin, green eyes and auburn hair. He also had a port wine stain on the right side of his head, just in front of his right ear, jutting out of the hairline, like the Iberian Peninsula. His perfect chest was covered with dark hair, which grapevined down to his navel and then snaked down his pants, although Joe did not know that right away. When Joe first saw him he was wearing spattered painter's pants and a white tee shirt standing next to the cigarette machine at the 1270, a gay dance club in Boston. Joe was on the other side of the room waiting for his friend, Harris, to get bored so Joe could go home and go to bed. Joe had just flown in from San Diego from a conference that was as boring as oatmeal. Because the Chief Justice of the United States Supreme Court was speaking at the conference to the chief justices of each of the fifty states Joe was also there. Joe had a job cultivating chief justices at that time. He had jet lag and all he wanted to do now was to sleep.

Harris, who was prowling the dance floor, had taken the bus down from Oneonta, New York, where he was still being a hippie, except that he didn't take drugs, which to Joe kind of defeated the purpose. Harris taught Art History, wove shawls, scarves and blankets and tended his vegetable garden. Even though he'd spent the afternoon in the dirty movies, Harris was still horny. Joe thought that it was his duty as a host to get Harris laid, and Harris thought so too. This was the second bar they had gone to and Harris wasn't having any more success here than he had in the first one. Joe's next step was going to be to leave Harris at the *Shed*, the leather bar down the street, and let Harris find his own way home.

Just as they were leaving the guy in the painted pants came across the floor and said to Joe, "Where are you going?"

Joe couldn't believe his good fortune and came to life. "I'm dropping him off at the *Shed* and going home to bed."

"Can I come?" the man asked with a smile.

"Joe, let's get out of here," Harris said, a little irritated that he wasn't going to be the center of Joe's attention any longer.

Joe ignored Harris and said to the interloper, "Are those paint spots real?" They were selling pre-dripped painter's pants in some stores for the hippie wannabees.

"Yeah, I'm the real thing. I'm a painter. My name is Arthur Bruce, Arthur Gentilini Bruce. I'm at the Museum School."

"Let's go, Joe," said Harris again, now whining.

"Sure you can come with me. I'll drive you home," Joe said to Arthur Bruce and they all went to Joe's Volkswagen bug. Harris sat in the back. He was quickly dropped off at the *Shed*, the leather bar with a back room for sex.

That began a year of joy and misery for Joe. Although Joe had never seen him before, it turned out that Arthur lived around the corner from Joe with a woman named Annie, who doted on him and with whom Arthur was sleeping. Joe was only the second man Arthur had ever been with. Arthur was a painter in his fifth year at the Museum School.

For a time Arthur loved Joe and would do anything Joe asked. That was not what Joe wanted, however.

At that time Joe thought that love, like making art, was all about suffering. He didn't know how to be happy. He was in a dead end job, an associate at Swords, Healy and Fiske, a big law firm, in their litigation department preparing and conducting depositions in what seemed to be an endless variety of boring cases. It was a good thing that he had spent three years in a courtroom as an Assistant District Attorney because he hadn't worked alone on a case in court in four years at the firm. As an Assistant District Attorney he had prosecuted everything but a murder case and he had second seated one of those. He assisted the old prosecutor who was trying the case, keeping track of the evidence, rounding up and interviewing witnesses and did research as necessary.

But he had burnt out as a prosecutor. The wins became hollow while the losses remained heavy. Furthermore, the pay was only $14,000. and it didn't look like it would go up. One of his mentors had told him to be an assistant D.A. for three years and he wouldn't regret it; that if he did it any longer, he'd be stuck. Joe thought that if he had any balls, he'd give the Law up and go to Art School. But now he had a house in the South End to pay for.

One of the reasons Joe liked Arthur Bruce is that Joe could live as an artist through Arthur. Another reason was that Arthur was beautiful beyond belief. Arthur's mother was Italian; thus the dark hair and the hairy chest. Arthur also was young, undefeated, alive, vibrant, full of piss—ready to take life on.

Joe felt like he had given up. He went deeper into the closet when he joined the big law firm. The year before, 1973, a brave associate of another big law firm, who lived on the flat of Beacon Hill with his lover, went to the managing partner of his firm and told him that he was gay. He figured that the information would soon come out anyway. Some of the firm's clients were his neighbors. The managing partner, may God forgive him, said, "You'll never go anywhere in this firm." The Associate jumped out a window that evening.

Arthur liked Joe for all the reasons Joe didn't like himself. Arthur saw the solid middle class lawyer with the house in the South End. Arthur wasn't gold digging exactly, but he wanted a reliable base. Joe didn't give him money—until the end and then he would have given Arthur anything to keep him. Joe thought that he couldn't live without Arthur and that Arthur's destiny was to make Joe's life complete. Joe had started to see a psychiatrist a few months after meeting Arthur. Even though it was clear that Joe was depressed, the psychiatrist put Joe on Valium, the wonder drug of the seventies, also a depressant.

The burden of Joe's dependency made Arthur dislike Joe more and more. Joe wasn't the pillar that Arthur sought. After a year it sent Arthur off into the arms of Joe's best friend in New York. Joe had a breakdown. He tried to take a leave of absence from his firm but they didn't grant it. He couldn't tell them the particulars. He had to resign. Fortunately he had rents from the tenants of the three upper floors of his house and the firm's health insurance carried over for a while. Joe went to McLean Hospital for a month and began to heal. They withdrew him from the Valium and gave him a new psychiatrist, who gave him no medications. But he had to have a job. And it wasn't easy in 1975 to find one. The firms he applied to saw him as damaged goods.

Joe had never come out to his parents. He sensed that his mother knew. His father was always interested in something else, like Cicero or Catullus, so the information wouldn't have registered anyway. However, Joe felt that he had to tell them to free himself. The psychiatrist, who was straight, told Joe that he had to accept himself.

Easier said than done.

14 The Endurance and Changeability of Love

Arthur Bruce stayed in New York. His affair with Joe's friend didn't last more than a couple of months. Arthur soon found someone else, Lou, who Joe met and actually liked. Not that Joe didn't want Arthur back, he did, but Joe didn't mind that Lou, Arthur's new lover, would take care of Arthur until that inevitable happy day when Arthur would see the light and come running back to Joe.

For a long time after he left, Arthur Bruce was the paragon against whom Joe measured all other potential romances. That only stopped about seven years later when Joe met Michel, a poet who also was a competitive swimmer. His broad shoulders matched Arthur's and his wit exceeded most everybody's. Somehow, while breaking up with Michel after a year, Joe was able to put Arthur in the past as well.

Joe never understood how that brain trick, obsession deflation, happened. In his usual self critical way, Joe thought the fact that it happened at all indicated shallowness in his attachments. Arthur was to be forever. Joe hadn't ever wanted to let go of Arthur. But the good news and the bad news were the same—Joe got over Arthur. Or at least he thought that he had.

In the meantime Arthur Bruce, child of the seventies that he was, became addicted to more and more drugs—finally to heroin. Because he was financially able to keep up appearances he got away with it. However there were jackpots. One of the last was a suicide attempt while high that sent Arthur stumbling down Greene Street in Soho in Manhattan in full daylight with his wrists gushing blood. The cops picked him up and sent him to Bellevue. Soon after, Arthur got clean.

Mindful of Joe's own crackup and recovery, Arthur called Joe and Joe flew down to New York to talk to Arthur.

Arthur looked whipped. The famous shoulders stooped and his face was drawn but his eyes were clear. Arthur still had it and when they stopped in a restaurant in the East Village for a bowl of soup all eyes gravitated to Arthur.

Arthur was soon on the mend, going to AA and NA. He kept in touch with Joe periodically, but soon married a woman, also in recovery. They moved to Florida and after a while they had a son, who looked just like Arthur. One summer they vacationed in Manchester by the Sea and Arthur took the train down to Boston to meet Joe for breakfast downtown.

Arthur had never looked more beautiful. He was tanned, rested and full of the energy that Joe had loved when they were together. Arthur loved being married, being a father and he was painting again.

Joe was more envious than desirous. At that time Joe was still in the law firm, albeit now trying complete trials on his own, writing briefs and doing appeals. Arthur had no idea what Joe was talking about when Joe discussed his work. He was impressed with Joe's gay activism, however. Joe had just been appointed to the City's Human Rights Commission. Joe had finally been able to come out. As a matter of fact, he was one of the founders of the Massachusetts Lesbian and Gay Bar Association, and was chair of its Big Firms Section. Even his firm liked that; it made them look liberal, always a virtue in Boston. Although Arthur was now a husband and a father, he didn't see himself as a straight man.

Joe particularly enjoyed it when, as they sat at a table in the window of the Ritz Café, a famous old Boston political figure, formerly a judge, always rumored to be gay, but deep in the closet, came by and stopped dead in his tracks staring at Arthur. He didn't even see Joe, who got up and said, "Good Morning, Judge." Joe then introduced the poor man to Arthur, who turned on the charm for Joe's benefit. "It's a pleasure to meet you, your honor. I've heard so much about you."

Joe knew that he just went up 25 percent in the retired Judge's book.

Once the judge passed, barely out of earshot, Arthur said, "Who's that old goat? Should I know him? Can he help you?"

"If he lives long enough for me to make my move, you just helped me a lot," Joe replied. "He's a political broker here. He brings people together. He knows everybody. He's very closeted and lives with his sister around the corner in the Back Bay. He knew one of my uncles and I once went to see him to ask a favor. I think that I scared him because he knows that I'm out of the closet. The only way people came out in his day was when they got caught with the bellboy. Being outed is his worst fear. He used to take his business to New York," Joe explained.

"This town is so provincial. Who cares if you're gay? Look at me! I'm so gay I married a woman. I've always liked sex with women too. You know that. Who fucken' cares if you're gay!?!" Arthur shouted, stopping the waiters in their tracks.

After breakfast Joe had to get to his office. He walked Arthur to the Park Street Station so Arthur could go to North Station and get the train back to Manchester by the Sea. Arthur grabbed him and kissed him right there, right in front of the Park Street Station, the hub of the universe, if you live in Boston.

"Keep it up Joe!! You're looking great and you sound great," Arthur shouted." You're doing great things with your life. I love you."

◊ ◊ ◊

Three years later, in 1991, Joe came home from work to a message on his answering machine that said, "Joe, this is Arthur. I'm moving back to Boston. I'll be there in two days. My brother and sister are driving me up. I'm not doing too well. You may have heard. We'll talk later. I really want to see you."

Joe had heard a rumor about Arthur's health, but denial and the distraction of other people's illnesses had deflected Joe's attention. Besides, rumors were rampant about a lot of men in those days. It was too difficult to track all the rumors down. But this message was too clear to ignore. Joe waited impatiently for three days. On the third day, in the early evening, Joe got a call from Arthur. "I'm at the Prudential Apartments. Can you come over? We just finished moving in. I'm in Apartment 16E at the Boylston, the building closest to the City."

When Arthur answered the door Joe reflexively stepped back.

"I know, I know, I look like hell. Part of that is the fucken AIDS, but mostly it's because I just finished chooching this apartment up an hour ago. My sister was here. It's a good thing she's a dyke. She moved all the shit."

The "shit" was lots of beautiful Italian Modern furniture and some wonderful art. Arthur showed him around the apartment, which was already perfectly done, even though Arthur had just moved in. Furthermore, the apartment had a great view of the Back Bay.

Joe tried to meet Arthur where he was. Joe knew from experience with other sick friends that he couldn't default to his usual Irish morbidity. And Arthur wasn't going to let him. As they approached a beautiful sexy pencil portrait of the shirtless Arthur leaning on a mighty bicep, Arthur said, "Yeah, that's me just after I fucked the artist."

Eventually Arthur calmed down and told Joe the story of his diagnosis. He even told him who he thought had infected him. Joe had met the guy, who was now dead, a couple of times. For a short time he'd been the boyfriend of another friend, who had died two years before.

Arthur had gone to Rome to do sets for a famous photographer who was shooting photos for a famous designer's twenty-fifth anniversary in business. While there Arthur noticed that a bump had developed on his neck. When he returned to Florida he had it looked at and as a precaution the doctor gave him an HIV test. He tested positive. The doctor told him that he probably had six months to live—but not to worry because they had lots of morphine. He lived under that sentence for a few months until his family and friends convinced him that he could get better care in Boston. So he decided to bolt. He and his wife had separated about a year before. Arthur hated being away from his kids; they had adopted another boy about three years before. However, his Boston doctor was the best, and he was feeling optimistic. He had bursts of gallows humor like tonight when he said, "Some fucken AIDS victim I am! I carried that goddamned sofa up the ramp with my butchy sister."

Joe introduced Arthur to other men in Boston with AIDS. Arthur became friendly with a lawyer named Mike, who had retired on a disability. As Arthur got healthier and spring came Arthur and Mike rollerbladed across the river from Boston's Back Bay to Harvard Square, shouting, "Look at us; we're AIDS victims. Ha!"

Joe took Arthur to Provincetown and introduced him to artists down there. Arthur loved it and for a while he stayed in a little apartment that Joe had rented for the long season. Arthur then rented a place of his own and stayed down through the winter. He even shared a studio and painted again. Arthur wanted to leave a legacy for his kids.

One day he said to Joe, "Did you ever notice how a lot of Provincetown paintings look like salt water taffy? Well, now mine do too." The sharp, expensive, hard New York edge, the painting on gold leaf was gone. Although still abstract, his paintings were softer, freer, almost musical.

Arthur returned to Boston when he got sick or to see his children when his wife brought them up from Florida. One summer afternoon, while Joe was sitting as a Single Justice, he was slipped a note by a court officer, "Arthur Bruce is at the Deaconess Hospital Emergency Room." Joe finished the sitting and rushed to the hospital.

Arthur was fully dressed, wearing a heavy sweater, curled up on a bed in the back of the Emergency area. He had pneumocystis. He'd taken the slow boat up from Provincetown, wrapped in sweaters on this hot day. Eventually, the hospital admitted him, but after a few days he developed "rigors," as he called them, and left the hospital against medical advice because nobody was paying attention to him.

He returned to Provincetown, rigors and all. The town nurse, Alice, who was an old friend of Joe's, the local doctor and his new friends nursed him back to health. But in April of the next year the Kaposis had gone to his lungs, and Arthur knew that he didn't have long. He wouldn't let other people mourn before he was gone. A handsome young college student, who met Arthur while preparing a supper for people with AIDS fell in love with Arthur and would come down from college in Boston just to be with him on weekends. The young man burst into tears when Arthur told him the latest diagnosis.

Arthur said, "Get out!! I'm not dead yet and I don't have time for that."

One Saturday in early June Arthur called Joe and asked him to come over. When Joe arrived Arthur said, "I'm really bad and I don't expect to last more than a week or two. My mind is going. Yesterday I found myself out in the yard and I didn't know why. My sister's coming to take care of me. I have to have someone here all the time. If I don't pay much attention to you, that's why. I love you Joe. You've been very good to me, especially since I came back up here."

Joe wanted to shut his ears. He thought that if he acknowledged what Arthur had just said, it would be true. Joe stayed silent for a bit and then muttered, "You've been very good to me too, Arthur." Joe wanted to say, "Don't talk like that. Don't even think that." But, of course, it was to himself he would have been talking. They hugged silently and Joe left. Joe refused to believe that this was the last time they'd see each other.

Arthur's mantra in his last days was, "Nobody's gonna hold my dick while I pee," and nobody did. On the night he died Arthur climbed the stairs to the bathroom and then returned to bed on his own. He died on Father's Day in 1993 surrounded by his parents, the ex-wife, the ever faithful town nurse, Alice, and a few other friends, as well as 1,000 or so candles he had placed around the room the day before. He went out to music of his own choosing.

Alice, Joe's old friend from that fateful Saint Patrick's Day party in 1965, opened a window to let Arthur's spirit out and an hour later she called Joe to tell him the news.

15 More Mystery in the Homeland

Josie wanted to sleep in her ancestral territory. If Nora had even hinted at it, Josie would have moved onto the farm. Josie would have slept in the barn! But Nora didn't ask them to stay over, even though they probably had as much right to the place as Nora did, maybe even more, being Lavins by blood. And Josie didn't hold it against Nora for not asking her to stay. "We had never met before today, for God's sake." Joe could have cared less about being Nora's guest. He was about to go on a mission.

So they stayed back on the main road in what had been the Big House for the area—the successor to the house that had been burned down. The main section was a big Neogothic pile. There were modern motel-like additions in all directions. The place was now called Dunbukulla. Joe wondered if his ancestors had been servants there like they were in Newport after they emigrated. Dunbukulla wasn't as fashionably done up as Ballymaloe, but it was comfortable and had large bathtubs. Again Josie and Joe had a two bedroom suite. After long naps they ate in the hotel dining room which was almost empty. The next day they planned to go to the cemetery on top of the hill in nearby Faughart where their ancestors were buried.

Nora's husband Dan was buried there with a new gravestone because there was no more room in the old plot or on the old stone and it was crumbling. Nora wondered if she should have put the Lavin crest on the shiny new stone, like the older Lavin stones. It was obviously a matter of great concern to her. Somehow it didn't gibe with the times, crests on gravestones, but the Lavins had a history in the area and "it should not be forgotten. If the children wanted to put the crest on, they could," was how she finally resolved it. She wasn't going to worry about it anymore, but, of course, she did.

Nora was such a preserver of the Lavin flame. When Joe asked her what happened to the Lavins during the Famine, she replied that they gave the land to their tenants, 30 acres of it. That was a nice way of saying that they lost the 30 acres, Joe realized. Nobody gives up 30 acres unless they can't support it or get the rents from it. Only recently did the Lavins get it back, bit by bit so that they again had 60 acres.

The meal at the hotel was so-so, overdone lamb, three kinds of potatoes, of course, turnips, which Joe hated, and wonderful fresh green beans, not over cooked. There was a delicious trifle for dessert. After the long and emotional day Joe and Josie wanted to go to bed. They had no interest in the almost empty common rooms. There was none of the stylish, travel magazine gaiety of Ballymaloe, nor the formality of the Shelburne.

Even though the scenery in Louth was pretty, it lacked the dramatic spectacle of the West and the gentle roll of Cork. There was no Ring of Kerry or Cliffs of Moher. The terrain was lower, flatter, more worn down, perhaps due to its proximity to England and the rest of Europe on the non-Atlantic side of Ireland. The hotel was patronized principally by golfers and the few who were there then were not an interesting bunch. Because there was a golf tournament down in Kerry there weren't even many of them there when Joe and Josie arrived.

Peculiarly, their suite had televisions in each bedroom but not in the common living room. Josie retired, saying, "It's been a long day. It was a long drive up here but I'm glad we came. She is a dear, that Nora. How nice that she has all that lore. And how lucky for her to have all the children nearby! She probably has had enough of us. Did you bring tracing paper for the graves? I'd like to get some of the names and dates down."

Joe couldn't stop thinking about Tim Ronayne, the Red. How could he find him? It wasn't such a big town, Dundalk. And there weren't that many people there. Could he just drive into Dundalk, stop at some pub and with Yank naivete ask, "Is there a Tim Ronayne around here?"

While plotting Joe fell asleep. *Tomorrow*, he thought. *Tomorrow, I'll think of some reason to go into Dundalk. Maybe while Josie naps.*

Late that night it rained heavily and the rain on the metal roof of the porch outside kept Joe awake. He took the wakening noise as a sign to get out of bed and find Tim Ronayne the Red. Joe dressed in the dark and wandered into the living room of the suite. He looked in the little refrigerator mini-bar for a Coca-Cola, some caffeine to keep him awake for the drive into Dundalk.

When he opened the fridge door, right there, sitting on the shelf next to the tiny freezer was a teddy bear, with one of its button eyes missing, the right one, in fact. Joe picked it up. It was not particularly cold for having been in a refrigerator; it hadn't been there before dinner when Joe had taken out a bitter lemon soda. Underneath the bear on the wire shelf was a 4″x5″ pasteboard card.

Written on the card was, "Why don't you give it up, Joe? There are things you'll never understand about us. I still want you." And then it looked like the writer was going to sign the card. There was a vertical line below the message where a signature would be.

Had someone interrupted the message sender? Had he heard Joe come into the room? Was he going to reveal himself if he'd had the chance?

Undeterred, Joe went down the stairs. He stopped at the desk, woke up the old man who was sleeping behind it and asked, "Excuse me, but do you have a telephone book?"

"What's that?" the man replied.

"A book of telephone numbers."

"And who would you want to call at this hour? I know all the telephone numbers around here. Give me a try."

"Never mind, thank you," and Joe walked out to the car park by the side of the hotel. He had forgotten to bring an umbrella so he pulled his jacket up around his head to protect himself from the rain.

As he approached the Mercedes he heard a man's voice say, "Judge Lyons, Judge Lyons, Joe, isn't it a little late to be taking a ride?" The voice was rough and gravelly, yet soft at the same time. Joe turned and lowered his coat to see who belonged to the voice. They had registered at the hotel in Josie's name. How would anyone know he was here?

It was difficult to see the man, but he was about 5′9″, trim and solidly built. He was wearing a Scally cap and a green oilcloth coat, an expensive English Barbours, Joe noticed. It's funny what goes through your mind even when you're frightened. And Joe was frightened. The man carried a flashlight which he held down to the ground but it still illuminated his front.

Joe didn't like being recognized as a judge, even on the street in Boston. He liked to be anonymous. It gave him freedom, freedom to look at other men, among other things. So to be spotted here, in the countryside in the North of the Republic of Ireland in the dead of night, and to be called both by his title and his nickname was unnerving.

"Don't worry, Joe. Don't worry. I mean you no harm. You're safe with me. I'm the man you've been looking for. I thought that I'd save you the trip. It can be a little dangerous in Dundalk late at night looking for a man. They aren't a trusting bunch there."

"How did you know…how did you know that I was looking for you?" Joe was dumbfounded. He didn't even know his interloper's name yet but something in him told him who this was.

"Let's get in out of the rain. Let's sit in your car and I'll tell you."

Joe pressed a button on his key chain and the car's interior lights went on. The doors unlocked. Out of habit Joe got in on the left side. The visitor got in on the right, the driver's side in Ireland. Neither of them attempted to change seats. They said nothing for a minute.

Then the visitor said, "I'm Tim Ronayne, 'Tim the Red.' I'm a friend of your cousin Nora, and she's a friend of ours. She told me that you were curious about me. She didn't know why, but she doesn't ask questions and she thought that I ought to know. It's an old loyalty, going back generations. She passes on information that she thinks we might want to know. It's amazing what an old lady with good instincts can pick up. She doesn't know that we'd met before." With that he took off his cap. His hair was mostly white but there was still some red.

"Let's take a ride, Joe. I'll drive. I'll show you the sights of Dunbukulla. Did you know Dunbukulla means *Boys House*? Its proper name in Irish is *Dunbuachailla*. This whole area is very manly," Tim smiled slyly. "The town's name, Ballyfirglin, is a corruption of Bailefirgohailainn, the Place of the Beautiful Men."

"I had no idea and I didn't know there were any sights here," Joe quipped nervously.

"There's only one. Have you read of Diarmuid's Dolmen?"

"Josie talks about it," Joe said, assuming that his passenger would know who Josie was as well.

"It's very ancient, before Christianity, and not far from here. Behind those clouds there's a full moon. Maybe it'll stir some ancestral pagan feelings in you." Tim smiled at the last sentence, pulled a football pin out of his coat pocket and put it in his mouth. The Dublin angel had reappeared, a bit older but still sexy nevertheless.

They went through the car park onto a road that soon became dirt. On the left as the road ascended there was a gate. Tim stopped the car. The rain had stopped and the moon lit up the now fragmented, fast moving clouds.

"We'll take a little walk up through the gate, Joe."

"Is it safe here?" Joe asked.

"Safe as church, Joe. Safe as church," Tim replied softly as he smiled at Joe while opening the gate. "It's even safer than a certain green in Dublin once was."

Joe, who had been stunned by the events of the past twenty minutes, almost fell down. He'd been right. His intuitions were correct. He who hadn't trusted intuition for years, living the life of reason as he had to do in his work, he who had been tied up and robbed when last he dared to lean on instinct was so relieved. He felt alive again, more alive than he'd felt in thirty years, certainly more alive than he had felt since he became a judge fifteen years before.

Joe followed Tim through the gate up the hill.

At the top of the low hill there was a clearing. In fact it was the hotel's golf course, although Joe didn't know that then. In the center of the clearing was a large lump of rock about 15 feet across and seven feet wide balanced on three other rocks, two of which went up seven feet above the ground. The third was a little taller. Joe walked around the dolmen in the moonlight while Tim stood leaning dangerously against the tallest of the three vertical stones. Something stirred in Joe; it may not have been the dolmen. Tim took off his coat and laid it on the ground under the capstone. Tim wore a white shirt which glowed in the moonlight even under the shelter of the capstone. His sleeves were rolled up revealing strong, red-haired forearms.

Tim took the football pin out of his mouth after Joe's third circumambulation of the ruin and said, "Come in here with me Joe. It's starting to rain again. It's been too long. I don't want to wait any longer. The sun'll be up in a few hours."

Joe moved in under the capstone with his back against one of the portal stones facing Tim. The way they had to squeeze in together was exciting and scary at the same time. It began to thunder. Joe thought that if either of them breathed too hard, they'd bring the whole thing crashing down on themselves, 5,000 years of its standing notwithstanding.

They kissed, at first gently and then more passionately. Joe opened Tim's shirt. Tim's coarse chest hair, which now went up to his neck, was still red and it still glowed against his white skin. But it was a man's body this time. Tim stuck his right hand down Joe's pants. Joe was hard. He hadn't been this hard for a long time, not since the robbery. It frightened Joe to be hard. Tim opened Joe's pants and wriggled himself down to his knees between two of the portal rocks. Tim began to lick Joe's balls and then took Joe in his mouth. It didn't take much. After a moan or two Joe came all over Tim's chest. Tim rubbed Joe's gism into his chest hair, rose up and kissed Joe again.

Joe put his hand on Tim's crotch. This time Tim did not remove it. Joe was too tall and too old to go to his knees in that small space but he opened Tim's pants and with his hands Joe pushed the pants to Tim's knees, then to the middle of Tim's calves with his raised left foot. It wasn't easy to maneuver amongst the rocks but Joe spit on his hand and was able to rub the head of Tim's cock. Joe began to jerk Tim off. As Tim moaned and as his cock began to throb Joe slowed before Tim could come. Joe did that twice. Finally, Tim could stand it no longer and he said, "Don't stop, Joe. Don't stop now. Finish me off."

Joe did. The lightning flashed, illuminating Tim like a flame inside their coven. Thunder followed, as it always does.

"I'll see you tomorrow. I'll be your guide," Tim whispered as Joe got out of the car at the parking lot before Tim went off into the shadows of the night.

◊ ◊ ◊

The next morning Joe met Josie in the dining room for breakfast. She was off in a corner by herself.

"Good morning, darling. How did you sleep? I thought I heard someone go out in the middle of the night. You didn't take the night air, did you? Nora told me that it's difficult to find the Faughart

Cemetery so I engaged a guide at the desk. You don't mind, darling, I hope? We can use our nice little car, if you like."

As usual with Josie, Joe could take his pick of which questions to answer. He surely wasn't going to tell her what he did last night. "No, Josie, I don't mind using a guide. I think that's a good idea. We rushed up here and I am tired of driving."

By this time, Joe realized that Tim Ronayne's parting words of the night before were not just metaphorical.

"The guide will be here at 10:00 a.m. The hotel manager says that he's a very good driver and that he knows this area like the palm of his hand. I'd like to see that Diarmuid's Dolmen they all talk about, although I'm told that it's a puny thing compared to Newgrange and other wilder places. Did you know that if you throw a stone up on it and it doesn't fall off, you'll be married within the year? Well, neither of us would want that. Wear a jacket. We'll be up on a hill and there may be a breeze. Bring tracing paper to make rubbings of the graves. My Grandmother Hogan's family is up there too, you know. They had a one storey house, according to the 1905 pictures. They weren't as important as the two storeyed Lavins, but they were respectable."

Joe went upstairs to get the tracing paper and the jacket. Just as he got to his door Tim Ronayne came out of the next door down, the maids' closet. "As I told you last night, I'm your trusty guide, your man Friday, if you will. We have to talk but we can't now. We'll find a time. Things will make sense. Don't be afraid. We're all in this together. I'll pretend we never met." There was a pause and then he added with a smile, "And she's right, bring your jacket. There's always a breeze up at the graveyard."

Joe had given up trying to figure out how these people knew his every move and now even his private, albeit in a public room, chats with his maiden aunt. He was on a journey and he had no control over where it was going. It now appeared that he had protectors, although Tim's apparent obsession and passion scared him.

It's been over thirty years since we first met, Joe thought. They have long memories here, too long, Joe told himself as he and Josie walked out to the car. He wore the jacket. Josie wore a long black and white tweed coat, kind of old fashioned; it pinched at the waist and had a skirt. It wasn't at all what women were wearing, but it was appropriate to the day and the occasion. In the gray morning she looked like an old black and white photograph.

Tim Ronayne was standing by the car smoking a cigarette. Joe's heart jumped a beat. Tim dropped the cigarette on the ground and stomped it out. He held the front passenger door open for Josie, introducing himself at the same time, "I'm Tim Ronayne, ma'am. Good to meet you."

"And I'm Josie Lavin and this is my nephew Joe Lyons. My people are from here. We want to go to the cemetery at Faughart to see the graves of my family."

"The Lavins of Ballyfirglin are a very important family, Ma'am. I'm happy to take you there."

"Tim Ronayne, Tim Ronayne, why is that name familiar to me? Do you have relatives in Rhode Island, in the States?" Josie asked. She was very proud of her ability to place people and once started, she wasn't happy until she had done so. It seemed that she knew every Irish family in Rhode Island.

"We're a big family, Ma'am, originally from Galway, in the eighteenth century. I'm sure there are some of us all over America."

"Yes," said Josie, dissatisfaction at her inability to place Tim softening her voice.

"We'll go to the cemetery first. It's a twisty ride but well worth it," Tim said as he deftly maneuvered the little Mercedes up the hill's curving roads.

They parked in the car park to the right of the cemetery. It had a beautiful pastoral view over the fields and out to the sea. At the far end there was the burnt out skeleton of an automobile. Joe didn't want to ask Tim but Tim said, "T'is a good place to get rid of the evidence. It also makes a spectacle from afar way up here—sends a message, if you will. Like your Indians we've always had signal fires here."

Joe wondered what they might have been signaling, but it seemed intrusive to ask.

To their left at the broken down steps leading up and into the cemetery were two graves. Josie recognized the Lavin crest on one of them. "Did you bring the tracing paper, Joe? Rub that one. What does it say?"

"Let me get a better look," said Joe as he moved closer.

"This monument is erected by Peter Lavin of Ballyfirglin and Dundalk in memory of his wife Anne Lavin who departed this life on 20th of October 1817 age 69 years," said Joe as he rubbed at the familiar crest with the rubbing crayon—three boars over a bar pointing up in the middle, in which there were three crosses.

"Peter is probably there as well," said Tim Ronayne, who had been standing back quietly. "Whoever died first got the name on the stone. Which is hardly a reason to die, of course, but it is a small reward. The crest is unusual. You won't see many more in this place. There weren't many Catholics who still had crests in 1817. They're a fine family, the Lavins."

They climbed the three crumbling stone steps up into the cemetery and looked at the grave from behind. It was sunken. Joe couldn't believe that they had hit on it right off. He was correct. There were a lot of other Lavin graves, including a new one for Nora's Peter. It was shockingly white, shiny and modern with black lettering.

The cemetery also contained the ruin of a church and a holy well to Saint Brigid, who was supposedly from the area, as well as some overgrown bushes, one of which had scraps of cloth tied to it.

Tim said, "Those are for the well. They're called 'cooties.' The scraps represent a petition. Do you want to see the holy well?" He then led them around the bush. Below them appeared a hole in the ground, its sides covered with rock. It was almost like a funnel. You could fall into it, like Alice in Wonderland.

Josie charged down and tried to squeeze in the doorway made

of stone. Momentum was behind her. It looked like she'd either disappear or get stuck in the gratefully narrow opening.

"Be careful, Ma'am! You could fall in!" shouted Tim Ronayne as he went to rescue her. He grabbed her by the waist and, like an impetuous, little kid, she leaned into the hole knowing that he'd hold her back. It was an act of faith.

"It's dark and I don't see any water. It'd be nice to drink the water or bring some back to your mother, Joe. How can I get some water, Tim?" her voice echoed from within the well.

"I'll get some for you. Stand aside." She did and he lay down flat on his stomach, a bit of his pale, musclely back showing where his shirt and jacket had pulled up. Slowly his upper body came back up, his hands cupped in front of him. He rose to his knees, then to his feet, the water in his hands barely rippling.

"Perhaps you ought not drink it, Ma'am. It's a little brackish, but you could bless yourself with it."

Josie dipped her fingers in his cupped hands, as if it were a lavabo, and blessed herself. She then took a white linen handkerchief out of her pocketbook, one of those she bought every year at the fancy Linen Shop on Bellevue Avenue in Newport, ripped it in strips and dunked each strip in the water. "Now come here Joe, I know you're almost a pagan, but at least get wet with it. Your ancestors' bones have probably been soaking in this water for centuries."

Tim walked up to Joe, Josie at his back. Tim looked up at Joe, right into his eyes, smiled softly and Joe put the four fingers of his right hand into the holy water font that was Tim's hands. Joe rubbed his hand across his mouth kissing his own fingers as they went across. Tim smiled more broadly and then turned back to Josie.

"Can you bring the rest over to poor Peter and Anne, over here, Tim?" Josie asked. Josie had decided that they were the antecedents, even though there were other Lavin graves. The crest had convinced her.

Tim walked back to the first grave they had seen and at Josie's direction spilt the water over the sunken plot as Josie blessed herself again. She then returned to the bush with ribbons on it, began attaching three of the strips of her handkerchief and said, "I hope that you boys prayed for something because I am leaving one of these ribbons for the intentions of each of us. And that includes you, Mr. Ronayne. Surely you must have something to pray for."

Joe and Tim looked at each other conspiratorially. They may or may not have been praying, but they did have intentions.

"Ma'am, did you see Edward Bruce's grave up here?" Tim said. "He was the brother of Robert Bruce, the King of Scotland. Edward Bruce was named the King of Ireland at Dundalk on May Day in 1316. Robert came over to help him conquer the country. They couldn't take Dublin, however. They say Edward Bruce is buried here. He was killed at the battle of Faughart in 1318. Other histories say that he was drawn and quartered and his body was taken in pieces to Edward ll in London. Still others say that they only took the head to London to show to the bastard there. Sorry, Ma'am."

"Don't apologize. You can't say enough bad things about the English in my opinion. Joe thinks that I should be more temperate, but that's because he went to the Protestant schools and then studied Law. I've kept him from taking the soup, however. Haven't I, Joe?"

Joe shivered. Whether it was at Tim's story, Josie's chide or hearing the name Bruce, he was not sure. Josie always liked to think that Joe was on the verge of conversion, of taking the Protestant soup like some poor people during the Famine, who had to convert in return for food. It was her pride that in the face of all the Protestant allures, Saint George's and Harvard among them, she had kept Joe from turning Protestant. That his people and Arthur Bruce's ancestors should be in the same graveyard was too eerie for Joe, however. Like a tsunami, nostalgia came over him for things he could not even name. He walked back towards the car alone.

He stopped and looked at the view over the fields and farms

to the Irish Sea. Joe knew that just a few miles to the North was Northern Ireland and to the East was Scotland. How did his people survive here, he wondered? And how brave of his great grandfather, Henry, to leave!

Josie walked to the other end of the cemetery, her little notebook was now out and she was taking notes. Tim came over to Joe.

"When she takes her nap, you come down to the lounge. I'll tell you everything. Don't worry. It will all make sense, Joe."

After they drove back to Dunbukulla, Josie went upstairs for her nap, protesting all the way, "I don't know why I always want to take a nap over here. I never do at home and I'm much busier there. Maybe it's the emotion of it all. Imagine being on the same soil as my ancestors! God knows when the Lavins got to Ballyfirglin. That will be the next project. You go talk to that Tim Ronayne. He seemed to interest you. Was Arthur Bruce really related to Robert Bruce? I remember that he told me that, but I never trusted him after he ditched you. Of course, he was young and what do the young know about love." Josie talked her way right into her room and onto her bed.

Joe rushed downstairs to the lounge where tea was served in the afternoon. It was grand but still cozy, chintzy and comfortable with lots of stuffed chairs and sofas covered in faded roses arranged in conversational groupings. Joe took a seat on a sofa that had a view of both the front door and the check-in desk, which was in what had been the front hall of the old mansion.

After a while a young woman came out of a swinging door to his left, presumably from the kitchen, wiping her hands on her apron. "We don't serve tea until 4:30 but what can I get you now, Judge Lyons?" she asked in an Irish accent, more specifically a Northern accent. That she knew who he was alarmed Joe. She had red hair like Tim Ronayne and looked like she could be his younger sister. That seemed to explain it, but still it was creepy. He felt like he was being followed. She also looked like someone else but he couldn't put his finger on whom.

"Just a cup of tea with milk, thank you," Joe replied, trying not to sound threatened.

The woman left through the door she had entered. Joe picked up the *Irish Times* and began to read it. He was surprised at all the graft and political scandals in Ireland and all the investigating commissions. Somehow, he had thought, Holy Ireland wouldn't have any of this. They had no need to, he thought stupidly. He was among those American Irish who distance, in time and space, had made fonder of Ireland; he romanticized and idealized Ireland. It may have been a generational thing. His grandparents and great-grandparents had no illusions about Ireland. They were happy to be out of it. Of course, it was a much more miserable place then.

While reading the *Irish Times* Joe also marveled at the libel suits. In the second section there was a feature on the best Irish barristers, most of who seemed to specialize in libel. He thought that was a wonderful thing and hoped that the United States Supreme Court would reconsider New York Times v Sullivan, the case which made it difficult for "public figures," which included judges, like Joe, to sue for libel. Some of his colleagues on the trial bench had recently come in for a lot of gratuitous abuse over sentencing and one of his appellate colleagues was getting skewered after being arrested on a drunken driving charge. It's hard enough being a judge, Joe thought, without being able to fight back because you're a "public figure." Although there had been a little publicity when he was appointed because he was openly gay, Joe felt the media's sting for only a few days. In general, the newspapers had tried to outdo each other in liberalism. After saying the obvious and what everyone knew already—that he was gay—they went on to something else.

As he was mulling these weighty thoughts and thinking he shouldn't worry himself by them while on vacation, Tim Ronayne came through the swinging door from the kitchen with a tray bearing a pot of tea, two cups and saucers, a pitcher of milk, some sugar and some fresh strawberries.

"My niece just handed this tray to me as I came in the back door. Is this what you ordered?" Tim said, smiling as he put the tray on the coffee table in front of Joe's couch. That solved one mystery, Joe thought. Tim then pulled up a chair to Joe's right.

They both had a view of the front door and the check-in desk. Tim sat in the chair he'd just pulled up.

"Listen Joe, I'm going to tell you the whole story."

Just then a car pulled up in the driveway outside. There was a commotion outside the front door, car doors slamming, women's voices. Tim got up and looked out the window onto the front porch. "Ooh, they're early and she's in a Daimler, with a driver. Well, she was never one to go on the cheap. Stay here, Joe, I have to greet the in-laws."

Tim then went to the unmanned desk, stood behind it and smiled. He rang a bell on the desk and a redheaded boy about seventeen ran out of the kitchen door through the lounge and out the front door.

"Jesus, the boy looks familiar too," Joe said to himself, "Is everybody related up here?" Joe started pouring his tea, added a little milk, took one sip and looked up at the check-in desk. Tim had gone around it and was hugging a woman in a fox stole over a fawn-colored suit, wearing a big hat from which pheasant feathers streamed backwards, as if the poor bird had landed on her head. Joe could only see her back but he recognized the voice.

"Darling Tim, it's so nice to see you. You remember Virgilio, don't you? And we brought sweet Maureen up from Cork. Doesn't she look marvelous? Her Irish skin has been restored now that she's out of the North End of Boston. My son Vito certainly married well when he found your sister. Maureen has been studying too much. It's only her first month but the poor thing is living on tea and scones at that university in Cork. Dino sends her money but she only uses it to buy books about Irish art."

Just then a young woman with a great head of red hair, younger than the one who took his tea order, rushed up to Tim and said,

"Oh Uncle Tim, it's so good to see you! I've missed you. How are Auntie Louise, Auntie Kit, Auntie Alice and all the cousins?"

"Well, one of them is hauling your luggage right now. Give James a good tip. He wants to buy a Manchester Guardian's shirt. Another cousin, Eileen, is in the kitchen preparing tea for you. She made a lemon cake. She remembered you liked it from your last visit. How is your uncle Dino? Did he give you a package for me?"

Joe froze. The cup didn't reach his mouth for a second sip. It remained suspended in midair about a foot from his mouth. He couldn't move.

They marched into the lounge and spread themselves around Joe. *Like octopus tentacles*, Joe thought.

"Good afternoon, Judge," Giuseppina said, "And how is your charming aunt? Did you have your talk with the Judge yet, Tim? Did he remember you fondly?" she added with a little smile addressing Tim, who was now sitting close to Joe on the couch.

"Ooh, he remembered me, after a bit, but the talk was just about to happen when you all arrived. And glad we are to see you! Aren't we, Joe?"

Glad? Joe thought. *I've never been so scared and confused in my life.* He was still in shock and could say nothing in response. Giuseppina descended into the big stuffed chair to Joe's left. The Count, Virgilio, pulled up an ottoman next to her and in front of Joe and Tim on the couch. Maureen took the stuffed chair on the right. She had been staring at Joe quizzically from the time she entered the room.

"Michael, go get your cousin Eileen and help her bring in the tea. Would anyone like a drink instead?" Tim asked.

Virgilio said meekly, "Do you have any Cinzano? I think that Pina and I would like that."

"Yes, I've been drowning in tea since we arrived. It's very nice but too much of a good thing, you know," said Giuseppina, looking a little pained at the prospect of another cup.

Tim replied laughing, "We understand your foreign ways, Madame. We do have some Cinzano. We stocked it for an Italian racing car driver who stayed here last summer. He was not so kind about our tea. He called it *'urina de gatto.'* He spoke in Italian, of course, so we could not understand him, or so he thought. He didn't know about the marriage of our families and our international savvy," Tim added with a smile.

Joe still hadn't moved except to put his cup back down on the coffee table into its saucer. He was still white with shock.

"Joseph, enjoy the tea. It will all become clear soon," said Tim, "You have nothing to fear here. We are all family."

"Now I know. Now I remember," said Maureen, who had been sitting quietly staring at Joe. "You were with the old savage who chewed me out about my dishy waiter at the Acquitaine. Of course, he was right to do so. Some queens are just too regal, and they're too often waiters."

Aha, Joe thought, *that's the connection.*

"And I saw you before at that little café on Charles Street. You were sitting behind Uncle Dino and me. I went back to tell Dino one more thing about my coming to Ireland and through the window I saw him chatting you up. So, I left without coming in. What are you doing here? And how do you know my Uncle Tim? Who are you? Are you friend or foe? I know that one of my uncles is a gerontophile but are there two? One on either side of the pond? And what is this mysterious packet I just delivered from the one to the other? Are they trading old guy pornography?"

"*Che significa* 'gerontophiles'?" said Virgilio to Giuseppina. "*Che dice la ragazza?*"

"I never stuck my nose in my husband's business and I'm not going to do it with any of my sons'…enterprises. I think that Virgilio and I will retire to our suite. I understand that we have a view of the golf course and of the archaic ruin. What do you call it, Tim, a 'dolomite'?"

"It's a dolmen, Pina, Diarmuid's Dolmen. I showed it to Joe last night. It's quite interesting. If you throw a stone up on top of it and it stays, you'll be married within the year."

"I was married once and that was quite enough, thank you, Tim. I'll not be throwing any stones. Take my granddaughter. Maybe a husband will calm her down. Can James show us our rooms?"

"He's taking your bags up as we speak. I'll take you up. There's a little elevator behind the front desk."

Off they went leaving Joe and Maureen, who was still staring at him much to his discomfort.

"Well," she said, "Did the cat get your tongue? I shouldn't be so nosy. I'm Italian enough to know that, but at least we can talk. I'll find out what I'm supposed to find out someday. Everybody seems to know you except me."

"I'm from Boston, but I met your Uncle Tim in Dublin a long time ago. My mother's family is from Ballyfirglin down the road. I am visiting them with my aunt who's sleeping upstairs. You remind me of her, your…inquisitive nature. As for your Uncle Dino, we had just met when you saw us."

"Well, I know that you're Dino's type. The only thing that would've made you more desirable to him would be a cassock and a Roman collar, preferably with a touch of magenta at the base of the notch. He has a thing for the Monsignori. My grandmother pretends that she doesn't know what's going on, but she knows everything. That's how she survived. She's quite the modern woman. No sooner did her husband die than she was out of the kitchen in Revere and off to Rome. Do you think that she and the Count have sex?"

"Oh, the impertinence of youth! Of course they do," said Josie as she entered the room on Tim's arm, "but it's none of your business."

"Joe, you and I are going to take a walk," Tim said. "Josie Lavin, this is my niece Maureen Randozza. You are kindred spirits. I'm sure that you two can find things to talk about while Joe and I sort out the rest of the world. Either that or you'll kill each other," Tim added *sotto voce*.

16
Down Mystery Lane

Tim and Joe walked down the Dunbukulla driveway, out to the highway, past the Protestant Church and then up to the road which led to the Lavin house on the other side. They said nothing until they turned right onto the Lavin's road.

Walking, Joe noticed the road more than he had the day before when he drove down it in search of Nora's house, the ancestral farm. The terrain was flat and the bushes were a little overgrown on the sides of the road until they came to a modern house with a small lawn, which looked incongruously American suburban to Joe's eyes. Then there was overgrowth again and then another modern house. There were four houses in all. Each house had a lawn and two even had low white picket fences. Joe now knew that these were the houses of Nora's children, none of whom worked the land, except to care for the few cows remaining in the fields at the end of the road near the marsh. They were either tradesmen or worked in the factories over the border in the North.

Two houses down on the right, Tim pointed to the ruins of a cottage. He said, "That was my family's house. My great-grandfather was born there. My family had lived there for as long as anyone can remember. During the Famine they were evicted by the landlord who lived in the old big house that was then at Dunbukulla, where you're now staying. What a beautiful house that was! The landlord evicted us, burnt the cottage and turned the fields into grazing land. Your ancestor was the tenant of the landlord. My great-great-grandfather was one of his subtenants. Your ancestor stopped collecting the rents when the potatoes went black. He'd always been good to us. With no rents coming in the land reverted to the landlord, who spent most of his time in England. He left a bastard of an agent to do his dirty work." Tim's voice broke and he paused.

After a bit Joe asked, "What did your family do then?"

"Well, after the eviction your ancestor and his wife let my family live in one of their barns and they shared food with us. In fact, my family lived in the barn where the Cat is painted. My great-great-grandmother and two of her children died. Two others emigrated to America. My great-grandfather was the only child left in Ireland. Other families all down this road were evicted as well." Tim sounded bitter but controlled. He wasn't looking at Joe but off to the horizon, to the sea, maybe to England. His rage was just below the surface.

"In 1847 my great-grandfather and some of the other young men, who were then living in the hedges and eating grass, burnt down the Big House after taking the page from *The Book of Kells*. There were eight of them. After the fire they were called 'The Fireboys,' even though nobody was sure just who was in the group because, of course, they took an oath of secrecy. That alone, the taking of the oath, could've gotten them a sentence to Australia. They divided the page up into eighths and then most of them left Ballyfirglin. Some went to America, some to England. One even went to South Africa and another to Argentina. They each took their 'One Eighth' with them.

"Your great grandfather was suspected of being a Fireboy. He wasn't, but the authorities were on his tail. He went to Cork and then he left for America where one of his brothers had gone before him. He entered through Canada because they weren't letting the Irish in the States just then. He walked down through Maine and Massachusetts to where his brother was farming in Rhode Island."

Joe knew the story from there. After walking across the border from Canada because at that time the Irish were denied direct entry to the United States, Joe's great-grandfather saw a man working in a field in Middletown, Rhode Island.

"Is that you James?" shouted Joe's great grandfather. It was James, his brother. They worked together on various farms, pooled their money and after a while they bought the farm James had been working on that fateful day. Their son started the construction company.

Tim continued, "Your great-grandfather did not approve of the torching. He probably knew who did it but he didn't tell. Your family was part of the old order that survived the English invasions. The Lavins had been chiefs of this whole area. Their lands were confiscated in Cromwell's time but they remained as tenants. What else could they do? And they had been here forever. The Lavins were always good to their people, their subtenants. There was a loyalty between them. There's still loyalty among those of us who are descended from the Fireboys," Tim added.

Tim continued, "I knew who you were when I met you for the first time, back in 1969. One of the maids in that little hotel on Harcourt Street was my sister. She told me, 'There's a Lavin in my hotel and he looks like the men from the Marsh.'

"She asked you what your name was and where your people were from. You told her you weren't too sure but had heard that they were from near Dundalk. She asked if your name was Lavin. You said that was your mother's name."

Tim went into a reverie, like he was sleepwalking and talking at the same time. They continued down the road towards the Lavin Farm. Clearly he had told the story of meeting Joe many times before, if only to himself. The road took a bend to the left and then there was a little nest of buildings, one of which was Nora's house where Joe and Josie had visited the day before.

Tim looked at Joe, smiled and then said, "I went to the hotel to take a look at you myself. I filled in for the busboy. You don't remember, do you? You asked what the big fork was for. I told you 'the spuds.' You smiled. It may have been patronizing, but there was kindness in the smile I thought. You were reading a book by Brendan Behan at the table, all by yourself. It was *Borstal Boy*. We loved Brendan. He was a rebel. So was his mother. God rest their souls. I didn't stay around you long; you were too good looking. I knew that it was destiny that you had come here, to Ireland, to that little hotel on Harcourt Street."

Joe shivered at all this. It gave him the creeps. He was in this Irish rebel stuff for a dime, but not for the dollar like Tim was. That anyone should remember his every gesture from so many years before frightened Joe. He simply wasn't that important to be remembered so precisely, Joe thought.

Tim continued, "I hung around until you went out, then I followed you to the bar. You took a long time getting ready. I was going to go to your room on some excuse—to see if you had enough pillows or needed more towels; you Yanks bathe a lot—but instead I waited, cleaning up the dining room after supper. My sister didn't know what I was up to. She liked you but thought that you were haughty. She didn't know that was how you fended off women. I did. I'd done that myself. I followed you to the bar, to Bartley Dunnes. I hoped that was where you were going, to the 'theatrical bar.'

"I watched you in Bartley Dunne's, talking to that drunken *Irish Times* reporter who was obsessed with respectability. I even saw the big boyo from Tipperary, the sheepshagger, follow you into the loo. If you hadn't come out when you did, I would have gone in and beat him. I knew what he was after. It was crazy—this combination of desire and brotherhood that I was having. And you didn't even know!!"

Quietly Joe said, "I do remember the rest. I remember leaving after the reporter passed out and seeing you on the sidewalk whistling through the football pin in your mouth and you reading *Newsweek*. I remember everything from there on." Joe was also beginning to breathe the nostalgic, peaty smoke.

"But why did you give me the 'One Eighth?'" Joe asked, breaking the cloud.

"I'm not sure. It was a combination of impulse and intuition. I always carried it on me. It was part of your history too. With the trouble up North coming the 'One Eighth' wasn't safe with me anymore. We'd guarded it for more than a century. It was your turn now, I thought. You and I were connected before we met, at least in my mind. It may have been just sex for you, but for me, we went back centuries, beyond memory. The 'One Eighth' had come to me from my father and his father before that and his father before that. And your great-grandfather was part of all this, if only on the sidelines. Your family had taken mine in and saved some lives. That's the way you think when you're young and Irish. Maybe all you have to be is young. Surely, you must have felt that way about somebody. Maybe you still do."

Joe immediately thought of Arthur Bruce, but he said nothing about that. It seemed unseemly. He stooped and picked up a rock from the road—to bring back and, like the Jews, put on Arthur's grave perhaps.

"But why did you have to take the 'One Eighth' back? I presume that your people, whoever they might be, were behind the assault on me and the theft from my home. So, let me get this straight, Dino Randozza is your brother-in-law, once removed or something?"

"Let me explain, Joe," Tim said.

"And why did you have to take it back so violently? Why couldn't you have just asked for it? Why all this high Italian intrigue?" Joe interrupted.

Tim said softly, trying not to be accusatory or judgmental, "We were never too sure that you believed the 'One Eighth' was real. You know you were rather casual about it, 'negligent' some said, keeping it in a drawer with your socks. Sometimes you put it in the next drawer down with your boxer shorts."

Joe was astounded. "How do you know that?" he asked.

"Do you remember Liam, the carpenter, who built your bookcases in 1970? And Eileen, the woman who cleaned your apartment for so long? And Bridie, who cleaned it in the '90's? And Guadalupe, who cleans for you now? And do you remember the crew from Jordan Marsh who came to wash the rugs? And Kennedy, the plumber? Well, they're all with us in one way or the other and they checked on the 'One Eighth' every time they came to your house. You moved it from the underwear drawer back up to the socks. But it never looked like you valued it. We were worried."

Joe was both indignant and frightened at the violations of his privacy. "You bastards," he said. "Have you no decency, no respect for anyone's…anyone's…privacy?" Joe had never worried about things this close to home.

Joe continued, "I didn't know what it was. I thought that it was some souvenir from Trinity College that you'd picked up —like a bookmark, and that you made up all that stuff in the note because it was so romantic. I thought it was a scam and that you'd come back and want something from me. I could see that the decoration and script were well done, but I had no idea that it was real."

Tim ignored Joe's protestations. "And we needed it back. We need all the pieces. We have them all except for two. We know that one other is in Venice. Its guardian was Andrew Hayes, who was from here but left for America. He deserted from the American army during the Mexican War and fought in the *Batallon de San Patricio*. Do you know about them?" Tim asked, and then went on without waiting for an answer.

"They were Irishmen in the American Army. They were treated badly because they were Catholics and immigrants. They realized that they had more in common with the Mexicans, so they crossed the Rio Grande and joined the Mexican Army. They're heroes in Mexico. There's a square named after them in Mexico City and a lovely plaque in Spanish and English.

"Andrew Hayes was killed by the Americans when they defeated the Mexicans. They hung him along with 49 of his colleagues. Others they branded with a 'D' for deserter on the cheek. Andrew Hayes left his 'One Eighth' with the Italian priest who heard his last confession. He'd already told the priest about burning the big house, but as he stepped up to the hangman he told the chaplain, Father Gentili, that his 'One Eighth' was hidden under the statue of St. Joseph in the little church in San Angel, called *Chimalistac*, in the Square in Mexico City near where the plaque to him and the rest of the Battalion is today. Father Gentili had been part of the Papal Nuncio's staff in Ireland and spoke English. He was next sent to the Papal Nuncio in Mexico. The Gringos didn't trust any of the Mexican priests to minister to those they were about to hang. Truth be known, they didn't really trust any priest. But the Papal Nuncio, thanks to Father Gentili, who loved the Irish, was making a stink about the hanging so they let the Nuncio send his man to talk to the poor lads before they were hung.

"Father Gentili retrieved the 'One Eighth'. He later returned to Italy and became the rector of a church in Venice called *San Sebastiano*. We know that he hid the 'One Eighth' there but we have yet to find it. They're renovating the church and a couple of our lads who do plastering—their grandfathers learned it from the Italians years ago in Merrion Square—are over there helping the Italians out, and snooping around. Did you know that Brendan Behan's father was a fine plasterer? We've preserved the skill in Ireland and with the EEC we can now go anywhere in Europe to work. The boys already scoured the sacristy. Now they're taking a careful peek around the church. There's some kind of code as to where it's hidden. Before he died Father Gentili wrote Andrew Hayes' family. He told them about Andrew's brave death, his messages of love to his mother and sisters. Then in a postscript he said,

"**'Look for the cats under the backside of the dog in the temple.'**

"Now what the hell does that mean?" Tim burst out. "That's so fucken cryptic! We'll find it though. Have you ever been to Venice,

Joe? Do you know this church?"

Joe said, "I've been to Venice and I may have been to the church. I went there years ago, when I was more pious, just after college. I went to a lot of churches. I have a friend there. He showed me around. He has a lot of money and studies the great Venetian painters, Titian, Tintoretto and Veronese."

"I've heard of them," said Tim abruptly. He then continued his dissertation, "The last missing 'One Eighth' may be lost or it may be right under our noses. The guardian of that piece had a cottage on this very Marsh Road, but it was knocked to the ground in an eviction and maybe his 'One Eighth' with it. Don't worry, we know the location of the house and it's safeguarded, but we can't go digging yet. There may be a new garden down here soon, however. Maybe the 'One Eighth' will come up with the daffodils some spring." Tim smiled slyly as he said this.

"But why did I have to get tied up and why did 'the Mob' have to get involved?" Joe asked. "Why couldn't you just have had one of the cleaning girls pinch it, or the plumber? You're right. I didn't take it, or you, seriously. I never thought that it was for real. You were just a kid. What would you be doing with a piece of *The Book of Kells*, for Christ's sake? I thought it was just an exuberant, impulsive, little love present. You didn't even want to get off. The whole event was weird, lovely but weird. The 'One Eighth' looked old, but it seemed too bright to be real. And what fool would cut up a page of *The Book of Kells*? I should have taken it and you more seriously but I was a bit of a jerk then. I thought that I was the cat's meow."

Tim smiled and said quietly, "You were, Joe. You were. You're not bad today, a little long in the tooth, but still a handsome man. We were afraid that if we stole it, you'd go to the police, and even though we have friends there, we didn't want to have to deal with them."

"But I did go to the police," Joe said proudly.

"We didn't think that you would, considering the circumstances of the…he 'One Eighth's' removal," Tim said thoughtfully.

"You hadn't taken into account the present level of Gay Liberation in Massachusetts then," Joe said ponderously. "We are everywhere and we will be free," Joe said smugly with just a little irony.

"No, no, we hadn't. We didn't know about those things," Tim replied trying to conceal a smile. "The status of Gay Liberation in Boston is not in our Intelligence yet; it's not our forte, as it were. Our intelligence is pretty keen, but the idea that you'd go running to Sergeant Detective Shaughnessy never occurred to us. But, of course, you never told him about the 'One Eighth.'"

"How do you know that? How do you know the name of the detective I talked to?" said Joe. "And just how do you know what I said to him, to the police? That's confidential. It's a crime for the police to reveal confidential information. How dare you!!"

Tim just smiled. He then said, "Take it easy, Joe. It'll be alright." They walked about ten more paces and then Tim added, "Do you know who lived in that house?" And he pointed to the only other still standing old house on the road.

"The Shaughnessys lived there. They emigrated to Boston about 1925. And wouldn't old Dan Shaughnessy be proud that his grandson is now a Sergeant Detective on the Boston P.D."

Joe's jaw dropped and he sputtered in indignation as they proceeded on down the road. Just before they arrived at the back of the Lavin homestead Tim took a right through the gate into the pasture with the cows, towards the Marsh. It was the same pasture Joe had been in with Josie earlier. Dundalk was before them across the shallow water. Joe remembered Nora Lavin telling them that Peter Lavin, her husband's bachelor uncle, used to walk across at low tide to visit Tim's uncle, Padric Ronayne, in Dundalk. *Were they lovers,* Joe wondered?

"Where are you taking me now?" Joe asked. "What is this craziness? I don't give a fuck about your goddamn page of *The Book of Kells*. You've ruined my life. I have the mob chasing me. Lucrezia Borgia and Marcello Mastroianni are back there cozying up to my dotty aunt. Some crazed stud is sending me mash notes with dismembered teddy bears and you tell me to take it easy!"

Tim remained silent during this rant. Joe thought that he could see a small smile, which irritated Joe even more. "What am I supposed to do? I don't want any part of your Mucka craziness. You're all nuts. No wonder all my great grandparents left and only one came back—for a short visit. Why have you shut up? You'd think we were going to Church you're so quiet. Say something for Christ's sake. Reassure me."

"Take a left, Joe," Tim whispered. "We're getting close."

Joe took a left, as did Tim, and they walked towards a small barn within the enclosure. To Joe it looked like the same barn he was in before, the barn with the rampant cat painted on the back wall. A couple of cows approached them. They frightened Joe, but Tim patted them on their soft velvety wet snouts. Joe thought that was disgusting. He realized that's how far away he was from the farm; he was ashamed for thinking that. He really didn't hate Ireland so much. He was threatened by the whole thing. That's all. And he thought that he was in some special relationship with Tim and that Tim could get him out of all this. That's why he dared blow up in front of Tim.

The little barn door was ajar. Tim pulled it open further and walked in. It was pitch black. Joe followed warily. If he couldn't trust Tim, he was doomed. Five steps into the blackness Joe heard, "Good afternoon, your Honor. It's good to see you again. How've you been?"

Joe really freaked and tried to retreat but Tim grabbed him firmly by the upper arms and whispered, "He's with us, Joe. Let your eyes adjust to the light. He may be a cop on the other side of the ocean, but over here he's with us. You'll recognize him in a second."

Joe didn't want to be a part of any "us" that Tim was talking about. He tried to pull away again but Tim knocked him down into the hay and fell down beside him. Tim rubbed Joe's head gently. The barn door slowly opened wider; Joe saw his salutatorian.

"It's Sergeant Detective Shaughnessy!" Joe exclaimed in horror.

He couldn't believe it. He'd never been particularly paranoid in his previous life, but ever since the robbery he felt little else. Now he just abandoned himself to his fear.

Shaughnessy was still pink-faced, boyish and a bit pudgy, but he had his swimmer's shoulders yet—'Butterfly' indeed. He was still dressed like a detective, however, an old tweed jacket, well worn gray pants but no tie. He was wearing thick soled black shoes, gumshoes. Over here he wore a Scally cap. Shaughnessy was smiling at Joe.

Joe tried to wriggle out of Tim's grasp. All he wanted was out, out of this barn, out of this town, out of this fucken nutty country. Not that he'd feel any safer back in Boston if the likes of Shaughnessy made up the Police Department. Maybe he could go to… Idaho, some uncomplicated place where there weren't any Irish.

"Take it easy, Joey. We're your friends. We love you. We aren't going to hurt you. We want to show you something. Calm down Joey boy," Tim said.

Nobody had called him Joey since Jackie Driscoll fifty plus years before and that appellation, as well as Tim's gentle tone, did calm Joe down. Shaughnessy had joined them in the straw and was holding Joe's other arm but Joe didn't even realize it until he looked to his left and saw him. *Just a kiss away*, Joe thought and then Joe said, "You're just a kiss away Shaughnessy, and so are you Tim. Why don't we just fuck and forget all this intrigue. What do you say, Sergeant Detective? Gay sex is not a crime in the EEC."

"Joe, come to your senses. The fucking can wait. We have most of 'The Page,' all but two eighths. Let me show you what we have." Tim released his hold; Shaughnessy didn't. Tim got up and opened the barn doors wider, letting in more daylight. Shaughnessy and Joe got up still holding hands. Peculiarly, Joe didn't mind. The grasp was affectionate now.

Tim went to the far side of the barn and returned with a cheap, cordovan colored, leather attaché case. Tim pulled over a rough wooden table from the corner of the little barn, dusted it off with his handkerchief, and put the attaché case on top of it. He then lifted the table and its cargo to the now well-lit doorway. He snapped open the case. Inside there was a lot of tissue paper piled in double folded sheets—like folios. Tim leaned over and began to peel them back. At the last layer he looked up at Joe and Shaughnessy radiantly. The lighting of the whole event was like a painting by de la Tour. The light was carefully, if not credibly, on the holy object and the person closest to it.

"Well, are you ready?" he asked.

"Of course we are. Cut out the drama," Joe said.

Shaughnessy laughed at Joe's quick recovery and return to curmudgeonry.

Tim lifted the last sheet of tissue paper. It seemed whiter than the others and almost transparent. There it was, THE PAGE. It had been cut down the middle vertically and then each side was cut into fours. But for two 'Eighths,' one at the top right and the other down on the left, it was complete. Joe's 'One Eighth' (which had also been Tim's 'One Eighth') contained the first words. They made more sense now.

> *ET misertusest super*
> *Oves nonhabentesp*
> *Cere illosimulta ETc*
> *Fierit accesserunt d*
> *DEsertusest locus hic etiamhorapre*
>   *terevit dimitte illosuteuntes in prox*
> *imas villas et vicosacemant sibicibos*
> *quosmanducent etrespondensaitillis*
> *date illis manducare et dixerunt ei*
>   *so'naris ducentis pa*
>   *s manducare ET dicit*
>   *abetisite etvidite*
>   *dicunt eiquinque*
>   *ET praecepit illis*
> *utaccumbere facerent omnessecondu*
> *contubernia superviri defenum etdis*

cumbuerunt in partes percente nos ET

Then on the other side it read:
*acceptisquinquepa
us intuens in caelum
anes et dedit discipu
nteeos et duospisces
divissit omnibus et manducaverunt om
nes Et saturatisunt etsustulerunt reli
quias fragmentorum duodecim cofinos
plenos et depiscibus Erantautem quiman
ducaverunt quinquemiliavirorum
ET statim coegit
 cendere in na
eeumtrans fretum a
ipsedimitteret pop
ET cumdimissise
 orare
ET cumsero esset idemeratnavis
 in mediomari etipsesolusinterra*

Striped tiger cats of various sizes and in different positions were scattered through the text—occasionally as a glorious initial letter but more often to form the Latin word '*ET*,' meaning 'and.'

"Mark 5," said Joe. "Particularly fitting in the time of The Famine…except there was no miracle to relieve the people's hunger then. Jesus did not feed the masses during The Great Hunger. There were no loaves and fishes for our great grandfathers. They stole the Gospel but they never got the bread…at least not in this place, which was God forsaken at that time."

"What are you talking about?" said Tim.

"Has he lost it entirely?" Shaughnessy asked.

Joe said, "I had eight years of Latin and was once very pious. THE PAGE is the beginning of the story of the loaves and fishes.

This is Mark's version. He wrote about it twice. Didn't you boys ever pay attention in church?" Then Joe leaned over the manuscript.

Joe read the Latin and translated aloud in a drone at the same time. He even knew the missing parts.

> And he had compassion for them,
> because they were like sheep without
> a shepherd and he began to teach them
> many things. When it grew late his disciples
> came to him and said, "This is a deserted
> place and it is very late. Send them away
> so that they may go into the surrounding
> country and villages and buy something to eat."
> But he answered them, "You give them something
>   to eat."
> They said to him, "Are we to go and buy
> two hundred denarii worth of bread and give it to
>   them to eat?" and
> he said to them, "How many loaves have you?
> Go and see." When they found out they said,
> "Five and two fish." Then he ordered them
> to get all the people to sit down in groups
> on the green grass. So they sat down in groups
> of hundreds, and of fifties. Taking the five loaves
> and two fish he looked up to heaven and blessed
> and broke the loaves and gave them to
> his disciples to set before the people
> and he divided the two fish among them all.
> And all ate and were filled and they took up
> twelve baskets full of broken pieces of the fish.
> Those who had eaten the loaves numbered
> five thousand men.
> Immediately he ordered his disciples to
> get into the boat and go on ahead to the other side

> to Bethsaida, while he dismissed the crowd.
> And when he dismissed them he went up
> on the mountain to pray.
> And when evening came the boat was out on the sea
> and he was alone on the land.

Then Joe looked up and at the men in in the barn. He said, "The big miracle happens on the next page—He walks across the water—which was also true for our ancestors. The miracle happened for many of us after we left here, after we got out of this place, after we crossed the ocean."

It was not lost on Joe that he had said, "After we left here, after we got out of this place, after we crossed the ocean." Heretofore he had tried to keep himself separate from Tim and his crowd, many of whom he didn't even know. But now, he felt solidarity with his great grandfather. For Joe now, like Tim always, the whole thing was of one piece. Joe was his great- grandfather. Joe was a 'Fireboy.'

Nor was Joe's change of heart lost on Tim, who said, "Joe, you have to help us find the Venice 'One Eighth.'"

"What?" said Joe, lapsing back into resistance.

"You have to go to Venice with Pina and the Count. They'll be staying at the Danieli." As if Joe would be lured by grandeur. "Shaughnessy will meet you there. He's a detective, for Christ's sake. He ought to be able to find a dog in a church."

"Sergeant Detective Shaughnessy to you," said Shaughnessy with a grin. "And I'm a cop, not a dogcatcher."

"What about Josie?" said Joe.

Tim knew he had him, "Bring her," he said.

"I can't get the time off."

Sergeant Detective Shaughnessy said, "Yes, you can. When do you sit next? Nobody knows what you guys do when you're not in court, and you're only in court every once in a while or so. How many of you are there now? Nobody knows who you are, or where you are when. You're called 'The Anonymous Court,' you know.

That's not to say you don't work hard. It's just that your court's work habits are a bigger mystery than the last message from Fatima."

"I sit on a panel in three weeks. There are now 25 of us. The Speaker of the House just added 11 new judges," Joe said meekly.

"Good, that Speaker Finneran is a wonderful guy. They'll never know you've been gone," the Sergeant Detective said.

Tim gently folded the tissue over the page, like a priest folding the holy linens after communion. He then closed the briefcase and took it with him. They returned to the hotel in Shaughnessy's rental car, which was parked discreetly behind the Lavin barn. To Joe it seemed pointless to protest. He was now part of this. It wasn't every day one saw and touched a piece of the national treasure of Ireland, its Holy Grail.

Back at the hotel, Josie had risen from her nap: she and Pina had already become great pals, as had Maureeen and Josie. Maureen was the kind of girl Josie had once been—no nonsense, full of spirit, and loving life.

"Joe, Joe, did you know that Maureen went to the Madames in Newton? We've just been talking. They still wear mantillas to Mass. Isn't that grand! And Pina went to the Sisters of Notre Dame in Dorchester, Saint Gregory's. Isn't that where that very nice lady judge you used to squire around went to school?"

"Polly Killeen? Do you know Polly Killeen," Pina said. "She was behind me in school but she was a hero to all the girls. She had more courage than any ten men, and that includes all of you. Do you know that she used to play Little League with the boys? She would tuck her red braids up into her hat and hit home runs. You could use her over here. She'd get this place moving. My sister, who was in her class, said that Polly Killeen was the 'coolest' girl who ever went to Saint Gregory's. I'm too old to know exactly what that means but I think that it's something admirable."

Josie interrupted, "I want to take Pina and Maureen to meet Nora. Wouldn't Nora like that! She's a good woman, Joe. She took care of her husband's old bachelor uncle, raised all those kids, ran the farm and even increased the land. She's still doing it at age 83."

"God bless her," Josie, Maureen and Pina all said in unison.

"Josie, we have to go to Venice. And we have to leave soon."

"But I have no clothes," Josie said.

"I'll treat you to the clothes," said Pina. "God knows, I have too many myself and it will satisfy my obsession to shop. I'd buy Maureen some new clothes too, but she is still in this absurd black mode. Why do the young have to look so morbid?" said Pina.

During her marriage, Pina had become used to impromptu changes in plans. As she said, she never asked questions. She always made the best of it. Fortunately now she had the money to do so. "There are lovely shops in Venice," she smiled. "We're staying at the Danieli. We have a suite in the front looking at San Giorgio. I'm sure you can stay there too. The Count will call. He knows everyone in Italy and everyone knows him. There are flights daily from Dublin to Venice. There won't be any problems. I look forward to showing you Venice, Josie dear."

17. Venice and Veronese

The next day, late in the afternoon, the four of them, Pina and the Count, Josie and Joe, were in a motor launch water taxi speeding through the fog from the Venice Airport to the Danieli's dock. The driver, who looked like Rossano Brazzi, jaunty in a peacoat and a knitted cap, was navigating through a passageway marked by a line of guideposts made of three boards bound together at the top with iron bands, spaced in the water every thirty yards or so. They looked like the supports for a tepee or some other conical structure. The guideposts, called *briccole* in Italian, stuck out of the water about 10 feet into the air. Sometimes there was a giant ball made out of slats on the top of a 4′ x 4′ as well, but for a long time, and for a long distance, there were only these triad guideposts. Joe tried to count them but too many had passed before he started so he gave up and watched the boat's wake behind them as they bounced over the waves. The spume jetted out straight and then split off to the right and left equally. When they bounced on a wave the straight foam diminished.

No sooner had he noticed this than they docked. The beautiful robin's egg blue and white striped posts of the Danieli flanked them on either side as they pulled into the hotel's dock. Josie, who had never been to Venice before, was agog. She had been talking all the way in on the speedboat, but even she could not be heard above the noise of the engine. Pina and the Count, old hands at this jaunt, simply sat back and smiled throughout the trip. It's a pleasure again to show people a place familiar to you but new to them.

Two doormen came running over to help them out. The driver of the boat took off his knit cap once they landed. He had a beautiful head of silver hair. He guided Pina and the Count up to the ledge of his boat with one hand and held onto the dock with the other. The doormen tied the boat to the pier. The Captain then gave Josie a little push from behind, thus fulfilling for her the legend of Italian men, about which Pina had instructed her—"They won't care how old you are, Josie. They'll pat your behind. It's terrible but that's the way they are. You'll get used to it." Josie gave him a smile and said to no one in particular as she looked back, "What lovely silver hair he has! There's nothing like Italian hair, I've always said."

The Captain did the same for Joe, pushing his sturdy bum tenderly up the stair to the ledge of the boat; he even held it a little after Joe hit *terra firma*. Joe looked back in surprise. He hadn't given the Captain a second glance after getting into the speedboat. The Captain gave Joe a big smile with his beautiful white teeth and tanned skin. None of Joe's fellow travelers saw this little exchange because they were all hurrying to the hotel door. Josie was *ooh*ing and *aaah*ing at every step and almost fell through the opened door of the Danieli onto an Oriental rug.

At the desk Pina said, "Now go upstairs to your rooms and come back here in a half hour. We'll have a wonderful lunch at Harry's Bar and then I'll take you shopping, Josie."

Joe said, "I don't think I'll be joining you. I have an errand to attend to. I'm going to leave my bags here. They can bring them up to the room and I'm going to get the *Vaporetto*."

"Oh Joe, you're no fun anymore," Josie accused. "You're too preoccupied. He works very hard. I bet that it's a murder case or something. Boats relax him, however. Leave me a credit card, Joe."

"Don't worry about that," Pina said. "They'll send the clothes and the bill here. I'm taking care of this. After all, I forced you to come with me to Venice, Josie," Pina said firmly.

Joe didn't like this arrangement but he was out the door in a flash. He caught the #82 Vaporetto just as it was pulling out and sat up in the front all alone.

He got off at the San Basile stop. After consulting the little map he had taken from the desk at the Danieli, Joe walked up an alley and then along a smaller canal past an older trattoria which had a couple of outside tables and then a smarter, more modern café which was jammed with people. Joe then took a left over a small bridge. There he was right in front of the *Chiesa de San Sebastiano*. There appeared to be some sort of school to the right of the church's entrance. Young people were going in and out of a big old door to the left. Joe thought this door was the church entrance until he got close enough to read the sign. Confused, he stood back and then saw a closed door at the front of the church. It said "*Chiuso fino alle 2:00.*" Although Joe's Italian was mainly the memory of Latin, he surmised that he couldn't get into the church through that door until 2:00 in the afternoon. Joe walked around the right side of the church into a big desolate piazza, or *campo* as they call it in Venice, and then to another church, which was undergoing reconstruction on the outside. Joe was looking for a side door to San Sebastiano but nothing appeared.

Joe decided to go back to one of the restaurants and have lunch. When in Italy always eat lunch. After all, that's probably why the church was closed.

The fashionable café was too crowded, so Joe took the few more steps to the *trattoria*. It too was crowded, but a busy young man at the front with an apron around his waist pointed to a table in the second room back. Joe walked to the table and sat down, looking out through the front door to the sidewalk and the people at the tables out there. The waitress, an older woman dressed too young for her age in jeans and a tight top, but not without style, came over and spoke to him in German.

Joe quickly responded without thinking, "No, English," and she threw up her hands, said "*Madonna!! Un altro Irlandese!*" She walked away to talk heatedly to the young man who had seated Joe. After a while the young man came over, apologized for the waitress' inability to speak English and took his order. Joe ordered pasta with a fish sauce even though the first time he had come to Venice he got sick after eating just such a dish. It was one of the two specials after all and Venice was famous for its seafood, he thought hopefully.

All of a sudden, as he was halfway through his meal, a bohemian looking young woman in a long hippy skirt came bustling through the restaurant with an accordion and went to a room Joe hadn't seen behind him to the left. Soon he started to hear tuning up and then *The Wild Colonial Boy*. Joe ate a little more, but curiosity got the best of him. He put his napkin on the table and walked back as if he was headed to the toilet, which was also behind him. He stared into the side room, where the music was coming from.

A big guy covered in plaster dust looked at Joe and said with a brogue, "And who are you?"

There were two other men in the room, also covered with plaster dust. One of them, the smallest of the three, was holding the accordion. The young woman also was there. They all were looking at Joe now.

Joe paused and then said, "I'm a friend of Tim Ronayne."

"Aahhh," said his greeter. "We've been looking for the fucken dog for days, high and wide. We heard you were coming. We're on our lunch, although we mainly drink it. Liam here hates Italian food. This is Anna who wants us to buy her accordion. Maybe we will. We're getting lonely here and hoping the old songs might cheer us up."

"Or bring us down further," said Liam as he lifted his glass of red wine.

The greeter said, "Forgive me. This is Liam and the other fella, with the squeeze box, is Tom. We call him Tom Red but you can't tell that for all the dust all over him. That's why they put us back here. They don't want us scandalizing the gentry in front. Ha!! Will you come back with us to the Church? Maybe you can find the fucken dog. I'm Harry, Harry Finn."

"And I'm Joe Lyons. My mother's people come from Ballyfirglin. As I said, I'm a friend of Tim Ronayne's."

"We know who you are and what you do and all your cousins in Louth, for Christ's sweet sake. Who do you think we think you are? Margaret Thatcher?" Harry said impatiently. "We're glad you're here and we'll take care of you. We hope you can help us out and soon. We're getting tired of being here. The money is good and the women are beautiful—but we don't know a fucken word of Italian except *pasta* and *fresco* and *impiastro* and a few other words like that—technical words. We'd rather be at home is what it amounts to. Tommy had never even been to Dublin. You understand that, I'm sure, Joe. You're away from home too. Let's go to the church now boys. Tell Anna we'll decide about the accordion tomorrow. Goodbye Anna, *Arrivederci Anna!*"

They all walked over to the church. From the first he heard of it Joe had in his mind's eye that Father Gentili's reference to a "dog in the temple" was to a statue of a dog in the church. He imagined that there would be a statue of Saint Francis of Assisi surrounded by animals, one of which was a dog. Joe could just lift up the statue and there would be the Venice "One Eighth." He had convinced himself of that, with little or no evidence to back up his belief. That wasn't very judicial of him, and he knew it.

He and Harry talked seriously while the other guys, Tom and Liam, bantered about the pretty, sexy, Italian girl students hurrying across the bridge. Joe wanted to know how much of the church they had been able to explore and if they were alone in the church.

"There's kind of a foreman, a curator from the Government, an Italian guy in a fancy suit. They call him *Maestro*. He wears dark glasses and a sweater over his shoulders, like your old aunt Nora. I don't know how he can see a fucken thing in there. He comes in once or twice a day, often with someone else, and they yack away in Italian. Then in English he tells us what area to do next. He shows us pictures of what the plasterwork used to look like, but we know what we're doing. We follow the lines of what's still up or what's on the other side. Sometimes we make a mold from the other side. We've had no complaints about our work yet. We started in the sacristy to the left of the nave and then went to the nave and now we're going down the left side. We're just about at the organ. There are a lot of paintings everywhere and we have to be careful with those. They're by some guy named Veronese and the *Maestro* guy tells us he's very important. The pictures are quite dramatic; they look like the holy cards the nuns gave out in school. The one of poor Sebastian is a fright. He's getting shot with arrows from all sides. He's got a nice build on him too. It's too bad. The Blessed Mother is above him in heaven so I guess everything worked out alright for him in the end. Maybe he couldn't feel the arrows. He looks pretty good for the abuse he's taking."

Over the bridge at San Sebastiano the door was now open. Before he and Joe stepped in Harry added, "There's also this woman, who sits at a desk and takes the admission. For extra money she puts on the bright lights. She's o.k. She has a crush on Tom and he flirts with her. She's kind of studious but a little plain in comparison to most of the girls around here. She sells books about the Church and the paintings in a number of languages. There aren't many tourists. We're a bit off the beaten path."

They all went in and Tom immediately shouted, (irreverently for being in church, Joe thought) "*Arianna, que bella!*"

The bookish young woman with thick glasses behind the desk looked up, beamed and quickly looked down at her book. Harry introduced Joe to her as their *amico Americano*. She smiled at Joe but asked him for the entrance fee, three euros, nevertheless. She didn't get much business, almost not enough to justify her existence and because the Irish plasterers were now in the church itself they kept the church's bright lights on all the time besides shining lights of their own. So she had lost her income from turning up the lights while the Irish boys were there.

Joe did a quick tour around the church as the Irish boys climbed up their scaffolding. He agreed with Harry about the altarpiece of Saint Sebastian in the nave. Sebastian looked pretty serene in spite of having been punctured with two arrows, one in the upper right thigh and the other just above a well-shaped left pectoral. Neither arrow seemed to have drawn blood, however. Maybe it was the seated Madonna with the *Bambino* standing on her lap in the clouds above which made Sebastian invulnerable. Or it could have been the Virgin being crowned in the ceiling. The paintings were beautiful. The well-muscled figure of Sebastian was surely inspired by an earlier Greek god. Mary was lovely and the baby Jesus was just the serious side of cute.

There was a funny rug with big roses on it laid before the main altar. It looked like a remnant from a discount store in a Latino neighborhood, Joe thought. It's an unusual juxtaposition of the vulgar with the sublime. But it also tells you that this is a real church, used by real people, a regular parish, not another Venetian museum.

Joe peeked into the recently replastered sacristy, which was now dark. And then he started up the left side. The doors in front of the organ were open. Veronese had painted on these a scene of something going on inside a classical building. The adult Jesus appeared to be on the right hand door consoling a greenish looking, almost naked man in a sheet. Joe didn't recognize the story. It could have been any one of a number of Jesus' miracles—curing the leper, raising the dead Lazarus, or healing a cripple. It was hard to see the organ itself through the scaffolding and it was hard to see anything very clearly, even with all the extra light.

Joe wasn't sure what some of the other paintings depicted, what the stories in the paintings were. He decided to buy a guidebook from Arianna. Maybe it would give him a hint about the dog and the missing "One Eighth." There was no St. Francis and no statue of a dog that he could see in his preliminary tour. He hoped that Arianna had a guidebook in English. Maybe that would show a marble canine. After a search Arianna found the last English guidebook under a table behind her. The illustrations were in black and white, however, so Joe had to buy the Italian version, which was in color, as well. He figured he could look up the picture in color in the Italian book, find it in the black and white English book and then read the description in English.

Joe decided to return to the hotel to do his research, but also to see if Shaughnessy had arrived. Two heads would be better than one on this quest, especially if one of them knew what he was doing, like Shaughnessy, the detective, was supposed to.

Joe said goodbye to the boys. Harry said, "Come back tomorrow. We'll be working around the organ doors so we'll have to move the scaffolding and shut the doors. Did you find anything?"

"No, but I bought a couple of books to do some homework and to keep Arianna happy. Shaughnessy should be arriving soon. We'll come back tomorrow."

"Oh, you made Arianna's day. She hasn't sold a book in two weeks. She may get promoted out of here if this keeps up. Then what would I do?" said Tom. He started to sing a song that began, "She is my heart's desire/She sets my heart afire…."

Arianna, whom nobody thought understood English, blushed.

18
A View of San Giorgio

Shaughnessy hadn't arrived. At least he hadn't made himself known to the desk at the Danieli. There were no messages for Joe. Joe went up to his room. As Joe approached the door there was something lying in front of it. It looked like a newspaper from a distance. When Joe got closer he reached down to pick it up. He couldn't believe it. It was a newspaper, but wrapped in it was a teddy bear punctured by two red arrows, one above the right thigh and the other above the left pectoral, just like the Saint Sebastian he had seen at the church.

Joe shook as he entered the room. There was a message on the phone. He was too frightened to pick it up and sat down in the big armchair facing the window opening onto the Grand Canal and the magnificent church of San Giorgio.

What is this? Why can't they leave me alone? Who are "they?" I thought that we were all in this together now? I'm traveling with Pina and the Count now. What more do they want from me? I can't take any more of this. Where can I be safe? I've got my job to protect. I can't go to the Feds. What if the papers get this? Those pricks at the sensation-loving Herald *won't let up. I can see the headline now.*

"JUDGE LYONS TIED UP AFTER LOVE TRYST." Then the next day, "LYONS HID NATIONAL TREASURE OF IRELAND FOR 30 YEARS." On the third day they'll say, "MOBSTER BINDS JUDGE IN BROOKS BROTHER TIES." And so on it went in Joe's mind. He would be condemned for having had the treasure and shamed for having lost it so ignominiously. And then his reputation would be ruined for consorting with the Mob. The most beautiful view in Christendom, which was right in front of him, gave him no relief.

Because Joe had already condemned himself, he decided to pick up the message and face the consequences. As he reached for the receiver the phone rang again. *Oh fuck*, he said to himself as he answered it.

"Hi, it's me, Shaughnessy. I hear that you met the Irish lads at Saint Sebastian's."

"I did," Joe replied, "And I bought some reading material for us to study. How's your Italian?"

"What have you found in the books? You know more about this Fine Art stuff than I do. We did have a course in the seminary in liturgical art but they mainly seemed concerned about not showing anyone, especially Jesus and his Blessed Mother, looking like any kind of sexual being. We used to call it Eunuchs 101. The funny thing was that the other courses were getting pretty radical and presenting Jesus in all his humanity. Although we read Kazantzakis' *The Last Temptation of Christ* and D.H. Lawrence's *The Man Who Died*, I guess looking at a Christ who might have had sex would be too much for us. You know, 'A picture is worth a thousand words.' So, there we were with these holy icons that looked like blocks. You'd never know there had been a Renaissance, never mind Classical sculpture."

Shaughnessy added, "Anyway, I think we should go to the church and count all the dogs inside and out and then start looking under them. Ha, ha! Check the books tonight and I'll meet you in the morning. Hey, you didn't see Dino Randozza around, did you? I could've sworn I saw him on the *vaporetto* coming in from the airport. Has he been visiting his sainted mother? I thought that the Feds had pulled his passport." All this was said nonstop, and much too cheerily for Joe in his present state of mind.

The last bit of information about the sighting of Dino Randozza sent Joe into a state. It almost pushed him over the edge. His knees were knocking but Joe couldn't tell if it was from fear or desire—or both. Would he again see his nemesis? What would he say to him? Would they have sex at last—without Joe getting tied up? Was that part of Dino's excitement? Would Joe have to get dressed up as a monsignor? Where would he get the outfit?

Joe said to Shaughnessy, "Get over here! When can I see you? Where are you staying? I just got another of these maimed teddy bears. This one is wounded like Saint Sebastian at the church. It's too much. I thought that I had joined the enemy. So why are they doing this to me? I'm going to leave and go back to Boston and right to the FBI. Fuck you all and your fucking Dago-Mick conspiracies. Who reads *The Book of Kells* these days anyway!? "

"I'll be right over," said Sergeant Detective Shaughnessy. "Don't move."

As he waited, Joe debated with himself whether or not to check the message which was still blinking for him on the phone. He began to reach for the phone a couple of times. Finally he decided to wait and let Sergeant Detective Shaughnessy retrieve it for him. Shaughnessy might even know who it was. Weren't they tape recording the North End mobsters in their social clubs these days?

Joe sat back in the chair and looked out the French doors to San Giorgio. In spite of his anxiety he could almost appreciate the beauty of the view. He adjusted his feet and tried to meditate.

Years before, in an attempt to stave off taking medication for high blood pressure, Joe had taken a meditation course. There was still a bit of the Sixties in Joe. Besides, he'd heard that the medication made an erection difficult; that gave meditation an added incentive. "Follow your breath," he said to himself. "In, out, in, out; feel your toes; feel your feet; feel your calves." Joe was almost up to his waist, and enjoying it, when there was a knock on the door. Joe assumed it was Shaughnessy. So he got up and went towards the door. Almost to the door, Joe realized that he should ask who was there.

"Who is it?" said Joe.

"You know who it is! I've been calling you for hours. Now let me in. I've got so much to tell you. It's me, your aunt. Open the door!"

Well, that solved two mysteries at once—the door and the phone message—Joe thought as he opened the door to a more glamorous Josie than he'd ever seen before. She was in a plum red nubby knit suit which would have been Chanel except that the waist was pinched. Josie was always proud of her figure and she still had a waist worth accentuating.

"I had such a wonderful day. First Pina took me to this wonderful shop at the other end of the piazza and I bought this beautiful suit. They tailored it while we went for shoes," and she pointed down to a pair of low-heeled pumps just a shade darker than the suit. "Then we returned for the suit and I wore it out of the shop. It does wonders for my coloring. This is the best suit I ever bought since that navy blue Carlyle suit I bought for your Cousin Kate's second wedding—the Protestant one—and then wore to your Uncle Mike's funeral. She deserved that nice Episcopalian she married; the first husband was a creep, Knight of Malta's son or not. He used to hit her. I don't know why I've not worn red before. The reds at home are too bold. They lack subtlety. They may be good for Nancy Reagan but not for me. This tone is perfect for my pale Irish skin and it's wonderful with my white hair. Pina told me that it brings out the pink in me.

"After shopping we stopped in a café in the Piazza. They gave Pina and me the best table, right out front, but back far enough so we wouldn't be ogled. She knew the *maitre d'* except they call them something else in Italian. And then the Count took us to the Correr Museum and the City Museum. They're down at that end of the Piazza too. We saw the treasures of Venice. The Count hired a guide, a little bit of a thing with a big voice. His name is Guido, Guido the guide. When we got to the Library he said, 'Anda now we have the pintings of Veronese. Paolo Caliari was the name he took in Venice but his real name was Spezapreda whicha means rocka breaker.' I heard more about Titian and Tintoretto and Veronese than I'll ever remember. Tomorrow we are going to Veronese's, and the guide's parish church where Veronese painted everything in sight, even the organ doors. Did you know that the Inquisition was going to punish him because he put animals in *The Last Supper*? They thought that was irreverent. They sound like Monsignor Phelan, who used to be at Saint Mary's in Newport. He was a stickler too. They told Veronese to paint the dogs out and put Mary Magdalene in but he outsmarted them and changed the name of the painting. I don't think that Mary Magdalene was at the Last Supper anyway. Veronese left the cat and the dogs in and called it *The Feast in the House of Levi*. It's in the Louvre these days. What did you do today?" She added unexpectedly.

Joe was ready for another ten minutes of monologue at least and was caught unprepared. "I went to the church that I think you are going to tomorrow," Joe said.

"San Sebastiano? Oh then, you won't want to come tomorrow?" said Josie disappointedly.

"Well, I might," Joe said, thinking that it might be a good thing to see the church with a knowledgeable guide. "I have some books here if you want to do a little homework," he added picking up the books he had bought from Arianna off the telephone table.

"Oh no," said Josie, "These are beautiful shoes, but new nevertheless. I'm going to go soak my feet, take a nap and get dressed for dinner. I have a new silk dress in a darker shade of this color. And a beautiful sky blue shawl if it gets cool, and even if it doesn't. Will you join us? We are going to some place called *Oliva Nera*. The Count swears by it. It's somewhere back from here. I'm sure he could fit you in."

As much as he was relieved that he didn't have to baby sit Josie, and as happy as he was that she was enjoying herself, Joe felt a little abandoned by her. She seemed to have forsaken him for Pina and her retinue. Joe hadn't told her about the shadier side of Pina's family, or his connection to it, but he was tempted by his jealousy to discredit Pina. However, he was smart enough to realize that to do so would leave Josie to his care and that he had another job to do.

Just then there was another knock on the door.

This time Joe just opened the door. He didn't ask who was there. Somehow he felt protected by Josie.

It was Shaughnessy.

"You remember my aunt, Josie Lavin, don't you?" Joe said.

"Of course, Ms Lavin, we met at Ballyfirglin, all too briefly," Shaughnessy said with a gallantry that Joe had never seen before.

Josie replied without acknowledging recognition, "Oh yes. Well, I have to go now. You boys enjoy yourself. I'm sure that you have business to do." It seemed that she had no memory of Shaughnessy and she really did think that Joe was over here doing mysterious Judge business.

Joe had no idea what she meant about "business" but now was not the time to inquire. Josie had her own take on things and sometimes it was better not to ask. Just as Pina never asked questions, Josie didn't always want to let you know what she thought she knew.

As the door shut Joe said to Shaughnessy, "I went to the Church of San Sebastiano today and snooped around briefly. I didn't have a clue, but now I may be on to something. Josie may have tipped me off. She's going to the Church tomorrow with a guide. I'm going too. You should come. First I have to check out these books from the church and see if they offer us anything. What are you doing now?"

"I'm at your service," said Shaughnessy with a leer. "Where's the teddy bear anyway? What's that about?"

Joe had almost forgotten about the teddy bear. He leaned over and picked it up and said, "As you know, I was getting these teddy bears with various states of injury both in Boston and in Ireland. I thought that they would stop once I joined up with Pina, but today, just an hour ago, there was this one outside my door wrapped in a newspaper."

"What newspaper?" asked Sergeant Detective Shaughnessy.

"What difference does that make?" said Joe impatiently.

"Well, it might let us know what your stalker reads, or at least what he buys."

"It's in the wastebasket. This bear was wounded with arrows in the exact same spots as Saint Sebastian in the painting I had just seen in the church. It's creepy."

"Was there a note, or a message, or anything?"

"No note, no message. There was a message on the phone. The light was blinking. It still is. I was waiting for you before answering it, but it's probably Josie. She said that she had been calling me for hours."

"Did it occur to you that there could be more than one message?" said Shaughnessy as he headed towards the phone. He pressed the blinking button.

"Joe darling, call me. I've had the most wonderful day." That was Josie and Joe looked at Shaughnessy with an "I told you so" glare.

There was a pause and then the phone clicked again, "Soon we'll be together again. You have nothing to fear from me. I've found religion. I love you and want you, my *cuzza grande*," all this was in the same guttural voice as the earlier calls that accompanied the wounded bears.

Joe fell into the chair, his head in his hands.

Shaughnessy went to the wastebasket and pulled the newspaper out. It was *Osservatore Romano*, the official Vatican newspaper.

"He's either a priest or he has a thing for priests," said Shaughnessy flashing the paper at Joe. "What does *cuzza* mean?"

"I have no idea," Joe said through his fingers, still concealing his face and his weeping eyes. He was in despair.

"Look, we can't worry about this creep now. We have to find the Venetian 'One Eighth' and if we could just figure out that cryptic message from Father Gentili, we'd be fine. **'Look for the cats under the backside of the dog in the temple.'"**

"What the hell could that mean?" said Joe petulantly.

"I'll stay with you tonight. I won't leave your side. You know I guarded the Polish Pope, John Paul II, when he came to Boston. I rode in that Popemobile with him all over Boston Common when he said Mass. They dressed me as a priest. I still have the cassock and the collar. It made my mother very happy. When she saw me on the television she even briefly forgave me for leaving the seminary. I'll sleep over here tonight and we can go to the church tomorrow with Josie and her crew or we can go earlier, snoop around and meet them there. O.K.? Whatever you want."

"I want all this to be over. I want to be out of here. I don't want to be stalked anymore. I want some peace and quiet. I'm going to bed. You can stay here. The couch is pretty comfortable. Give me an hour. Then we can call for room service or we can go upstairs and eat, although I don't feel like going to the bother. Wake me in an hour but don't leave me." With that Joe went into the bedroom leaving Shaughnessy the big chair and the view of San Giorgio as well as the guidebooks to San Sebastiano.

For a while Shaughnessy just sat watching the sun change the color of the water and San Giorgio's façade. Some writer he had read on the flight over had written about Venice being all façade and the sides and backs of buildings being of inferior stuff. Actually it was Mary McCarthy. Shaughnessy had bought her book in the Dublin Airport bookstore before leaving, thinking that she was some sweet, Irish travel writer lady. The bookstore may have too. He was pleasantly surprised by her brilliant and unsentimental observations. And then he read on the jacket that she had written *The Group*, and he'd seen the movie. From Joe's window he could see the side of San Giorgio and he could see that it was made of ordinary brick rather than the beautiful white marble which was on the facade.

He picked up one of the two guidebooks for San Sebastiano.

It was the one with pictures in color and thus the Italian one. He marveled over the Veroneses and tried to decipher the stories the paintings portrayed. He too had studied Latin, at Boston College High School and then at Saint John's Seminary. He could make out some of the Italian but mainly he just looked at the pictures. He had also studied Biblical and Church History and thought that he knew most of the stories. They certainly weren't registered in his mind in the wonderful, sensual, rich, dramatic way that Veronese had painted them. And whoever heard of monkeys, parrots or dogs in the foreground of so many sacred events?

With this thought Shaughnessy nodded off, forgetting that he was to awaken Joe.

Joe woke up on his own and after peeking in at his sleeping custodian he took a shower in the bathroom which was off his bedroom. Joe returned to the bedroom and was toweling himself dry in the middle of the room when Shaughnessy walked in, looked long at Joe and said, "I need to shower too. Do you mind?"

Before Joe could answer Shaughnessy had his shirt off. He had a nicer body than Joe had imagined. Joe had always seen him in baggy clothes and the circumstances of their meetings were not conducive to lustful looks on Joe's part. In addition, Irish men were not Joe's usual ideal. Shaughnessy's body was still youthful and it was pink and white, like Jackie Crotty's had been. You knew that he had been a butterfly swimmer by the big chest, round shoulders and powerful upper back. He was in great shape for his age. Shaughnessy was an Irish blond, which is to say not a pure blond, a little dirtier.

Shaughnessy dropped his pants with his back to Joe, his boxer shorts went down with the pants. He had a beautiful milk white bum, a little larger than was the fashion but strong, like a pony's. There was just a diamond of dark blond hair at the base of his back, like a satyr. That matched the bush surrounding his rapidly swelling dick as he turned to head to the shower. It was as if Jackie Crotty had grown up.

Neither of them said anything as Shaughnessy walked to the bathroom. Joe didn't conceal his looking, however, and Joe's pleasure was becoming apparent. Shaughnessy left the bathroom door open. Joe contemplated climbing in the shower with Shaughnessy. He decided to lie naked on top of the bed instead and let Shaughnessy make the first move. Joe always liked to be seduced. In the days when he used to worry about the sinfulness of sex he didn't have to be the one responsible for the sin if he was not the pursuer, or so he told himself. In reality, he usually seduced the seducer into seducing him, like the scene he had now set up.

Joe lay on the terra cotta and pink bedspread, himself white and another shade of pink. His body hadn't seen the sun in years. Joe was hairy-chested and fuzzy all the way down to his crotch. His legs were fuzzy too. Hair even grew on his upper back and shoulders. Joe didn't know where that hair had come from. He'd been pretty smooth through his forties, just a nice pelt between his pectorals, but at fifty the hair started growing everywhere. It was all white. Joe shaved what sprouted on the edge of his ears. He'd thought of getting some of the rest removed, but he read an article that said that was an act against nature and undignified—that he should wear it proudly, like a polar bear. So he tried to do that, but he was never quite sure he liked being a polar bear.

The room was pink and salmon, very Venetian, the pink of rich fabrics and Renaissance paintings, a luxurious pink, *Gaudate* Sunday pink and manly too, like a Brooks Brothers Oxford cloth shirt. There were aquamarine, pink, discordantly yellow, and milky white Murano glass sconces on the walls and a chandelier to match in the center of the room. The rug matched the walls.

Shaughnessy came out of the bathroom and stood underneath the chandelier on a towel he'd dropped on the carpet. He did a beautiful swimmers swoosh with his open hands down both sides of his body to get the surface water off. He even tossed his head, like a sheep dog, sending out a fine spray from his boy's regular, some of which hit Joe on the bed. Then Shaughnessy rubbed himself down with another towel, revealing the supple musculature of his back as he reached for his ankles.

Joe said nothing. He continued to stare, however. And when Shaughnessy finished the rubdown he looked back at Joe on the bed and smiled, his blue eyes twinkling. Shaughnessy said nothing as he walked to the bed, still smiling. Once there he quietly said, "Move over, Joe," and climbed onto the bed, his right side touching Joe's left at shoulder, hip and knee. They lay like that for a while, just breathing, and then Joe, shocking himself, rolled over to Shaughnessy and kissed him right on the mouth. Shaughnessy opened his mouth and kissed back. They remained in bed making love in the dusky light until they fell asleep.

19 A Dog Barks in Church

The lovemaking was a complication neither Shaughnessy nor Joe had anticipated. To call it "a conflict of interest" was an understatement. It was in so many ways that the ethical mind boggled—detective and victim, judge and police officer. Whatever Sergeant Detective Shaughnessy's rank was in the Fireboys, Joe was at best an ambivalent conscript. But in Venice, in Italy, in Europe, out of their respective roles and jurisdictions, what could it matter?

Because they'd gone to bed so early, Joe woke up early. Joe took a look at the sleeping Sergeant Detective Shaughnessy, vulnerable and boyish on his side curled up in the fetal position, his blond and white hair all messed up. Joe smiled. From the big chair in the living room, still naked and unshowered, Joe called for breakfast for two while watching San Giorgio brighten in the morning light. Joe had no supper the night before and the night's activities made him hungry.

Joe and Shaughnessy made up for hundreds of years of Irish sexual repression. It was as if Jansenism had never infected Ireland. For Joe the sex hadn't been so hot since his first sessions with

Arthur Bruce, or his night with a tawny Spanish sailor with jet black hair and eyes, who was on a tall ship docked in Boston Harbor for the Bicentennial. That was a night Joe thought could never be equaled.

Sergeant Detective Shaughnessy woke up and wandered into the living room. He didn't know where he was until he saw Joe, and even then he looked startled. Now Joe smiled and from the chair pulled Shaughnessy towards him. Shaughnessy came willingly. The chair tipped over slowly. The rug was soft but they weren't. Shaughnessy had Joe right there on the floor in front of the window looking out at San Giorgio. Joe gave as good as he got and soon came all over his stomach. Shaughnessy let go of Joe's right leg, scooped the gism up from Joe's belly, smeared it on his own chest, moaned, spasmed and soon collapsed on Joe. The light from the window shone on them, as did its heat. They lay like that until the bell rang with the bellman and breakfast.

After breakfast they met Josie in the lobby. Once Guido the guide arrived they went out the front door to the dock where Pina had reserved a motorlaunch, a long, sleek, partially covered, wooden speedboat which rode low in the water. Something had come up regarding Pina's son, Monsignor, hopefully about-to-be Bishop, Rocco Randozza. Pina, the Count and the niece were flying to Rome for the day, according to Josie.

The motorlaunch captains looked like gondoliers who had grown into their fifties—a little thicker, grey or white hair, but still handsome and sexy. The same captain who brought them from the airport was driving this motorlaunch. This time he wore no hat and his thick, wavy, white hair gleamed in the sun. He shot a big smile at Joe on the pier as he helped the others into the boat. Josie got another pat, which she ignored except for a little smile straight ahead. Joe was the last. The Captain said, "*Signore Giudice*, let me help you." This invocation of Joe's title prompted Sergeant Detective Shaughnessy, who had preceded Joe, without any assistance, to turn around. He saw the Captain hold Joe's left arm with one hand while holding Joe's butt with the other. Shaughnessy was not pleased. He grabbed and held Joe's right arm until Joe was safely in the boat. Joe thought to himself, *I am being treated like the Queen Mum. I am not this helpless, but the attention is grand.* Joe didn't even question how the captain knew he was a judge.

Sergeant Detective Shaughnessy and the Captain were left facing each other after helping Joe into the boat. Shaughnessy gave the Captain a look that could kill. The Captain came down to his place at the wheel. Shaughnessy moved back to sit next to Joe and across from Josie at the back, the open end of the boat.

"Isn't this marvelous, Joe," Josie said. "Can I stand up here?" she added rising up before waiting for an answer. "Joe, look at San Giorgio! And San Marco and the Campanile! Can Heaven be any more beautiful! Thank you, Joe! Why can't the Italians in America make places like this?"

Most of this was said to the air as Josie swirled around perilously at the back of the boat which was speeding and rising up in the water. Of course, as usual Josie knew the answers to most of her questions but didn't care to hear them. It wasn't only the Italians who got this treatment. She harangued Irish Americans as well, if not worse. When Bernadette Devlin came over in the Seventies to raise money for 'The Cause' Josie berated the finest High Irish in Rhode Island. "Do you realize what those barbarians are still doing to our people? Our ancestors will turn over in their graves if you don't give this poor girl some money." Most of them had no idea what "The Cause" was and thought Bernadette was a hippie with bad teeth and a brogue. But they feared Josie, and gave.

The boat slowed as they approached the San Basilico *Vaporetto* stop and the little canal of San Basegio. The Captain turned around and told the still *ooh*ing and *aah*ing Josie, "*Signora*, it would be better if you sat down. We have some bridges ahead in the little canal, *per favore*." He smiled at her with all his white teeth.

"Oh Joe, that was a marvelous trip. I hope that we never leave here. Even the tugboats have that little extra baroque curve. The barges are beautiful too. It's hard to believe they carry anything as mundane as garbage. I saw two banking boats. Can you believe that they cruise around and pick up the receipts? It beats waiting at the ATM or dealing with a surly teller. Of course, if we let our Italians pick up the money in Providence in boats, there'd be no money left," she added after a pause.

They arrived at a landing just after the San Sebastiano Bridge. Josie and Joe were the last to leave the speedboat, again with pats to the bum by the ever solicitous captain. Josie stood outside the Church of San Sebastiano and read aloud from the English guidebook, "This is the church of Saint Sebastian, decorated by Paulo Caliari, born Spezapreda, the rock breaker, in Verona in 1528, later called Veronese. From 1555 to 1570 Veronese painted almost everything in the church, even the murals and decorative scenes on the walls themselves. Look up at the ceiling…"

Then she stopped reading and said, "Let's play a game and count the dogs in the paintings. Veronese was always painting dogs, you know—even in the most serious scenes. It was so charming of him."

Joe and Shaughnessy looked at each other, wide eyed. "Dawns the light on Marblehead," they both thought! Neither Shaughnessy nor Joe could believe what they had just heard.

"Look for the cats under the backside of the dog in the temple."

Weren't they at the temple? Shaughnessy said with his best detective cool, "Just what do you mean, Josie?"

"I mean that Veronese put animals in his paintings, mostly dogs, even in the most serious ones. He painted a Last Supper with dogs, a monkey, loose women and a dwarf in it. The Venetian Inquisition told him he couldn't do that. It was irreverent. Veronese said, '*Lo depingo et fazzo delle figure.* I paint and make figures.' So instead of getting rid of the dogs he changed the name of the painting to *The Feast in the House of Levi*. I told Joe all this yesterday. Sometimes I think that he doesn't pay any attention to me anymore," Josie said impatiently.

"Well, uh, well…Let's do that. Let's count the dogs," said Sergeant Detective Shaughnessy, casting a quick conspiratorial look at Joe, which he hoped Josie didn't see.

She did see it, and said, "Are you toying with me? Treating me like a dotty old lady? Don't do that to me. I don't know you very well, but I'm beginning not to like you at all. You may be a friend of my nephew, and you are a detective, but that doesn't give you license to patronize me."

"Josie, Josie, he saved my life. Shaughnessy saved my life. He's a good man. He's protecting me, even as we speak. He's not patronizing you," Joe rushed to say.

"Alright, Joseph Lavin Lyons, if you say so. I know that you have a life that you have to keep secret from me. I respect that, what with all the gangsters and terrorists who come before you, but treat me like an adult, not a silly old goose. It's hard enough getting old without being talked down to. I've been around too."

This little *contretemps* went on at the door to the church. The passing students looked on with surprise. "Get on with you!" said Josie to a pair of miniskirted Italian girls clutching books who had stopped to stare.

The three of them, Josie, Shaughnessy and Joe, then went inside the darkened church. Their eyes had to adjust to the dark. Once they did, Joe greeted Arianna at her desk, who was smiling broadly remembering yesterday's big book sale.

Joe said, "This is my Aunt Josie Lavin. She lives in the United States and is an admirer of Veronese. And this is my friend Shaughnessy." He didn't give the title.

Sergeant Detective Shaughnessy was already off scouring the scene. Josie extended her hand to Arianna and smiled like a duchess, "So nice to meet you. My nephew has told me of your kindness." Joe didn't know what she was talking about, but so be it.

Arianna replied, "I will turn up *all* the lights for you. The guides ask. I don't do, but for you the best light."

Shaughnessy found the Irish *boyos* in front of the organ. They were taking down some of the scaffolding to put it back up a little to the right. They worked from site to site. "We have to move over to the tomb of this Veronese guy—not a bad painter, but I never saw dogs in holy pictures before. Give us a hand, lad," Harry said to Sergeant Detective Shaughnessy.

Shaughnessy took some scaffolding pipes to the floor below the bust of Veronese, a nice looking man with an aristocratic nose and a beard, balding a bit. The pipes came down from Liam at the top of the scaffolding to Tom at the next level, to Harry to Shaughnessy. From across the room, where Joe and Josie were standing, it looked like a ballet, with the Irish boys in their white jumpsuits stretching and bowing rhythmically as if to music. They left a wide platform of scaffolding and staging about 15 feet up from the floor and 6 feet below the painted doors, which when closed concealed the organ pipes.

"Ah, there's a dog!" said Josie looking up at the ceiling at *The Banishment of Vashti*. "He looks like a setter to me." Joe guessed that poor Vashti was the woman scurrying down the stairs. "And there's another, a greyhound, up there." Josie grabbed the guidebook out of Joe's hands. "That's *The Coronation of Esther before Ahaseurus*."

Joe and Shaughnessy looked up quickly at the ceiling, then down to the floor and then up and down again. There was nothing beneath these canines, unless it was the floor and there was nothing there but tiles. Perhaps the Venetian eighth was buried beneath a tile. How would they ever get to it? Shaughnessy immediately counted the tiles' distance from the wall, went over to those tiles that appeared directly underneath the dogs on the ceiling and, as unobtrusively as he could, scuffed an *X* on them with his gumshoe heel.

"And there's another setter on the organ door. It looks just like the dog the James O'Briens had in Newport. Actually it looks just like the one up there with poor Vashti. Vashti got bumped for Esther by Ahaseurus. I bet that old Paolo used the same dogs as models over and over, just like Picasso used his wives. I hope that Veronese was nicer to the dogs than Picasso, or Ahaseurus even, was to his women. You remember the O'Briens, Joe. She was Annette Hogan and went to school with your mother at the Madames. There were 12 kids…"

Unusually, Josie stopped the genealogy there. She was on a mission and her eyes darted around the church. They stopped at the main altarpiece. There was something white and fluffy in the lower left of the painting in which the twice perforated, but as yet unbleeding, Saint Sebastian, bound to a fluted column, looks up to the Blessed Mother on her throne above the clouds. Josie chose to see it as another dog but it could have been a lamb.

"That miniature poodle belongs in Miami or Hollywood," Josie said. "Mimmi, the big, beautiful Norwegian blonde who married your cousin Billy Lavin had a dog like that. She also had a white Cadillac convertible to match and a tiger skin bathing suit. She used to call you 'Snookums' and kiss you a lot. You loved it. You said that she smelled nice. She wore Chanel #5, never my favorite."

There were more dogs, mostly greyhounds and setters, all around the church and in the sacristy. The back end of the O'Brien's setter was weaseling his way into the crowd in the more gruesome *Martyrdom of Saint Sebastian*. The same canine appeared again, with his tail between his legs coming down the steps, in *The Exhortation of Saints Mark and Marcellus*. They were two brothers facing martyrdom who, after being exhorted by the armor-clad Sebastian, refused to abandon their faith to save their lives despite their parents' pleas.

Josie was triumphant. She had won at her own game of finding dogs. "Those Jewish women have always had spirit," Josie said. "Esther saved her people and so did Golda Meir. Golda wasn't as pretty as Esther but she had other talents. Don't forget Joe, that we have our own heroines, the Countess de Markiewicz and Bernadette Devlin most recently, but there were some great girls in the old days, Queen Maeve and Grania, who ran away with Dermot, and the pirate queen, Grace O'Malley."

Joe and Shaughnessy were dumbfounded. Father Gentili's dog

must be in a painting but there were so many dogs here that they didn't know where to start. Which was the right dog? Were any of them sitting down? Obviously they couldn't be digging up tiles or scraping walls while everyone was in the church, especially Arianna, the watchdog. Maybe they could put on white jumpsuits, join Harry's crew and search when nobody was looking, thought Sergeant Detective Shaughnessy.

Just then Harry shouted, "Hey, can you lads help me with these organ doors. We want to close the organ doors so we can get to the plasterwork around old Veronese's tomb. The doors are heavy and the hinges are old and rickety. We need all of yez." He gave a wave towards the doors.

They all went over to Harry and his crew, even Josie who, through no fault of her own, wasn't a lad strictly speaking. Arianna, who had no idea what "lad" meant, joined the crowd. Of course, for her any excuse to join Tom was welcome. "Alright lads, everybody up on the scaffolding. Use that ladder to the left." The doors were about 20 feet above the floor. "Joe, Shaughnessy and Josie, you three go to the door on the right. Liam, Tom and Arianna will be on this side and I'll direct from out front, like Toscanini. Be careful. These things are almost 500 years old."

It was only a matter of shutting the doors, but they were cumbersome. The doors were about 12 feet high and 5 feet wide. Each door was 3 to 4 inches thick. They were cut and notched at the top to fit within a marble arch with a triangular pediment when closed. The arch was supported by two marble Corinthian columns. The doors were painted on canvas stretched over wood. When open, the Corinthian pillars of the arch were continued in perspective in paint and led down to another arch and the open sky.

The crew, motley indeed, lined up on the staging platform facing Harry who was on the floor in front. "Now duck behind, reach up, get a good grip and walk them out slowly. I'll count and you take a step with each count," Harry said. Joe was at the near, the hinged end of the right hand door, Shaughnessy was next to him in the middle, and Josie at the far end. The sleeping setter was on the other door. Sergeant Detective Shaughnessy was hoping he'd be on that side so he could do a little closer snooping.

Patience, patience, Joe told himself. *There's time enough. We'll find a way—one clue at a time, one dog at a time.*

Arianna, the only outsider to this quest (if you don't count Josie, who would have thrown in with the Fireboys in a second had she known what they were up to) suddenly cried out "*I guanti, i guanti!!*" The others stood there puzzled. Arianna then climbed down the ladder from the staging, ran back to her desk and began searching through drawers and under tables. Finally, she returned with a dusty old wooden box which she carried in front of her like a monstrance. The box contained white kid gloves. "These are always used when touching Veronese," she said. "They have been in the *chiesa* for years. The *maestro* insists."

"That's right," said Harry. "I remember the snotty bastard telling me that if I ever had to touch a painting to ask Arianna for the 'gawanty.' I didn't know what the fuck he was talking about. Oh, excuse me, Ma'am," he added as he nodded apologetically to Josie. Arianna didn't count, if she didn't understand English, even though she had just spoken it.

Josie nodded back and continued to search in the box until she found a pair that fit. Finally Arianna came to Tom. She never raised her head.

"Now do you have anything there for me, Arianna darling, in that little casket? I bet there's a lot you could give me. Do I have to give anything back? I would with pleasure." Tom was never sure that Arianna understood him. He didn't care. She heard the music of his words in either case and blushed.

Arianna reached inside the box with her right hand and pulled out the finest gloves for Tom. They fit. Arianna beamed and then took a pair for herself.

"Alright lads, are we ready at last or do we have to change our shoes too, perhaps those velvet gondolier's slippers they sell in the tourist's shops? Liam, they'd never fit your big farmer's feet. Let's go now. Lift up your arms and get ready to walk and push. Gently! Gently! ONE, TWO, THREE…"

At step THREE Joe felt something moving in his right hand, something at the bottom of the door. At first he thought that he'd broken a piece of the base of the door, but he didn't dare stop walking in time to Harry's call. If he stopped and everyone else went forward, the whole door could split. So Joe extended his fingers higher to get more of the door above the part that seemed loose. The piece, which felt about an inch thick and was the width of the bottom of the door, about four inches, wiggled in his hand with each forward step. He continued on around the quarter circle arc to the front where he ended up facing the wall. He looked up at the other side of the door and there, right in his face, just above where the piece was loose, was the backside of a white greyhound, perhaps the same he'd seen earlier in the ceiling at Esther's coronation, but in a different pose, sitting on its haunches—his haunches, on his backside.

"Let go now lads. Step down. It seems we have another painting on this side."

"Of course we do," said Josie. "It's *The Presentation of Jesus in the Temple*, she added, still with her hands up against the door, which was invisible to her at that level and angle. "Haven't you ever looked at the guide book, Harry?"

Joe's heart jumped when he heard "temple." He still hadn't let go. The loose piece, which now felt like a block, moved in his hand. It felt like it would slip out like a drawer or a butterfly wedge between two boards. How could Joe remove it without being seen? The others released their grips and stepped back. They turned and walked forward, their backs to Joe. Joe gently twisted the block. It moved with his hand as the door stood still. He finally pushed and the block moved out of the door in his hand. Joe quickly slipped the block into his right pant's pocket. It was about five inches by seven inches; he could tell by the feel of it.

Joe thought that if he had loosened a fragment of the base of the door, he could glue it back later. But he also thought that the block might be something else. He remembered the cryptic clue of Father Gentili,

"Look for the cats under the backside of the dog in the temple."

In either case he didn't want to show the others his discovery right yet, or his shame if he had broken a piece of the door. Not just yet.

The painting on the right-hand wing of the now closed organ door depicts the infant Jesus in his mother's arms being presented to Simeon, the old priest in the temple. Mary is lovely with a blue veil slipping off her head. Joseph is old, bearded and drab behind her. He has his carpenter's hammer in one hand and a lit candle in the other. Mary is leaning over in profile placing Jesus on the lap of the seated ancient Simeon, who has his arms crossed in front reverently and is looking down at the babe. This was the event where Simeon made a prophecy about Jesus. "This child is destined to cause the rising and falling of many in Israel," Simeon said.

Simeon and a holy old woman Anna, who hung around the temple day and night, were both told that they would not die without seeing the Messiah. It may be Anna herself in the background holding a crozier, a shepherd's crook, later carried by bishops as caretakers of their flocks.

There are a lot of other people standing around holding objects, sacred things which would have been recognizable to Catholics in the 16th (and 21st) century. There is a young boy with a thurifer and incense boat in the front; another man looks up from a book while standing at a pulpit; his right hand is holding a pen on the altar. A woman on the left carries a cage with two turtledoves in it. Simeon wears a bishop's mitre, but sideways. Candlesticks with lit candles are on an altar as is a golden pitcher. Another little boy appears to be carrying more candles. A garlanded pole is in the background. One message of these old and new symbols seems to be the continuity between Judaism and Catholicism. After all,

Veronese painted one of the more risqué stories in the Old Testament, Esther and Ahaseurus and Mordecai, onto the ceiling of this church celebrating the almost naked Sebastian, one of Christianity's early martyrs, and the excuse for many homoerotic paintings throughout the Renaissance.

Meanwhile, whatever theological message Veronese intended, the greyhound in the foreground, at the bottom edge of the painting, oblivious to the solemnity of the occasion, sits solidly on the floor, and looks the other way, out of the picture, like he is just getting ready to lift his right front paw and scratch.

Josie said, "I thought that the Presentation was when Jesus was about 12 and he went to the temple and wowed the priests with his wisdom. I don't remember this business. I must be wrong; this painting certainly is beautiful. It's like we're peeking in at something happening at a side altar. Look at the sky in the back and the perspective of the whole thing! What gorgeous fabrics! Now I know what inspired my beautiful new Venetian clothes. Joe, look at that guy in the turban! You'd look good in a turban, Joe. And do you see that all the men have beards except the two movie stars in the back, showing their perfect profiles. Joe you should grow a beard. It'd be very distinguished in a slightly unconventional way, just like you are, you know, just a little out of the norm."

Joe just wanted to be out of the Church so he could discover what the block in his pocket was about. It was burning his thigh. Could it be the Venetian "One Eighth"? Joe wanted to go to his room, close all the curtains and examine the block. His patience had vanished; he wished that Josie would shut up. But Josie did as Josie does, and she went on about the painting. And when she finished her dissertation on *The Presentation in the Temple*, she moved on to another painting.

Joe thought about signaling Shaughnessy, but he didn't know who else was watching. Sure, the Irish boys were in on the quest for the Venetian One Eighth, but Arianna wasn't and tourists might walk into the church at any time. Joe had to be somewhere secure before he pulled the block out. To him, the only safe place would be his hotel room.

Finally, in order to get to the hotel, Joe decided to feign illness. He began to moan softly. Shaughnessy heard Joe first and brought him down from the scaffolding to a chair on the right. Josie saw him sitting there and stopped her monologue.

"Josie, I think I have to go home. You stay with Shaughnessy. I'll send the motor launch back for you. It must have been that Arugula I ate. It didn't seem to have been washed very well."

"I grow my own Aguilera, you know," Josie said. "That Vecchione girl, the lawyer, who lives across the street, gave me some seeds years ago. She got them from her grandfather's plants that he started with seeds brought from his village in Italy. It can be a perennial, you know. You do have to wash it well. I wash it a couple of times and then spin it twice. We'll go with you. Won't we, Mr. Shaughnessy? That Captain of the motor launch is a frisky one. You may get sicker on the way, and he doesn't look like he'd be any help."

Joe knew that Josie had to work her way up to the matter at hand by talking ragtime for a while. This arugula soliloquy was a classic. The issue was whether Joe should leave the church, and with whom, but Josie had to talk, and presumably at the same time think, her way to that issue with her Providence Arugula or 'Aguilera' (as Josie would sometimes call it) connection. There was a purpose to her rambles, Joe knew but they were sometimes trying.

Joe wanted to leave and the sooner the better. He preferred to go alone but he wasn't going to fight. He could ditch Josie at the hotel. Nothing gained privacy sooner than the threat of diarrhea. That would be his next announcement, if necessary.

They got into the boat. Josie told the old smoothie Captain, "Take us back to the Danieli Hotel, *per favore*. My nephew is ill and we have to get him home promptly. Help Joe into the boat, Mr. Shaughnessy."

The return trip took only 15 minutes and was without any bum pats. Josie, Shaughnessy and Joe went up to Joe's suite, Josie in the lead. Once there, Joe rushed into the bathroom. He turned the water on and faked a retching sound. Then he sat down on the toilet seat and took the block out of his right-hand pants pocket. It was smooth on one side and appeared to have hardened glue on the other. There was a hinge inset at one end and a little notch in the middle of the other. With racing heart he pried with his thumbnail but nothing happened. He could see that the block was divided horizontally in two, although made of one piece of wood. From his shaving kit he pulled out a nail file and went at the block, first at the notch and then at the hairline space at the sides. He turned the block over and saw what looked like a filled hole on the bottom near the notch end. He pressed there and the top sprung up a bit. He pulled it the rest of the way.

The box was lined in green and gold brocade. Something appeared to be wrapped in green silk. He pulled it out gently and unwrapped it. The silk was a small flag with the Mexican eagle and the words, *Battallon de San Patricio* on one side and *Erin Go Bragh* and a golden harp on the other.

There it was inside the flag—one of the last two missing pieces of the Fireboys' page of *The Book of Kells*, written 1300 years before, and stolen, or liberated, more than 150 years before by Joe's great grandparents' neighbors. As a result of the fire that accompanied its theft Joe's great grandfather, unfairly accused, had to leave his farm and transplant himself to Rhode Island via Canada.

This piece picked up where Joe's fragment had left off, at the beginning of the gospel. On one side it read:

ereos quierant sicut
astorem etcoepitdo
umiam horamulta
iscipulieiusdicentes

And on the other side:

acceptusquinque pa
us intuens incaelum

nes et dedit discipu
nteeos etduospisces

Joe began to cry. He cried for having found the Venetian "One Eighth," for the man who was hung in Mexico, who was its first custodian after the torching of the big house, for the original and the present Fireboys, for his great great grandparents, for long suffering Ireland, for Father Gentili, for Arthur Gentilini Bruce, who had nothing to do with this business, for his other friends who had died of AIDS, or anything else, for the safety with which he had lived his life, for everything he had never dared do or say, for now being part of a cause larger than himself after having walked the middle road for so long, for the love of Christ as displayed in this miracle, and finally for himself. They were tears of joy and sadness.

Joe Returns to the Court 20

"Are you alright, Joe? Open the door! What's happening? Please, let us in! Joe, we'll take care of you." Josie said.

"I'm...fine. I'll be right out. Let me pull myself together and I'll be right out. Thanks. Just one minute," Joe replied haltingly. He stuffed the "One Eighth," the flag and the wooden block now box into his shaving kit and zipped it shut. Then he coughed a few times, hacked, spit, flushed the toilet, put water on his face and threw some on his shirt for good measure.

He came out of the bathroom red eyed but radiant. Shaughnessy knew something was up while Josie thought his glow was a fever. She never trusted foreign food, which meant anything other than American or Irish food, and she wasn't too sure about the latter. "I'm calling the hotel doctor, right now. He'll be here in a minute. Go lie down. Mr. Shaughnessy, I think that you better leave. Joe needs to rest and be quiet. Thank you very much for your help, but he'll be safe in my hands."

"No, Josie, I want Shaughnessy here," Joe said strongly.

Josie backed off. "Alright, alright, but he'll have to be quiet. Do you have any medicine here, something to calm your stomach? Let me check your shaving kit." And she headed towards the bathroom.

"No, Josie! I'll get it," Joe said rising from the bed, Lazarus like.

"Ooh, I understand. A man's shaving kit is like a woman's purse. It's very personal and private. Mr. Shaughnessy, will you go get Joe's shaving kit. We'll let him open it. Joe, you don't move from this bed."

"I have to do some business in there myself," Shaughnessy said modestly. "I'll be right back." He went in the bathroom and shut the door. He turned on the water and unzipped the bag. He thought that it was condoms and lubricant that Joe didn't want Josie to see. He was going to remove those for the protection of Joe's virtue. Instead he found the flag, the box and the Venetian "One Eighth." He knew what it was instantly. He put all of the contraband into his pockets, the "One Eighth," the flag and the box, flushed the toilet and exited the bathroom zipping up his fly, without having peed, as he came through the bathroom door.

Josie averted her eyes away from him. Shaughnessy winked at Joe and brought the kit over to him. Joe opened it and found a bottle of Pepto Bismol, which looked jarring in the elegant, gently sybaritic room. Unlike the sheets there was no subtlety to its pink. Joe took a couple of belts of the Pepto Bismol, lay back and said, "What do we do now?"

Josie said, "You are going to take a nap. I'm going to retire to my room. I'll check on you in a half hour and if you're not better, we'll call the doctor. Come, Mr. Shaughnessy. What are you carrying in your pocket?"

"My breviary, Ma'am, I was in the seminary once and still say my daily prayers. We're reading about the Miracle of the Loaves and Fishes today," Shaughnessy said, casting a sideways glance at Joe, who caught it.

"Oh, that reminds me. I almost forgot. I promised to call Pina in Rome. They were supposed to hear about Monsignor Rocco today. The Vatican was going to announce this morning if he'd be made a bishop. It's pretty much a certainty, but I ought to call.

"Joe, you stay in bed.

"Mr. Shaughnessy, you stay here and don't let him out of bed. I'll be back. I have to get out of this girdle and call Rome. I'm probably the only woman alive who still wears a girdle, at least the only one in Italy. You should see some of these women! How they jiggle! Pina is at her flat in the Piazza Navona and Rocco is at the American College. If it happens, if Rocco gets the Pope's nod, I think there'll be a party. All the family will be there. Can we go to Rome, Joe? It'll only be for a day or two. Can you take the time, Joe?"

"Let me think about it, Josie. I have to call my Chief Justice. He thinks that I'm taking care of my sick mother in Rhode Island. I'll do my best."

Of course, when Joe heard that the entire Randozza family (those who weren't in Federal custody) would be there he could only think of seeing Dino again. For a minute and a half he wasn't sure if he wanted that or not.

He wanted it. He'd bring Shaughnessy, for protection, he decided. Josie left.

Shaughnessy smiled. "That was pretty quick thinking, that bit about the breviary, wasn't it?" Shaughnessy said. He wasn't usually so self congratulatory. After all he was a detective and expected to think quickly on his feet. But this was something different.

"And so was my illness," Joe said, as he climbed out of bed. "Now how are we going to get the Venetian "One Eighth" back to Ireland? You can't bring it. I'll need you to go to Rome with me. You can be part of the Boston delegation. The Mayor will probably come over. He never misses a trip to Italy. He may be the next ambassador to Italy if the Democrats ever get back in the White House."

"Harry or one of the other plasterers can take it back. They're EEU, citizens of Europe, and itinerant workers. Their bags won't be searched like ours would be. I'll take care of it. I'll leave you the box and the flag," said Shaughnessy.

"I can't stay in Europe any longer," Shaughnessy added. "You forget that I have a job, Joe. We all aren't associate justices of the Appeals Court and paid to ponder. Besides I don't think that seeing Dino Randozza, as sexy as he might be, would be good for you just yet. You shouldn't even see him in church. He's not a nice boy, Joe. The things that your mother told you about Italian bad boys are true in Dino's case."

Frustrated at this attempt to curb his lust, Joe angrily replied, "My mother loves Italians. She's not some low-class Irish shrew who thinks every foreigner is a threat. I come from Newport, not Neponset, Sergeant Detective."

"No offense, your Honor, but don't be ruled by your dick and call it your mother," Shaughnessy said with a courtly bow. "Dino was working for his brother in law, Tim Ronayne, when he relieved you of your "One Eighth," but he also has other interests, which may not jibe with your lofty position. His people wouldn't mind if he was fucking a judge. They might even overlook his being queer for that. And although he stole your little prized "One Eighth" for his in-law, Tim Ronayne, he'd turn on Tim too, if it suited his real family. He's not your friend, or our friend.

"And he has problems, 'personal problems,' as they say. He loves old tads but he gets a kick out of violence in sex. It comes from having been molested by a high Irish Monsignor in toney Weston when his father moved there to try to look respectable. The bigoted old queen, the Monsignor, wouldn't let Dino be an altar boy because he was too tawny for that very white and blonde suburb, but the Very Reverend didn't mind giving Dino blow jobs in the rectory. Honest! As is the peculiar nature of these things, Dino has had a love/hate thing for sturdy Irish gents over 60 ever since. I think the shrinks would say that he is still 'working it out.' I don't want him to work it out on you any more than he has already."

"But…" Joe protested.

"No buts," Shaughnessy interrupted. "I told you that I thought that I saw him when I was coming in to Venice. He may just be visiting his mother but he also likes to tease and torment you. Witness the maimed teddy bears and weird messages—even here. Now, you just forget about Dino for a while. I know all about the forbidden fruit, you should pardon the pun, theory of sexual attraction; I've done it myself. In my case it's Irish lads to be specific. We'll find you some other tawny playmate, who'll love you to pieces."

Joe was stymied by all this candor, both his own and Shaughnessy's. He also felt a little guilty about his slur at Neponset, a middle class but insular section of Boston. He had no idea where Shaughnessy came from but Neponset could be it. Joe knew the remark was hurtful. He tried not to be a snob. However, he had been raised in Newport and gone to Harvard. He didn't have to buy every shanty prejudice that the self-appointed defenders of his national heritage tried to lay on him. He knew more about Irishness than most of them. Some of them, and that included Shaughnessy at this moment, were worse than the thin-lipped nuns he had to listen to in Catechism class on Saturday mornings. "You'll lose your faith if..."

Joe knew that it was crazy that he wanted Dino. Joe thought he could make Dino good. However, Joe couldn't escape the truth of Shaughnessy's observation that for Dino, the original encounter was a business deal, with twisted romantic and sexual desires thrown on top, like confetti.

Joe had made similar, albeit less dangerous, romantic mistakes in the past. Most recently there was that Mexican/Swedish artist from Los Angeles. He sent Joe back into therapy. Even the now beatified Arthur Bruce was not the healthiest of love objects at the time of the romance, although it matured into a love story of sorts 12 years later. Joe had learned that much in therapy. It was one thing to be somebody's romantic type but when the type-casting was for a role that you couldn't play, and really didn't want to play, disaster struck. The more that Joe looked like a daddy the less he wanted to be one. Joe wanted to be taken care of too. And a hot Italian daddy, twenty years younger, could do that very well.

So after dinner with Shaughnessy at the *Osteria Oliva Negra*, an expensive faux rustic restaurant back in the alleys behind the Danieli, Joe decided to send Josie to Rome for Rocco's certain consecration and to return to Boston.

Joe was scheduled to begin a Single Justice session the next week where he would listen to emergency matters from the trial courts. Because he had no kids and had often filled in for his parenting colleagues, particularly on school vacations, he knew that he could call in a chit and get someone to take his turn or part of it. Nevertheless, he decided to calm his life down and return to work. He was also scheduled to preside over a panel of three judges the week after that and he really should do some homework, if only to learn about the two cases that would be his to write the decisions.

Contrary to his worst fear, when he arrived back to his apartment in Boston there was no wounded teddy bear at his door. The very efficient new concierge, a young, handsome, Latino man who went to business school at night at Northeastern University, had put Joe's mail into three piles, bound them each with a thick red elastic, and neatly labeled each pile—"junk mail," "magazines and catalogues," "serious social & professional correspondence." Joe thought *it's a good thing that I didn't get any dirty postcards; I wonder how many letters he held up to the light.* Joe went through the piles cursorily, threw out the obvious junk mail and the catalogues, placed the magazines on the coffee table and put the "serious" pile on the seat of his favorite chair so that he would have to go through the pile before sitting down again.

He then, with a little trepidation, checked the phone. It was a portable so he could walk around while listening to it, take off his traveling clothes, pee and get a glass of Pellegrino from the icebox. The telephone messages were banal—except for one.

Peter, one of the few men from college with whom Joe had contact, maybe every two years, wanted to know if Joe would go to their Fortieth Reunion, which was going to be over a weekend the coming October. For some reason this reunion was not in June at Commencement like all the big ones.

Joe had no interest in going to the reunion except to see Peter, who he had always liked. Peter had never judged Joe and had always encouraged him to be himself—whatever that was at the time. When Joe came out to Peter, Peter said, "You know, I used to think that if I were ever to be gay, I'd be in love with you, Joe." Joe also was curious about some college crushes, like half the wrestling team. Frankly, he wanted to see if they still turned him on after all the longing he had expended on them forty years before.

Peter was definitely straight; he loved blonde women. He had won and taken a fellowship after college because it let him study anywhere in Europe. He went to Scandinavia where he thought that the blondes would lust after his black hair, dark skin, doe-eyed Sephardic self. He was right because he came back with a busty, blonde wife. Peter taught a little, wrote a lot and was now beginning an acting career, in his sixties. As an undergraduate Peter wrote poems, some of which Joe had saved, but now Peter wrote timely articles about the U.S. for European magazines, while working on a novel. He and his wife had a boy and a girl.

The boy sounded just like Peter when Joe called back the number that was in his phone book. The boy said, "He doesn't live here any more, but I'll give you his number. He should be home now."

Joe called Peter, who said, "Yeah, we split up. My son lives with her. He's dropped out, but he's a good kid. My daughter is in California. She'd dropped out too but now she's studying medicine in San Francisco. My father left them some money. I'm a trustee but I let them find themselves. Speaking of that, don't you go to Provincetown? We used to go to Truro and I really love it down there. Would you want to go to Provincetown this month? I know a guy, a gay guy, who has a house there and he said I can use it. He's directing a play I'm acting in. He thinks that I'm still married. It's a great house and a great offer. If I tell him that I am going with a gay judge, that'll be better than a wife and two kids. I'd like to take him up on it. All the people I know and like down here go to the fucken Hamptons or Fire Island. Besides I'm tired of New Yorkers. Say you'll think about it. The week after next is a good time for me."

Joe wasn't too sure what the transition from Peter's kids finding themselves and Provincetown was, but he let that go and told Peter, "I've just been in Europe for a while with my aunt. It was no vacation. It was nuts. I'd like to talk to you about it. I'm not sure that I can take the time off for Provincetown now. Although I'm almost caught up on my decisions, there'll be a new round beginning next week. I sit on a panel on Tuesday, August 19th, but I could get free after that. I'll bring my laptop and I'll have to work at least in the mornings. I really shouldn't but at least I'll be in the jurisdiction, in Massachusetts."

"Live a little," said Peter. "Sure, work if you want to. It'll be good to see you."

What Joe really thought was that he could hide in Provincetown, especially if he was with a straight guy. Joe hadn't gone to the gay clubs since his appointment and he had no need to parade himself around town. Provincetown wasn't exactly the place for men his age. Peter was a smart guy, and may have some insight into Joe's present dilemma. Joe wasn't too sure how much to tell Peter. After all, although he hadn't taken the oath, Joe was almost a Fireboy himself now, having been the source of the return of two of the "One Eighths." He'd worry about that later. Just as Peter was fed up with New Yorkers, Joe had had it with the Boston Irish and Italian Catholic and/or gay crowd. A little high-toned, well-analyzed, heterosexual, New York Jewish wisdom would be a good change.

Joe was in for a surprise.

Joe's Ethical Dilemma 21

There wasn't a lot doing at the Appeals Court in August. Not many lawyers were rushing up to seek emergency writs. Nevertheless, Joe had been assigned to be the Single Justice for the month, to deal with emergency matters. The reality was that he had to hang around his office all day. He got a lot of reading done.

Almost daily there was an emergency request regarding the custody of children in divorce cases. Joe could handle those, even though he hated that part of the practice of law. One man from the North Shore wanted custody of the golden retriever as well. Some seekers of restraining orders were dissatisfied with the Superior Court's denial of their petitions. One was the father of a Hindu woman who was about to marry a Catholic. The Catholic spouse-to-be had promised to have a Hindu ceremony, but then he had reneged. The pious Hindu father was trying to enjoin the priest, the pastor and the Cardinal Archbishop of Boston from conducting the Catholic ceremony. The distraught man asked Joe to recuse himself because he presumed that Joe was a Catholic and on good terms with the Archbishop. If he only knew. Three criminal defendants who had been held without bail for various reasons by judges of the District Court understandably wanted to get out of jail. Two were released, thanks to Joe.

Otherwise Joe sat in his office and acted on the papers, granting leave to file briefs late or allowing stays of sentences imposed by trial judges while an appeal was pending.

On the second day back, a Tuesday, Joe began to read the cases that would come up the next week before the panel of three judges that he was presiding over. Joe hadn't read them before he left for Europe and he didn't call them up on the computer while he was gone because he hadn't brought his computer with him. He didn't even know the names of the cases. When he did read the files he discovered that one of the cases was <u>Williamson v. Randozza Enterprises, Inc.</u>, a dispute over some land opposite Revere Beach on which a condominium was supposed to have been built. Williamson was a heavy investor. He had been a halfback for the New England Patriots and he poured money into the foundation hole of the condominium relying on the promises of none other than Dino Randozza, President of Randozza Enterprises, Inc. Williamson said the whole scheme was a fraud. The building never was built; it wasn't even begun. Before trial Williamson sought to attach the valuable land where the condominium complex should have been for the amount of his investment, $800,000. A trial judge allowed the attachment and Dino's company appealed.

What was Joe to do? He couldn't hear the appeal. How would he explain himself if he recused himself? Did he have to say anything at all? Couldn't the record just read "Justice Joseph Lyons did not participate in the hearing or decision of this case?" Joe thought that he had seen this once or twice in the reports of other decisions. Maybe he saw such a note in one of the Harvard cases when their former General Counsel, later Chief Justice of the Supreme Judicial Court recused herself. Joe was sure that no explanation was given in those cases. It didn't have to be; everybody knew her history. But they didn't know Joe's; at least not the particulars, like

Joe's lust for Dino Randozza's hairy chest.

Should he say, "Justice Lyons cannot hear this case because as he was lying naked on his stomach on his bed waiting to have hot sex with Dino Randozza (whom he met on the *Gray & Gay* network on his computer and who was known to him as 'Felix') Dino tied Justice Lyons up with expensive neckties and robbed him?" How would that read in the *Boston Herald*?

Or could he get away with just leaving when the case was called? But then how would he do it? Would he stand up dramatically and go through the curtain, sending someone else in so that an odd number of judges would hear the case?

He remembered one of his favorite women colleagues saying that she employed the "Bop Rule" for recusals. If she'd had sex with one of the parties or their lawyers, she'd get out of the case. If it had been just a couple of dates and a smooch or two, she'd stay in. If she had sex with both sides, she'd stay in—but only if the sex had been equally good with each side. If it had been awful in both cases, she'd leave because they'd each know that and each assume prejudice. The latter two situations had never arisen, by the way.

Joe decided to tell the Chief Justice that he was recusing himself on the Williamson case. He called it that because he didn't want to draw attention to the Randozza side. Usage created the popular name of a case.

If the Chief Justice asked why Joe was recusing himself, which was unlikely—there was a gentlemanly protocol to all this—Joe would say that his aunt was friendly with the mother of one of the principals. If the Chief probed more and asked who the mother was, Joe would come clean and say, "Giussepina Randozza." He hoped that the Chief Justice didn't know about the Randozzas.

It was while preparing these explanations in his mind that Joe realized why Giuseppina had called him by title back at Ballymaloe House in Cork. The wily old dame must have known about this appeal and also known what Joe looked like. She did her homework. "Know your judges," is a maxim for both appellate and trial practice.

As fate would have it, the Chief Justice was on vacation, so Joe was spared a personal visit. However, the Chief had to be told. The Chief hated to be interrupted on vacation. He was about to retire and lived for his escapes from the Court, which had this year weathered a small scandal over one of the justices who was arrested for drunk driving, budget cuts, expansion, and relocation in addition to the usual problems of dealing with 25 *prima donna* justices. Joe called the Chief Justice at the Chief's summer cabin in the Berkshires. The Chief had reluctantly gotten a cell phone the year before. The Chief Justice's secretary, Miss Mary Margaret Managhan, (emphasis on the "Miss") jealously guarded the number, but gave it to Joe after seeing how anxiously he asked for it.

Joe interrupted the Chief Justice while the unshaven Chief was sitting naked on a rock scaling a trout that he had just caught. The Chief asked no questions. He simply said, "Tell Mary Margaret and we'll throw someone else in. Goodbye, Joe. How ya been?" The Chief hung up before Joe could lie to him.

◊ ◊ ◊

When Joe returned home from the Courthouse that Tuesday, he decided to check the "Serious Personal & Professional Correspondence" that he had left on his chair. He'd already thrown out the ads and the junk mail. He rifled through the whole pile before opening any of it. That kid did a good job sorting this stuff; he'll go places, Joe thought. One envelope caught his attention. It was almost square, like a wedding invitation, and was addressed to him formally, like an invitation would be—"The Honorable Joseph Lavin Lyons." There was an ecclesiastical crest on the back flap of the envelope, complete with the bishop's flat hat over it, but no return address.

Joe opened the envelope. The crest reappeared on the top of a card. The crest contained three rounded rocks on the dexter, the right, and a lion rampant holding a sword on the sinister, the left, and the flat bishop's hat above the escutcheon. The card was an invitation to the installation of His Excellency, Bishop Rocco Randozza as Auxiliary Bishop of the Archdiocese of Boston at the Cathedral of the Holy Cross on Thursday, September 4th.

Joe, who in his collegiate medieval days had been very interested in heraldry, couldn't identify whose crest was on the top of the invitation. He thought that he knew the Cardinal's and that this was not it, which was strange since the invitation was from the Cardinal. It must be Bishop Randozza's. Why the lion rampant with the sword, very similar to his family's two lions rampant both holding the one sword, he thought? The three rocks had something to do with the Crucifixion and the two thieves on either side of Jesus as well as the Trinity, Joe thought, and the rock, which was Peter, represented the Church. "You are Peter, the rock, and upon this rock I will build my church," Christ said, justifying both the Church and the apostolic succession of bishops, even Orthodox and Episcopalian bishops, if the latter is not redundant, as Evelyn Waugh once noted.

There was no R.S.V.P. or reply card. On the back of the invitation, neatly written in a variant of majuscule chancery script, very similar to *The Book of Kells*, peculiarly, Joe thought, was written the following:

> Dear Justice Lyons,
>
> I had promised to return your property within two weeks of our last meeting. I have been unable to do so. Would you kindly give me more time to get to the bottom of this? As you may know, I have been busy with other matters. It was a pleasure to meet your charming aunt in Rome.
>
> I am sorry that you were unable to attend the consecration. Your aunt was seated with my mother, nephew and brother under the *baldachino*, next to one of Bernini's twisted columns at the high altar. She is a wonderful companion for my mother.
>
> I hope that you can attend the installation.
>
> Yours truly,
> + Rocco Randozza

There was no address to reply to. Was it presumed that Joe would agree to the delay in the return of his property? Probably! Who could deny a new bishop? But Joe already knew that his "One Eighth" was in Ireland. He would like the other stuff, however, and the Florentine bag. That had been expensive.

In that same Tuesday's mail Joe received a postcard with a photo of Diarmuid's Dolmen on the front. It read:

> Harry brought us some beautiful paper from Italy. Thank you very much. We're about to clear the land for the new house on the Marsh Road. We'll let you know what turns up. I have fond memories of these stones.
>
> Your old friend, Tim

Joe was happy with the news about the safe delivery of the Venetian "One Eighth." He hoped that the Fireboys would find the last "One Eighth" in the ruins of the cottage on the road to the Lavin farm, as Tim had predicted. However, he wasn't as certain as Tim had been that it'd be an easy task.

Whatever! It was out of his hands now. He had let it go. No more conspiracy. Maybe back to a normal life now, whatever that was for Joe. He hoped that it wouldn't be loneliness and desperation, like it had too often been before all this began in May. He wasn't used to the ensuing excitement, but it had been "something to do." An old dame, who Joe knew, went out every night until the day before she died. When asked why at age 88 she was going to a pool party at the YWCA in Boston in the middle of a blizzard in January, she replied, "Darling, you don't understand. It's something to do."

Up to now Joe had been too busy to bemoan his fate as a single gay man of a certain age. Being a judge was a lonely job; being single and gay and circumspect (most of the time) made it lonelier. He couldn't be like two of his closeted predecessors. One took his business to New York and the other had fucked all over town in the bushes, bathhouses and tearooms, thinking that no one knew who he was. He was wrong. The towel boys at the baths announced his presence to anyone who'd listen, as if their listeners were interested in titles rather than dicks.

Both of these Honorables were now dead; the second from the virus and the first from old age at home with his doll collection in his closet with the glass door. Joe would at least have his dignity, even though he had given up any hope of privacy in cold, small town, gossipy Boston. He had been the first person to be "out of the closet" on his application for a judgeship and his appointment had been third page news for a few days, but Joe knew that they, the public, didn't want to know the particulars, like who put what where, and how.

22
Joe Goes to Provincetown

Joe hadn't seen Josie since she returned from Rome, but on the Thursday of his Single Justice week she called him at his office and left a message. "Oh Joe, it was wonderful. And the Pope only shook a little. So many candles! Pina showed me the best shop for mantillas and Vatican dresses. I looked better than Rose Kennedy. Of course, I'm taller and I'm secure enough so that I can let my hair go white—which looks so good under black lace. All that wrapping of women in veils is so silly. It's like Iran and the *purdah*, like the old goats would get aroused at anything, leastwise my ankle. Such silliness! In St. Peter's we sat under the *baldachino*, next to one of Bernini's twisted columns. I was with the family, Pina, of course, the Count, a nephew Lorenzo, very handsome, and a brother Dino, who looks like Bishop Rocco, but a little rougher—kind of Federal Hill, if you know what I mean. How does it stay up, the *baldachino*? Where are the stresses? I taught physics one semester and I was worried that it would fall the whole time we sat there. The Catholics still put on the best show. You would have loved the Swiss Guards. A very handsome one was assigned to just us. He escorted us to and from the altar. Please come and visit. Or I could come up there to show you the photos. Did you know that the Count is a photographer? Well, he should do something besides collect rents from poor Sicilian peasants and pay bribes to the Mafia. I've read *The Leopard* and seen *The Godfather*. I know how all that works. And Pina gave me a present for you. When will you be down?"

Then the patient machine clicked off. There was some logic to Josie's stream of consciousness—from rents to bribes to the present from Pina. Of course, Josie would know nothing about the case pending in the Appeals Court, and Joe wasn't going to tell her. Josie's life deserved a little glamour, even if it was the shady glamour of Giuseppina Randozza and her crew, after all Josie had been through. Forty years teaching school had its own rewards, but *baldachinos*, twisty columns and Italian Baroque glitz were not usually among them.

Joe waited to call until he knew that Josie would be out at a Sodality meeting—after 7:00 p.m. on a Wednesday. Josie would surely have something to say to the Sweeney girls, the Sullivan sisters and all the other high Irish dames of Providence after the Joyful Mysteries tonight, Joe thought.

Joe told Josie's machine that he would come to Providence the next Tuesday evening, after his panel sat and on his way to Provincetown. He would take her to dinner at the *Il Forno*, to continue the Italian motif.

Joe was so grateful that he could and would recuse himself from the Randozza case.

Just then the phone rang. Joe looked at the device that told him who was calling. It said "Boston Police." He picked up the receiver. Shaughnessy said, "How're you doing, Judge? I was right about your friend, Dino. He's turned on us. I don't know what he's up to, but he's got people sniffing around in Ireland for the seven Eighths. He's even using the niece Maureen to try to get information from her cousins. He's been seen in Rome in the company of some Irish monsignor who works in the Vatican. And I just read in the Cardinal's rag, *The Pilot*, that the Randozza Family gave $25,000 to Catholic Charities. Perhaps he's gone holy on us. We can't trust him. I told Tim Ronayne to watch out. Now go back to checking your messages."

"But wait! Wait Shaughnessy! I've got something to tell you." And he told Shaughnessy about the case in the Appeals Court and what he had decided to do about it.

Shaughnessy said, "You're a very wise man. Nobody ever said you were stupid—a little naïve, but not stupid. I've got to run."

The next day, Friday, there was another postcard from Ireland. This one had a photo of the Old Library at Trinity College Library on the front. It read:

"The plan is to sell it back to them. We're still digging."

Why did Tim send postcards? Did he figure that Joe's mail would be opened, but that cryptic postcards would be overlooked? Did Tim not know of the nosy concierge, for example? Or did Tim want Joe to be implicated and to let the postcards do it? Joe hoped that Tim didn't write about a murder in the next one. Joe wasn't going to reply. It was too risky. Phones could be tapped, Email intercepted, and never put anything in writing. As Boston's own famous West End ward boss Martin Lomasney had said, "Don't write when you can speak; don't speak when you can wink; and don't wink when you can nod." These words still held good.

Joe was curious about the excavation and the search for the last "One Eighth," however, and he plotted how he could find out what was going on without asking directly. Perhaps he could begin a correspondence with Nora Lavin, his old cousin on the farm at the end of the Marsh Road or maybe Josie could do it. Maybe he could pretend that he was interested in buying some property on the Marsh Road, like a house he heard was being built there and Josie could inquire. He didn't like using Josie in this way but she had gotten on swimmingly with Nora.

Three days later, on Monday, the 18th, a letter arrived from Nora Lavin. One of her granddaughters, thus one of Joe's cousins, was coming over to be a nurse at the Massachusetts General Hospital and to earn a graduate degree in Emergency Medicine. Could Joe look out for her?

The Massachusetts General Hospital, or MGH as it was known in Boston, was just over the hill from Joe. Its nurses' dormitory was on Charles Street, about two hundred yards from his apartment. He knew nothing about how to deal with young women, but this was fate, for sure. The grandaughter, Grainne, was to arrive in two weeks. Joe immediately wrote back with all his telephone numbers and told Nora to have Grainne call him immediately upon arriving in Boston.

Williamson v. Randozza Enterprise, Inc. was the fourth case to be called, right after the recess, on Tuesday, August 19th and Madame Justice Mildred Bailey, who was just Joe's senior on the Court, was was to replace Joe on the panel after the recess.

Joe presided for the first three cases in the center chair and conducted the session quite orderly. One young yahoo wanted to rebut, but he had already used his 15 minutes and Joe said quietly, "That won't be necessary, Mr. O'Hara. Your brief makes the points." Of course, it didn't, but the time schedule had to be maintained. Each side had 15 minutes unless all the justices agreed that more time was warranted.

As a rule Joe himself asked few questions, even when not presiding. Justice Firrfield, however, "the world's leading authority," a former law professor, who was sitting on Joe's right, wouldn't stop pontificating, especially on the second case, which involved *Bills & Notes*, the subject which Firrfield had taught at Portia School of Law. Joe let his colleague go on for a while, then thanked him profusely, acknowledging his expertise. "We are very fortunate to have you on this panel, Professor Justice Firrfield, but we must move on. Thank you as well, Counselor. The next case, please."

Joe saw both Giuseppina Randozza and Dino Randozza in the audience as soon as he came out on the bench. Giuseppina gave him the slightest of smiles and a nod. She appeared to know Martin Lomasney's maxim. Joe knew that she was too savvy to wink. Dino just stared at Joe unceasingly with his beautiful black eyes. Joe didn't even see him blink. Dino wore an Italian cut navy suit, and a dark tie on a white shirt, which made his tan darker and the silver in his hair glow. Pina wore a very tailored black suit and even a small matching hat, with a veil to her eyebrows. The outfit was appropriate for the widowed mother of a bishop.

Joe walked off the bench, through the curtain at the recess. Joe's only regret was that he couldn't see their faces drop when Justice Bailey replaced when the judges returned after the break. The Randozzas had seen the change in the order of the cases on the list outside the door but thought nothing of it.

When Joe returned after the <u>Williamson case</u>, as he preferred to call it, had been heard, Pina and Dino and their lawyers were going out the door at the back. Pina looked back and smiled. She admired people who could play the game well. For her, this was just another round. Dino, who was leaving behind her, just stared at Joe, the same as he had during the first part of the sitting. It wasn't threatening to Joe; as a matter of fact it was comforting. That might have been because Joe knew that here at least, in the courtroom, he was the one on top.

After the sitting and after lunch with most of his colleagues who were at the court that day (Justice Firrfield always ate alone; collegiality was not to his liking; one wonders why he went to a court that sat in panels), the three justices conferenced the cases they had heard. The <u>Williamson case</u> was going to be conferenced first so that Justice Bailey, who had kindly stood in, could return to the Vineyard and her partner Louise, a Zoology professor at Harvard, and their two adopted Latino sons. At the conference the panel would get a sense of how they would decide the case and the judge assigned to write the opinion would be able to begin his or her assignment. The judges had read the papers separately before the oral arguments, so up until the conference none knew what the other two thought.

One could not even be sure how someone was leaning by the questions at oral argument. Some justices, like Firrfield, just wanted to hear themselves talk. Others had genuine concerns and still others wanted to frame the issue to meet the concern of some other judge on the panel. Some judges liked to confuse the parties by appearing favorable at oral argument and then opposed in the actual decision. Questioning by appellate judges is an art form, and not always a very good predictor of the final result. That did not stop people, particularly newspapers, from thinking that it was.

Joe sat in his office and reread the morning's briefs as well as the summaries his law clerk had prepared. He scrupulously avoided the papers pertaining to the <u>Williamson case</u>. Just as he was called to go to the conference room his phone rang. It was Josie, in her usual nonstop fashion.

"Joe darling, can we get together some other night? Pina just called and she is going to New York and will be driving through Providence with her son Dino. He's very handsome, like Bishop Rocco but…sexy. He looks like an Italian movie star, like Marcello Mastroianni with backbone, a little like that handsome composer John Corigliano. Pina seemed distressed. She's been so nice to me. I owe it to her to be available. You and I can get together Thursday; there's no Sodality this week. I hope that's o.k.; she's been so good to me. I'm sorry to kiss you off. You know I love you."

Joe replied, "Of course, Josie. I'm busy Thursday but we can schedule something later." He didn't want to tell her where he was going. "Nora Lavin sent me a note. Her granddaughter, Grainne Lavin, is coming to study and work at the MGH. I'm going to take her to dinner. Maybe you can come up for that. But I have to go now. The Court Officer is at my door. They want me in the Conference Room. I'm late already."

"Oh Joe, I know you're so busy. You're a dear. I hope that your cases weren't too stressful today. Didn't you preside? I told Mae Sullivan, you know her, one of the Sullivan sisters, they're from

Newport too. Mae went to grammar school with your father; I told her that you were presiding today. Her nephew is on the District Court in Rhode Island. She's never at a loss. She said very haughtily, 'My nephew is a trial judge; he presides every day.' Of course, we all know that appellate judges are more important. Aren't they? You get paid more, don't you? And you can overrule trial judges, can't you? Bye darling. Such a snob she is. Be good to yourself."

This is great. I can get an early start to Provincetown. If only we can keep that Firrfield off his high horse. We're probably going to have to listen to his entire course on that Bills & Notes *case,* Joe said to himself. *Thank God, I can leave during the discussion of the* Williamson case. *At least, I'll be spared that discussion. Once I've recused myself my colleagues can't talk to me about it; nor can I say anything to them. That's how the Supreme Court of New Hampshire got in so much trouble. Various judges quite correctly recused themselves from cases during oral arguments and then stuck their noses back in behind the scenes. I'll be happy to read the decision when it's published. I'll read the advance sheet.*

The justices didn't finish the post court conference until five. Firrfield was true to form. Joe turned his back on him during the conference and was about to call him a "pedant," but Firrfield would have taken that as a compliment. Firrfield was one of those wonks who came to Harvard Law School from somewhere else, put on bow ties, tried to pass as Yankees and talked about how Boston had been corrupted by the Irish—as if their people would have been any more welcome. The Yankees, who had abandoned their public service to trust funds and scotch, were flattered at the imitation, but weren't really going to let anybody in. A few of the *parvenus* made the Yankee bastions, the Symphony board, the trustees of the Museum of Fine Arts, directors of the Athenaeum, the Country Club in Brookline and the Somerset Club, but never enough to take over.

Firrfield was not one who made it even that far, although he thought that he should have. He thought he should be on the highest court in Massachusetts, the Supreme Judicial Court, if not the First Circuit Court of Appeals. It was those damned Boston Irish hooligans, even the Kennedys, who were keeping him off. Meanwhile Joe and his colleagues had to suffer with him on the Appeals Court.

Joe rushed home, picked up his mail, packed his second best duffel bag, (Dino having stolen the best leather bag to purloin Joe's treasures) with summer clothes, and tried to figure out the best way to beat the rush hour traffic. There were three messages on his machine. He pressed the button. The first caller was Peter. "The address is 25 Marshland Road, near the Pilgrim Monument. It's a great house. You guys really know how to decorate. Great art! I'll be here. I'll make a reservation for dinner. How's the *Edwidge at Night* for you? I heard that it's very good."

The second call was from Tim Ronayne in Ireland and it sounded like he was next door. "Call me. There's been an interesting development. We need you again—over there. You won't have to travel far. I'm sure you've heard of Provincetown? It's near you."

The third was the old, familiar cackle, "I still want you—more than ever. You're more handsome than I remembered. Maybe it's the black robe with your pink face and white hair. I want to be under the bench the next time you're the boss judge."

Ever since Joe had figured out who his caller/admirer/assailant was, he was no longer scared. The thought of seeing Dino again didn't frighten him. He'd had too much else to do in presiding over the sitting and slipping off <u>Williamson v. Randozza Enterprises, Inc</u> to be frightened. He knew what was up now, or he thought that he did.

After he walked over the top of Beacon Hill to his old Ford station wagon at the Boston Common Undergound Garage, Joe opened the back of the car to put his bag in. Kneeling in a prayerful position right in the middle of the floor was a teddy bear, with downcast eyes, holding a small plastic Celtic cross. Although Joe had just congratulated himself on his new found lack of fear of his admirer/assailant, his heart jumped at this sight. Joe was comforted by the prayerful position and by the cross—perhaps Dino had indeed found religion. But Joe still had to take a minute and walk around the car to pull himself together before getting into the station wagon and driving off.

Joe drove through the Back Bay, the South End and South Boston to pick up the Expressway in Dorchester. That route avoided most of the traffic leaving downtown. He had brought the cell phone in order to call Tim once he got over the Sagamore Bridge. Joe drove on rehashing, digesting and casting off the day as he approached the Cape Cod Canal and the Sagamore Bridge. Once over the bridge he felt a lot calmer; he'd shut off the day's deliberations.

At Brewster he went off the main highway to get to Route 6A, the old King's Highway, so that he could see and feel the healing calm of village life on Cape Cod. He'd learned that trick years before when the main road, Route 6, was under construction.

The highway changed again after the Orleans Rotary and Joe was well relaxed as he drove through Eastham, Wellfleet and Truro. He'd forgotten how beautiful the vista was coming over the last rise on Route 6 in Truro with Provincetown laid below, the cottages lined up like Monopoly houses, the Pilgrim Monument modeled after the tower at the *Municipio* in Siena, the twinkling curve of the Bay and the early evening sun. And then, once down the hill, on the right there was Pilgrim Lake in Truro and the dunes, like moonscapes.

Joe decided to take the left onto Snail Road and drive down Commercial Street. It was a way of announcing his arrival (even though he wanted to be *incognito*, and thus wore a hat and dark glasses) while checking out who was in town. Right there on Snail Road Joe realized that he had forgotten to call Tim Ronayne. Until he got off the main highway the traffic had been so thick that he couldn't stop and then he went into a pastoral reverie whilst traveling through bucolic Brewster. Besides, he really didn't want to get involved in this Irish craziness again. He'd done his part, and more. So maybe it was a subconscious intentional lapse of memory. Nevertheless, Joe pulled over to the left on Snail Road, at the entrance to the Foss Woods and dialed. Miraculously, because cell phone reception in Provincetown was notoriously lousy, he got through.

"Tim, this is Joe. What's up?"

"Nora Lavin is sending her granddaughter Grainne over. She's coming with a friend, Maeve Sand— her lover, in fact. They'll be in Boston but first they're going to Provincetown. We think that the lover knows where the last 'One Eighth' is, although she doesn't know she knows, or even what it is she should know. Am I being clear, Joe? The last 'One Eighth' isn't at the site of the fallen down house—at least we couldn't find it there. Maeve Sand is a descendant of the original owners. She is the only descendant. There was a box of family stuff taken out of the house before the evictors tore it down in 1886. The box was kept at the Lavins', at Nora's but, of course, Nora never thought of opening it. She looked at it many times but never opened it. You know these Irish women; they'll gossip forever, but give them a real secret and they'll die with it. Nora knew about the box and that it was behind a wall in the big bedroom. She had no idea what was in it. Her husband's mother told Nora about it. One of our researchers found a big Eviction book in the archives in Belfast. They took meticulous notes even as they destroyed us, the Brit bastards. There's even an account of the eviction. 'And Mrs. Sand, the elder, left the premises carrying a box and retired to the Lavin homestead,' like she was visiting the neighbors for a cup of tea! The bastards!"

Tim went on, in the rambling Irish way, as if they had all day, "The box was a Lavin secret passed on by the women, one of the many secrets they carried. Nora Lavin gave the box to Maeve Sand, Grainne's girlfriend, when Maeve turned 21. Nora moved the big bed and opened a little door and there it was. Maeve's father was killed in the North in 1978 and her mother died shortly thereafter of a broken heart. It's a terrible story but Maeve and Grainne are lovely girls and your cousin Grainne is a saint. She and Maeve went to school together in Dundalk; they've been together ever since. They moved to Paris a while ago. Grainne became a nurse and Maeve is some kind of artist. It's not easy to be gay over here, Joe, but it's easier for women to live together than it is for men, unless you're a priest or something."

"So, what do you want me to do?" Joe said impatiently. "Am I supposed to pry the family treasure chest out of her hands?"

"Now, calm down, Joe! She doesn't even know she has the last 'One Eighth.' We don't know that she has it, but if it's anywhere, it's in that box. I'm certain of that. We think Maeve brought the box to America with her. We checked her apartment in Paris with a little B&E; they took the T.V. to make it look good. There's nothing nowhere. And we can't find the 'One Eighth' anywhere else. We've sifted the soil at that goddamned site for days, pretending to make cement. You'd think we were panning for gold in *Californyeeay* in 1848."

"So, let me ask again, what do you want me to do?" Joe asked.

"I want you to cultivate Maeve Sand, find out where the box is, if she knows what's in it, and report back to me. If she has the box, we can put one of our boys on it and get the 'One Eighth.' We can make up a phony substitute to put in the box; we know the text. I bet you didn't know that Harry the plasterer, from Venice, was in the Seminary and learned how to write in Insular majuscule script and turn a sheepskin into vellum. You thought that he was just a sheep shagger, like your Tipperary relatives. Ha!"

"I didn't know that Harry was a sheepshagger. And then he writes on the sheep?! How resourceful! Does he write the script while he's fucking the sheep?" Joe said nastily. "And how the fuck am I going to find two Irish lesbians in this town at the height of the season? And how am I going to explain that I knew they'd be here? I am supposed to see Grainne next week when she gets to Boston. Nora has been in touch, but I wasn't told that Grainne had a…a companion, or that they were coming to Provincetown. By the way, does it strike you funny that I am just now driving into Provincetown? It does me. Are you guys psychic, or do you have spies everywhere? I'm here visiting a friend, a straight friend," Joe felt compelled to add, for reasons which weren't immediately clear to him

Maybe he wanted to get another chance at Tim and didn't want to make Tim jealous by having him think that he, Joe, was off lollygagging at a queer resort with another man with whom there was the possibility of sex. Joe was old fashioned that way. He wanted all his tricks to think that they were the only ones, no matter how long ago they had coupled.

"Well, isn't that fortuitous!" said Tim, with a laugh. "I'm sure that you'll find a way. It's a small town, isn't it? That's what the computer says. They're staying at a place called Gabriel's Guest House on Bradford Street. I think that it's a Sapphic retreat. Toodle loo, Joe."

Joe drove on fuming, almost hitting a man on a bicycle in a nun's outfit, a Sister of Charity, complete with winged hat, at the intersection of Snail Road and Commercial Street, just where the Bay comes up and takes your breath away. You can go right to the center of Provincetown, left to Truro, or straight into the beautiful bay. Joe stopped, told himself that he could do what he wanted, that he wasn't in thralldom to Tim Ronayne and the Fireboys, that he hadn't taken an oath, and that he was in Provincetown to have a quiet time with Peter, his old college chum. In any event, he was going to meet Grainne, and presumably, Maeve, the next week or so in Boston. If he ran into her or them in Provincetown, he'd do what he could for the fucking "Cause"—whatever that was these days—but he wasn't going to go out of his way.

Joe took a right to the center of Provincetown.

23
A Surprise Family Reunion

Contrary to his minute old declaration of independence from Tim Ronayne and all he stood for, Joe drove down Commercial Street looking for two Irish lesbians. *Should I look for two big, pink cheeked girls in Aran Island sweaters with red hair, blue eyes and thick ankles,* thought Joe? *No, those girls would be from Attleboro. Maybe I should look for women in foreign clothes, but what are those these days when all young people from everywhere around the world dress alike in jeans and Tee shirts, usually black?* His eyes scanned the road past Norman Mailer's house and the little waterfront converted garage Roy Cohn had rented before he died. He passed the Packard painters' houses, the daughter's on the right, the mother's on the left. There weren't many pedestrians until he got past St. Mary's, the beautiful wooden Episcopal Church on the waterside. *The Irish girls wouldn't be going there,* Joe thought. Episcopalians still prayed for the English Queen, in spite of their other laudable tolerances.

Two attractive women were leaving the Schoolhouse Galleries on the right. They glowed in the streetlight, stylish in pretty pastel sundresses and delicate sandals; one was carrying a sweater and the other wore a Pashmina shawl. The taller had thick brown hair and wore glasses, the other was blonde. They were dressed enough alike for you to know that they had checked with each other before going out. Maybe they were sisters from Chatham up for the night, Joe thought. Their blazered, sockless husbands were probably still inside the gallery drinking wine, Joe decided.

Joe remembered that he'd read in the *Globe* about some drawings at the Schoolhouse Gallery. A trial judge Joe knew drew quite nicely and his recent drawings from an Italian trip were showing at the Schoolhouse. They'd been well reviewed. Joe wanted to see the show, but there was no time for that tonight. Joe drove on.

A lot of people were going into the Art Association. There must be an opening, with cheap wine, seltzer water, pretzels and peanut—if you got there early. Most of these patrons were elderly East Enders, many of them New Yorkers, who had long been promoters of Provincetown as an art colony. Some of them dabbled in painting or wrote themselves, but most had made money in more conventional ways. They liked to be Bohemians in the summertime. They weren't too sure what they thought of the gay takeover of the town but they were liberals and suffered most every aberration, particularly if it had a political aspect.

Further on were more gallery goers. Dinner in town and the Friday night openings had become a ritual. The East End became a giant traveling wine and cheese party. Some art even sold behind the chatter, but there were also some hangers on, old hippies, who cadged a few drinks and suppered on brie every Friday night.

Down the street the daytrippers with sleepy children returned to their cars.

It was too early for the gay men to parade to the bars; some with codpieces and their asses hanging out of leather chaps; others leading the mate on a chain; a few in gauzy, see through outfits from the Casual Male catalogue; and many shirtless without shame, although a few should have known better. That strut didn't begin until 10:30 p.m. and was best seen at the other end of town from a bench on the brick patio of Spiritus Pizza.

Pedestrians were now all over the street and it was hard to move forward in a car, so after a few minutes delay Joe decided to get off Commercial Street. The detour would also let him pass by Gabriel's Guesthouse for a reconnaissance. He took a right on tiny Washington Avenue to get over to the parallel Bradford Street. It made him smile to drive up this street. It's so narrow that there are bumpers on the houses on either side to prevent cars from scraping them, yet it's an avenue. Joe realized with some chagrin how soon his noble and healthy intention to detach from Tim Ronayne, the Fireboys—and his own Irish heritage—had vanished, "But there you are," he thought to himself. "I can't help the way I am," as the song went.

Nobody was outside Gabriel's Guest House except one very small short-haired woman in full leather, plastic bag in hand, holding by a leash a giant Great Dane, which was leading her rapidly to the little *Bas Relief* Park that depicted the arrival of the Pilgrims at Provincetown in the autumn of 1620. In Joe's salad days, before the prudish Town officials put up a fence, men used to wander into the woods behind the *Bas Relief* for a little sexual sport. Now they went to the "Dick Dock," in the West End beyond Spiritus Pizza. Joe had never been there himself, of course, but he knew people who had, including a couple of men who called him looking for lawyers after being arrested under a dory, naked, in *flagrante delicto*. They have been together ever since.

There were still no Irish girls in sight, at least according to Joe's preconceptions, so Joe went up the hill on Marshland Road. In front of the High School Joe saw two plain looking, hefty women, in Provincetown sweatshirts, holding hands walking down the hill.

Joe decided to take a chance they might be the lasses. He stopped the car, rolled down his window and said, "Excuse me, is there a big monument on this street?" He felt like his old law school friend, Marko the lady's man, who'd stand knee deep in the pond at Wellesley College and ask pretty girls passing by, "Excuse me, is there a big lake around here?" The very handsome Marko would have them in his car and off to his bed in Cambridge in ten minutes.

"It's right beside you, fish queen. Open your eyes!" said the huskier of the women in an accent more Bronx than Irish.

"Thank you very *much*," Joe replied, emphasis on the much, and he slowly drove to the top of the hill now looking for house numbers rather than lesbians.

He didn't have far to go. There it was, #25, a kind of Victorian house, behind a very clipped privet hedge. The house had a handsome glassed-in porch across the front and a windowed turret of sorts jutting out on the second floor in the corner looking out to the harbor. Joe pulled the car into the little driveway behind a shiny new, black Saab convertible. He dared not park in the street. Provincetown's budget relied on parking fees and fines and its meter maids, most of whom were men, were ruthless.

The front door, although mainly glass, was covered on the inside with a white curtain as were the bottom halves of the windows on the porch. Joe couldn't see inside. He found the doorbell and pushed it. Joe heard some giggling, women giggling. *Oh shit*, he thought. *All I want to do is sit down and relax for a bit. Do I have to be entertaining? I bet they're blondes. Peter always liked blondes. How did he score so quickly—and in this town?*

Peter opened the door; he had a big grin. "Come in! Come in! I want you to meet some new friends of mine, ladies from Ireland. You'll like them."

In the living room Joe was amazed to see the two women he'd just seen leaving the Schoolhouse Gallery, as well as a young, tall, very handsome man with prematurely silver and black hair. He was chicly dressed all in black. His mostly unbuttoned shirt revealed a beautiful, black, hairy chest and the top "cans," if you will, of a six-pack stomach. He smiled at Joe.

The woman closest to him, the blonde, in pale yellow and baby blue, stood up and extended her hand, "Hello, I'm Maeve Sand," she said with a light brogue.

The second, the taller woman, with the glasses and the thick brown hair, who was wearing a chalcedony blue dress, said, "And I'm Grainne Lavin."

The young man sat grinning, but finally rose halfway and said, "I'm Lorenzo Randozza. It is a pleasure to meet you. What is your name?"

"My name is Joe, Joe Lyons. I'm a college classmate of Peter. We've been friends since college."

"And you're my cousin!" Grainne Lavin said with surprise.

"I know that. I just realized that. I was going to call you in Boston next week. Nora, your grandmother, told me you were coming over. I didn't expect to find you here, in Provincetown, I mean, or in this house, for that matter. How are you?" Joe replied meekly.

Maeve Sand looked at Grainne quizzically. This was too much for her. She didn't know it, but it was even more of a surprise for Joe. Peter was confused, but happy to have two pretty women, one a blonde, and his old, college chum all in the same room. He could have done without the Italian stud but he hoped that everything would sort out. Lorenzo Randozza just continued smiling slyly, like he had the secret to something.

Maeve Sand decided to put some of it together for Joe. She said, "This is my Uncle Johnny's house. He lives in New York. He's a director in the theater. We came over on the boat from Boston yesterday. We met Lorenzo on the boat. He keeps a place here and that's his beautiful car outside." She looked at Joe and Peter like they weren't following her. "I thought we could drop in on my uncle but it seems that he's lent the house to Peter, who was in one of his plays—*The Playboy of the Western World*, as a matter of fact. That could be you Lorenzo, in an Italian version, of course. Peter played Pegeen Mike's father, the publican. Anyway, we just arrived here a minute ago and now we find Grainne's cousin here as well. It's Kismet. Well, if not my Uncle Johnny, Grainne's Cousin Joe is a grand surprise. What do you think of all this, Lorenzo? Have you followed me, Lorenzo?"

Lorenzo said, "Perhaps your Uncle *Gianni* will arrive and make the circle complete. I'm from Rome. Usually all roads lead to Rome, but today they seem to have led to Provincetown and this charming house. Nothing surprises me. *Me piaciono famiglii e misteri.* Maybe my uncles will appear. I am sure that at least one of them knows the charms of Provincetown," Lorenzo added with a knowing—and telling—grin, while looking at Joe.

"Well then, now that we've solved all that serendipity, would anyone like a drink?" Peter said, getting up from the couch between the two women. He was trying to figure out which of the girls was with Lorenzo so he could pounce on the other, even though he preferred Maeve, the blonde. Maybe the drinks would solve that mystery; maybe not.

Peter didn't know the half of it. Nobody there did really, except Lorenzo—perhaps. Peter prepared gin and tonics for himself and the Irish girls. The girls declined ice. Joe wanted plain soda and Lorenzo asked for Campari & soda.

"Well, isn't this the coincidence," said Grainne. "Peter is so kind to entertain us. We just burst in on him. He heard our brogues and told us to wait for you. Of course, he didn't name you. He just said, 'Wait for my friend. He's Irish too.' I'm sorry we missed you when you were back home at the farm. Maeve and I were in Italy." Grainne smiled at Maeve. "She has friends in San Donato, a little town southeast of Rome. It was cool there in the mountains and the food was delicious. Lorenzo has never heard of San Donato, but he's so cosmopolitan. He only leaves Rome to go to Capri, Ravello or Positano—or Provincetown, it seems. He's such a prince. We've been teasing him all day." Grainne looked at Lorenzo, who gave a charming pout.

"I'll be getting a degree in Medical Emergency Care at the Mass General. You people have the best hospitals for that. Tell me about the Mass General, if you can. Maeve is getting a Masters degree in Art Education at Mass Art. Is that what you call it? Mass Art and Mass General—such funny abbreviations! We visited the galleries here earlier this evening. There's a nice show at the Schoolhouse gallery, the one way down the main street, lovely drawings in Japanese ink of Italian landmarks and beautiful watercolors of the harbor at night. Don't you agree, Maeve? Both artists have Irish names too. There are a lot of us here! Where's your Aunt Josie? Did she come with you? She's been writing to Grammy for years. Nora used to read us her letters. She's such a correspondent. I feel like I grew up with your family in the next town. Well, in Ireland we say that Boston is the next parish. Is Providence near Provincetown?"

Joe wondered if Josie's scattershot conversation style was genetic and if Grainne had it as well. Maybe it only occurred in the female line. It was very socially generous in that it included everyone in the room (and many people out of the room) in one paragraph—if you could call what Grainne had just spoken a paragraph.

Joe decided to start at the end. "No Grainne, Providence is about 150 miles away. It's fifty miles south of Boston. Josie's there, as we speak, and is anxious to meet you. I thought we all could have dinner together next week. Aunt Josie loves to take the train up to Boston. Where are you staying here? How is it? Did you leave some of your luggage in Boston, or did you bring it all with you? Perhaps I can drive it—I mean you both—back to Boston. How long are you staying?"

He hadn't meant to say so much, or to get quite so quickly to the luggage they might be carrying. Maybe he had "The Josieitis," as his mother called it, as well. It could be contagious.

"Thank you very much. Lorenzo is going to get us back to Boston in his lovely car. We only brought the essentials down here," Grainne said.

"And the family treasures, of course," Maeve added with a laugh.

Lorenzo said, "Josie? Aunt Josie? Josie from *Providencia*? I met a Josie in Rome last month with my grandmother. She was at my Uncle Rocco's consecration in *San Pietro*. She's very charming. My grandmother loves her. We called her '*Zia Josi*.' What a lovely woman—and smart too. Is this another coincidence?"

"Yes, Lorenzo, my Aunt Josie is from Providence. And I was with your grandmother in Venice," Joe said. "I also know your Uncle Rocco, the bishop. He spoke of you. Did you like Boston and the Kennedy School? I've also met your Uncle Dino and your Cousin Maureen. Which uncle, or uncles, were you expecting here? It's indeed a small world. Your family's well known in Boston."

Joe wanted to say something that would wipe the grin off Lorenzo's beautiful face. He wasn't going to let Lorenzo possess all the mystery or all the answers. He'd give him something to worry about, even if it was only that Joe knew Lorenzo had dropped out of the Kennedy School much to his family's disappointment.

Lorenzo was a cool one. His smile diminished slightly for a second but that was barely noticeable. Joe had seen the same fleeting look of discomfort on lawyers during appellate argument when he'd ask a question they didn't want to answer. Lorenzo straightened up in the chair and said, "Ah, Judge Lyons, of course. You are well known to my family. The Count admires your jurisprudence. And my grandmother found you charming. Of course, your aunt adores you. You would think that there's no more important judge in the United States. I haven't talked with my Uncle Dino in a while. He was in Rome with us but rushed off after the ceremony and before the reception. He had an appointment in the Vatican Library with an Irish monsignor. Uncle Dino has become very pious. Perhaps he has a delayed vocation. He seems to have become very interested in illuminated manuscripts. That's a strange interest for a gangster from the North End. No? Perhaps he's gone 'straight,' as you say."

Joe gasped. Conversation stopped. Peter returned with the drinks.

"Here we are, gin and tonics for the ladies, a Campari for you, Lorenzo, and your seltzer, Joe. Now did I miss anything while I was gone?" asked Peter.

Joe was still digesting Lorenzo's last comment. *He's an ungrateful twerp*, was Joe's first thought. *He wouldn't be sitting here in his fancy Italian silk shirt if his uncle weren't a gangster. Where does he think his money comes from? Does he know how his father died? Has he been that sheltered? And what about that car, the shiny, black Saab convertible, in the driveway? What dubious enterprise is paying for that?* But it was interesting to hear again, and from Lorenzo, of Dino's interest in illuminated manuscripts.

This wasn't entirely news to Joe. During a follow-up visit to the courthouse cafeteria the day after his last call to Joe, Shaughnessy told Joe that only after the robbery did Dino realize the value of what he had stolen from Joe. In a burst of naïve enthusiasm, thinking that Dino was a loyal member of *his* family and not just an in-law, Tim Ronayne had given Dino a crash course on *The Book of Kells*. Dino had listened—and learned. Shaughnessy also said that before Rocco's consecration Dino had gotten a little religion, so to speak, from the handsome Irish silver-haired monsignor in the Office of the Propagation of the Faith at the Vatican, and that in gratitude Dino might now be trying to rescue the entire page for the Vatican Library. The Monsignor had told Dino about the Borgias, and that they were no saints, yet they were glorified by having their name spread across Saint Peter's architrave like a billboard. Many the bandit had bought holiness, and maybe even redemption, with gifts to the Holy See. It made sense to Dino. The Randozza family had enough money. Dino was trying to go "straight," in Lorenzo's sense of the word. That pleased Dino's mother, and Bishop Rocco too, now that Respectability was within their grasp.

When Joe met Lorenzo his first thought was that Lorenzo was covering the Irish girls for Dino and that Lorenzo was out to steal Maeve Sand's "One Eighth." Then, somehow, in a way Joe couldn't entirely imagine, the Randozzas would parlay that "One Eighth" into the whole thing, the whole page of Mark's Gospel of the Loaves and Fishes, and give it to the Vatican library ensuring that Rocco would be at least an archbishop, if not a Cardinal within five years. Sainthood for Giuseppina or the martyred brother Aldo, Lorenzo's father, could come later. The bishopric of Hartford, let's say, would do for Rocco—for the time being.

Lorenzo's disloyal comments about his uncle, who of course Joe still felt warm about, if not hot for, shot that theory—unless it was just a diversion by Lorenzo to throw Joe off balance or a burst of pique, an attempt to be released from under the avuncular thumb.

Joe assumed that all the Randozzas were a team and that the real leader was Giuseppina. He assumed that what one knew they all knew. He didn't think of them as separate individuals, but as one octopus with one brain and as many tentacles as there were relatives. Maybe the more distant ones, like the grandniece Maureen, weren't in on everything but each of the named Randozzas had to know it all. Joe couldn't imagine the estrangement of any one of them from the other. That only happened in Irish families. And if each of the Randozzas knew everything, each knew about the ignominious robbery of Joe, naked, bound by neckties, on his stomach as the semi-tumescent Dino went out the door with "One Eighth" of a page of *The Book of Kells*, the most sacred national treasure of Ireland.

This Rome/Ireland conflict was nothing new. The Irish Church had almost been excommunicated in the ninth century for failing to conform to Rome's dictates. The Irish had been running their own show, with their own saints, married clergy and their own feasts (suspiciously similar to Byzantium's) for years. Such independence made Rome very nervous.

The Church at Rome had sacrificed Ireland to its own interests ever since Dermot McMurrough first brought the Normans into Ireland in the 12th century. Years ago, when he was pious, Joe had been with Rome. He liked the catholicity, the universality, of the Church, or at least the pretense of universality. It had been marvelous to see Africans, Asians and South Americans at mass at Saint Paul's Church in Cambridge saying the same prayers as the old Irish ladies and the Catholic Harvard students, many of whom, as Joe remembered fondly, were handsome athletes on scholarship.

But for the last thirty years Joe could not have cared less. The catholicity was probably just colonialism in a mantilla, Joe thought, when he cared enough to think about it at all. The Church could bury him, but he was gay and the Church was twisted about sex—for everybody. Now, ever since the robbery, due to some strange combination of coincidences, he was tied up to his ancestors, to Ireland.

He'd really prefer not to be with either Rome or Ireland. But there wasn't much else to choose from. As James Joyce said, when asked if he was going to become a Protestant, "I may have lost my faith, but not my reason."

He flashed back to a scene from the weekend just before September 11, 2001, and the strange piety that his agnostic, artistic friends had displayed as they reverently tiptoed into a gallery in a museum to watch Tibetan monks make a gorgeous mandala out of colored sand. In contrast, the monks chatted and laughed as they reached over each other for the brass cones containing the violet or mustard colored sand, which they needed to make the next part of the ancient pattern. The monks knew that they were going to destroy the mandala. They'd made hundreds of these and seen them all go. That was the point—the impermanence of things.

Were they like the monks who scrivened *The Book of Kells*, who had drawn animals at play—even tiger cats—in the illuminations and jokes in the margins, Joe wondered? Those ancient scriveners had probably worked in the scriptorium, laughing and chatting just like today's Tibetans. The fruits of their labors were supposed to last longer, and some like *The Book of Kells* did, but the Irish monks knew that many of their books would be stolen by the Danes, lost, or burnt. They might not have anticipated the farmer who found *The Book of Durrow* in the bog. Before more serious connoisseurs rescued it for posterity and "forever," the farmer used to dip the manuscript in the water he poured to heal his sick cows. Like their Tibetan successors, the monks of Kells and Iona must have known that nothing lasts forever in this world.

The flyer for the Tibetan monks in the gallery at the art museum said that "The destruction of the beautiful sand drawing was to illustrate the transience of this life and its vanities." It was the same message as the faggots of wood burnt before a newly crowned Pope were meant to give while the new Pope was carried around Saint Peter's Square on a *sedilla*—to remind him that *Sic transit gloria mundi*, thus passes the glory of the world, or the ashes rubbed on the foreheads of the rest of us at the beginning of Lent, *Pulverem pulveris*, from ashes we come and to ashes we return.

Some of the Western spectators in the museum gallery, an artistic, hip bunch, had dressed themselves up like Tibetans, and looked ridiculous. Most of them had rejected their own homegrown religious heritage and scorned those of their neighbor's, but there, that day, they were more reverent than a convent of Discalced Carmelites on Good Friday from twelve to three. They had attached their long lost, or never before discovered, piety to the far off East. It was an easy jump to exoticism.

Joe smiled at that piety then and smiled again at the memory of it. Perhaps he was being patronizing. After all he had nothing of his own to offer; he was no shining example of the veracity of the "One, Holy, Catholic and Apostolic." Shouldn't others be able to get their spirituality where they could? And if it took saffron robes and colored sand to do it, so be it.

All this ran through Joe's mind in the living room as he sipped his seltzer and tried to figure out how to get Maeve Sand's "One Eighth" before Lorenzo Randozza could grab it for his monsignor-shtupping Uncle Dino as a love present for his newly found Irish dignitary in Rome.

"We really must be going." Lorenzo said as he rose entirely, all 6′2″ of him, from the little low chair next to the couch. "I made a reservation for dinner for the three of us at Chester's. They squeezed us in or I'd ask you to join us. Do either of you know the place? The room looks wonderful—very salty and nautical. The bar is an old dory, the manager told me. And the place is named after his dog. How charming! And the dog is a mongrel—even more droll! Perhaps we will see you tomorrow."

"The telephone number at our guest house is 3172," added Grainne. "Please call us, Joe."

"And our number is 3173. How coincidental," said Peter, hoping Grainne would call him.

They processed out of the room onto the porch, Lorenzo in the lead. Before going out the last door Grainne returned and planted a kiss on Joe's cheek. "I'm so happy to meet you. It's nice that we share so much." She then looked at the departing Maeve's back lovingly. Peter looked crestfallen until she kissed his cheek too. "Thank you for your hospitality. You're very kind," Grainne said with a charming smile.

Joe and Peter returned to the living room and sat down. As he returned to his spot on the couch, Peter said, "Well, they're very nice—and very attractive. I hope that Italian stud isn't sleeping with *both* of them. There were so many coincidences in this reunion. Isn't that interesting?" said Peter bemusedly.

"You don't know the half of it," Joe replied. "That's a plot too thick to stir."

"Oh, you Irish and your plots! You'd think you were still fighting the Revolution. Wasn't that over in 1910?"

Joe said. "You mean 1916, and it's not over yet for a lot of people. Where am I sleeping, Peter?"

"Oh, I'm sorry. I was so distracted by those girls. You know me and Northern European women. I think that I'll put you in the 'Lilac Room.' In case you can't tell which room it is, there's a little plaque on the door, just like Lady Whoozywhatzy's in Newport. This place is a hoot. You gay guys really know how to doll it up, don't you?"

Joe resented at least three things about Peter's last remarks; First, the presumption that the women were heterosexual; second, that because they were heterosexual Peter could make moves on them; third, the clichéd notion that all gay men were interior decorators.

Joe also was very discomfited by the presence of Grainne and

Maeve in the company of Lorenzo Randozza, which could not have been a coincidence. Joe did not want to reveal what he knew about the Irish girls' sexual tastes. That would lead him down a path he didn't want to take Peter. So, his discomfort came out this way.

"And why do you think that I can speak for all gay men? I don't even know the man who owns this house. You're like my colleague Firrfield, who comes to tell me every time a priest is arrested for molesting an altar boy. He thinks that he has me on all counts, the gay one, the Catholic one and usually the Irish one as well. I told him that I'm not responsible for every Father Mary Doogan in the world any more than he is responsible for Woody Allen, Ariel Sharon or Eliot Spitzer."

Peter said nothing to this.

"I'm sorry to be so testy," Joe apologized "but there was something about that Lorenzo character that I didn't like and I fear for my cousin, even though I just met her. I can understand your attraction to Irish women. There is something wonderfully refreshing about them. They don't put up with much nonsense, but they're very sweet and forgiving to their menfolk at the same time. But here I am generalizing, just what I criticized you for. It's been a long and a hard day. Where would you like to eat?"

"Let's go to *The Mews*. I read about it last week in the *New York Times*. I made a reservation for 8:30. Would you like to take a nap before we go out?" Peter said, good naturedly ignoring the criticism in the apology.

"Is that a proposition or a suggestion, Peter? Has the Provincetown air turned you?" Joe said with a smile, trying to erase his earlier pique with an attempt at humor.

Peter replied very seriously, "You know, Joe, in college when I was experimenting with sex I would have gone to bed with you in a minute. You were too up tight."

Joe said, "Experimenting! That was the problem. You probably gave it up to one of those reptilean Adams House English tutors—and just to see what it felt like. I couldn't believe you guys, smoking dope, dropping acid and having group sex. Did your roommate Caspar ever do it with a guy? I really liked Caspar. Do you remember the *Anniversary of the Surrender of Fort SumterParty*, in 1960, when we were all looking out the top floor windows of Quincy House at the couples dancing quadrilles below in the courtyard—the girls in big hoop skirts? I knew Caspar was leaning behind me to look out the window and I put my hands behind my back so I could feel his crotch. It felt like he enjoyed it."

"I doubt that Caspar even noticed. He was probably groping a blonde farm girl while you were feeling him up. He liked that type," Peter said.

"If you had gotten me drunk," Joe continued, "you could have had me. I just couldn't do it as clinically or scientifically as you people did. For you guys it was like you were taking another course. I had paralyzing crushes on a number of your friends but I needed something to unfreeze me. And furthermore, you guys were also sleeping with women, and I didn't believe that women really wanted sex. It was my way of avoiding having sex with them. It's all about the Virgin Mother."

Peter said, "Caspar is as straight as a string and always has been. He's had two wives and is working on a third. He's a little oblivious, just like he looks. That's part of his charm—the hayseed Down Mainer. He probably had no idea what you were doing. Sorry to disappoint you after all these years." That was Peter's revenge for Joe's previous chastisement.

Joe saw it for what it was and said, "I'm going to take a quick nap. I'll be down in 45 minutes." Joe went upstairs. Soon after Peter heard Joe say from upstairs, "What faggot got out of control in this room? 'When Lilacs last on Marshland Road bloomed….' Is Walt Whitman hiding in the closet?"

24 An Angel at the Meat Rack

One of the difficult things about being a judge is that a lot of people want a piece of you. They aren't necessarily trying to corrupt, but they think it's good to know a judge, just in case. There is a big gap between the popular notion of corruption and the prohibitions of the Massachusetts Canons of Judicial Ethics. People weren't evilly intended. Some just wanted to have the judge in their Rolodex, should a problem arise.

Joe had learned this over the years. He thought that he now knew how to determine whom he could trust. A videotape given to all new judges made some suggestions, including "Don't make any new lawyer friends." Joe had developed his own guidelines. Depending on their tone, he was skeptical of people who called him "Your Honor" outside of the courtroom. Somehow it was o.k. to call him "Judge," but "Your Honor" was too obsequious. He figured that they either were only interested in his title or they were mocking him.

Conversely, he didn't trust lawyers who, outside of the courtroom, didn't call him "Judge" in the presence of others. He distrusted lawyers who assumed they could call him by his first name in social situations. A couple of incidents cemented this caution. At a party he met a third-year law student, who insisted on calling him "Joe." Joe thought that the kid would know better once he became a lawyer. He didn't. For a couple of years after passing the bar the man continued to call him "Joe," even in the hallways of the courthouse in front of other lawyers. A few years later at a cocktail hour before a professional dinner they found themselves standing next to each other. Everyone else who had been in the group had moved on. The young lawyer began to talk to Joe about the facts of a case that was pending before a panel that included Joe. Joe tried to shut him up but the brat wasn't hearing it. Joe said, "Mr. Thickhead (not his real name), you can't talk to me about a pending case."

"Oh, Joe, everyone knows the facts of that case. The whole story was in the *Globe*."

Joe anguished over the matter, but after a call to the Bar Counsel he was told that he had to report the boob to the Board of Bar Overseers, where they lectured, but didn't discipline him. Joe hated to have to do it and it upset him for days.

Another old friend, actually a short term boyfriend from the days before Joe became a judge, called Joe in the middle of the night from the Massachusett Bay Transit Authority lockup. He'd been arrested for having sex in the Men's room of the Back Bay Station. "What can I do, Joe? What can I do?" he cried.

"You can get a lawyer. Keep your mouth shut (that advice should have been given before the guy went into the Men's room) and get a lawyer." The miscreant couldn't understand why Joe kept his distance thereafter. Had he told the cops he was calling Judge Lyons? Probably.

Other people seemed to think Joe was a public resource and they called him up for legal opinions. "I can't give legal advice. Call a lawyer," was Joe's response. He would say it in different ways, of course, depending on whether or not he liked, or wanted to talk to, the person again. Many people just never thought about the delicacy of Joe's position. Maybe they could be pardoned but many others, who would never call a doctor for free medical advice, for example, should have known better.

Some people at cocktail parties would say upon meeting him, or better, meeting his title, "Oh, now I know who to call to take care of my traffic tickets," and then smile at their wit. They were usually businessmen, who were used to paying for everything. Joe had developed a particular glare for this gaffe, but at times he really took them to task. "Do you think that remark is amusing? Do you really think that's acceptable?" he would sometimes say. He gave much the same to people who sought instructions as to how to get out of jury duty.

The cumulative effect of all this over the years was that Joe had become a recluse. He was uncomfortable meeting new people. He worried that he was becoming a stuffed shirt, but he knew no other way. He wasn't a stuffed shirt, but he couldn't laugh off people's *gaucherie* in this regard. It bothered him to be confrontational, outside of the courtroom. So he narrowed down his social life.

He still went to some gay charity events; the political soirees were forbidden, thank God. While Arthur Bruce was sick, and for a while after he died, Joe was active in AIDS charities, like the Boston Living Center and the AIDS Action Committee. The *Canons of Judicial Ethics* prohibited him from raising money for any charity, but he could give money and attend events. Recently, however, he dropped even that. His interest in the charities waned. Maybe it was because Arthur had died or because protease inhibitors took the urgency out of the crisis. Most of his friends who'd been infected had died and the others were on the cocktail. AIDS didn't seem to be the crisis it had been in the late eighties and early nineties.

Or maybe Joe really was a hermit at heart. If so, he didn't like it. He didn't want to die a lonely old man. The computer search had been an attempt to get out of himself. It wasn't only lust. Honest.

◊ ◊ ◊

When they arrived at *The Mews* the owner was at the desk. He greeted Joe and seated them at a table next to the sliders looking out at the Bay. Joe knew the owner through a mutual friend, who ate there all the time with his retinue and Joe had been a patron years before when the restaurant began in a shack out on the pier. He also knew the *maitre d'*, who once was the young boyfriend of a well known Boston lawyer.

That Joe was a judge may have entered into the seating choice, but not because Joe raised it. Early on in his tenure the fact that some people treated him better than others bothered Joe but now he was more used to it. He worried about what seemed to be a loss of scrupulosity, but not as much as he used to. By and large, he was powerless over other people's response to him, he'd decided.

They arrived at their table just before the sun set on the opposite, the ocean side of town. The setting sun painted the Bay's water pink, violet and pale blue. For a few minutes the diminishing sunlight shone only on the moored boats making them almost fluorescent against the darkening water and shore. As the meal progressed, the lights along the Bay came up and twinkled down the nautilus-like curve that is Provincetown, Truro and Wellfleet. Peter, who was usually more verbal than visual, and usually more articulate, couldn't stop saying "Wow" as the light and colors changed with every course. Joe, who had seen it before and too often took such a display for granted, joined in Peter's fresh delight. Joe was glad for Peter's company now.

The conversation was nothing heavy—reminiscences about classmates, like Joe's college roommate, who Joe couldn't abide (because of a homophobic remark in their Junior year, long before Joe was out,) but who had helped Peter through his divorce and won Peter's gratitude forever. Who was and wasn't gay in their class always came up. Joe outed nobody but Peter seemed to know most of the players, at least the New York ones, proving to Joe once again that straight men were just as gossipy as gay men. One great chestnut-haired beauty, who Joe had last seen dancing in the late sixties at the Boatel in the Pines on Fire Island surrounded by bare-chested admirers, was now dead, Peter announced. It was the virus, of course.

Finally they got around to Peter's life, his ex-wife and their kids. The daughter was going to medical school and the son had dropped out. What could Peter do? The mother indulged their son. Peter was writing a lot, which Joe admired. Joe opined that if he were left on his own all day, he'd never do anything. Joe needed a job for structure; Peter wrote every day no matter what. Joe thought that was wonderful.

By this time they'd finished their lobsters. Joe said, "Let's skip dessert here and walk down to Spiritus Pizza and have some ice cream. We'll see the town. It's a hangout."

After they'd walked about three hundred yards down the road, to "The Meat Rack," the benches in front of Town Hall, Joe saw Grainne, Maeve and Lorenzo seated on one of the benches. They were very dressed up, much more suited to St. Tropez than Provincetown. The girls wore pretty, flimsy little black and white patterned dresses with short skirts and high, high heels, like drag queens. They must have changed after dinner. Lorenzo, who slouched in between them, with leather pants and a white lace shirt, revealing his perfectly hairy chest and open to his well worked abdomen, didn't look too happy.

"What's up?" Peter said to the girls with his best schoolboy smile.

"This town is very strange," Lorenzo replied seriously. "We ate too early and now we're waiting for eleven o'clock so we can dance for two hours and then go give burning glances to some half drunk, adorable twink in front of that Pizza parlor up the street at one o'clock in the morning. This is not Capri."

The Irish girls just smiled. They liked watching the people, and many of the people liked watching them—both men and women. The Irish girls were well brought up and smiled politely, but without commitment, at the attention they received. Lorenzo wanted the attention for himself. Perhaps he shouldn't have agreed to squire them both day and night.

Peter said to Maeve, "May I sit down?" as he squeezed in beside her and a fat guy in a muu muu, with lots of gold, and two snarling papillons in his lap. On the other side of Lorenzo, Grainne moved a speck and pulled her tiny skirt closer to her upper thigh as if to make room for Joe on the bench. The woman next to Grainne, with a dirty blonde mullet haircut, carpenter jeans and work boots, closed her spread legs and moved down the bench sheepishly to make more room for Joe. Her similarly dressed and coiffed, but slightly more femmy, girlfriend accommodated the move with approval. The butcher mullet had been getting very close to Grainne and the femmy mullet didn't like it. She was very happy to see Joe move in and create space between Grainne and her butch.

Grainne said, "Joe, it's so nice to meet you at last. I should have called as soon as we arrived in the States but we'd been planning this side trip for a bit—a little second honeymoon, as it were."

Joe was surprised by her candor. Before he could respond Lorenzo stood up revealing the tightest leather jeans Joe had ever seen. *You can tell what religion he is*, Joe thought.

"I'm going over to the Crown and Anchor to see if we can get in. If there are more than ten people there, I'll stay," Lorenzo said to Grainne and Maeve. "Please join me. That place has the best music. I'm sure you'll enjoy it. Joe, you and Peter are welcome too. I will have paid the admission fees. Mention my name to 'the Kevin' on the door."

Joe smiled at the last remark. Because Irish Catholic Boston was the nearest city to Provincetown, the houseboys, waiters and staff people in Provincetown were referred to as "Kevins." In fact, more often than not, that was their name. The bartenders, on the other hand, had names like "Rocky" or "Brick" or "Stormy." That included the women.

Lorenzo walked away, attracting a lot of attention as he swaggered up the street in his Italian cowboy boots. *He looks pretty good*, thought Joe, *even if he's up to no good. That's some hairy chest and the bum is nice too.*

Once Lorenzo was out of earshot Grainne said, "We don't want to go dancing, but he's been so nice to us. He took us to dinner. It was lovely. He knows that we're lovers and we know that he's gay, although nobody has really said it. He really is very controlling. He wasn't too happy meeting you, Joe. I think that he thought you'd take us away from him. For all of his glamorous swagger he's very lonely. He's in love with a boy from Boston named Brendan, but they split up at the beginning of the month. He keeps on looking around as if we were going to run into Brendan and he puffs himself up like a pigeon for the encounter. I don't know what to do."

By this time Maeve had moved over. Peter was hot beside her. Maeve overheard the end of what Grainne said and added, "He seems very anxious to care for us as long as we're here. He has plans for the whole weekend. I just want to take a tramp in the dunes, roll in the sand, make wild love and then swim naked in some secluded tidal pool. But Lorenzo's arranged everything including a ride back to Boston for us in his convertible. It's creepy. I hope he runs into Brendan and that they go somewhere and fuck themselves stupid and then he leaves us alone."

"I'll take care of you," said Peter, earnestly, excited by Maeve's recitation of her list of desires, not yet knowing that they would not likely include him.

"Oh sure!" said Joe in response to Peter's solicitude.

"Now Peter," Maeve said with a laugh, "Don't be naïve. We have to get something straight…and it's not Grainne or me. Why do you think that two simple Irish girls, inseparable friends since childhood, who'd just spent the past two years in Paris getting *bon tonned* came all the way across the Ocean to this remote, little Portuguese fishing village, this nest of Gaiety, as opposed to…Atlantic City or San Tropez, for example. Please!!"

Peter looked quizzical for a moment, and then his jaw dropped. "I had no idea," he said finally, being patronizing in that way only heterosexual liberals can. "Why, you don't look like lesbians."

Grainne smiled, trying to be not too hurtful to Peter in his discomfort. Joe roared at the comeuppance. Thinking he was being too raucous, Joe then looked embarrassedly over to his left. The mulletted couple had left. They were replaced by a well packaged, small young man in blue jeans, flip-flops and a tight, plain white tee shirt, who grinned up at Joe. Then he lifted his toned arms above his head, thrust out his pelvis along the bench and moaned as he stretched. His tee shirt pulled up even more, revealing a muscled concavity of a stomach, and a silken treasure trail beginning a little above the navel, descending down beneath the belt line to what looked like a considerable basket at the crotch. He gave the stretch an extra pull and Joe saw the beginning of a Celtic cross two inches below his navel. The little beauty looked up at Joe, smiled again and said, "My mother's from Galway," as if that were an explanation.

Joe couldn't think of a smart reply fast enough, so he asked, "And your father?"

"He's from Italy. I got the Sistine Chapel 'Touching Fingers' somewhere else," and the cherub grinned again.

"One hesitates to ask where," Joe said, getting into this game.

"Take a walk with me. I'll show you."

By this time all attention had shifted from Maeve and Peter to the pale skinned, beautiful, dark-haired young man. Grainne said, "Can we all go?" She wasn't going to let her newly found cousin wander off with a stranger, no matter how adorable—or half Irish.

"Sure, you're all welcome. I sat here 'cuz I love to hear your brogues. I could listen to you girls all night," the young man said.

"Not likely, my pet," said Maeve. They got up off the bench in unison, laughing and followed the darlin' down Commercial Street over to the little alley across from Adam's Drug and Gosnold Street. They then headed out towards the harbor beach and Julie Heller's Gallery, which was lit up and still open. Joe was happy to see that. He knew the alley and as soon as they entered it he'd decided that they weren't going to walk any further than Julie Heller's

Gallery. Although there was only one of the beauty, and him small, who knew who or what was waiting on the beach. Joe knew that it was dark down there.

It turned out that they didn't have to walk even as far as Julie Heller's Gallery. At the end of the Tee Shirt shop, which flanked the alley on the right, the young man stopped under a small light attached to the back of the building. He took off his tee shirt, turned around, giving Joe and his friends his beautifully muscled back, unbuttoned his already low slung jeans, and pulled them down a bit more than halfway over his creamy white perfectly rounded butt. There, on the upper crescent of his lovely bum, were Michelangelo's hands of God and Adam touching fingers, just like the Creation scene from the Sistine Chapel ceiling. Adam's limp hand on the left cheek reached up to God on the right and they touched just at the top of the crack. As if to illuminate the electricity of the moment, there was a little diamond shaped tuft of blond and black hair at the point of contact. The beauty turned his head back to them and grinned as they looked. Joe wanted to trace the tattoo with his own index finger, or better his tongue.

"How's that!?!" said God's own creation.

"Fantastic!" said Peter.

"Did it hurt?" asked Grainne, ever the nurse.

"Brilliant!" Maeve the artist, added.

Joe just smiled in amazement at the whole performance.

The boy then turned around, buttoning up his pants, and said, "Now I'll tell you why I brought you all out here. You know that guy you girls have been with the last few days and were sitting with tonight on 'The Meat Rack?' Lorenzo? Well, he's trouble. He's out using again, crystal meth. It's a good thing he has a lot of money or you'd be penniless now. He's after you girls for something. I have no idea what. He takes his orders from his uncle Dino, a hood, in the North End, who's a trip himself. Dino goes for the older Irish guys. You," the angel said, nodding to Joe, "You're Dino's type all the way. Are you a priest? He loves priests; monsignors are even better. Be careful. And when you see Lorenzo again, don't tell him I said anything. He left you to score some more crystal and he's probably dancing his head off now. So, you're safe for a while."

"And who are you and why are you telling us this?" Joe asked.

"I'm Brendan, Brendan Pastorelli. I used to go with Lorenzo. We met in a halfway house in Dorchester and were together for a while but then he had a slip and I had to let him go. He's a good guy when he's clean and away from his family. But he's a mess if not. Take care! I love the Irish!" Brendan said smiling at Grainne and Maeve.

Then the messenger turned and ran off towards the beach, kicking off his flip-flops and catching them in his hand as he ran. Joe was sure that he saw little wings on the back of them as they flew in the air.

"Alright Peter, you're on your own now," Joe said. "I have to talk to my cousin and Maeve. There's a bar down the street to the right called *The Governor Bradford*. There'll be a straight girl in there—at least one. If you've become a 'fish queen' and are looking for lesbians, there's another bar off to the left called *The Pied Piper*. But whatever your choice, you have to disappear for a bit. I need to talk to the girls and we should go up to your house, Maeve's uncle's house to be correct, to do so. It's a family thing, an Irish thing, a Catholic thing. Don't take it personally. So, please give me the key before you leave. I'll leave it under the flower pot on the front porch, should I go to bed before you return," Joe said.

The girls and Peter looked in shock, not only at what Joe had just said, but also at the information Brendan had so dramatically delivered. The night was becoming much too heavy.

Peter, however, rose to the occasion and said, to everyone's relief, "Just where is *The Governor Bradford*, Joe? Will an hour be enough time for you?" as he handed over the house key on its metal-plated sand dollar key chain.

Grainne, Maeve and Joe marched up Marshland Road, up the hill. Joe stopped to get his breath at the High School. "Doesn't this look just like the high school in a Hollywood fifties movie, or an

Archie and Veronica comic book?" Joe asked. "Look at the lamps of knowledge up at the roofline. I hope that they teach the kids some tolerance. There used to be a lot of homophobic hoodlum kids on the streets here in the old days when I came down here more often."

The observation about the high school was lost on the Irish girls educated at a convent in Ireland, but Grainne, ever the nurse, knew that Joe probably had to stop, that he was winded. He was a bit overweight and getting up there in age, whatever else he might say.

Joe tried to disguise his discomfort. If he could just rest a bit, it would be o.k. The pain in his teeth that preceded the pain in his chest would go away. Joe pretended to look around and then pointed to the Pilgrim Monument on the hill to the right of them. "This monument, based on the tower at *Il Municipio* in the *campo* in Sienna, is a testimonial to the Protestant Ascendancy in New England—kind of ironic that the Prots had to go to Catholic Italy for the model."

The girls looked up. "We went to Sienna the summer before last. We never got to Pisa but loved Venice. Didn't we Grainne?" Maeve said.

"Maeve loves the Venetian painters, Tiziano, Tintoretto and especially Veronese," Grainne added.

"I love the dogs and other beasties in the paintings," said Maeve. Did you ever see *The Marriage Feast at Cana* in the Louvre? It's got a setter, two greyhounds and a chihuahua walking on the table. It's brilliant."

They proceeded a little more slowly up the hill. Grainne had clasped Joe's arm in what was meant to look like affection, but was really a ruse to feel his pulse. Grainne was worried that her newfound cousin might have a heart attack on the last rise to the top of the hill. It had been an exciting last half hour, never mind the hill.

They arrived at 25 Marshland Road and after a little fumbling Joe opened the door. "I'll make some chamomile tea," Grainne said. "Your uncle was always drinking Chamomile tea, Maeve, ever since he went to Italy. There must be some here." She headed to the kitchen.

Maeve sat on the couch, tugging her mini skirt down her long legs. Joe took the chair to her right. Grainne returned with a tray of cups, teaspoons and pink cloth napkins. "The tea will be right out. The water is about to boil," she said as she sat down next to Maeve, on her left.

Joe said, "I'm not sure where to begin. Do you girls know Tim Ronayne from Dundalk?"

"Of course, we do." Maeve answered. "He's almost family. He probably is family, the way everyone up there intermarried. It's lucky we're not walking around with three eyes and tails with all the intermarrriage. Tim's a handsome man. Is he not, Grainne? His sisters are handsome too. You always had a shine for the older one, didn't you, Grainne, the one who went in the Ursulines? She was very pious."

Joe interrupted before this chat really got off track. He had to tell them about "The Page," but how to do so in the briefest and most unrevealing way possible? "Well, Tim Ronayne discovered that many of the families of Ballyfirglin, many of them on your road, Grainne and Maeve, had a very important treasure. The first year of the Famine eight men came into possession of a page of *The Book of Kells*. You know that there are at least 60 missing pages, 30 folios, and that there were even some duplicate pages?

"Well, anyway there were," Joe added when he got blank stares from the girls. "The circumstances of the way our people came into possession of 'The Page' resulted in great changes in their lives." Joe didn't want to tell them they were descended from arsonists.

"One of them is why I am an American. But I won't get into that now. The page was divided into eight parts and each part was given to one of the men. Tim Ronayne is trying to bring the eight pieces of 'The Page' together again. There are others who are trying to capture 'The Page' for other reasons, maybe to give it to the Vatican library—at least to keep it away from Tim and the other descendants of the men who divided it originally. And, Maeve, people think that you have one of the pieces, that you inherited it and maybe don't even know it and that you may have brought it over here with you," Joe said solemnly as if he were in court making a ruling.

"I was going to approach you about this subject when we met in Boston. The family of Lorenzo Randozza is interested as well, but for the other side. They were originally Tim's allies but no longer. One of them may have gotten religion—well, at least a monsignor—and he may want to buy respectability by giving it to the Vatican Library. That would be Dino, Lorenzo's uncle, who the angel Brendan Pastorelli mentioned. I've met him; he's very attractive, but not always nice, particularly when you have something he wants. That's the short story; it will have to do for now. Do you know that you might have 'One Eighth' of 'The Page?' Did you see it in the family box you rescued from Nora's house?"

"How do you know so much, Joe?" Maeve said, meaning *why should we trust you?*

"I had a piece myself," Joe answered. "Tim has it now. Tim gave it to me years ago when we…when we first met. Tim told me all about it after he took it back a little while ago."

"Took it back? What does that mean? Did you not want to give it back? How do we know that you don't work for the bad guys—for the Ronzonis, or whoever they are, and the Vatican?"

"You'll just have to trust me. What we have to do now is safeguard the piece that you have, which by the way is the last piece, all the others have been recovered, and keep you two safe. These Randozzas have been known to be violent. And I don't trust anyone on crystal meth."

"Well, I did bring a batch of things from the satchel with me. They looked like letters and documents. I was going to sort through them over here and send them off to other people if appropriate. The portfolio is in the lingerie bag, which fits in my suitcase at Gabriel's Guest House. For some reason I hid the lingerie bag in the room. Don't ask me why. A premonition perhaps. Or maybe I thought that one of those butchies who clean the rooms would sniff it. So I hid it."

"Is it safe?" Joe asked.

"I hope it is. I got me knickers out of it before going out tonight and I'll need a fresh pair tomorrow, especially after the night we're having. There's a lot of pretty stuff in there. I'm very fond of lingerie. Old Grainne would wear her brother's Jockey shorts but I like me lacey bloomers and brassieres."

"If we retrieved your 'One Eighth' tonight, where could we hide it?" Joe said thinking aloud. "I don't want Lorenzo to know we're onto him. He's probably just waiting for a time to pounce on your luggage—probably when he drives you back. What if I walk you down the hill to Gabriel's and you give me the portfolio? I'll hide it in this house somewhere. Do you mind if I look through it? I know what we're looking for."

"*We*, your honor? Have you joined the Fireboys too?" Maeve asked.

"You know about the Fireboys? How do you know about the Fireboys?" Joe said in alarm.

"We were raised in the bloody village, Joe. We've heard its lore since we were big enough to crawl beneath Diarmuid's Dolmen. Did you know that's where theFireboys took their oaths? It was a sacred ceremony almost like exchanging blood, like your Indians. It all sounds very queer these days, the bodily fluid exchange. And we know about the burning of the big house and the flight of the Tiltons back to England. Good riddance to them and their tyrannical thievery. Yes, you can look through the portfolio. Maybe you'll find what you're looking for; maybe not. You'll probably appreciate the legal documents more than I would. If there's a pair of panties that got mixed in, don't throw them away. And you can't wear them either. You're too big for my stuff. Should we go now?"

They were almost at the bottom of the hill when a car pulled in to Marshland Road. It was Lorenzo in his black Saab. He screeched loudly to a halt.

"Where did you go? I've been all over town looking for you. I almost got murdered by this bruiser at the Pied Piper or whatever they call the dyke bar these days. She thought I was straight and cruising for girls. Where have you been? Why didn't you come dancing? I was very worried about you two. Where are you going now?"

"Don't worry, darling," Maeve said sweetly and sulkily. "We just went up to my uncle's house for a nightcap. We were too weary to dance. We're going home to bed, just around the corner, to Gabriels."

"I just looked for you there. I thought that the crew-cutted blonde in charge was going to shoot me for leaning on the bell so long."

"We'll catch up tomorrow morning, darling. We'll meet at the Café Heaven at ten o'clock for breakfast. They have the best French toast, darling. Sleep well my pet." Then Maeve leaned into the car and gave Lorenzo a kiss.

"Joe, do you want a ride back up the hill?" Lorenzo asked.

"No, I'm going to walk the ladies to their door. Thank you though."

"I'll turn around and pick you up," Lorenzo said as he did a U-turn in the middle of Bradford Street at the intersection of Marshland Road. And wasn't there a police cruiser coming up Gosnold Street to Bradford? And didn't she put on her wigwag lights, her siren and everything else that lit up or made noise?

Lorenzo pulled up on Bradford almost in front of Gabriel's.

Joe saw his opportunity as did the girls and they hotfooted it over to Gabriel's. Maeve ran upstairs to her room. Grainne stayed down with Joe. Maeve returned with a red leather portfolio, tied with a red ribbon. She handed it to Joe. Joe kissed Grainne and walked away, leaving Lorenzo to the dubious compassion of Officer "Meany" Souza, the fourth and toughest daughter of the harbormaster, Clemmy Souza. Meany was about five feet, two inches tall, stocky and she had a jet black unibrow as well as a not so faint mustache. She also had a gun and she knew how to use it. Her favorite pastime was shooting squirrels in her father's back yard in the Truro woods. "Good luck to Lorenzo," Joe thought.

Joe walked slowly up the hill, wondering where he could hide the portfolio. Or should he look through it now? He didn't look back. Joe went behind the school. All the ice tea had bloated him. He had to pee. He knew the back way to the house. There were lights *en route* if he chose to open the folder, or he could take a pee in a dark corner and proceed home.

Just as he got to the top step of the stairway behind the school, which would take him to a path behind the house, he saw a skunk sniffing along the edge of the right side of the path and heading towards him. Should he turn and go down the stairs and around to the street? Joe stood his ground, leaning against the left wall of the stairs, barely breathing, pretending to be a tree, as the skunk descended the stairs on the right.

The skunk stopped two stairs below Joe, hesitated and then turned around to return up the stairs.

Joe pressed himself into the wall, as if he were a caryatid. The skunk did return, passing three feet in front of Joe without so much as a glance. This guy, if guy it is, is just like the skunks at Spiritus Pizza, who wander right through the crowd of posturing silly billies, then under the gate to the boccie court in the back. What brass these Provincetown skunks have, not unlike the New York tourist queens they've just frightened.

As soon as the skunk got to the top stair and the flat of the hill above Joe heard footsteps, more like boot steps, to be precise. And then shortly after the skunk disappeared Joe heard, "*Jesu Christu*, the bastard got me!" He then heard the boots running in the opposite direction. The voice sounded familiar, but in the excitement of the moment Joe couldn't place it.

Joe had to decide whether to make the last dash behind the back yards to the Marshland Road house, or to retreat and go down, around and back to the more visible street to approach the house from the front. He was tired and chose the easier route—the back.

And he still had to pee. He did that right there on the steps, hoping that his urine might keep the skunks away, like fox urine is supposed to repel deer.

Furthermore, he thought if Lorenzo were looking for him, he would come by the street and how could he, Joe, secrete the portfolio on the street? He could drop it in the bushes here in the back. Four footsteps from the top stair, about ten feet ahead, he saw a white cloth in the middle of the path. As he got closer he realized that it was Lorenzo's see through lace shirt, that shirt which had revealed more than it covered Lorenzo's puffed and pelted pectorals and his finely chiseled stomach. He realized that the voice had been Lorenzo's. The shirt stank of skunk, however, so Joe gave it a wide berth. He thought of climbing over the four foot chain link fence into the backyard but he'd probably rip his pants. Besides the skunk, or Lorenzo, may be in the bushes. Joe walked around, slipping into the driveway, went through the gate and into the back door of the house.

He locked himself in the downstairs bathroom, sat on the covered hopper and began to leaf through the portfolio. The documents themselves were tied with another red ribbon. They were mostly deeds and letters and they were interesting, but Joe knew what he was looking for and refused to let his legal curiosity stop his search. Almost exactly in the middle of the papers there was a very thin, maybe 8" by 6" fold of old parchment paper. Just as Joe hit on it, the front door to the house opened noisily. Joe put the fold in his right pants pocket, pushed the other papers back into the portfolio, and tucked the portfolio into the shelf in front of him behind multiple rolls of toilet paper. That should do for now, he thought.

Joe stood up, flushed the unused toilet, ran some water, washed his hands, looked down and saw the red ribbon at his feet. He picked it up, put it in his other, the left, pocket, and marched out to the living room.

There was Peter with a big grin and a small, very young blonde, about the same size as Peter. Joe hoped she was of legal age. It wouldn't do for a judge to be in the house during a statutory rape.

Peter said, "Jill, this is my old friend Joe Lyons. Joe this is Jill. She is at the Fine Arts Work Center, studying Fiber Arts."

"Nice to meet you, Jill," Joe said, having no idea what Fiber Arts was. "Joe, I was just about to make Jill a Campari and soda. Would you like something?"

"I'll have the soda," Joe said. "Campari is too bitter for me. I'm a Cinzano man myself." Joe was really neither. He was trying to figure out how he could get back in the bathroom and retrieve the portfolio or get upstairs where he could open the fold.

Suddenly the doorbell rang. It was now well after midnight. Peter went to the door. He was the host; to him had been entrusted the house.

Joe heard Peter say, "Lorenzo! What happened to you? Why are you standing out in the street?" Joe couldn't hear the response, only Peter's side of the dialogue. "A skunk? Oh dear. I think there's some tomato juice here. I know that is what they put on dogs… or is it ketchup? I've also heard that vinegar works. There's only balsamic. There's a shower in the back yard beside the kitchen window. Go down the driveway and through the gate. I'll turn on the back porch lights and put the tomato juice, some ketchup and vinegar out by the shower. I hope there are no skunks out there. Put the tomato juice and ketchup and vinegar on first and then take a shower. Let it soak for a bit. Nobody will see you in the backyard. Stand behind a tree if you're bashful. The shower has both hot and cold water. Be careful! The handles are reversed; the cold is on the left and the hot on the right. It might take a few minutes to heat up. There's soap in the dish on the windowsill, lavender soap. That should help. I'll put some clothes out by the shed. We don't exactly have your size."

Joe heard Peter laugh a little at his own remark. "But I am sure they'll do until you can get back to your place. I thought that was your black Saab parked next door. I hope the neighbor isn't a grouch and that he doesn't have it towed. I'll explain the situation to him in the morning. You better not get back in the car. Maybe you should take a dunk in the harbor before going home."

Jill was listening in on this chat and tried to peer out the living room window, but all she could see was Peter's back in the doorway.

"Lorenzo is a friend of the owner's niece and of my cousin. They are visiting from Ireland," Joe explained, not entirely.

"Ooh, I love the Irish," Jill said gushingly. "I went to a weaving workshop in Donegal last year."

Joe could think of nothing to say. He was distracted. Contrary to his better judgment, he thought that he'd like to catch a glimpse of the naked Lorenzo in the backyard. But then Joe realized that maybe he would be safer if he remained invisible for a while.

Peter returned to the parlor. "I'm sure you heard all that. Lorenzo was sprayed by a skunk. He is standing out in the street shirtless in his leather pants and cowboy boots. Do you have any clothes we can give him Joe? I've an old pair of jeans. He's tall. They'll look like clam diggers on him."

"Well, he is Italian. Maybe Capri pants would suit him," Joe said.

Jill laughed. "I want to see this man. Will he really be naked in the backyard? Is he Italian? I love Italians. I spent my next-to-last semester studying tapestry in Florence. I speak Italian."

"Strawberries to pigs," Joe muttered.

"What did you say?" Jill asked.

Joe thought a second and then said, "It would be like giving strawberries to pigs for you to meet Lorenzo. He's gay and probably high at the moment, besides being stinky."

"How exciting! Is he beautiful? Gay men are so beautiful! I just love gay men!" Jill said.

Perhaps she'd attended a class in thong making in Cherry Grove, Joe thought unkindly, making him feel very old.

"I think that I'd better go to bed," Joe said as he rose from his chair. He went upstairs to the lilac room—which overlooked the shower below, by the way. Jill went into the kitchen to help Peter with the drinks. At least that's what she said she was going to do.

Joe took off his clothes in the upstairs bathroom and carried them into the dark bedroom. He lay down on the bed. Soon he could hear the running water of the outside shower. Maybe just a peek, he thought.

Joe leaned over on the bed and fumbled for his pants. He reached in the right hand pocket and found the parchment fold. He returned to the bathroom, turned on the light, and sat on the closed toilet. Smiling with anticipatory delight, he opened the fold. To his surprise, it contained a 100 pound bill with Queen Victoria's picture on it and a note on the inside of the parchment itself.

To whoever of my descendants finds this
you may need the money more than I do at
present. Good luck! I did the best I could.
Timothy Brennan   16/6/04

The money was well and good, and it must have represented a considerable savings in 1904, but where was the "One Eighth"? Could Joe have missed it on the first pass through the portfolio? Dare he go downstairs to search behind the toilet paper wall? How would he explain a return visit to the downstairs loo to Peter and Jill, and how could he get the 12"x 14" portfolio upstairs without them seeing it in his arms?

Joe returned to the bedroom and lay down on the bed again. Suddenly he got up and opened the closet door. He didn't want to turn on the light because Lorenzo may still be in the backyard, maybe naked, and Joe didn't want to remind Lorenzo that he, Joe, was in the house or show him where he was in the house. There was something on a hook on the back of the door. It felt like a robe, fuzzy, perhaps terry cloth or chenille. He hoped not chenille, but he had no choice. He put it on in the dark. It was a little short in the arms but it covered him with a bit to spare. He would go downstairs, and if there was anyone there, he would say there was no toothpaste upstairs, retrieve the portfolio from behind the toilet paper, tuck it in the front of the robe, hold his breath and return upstairs.

Joe tiptoed downstairs quietly only to see Peter leaning back in the little stuffed chair with Jill, kneeling between his legs, her head in Peter's crotch and his pants down below his knees. Peter looked horrified when he looked over and saw Joe almost down the stairs. Joe averted his eyes, even put his left hand up to his face to shield the view, or to let Peter know that he was not there to peep, and hustled around the corner into the downstairs bathroom. He turned on the light and saw himself in the mirror. He was wearing a pink and scarlet flowered chenille robe with white lace trim. Maybe the outfit was the reason Peter looked so shocked. Never mind, Joe leaned down and reached for the portfolio behind the toilet paper wall. Instead he knocked down the rolls of toilet paper, said, "Oh shit!" loudly, and crouched down to retrieve the wandering rolls.

From the living room he heard Jill say, "Who's that? Is somebody here, Peter? I thought you told me everyone was asleep. I'm going to go look to see who's here, Peter. Maybe it's that naked Italian gay guy." And with that she headed to the kitchen at the back of the house.

"Come back, Jill. Come back!" Peter cried. "I think that it was Joe upstairs. Perhaps he fell out of bed. Lorenzo is out back. The shower is still running. Come back, *honey*. Don't worry. We're safe here," Joe could hear Peter zipping up his pants as he followed her.

"No we're not safe, Peter. I'm going home. This place is nuts. Provincetown is crazy enough, but this house is just too strange. Take me home, Peter. I'm not even sure about you! Take me home! I live on Pearl Street, next to the Work Center."

"Maybe we could go upstairs, honey."

"Don't *honey* me. We just met," said Jill, who seemed to have forgotten that she had just been visiting between Peter's legs. "And I don't believe that Simone de Beauvoir always gave Sartre head either. I want to go home. If you don't take me, I'll run out the front door and scream."

Joe locked the bathroom door and reached far back on the shelf. He found the portfolio, put it on the shelf that held the sink above him, retrieved the toilet paper rolls scattered around him and put them back in two neat rows. He heard a door slam. Joe unlocked the bathroom door, looked out to the right and the left and then scurried up the stairs. It seemed that now he was the only one in the house, although Lorenzo may or may not still be in the backyard.

Once upstairs, Joe locked himself in the upstairs bathroom for the third time in five minutes. This time he turned on the lights beside the mirror over the sink. He laid the portfolio open on the sink, its ends resting on the flat of the sink. He looked carefully at each document but found no "One Eighth." He sat on the hopper, his head in his left hand, trying to figure out what to do next.

On the bottom shelf of the table across from the toilet there was a Teddy bear lying face down with its arms stretched out and its paws clutching a holy picture, Saint Joseph holding the baby Jesus, to be specific. Joe couldn't believe it. "How did he get in here? Where is he now? What am I to make of this?" Joe said aloud. "If he's become so holy, why can't he just leave me alone? I have to get out of this fucken Irish crazy business. This has to stop." Joe was thoroughly bewildered and sat on the toilet afraid to move a limb.

After much thought he figured out that he probably was safe, that Dino had sent many other threatening teddies—those with limbs pulled off or full of arrows—which resulted in no bodily harm to him. These ambiguously pious ones shouldn't threaten him either.

25 Passion at the Dick Dock

Finally, Joe went to bed, but not without a glance out the window. With the help of the giant lights guarding the school behind the house he saw Lorenzo passed out and naked on his back, in a chaise longue next to the hammock suspended from the two Chinese Elms in the backyard, Lorenzo's perfect long dick resting against his muscled right thigh, his chest covered with black hair like a pelt across his pectorals, the black hair grapevined down to Lorenzo's bush.

Joe was crazed with desire at the sight of Lorenzo. He knew that he touched Lorenzo at his peril. But there were "other fish in the sea" at this hour, more correctly sex-seeking men on the edge of the water at the Dick Dock under the Boatslip Beach Club and Hotel down Commercial Street heading to the West End. There was a time when Joe went to such places without fear, but then he had nothing to lose. Now he was a judge. He couldn't do what other men could. Usually he didn't want to either. But tonight was different.

He had heard that the police were doing "hands off" at the Dick Dock this year so long as the activity didn't move down the beach in front of the private houses to the west. When Joe had last been there years before his appointment as a judge, even before his ambition to become a judge, the sex scene was at the boatyard further west yet. The boatyard owner had complained to the police. Men were doing it under, on top of, and beside boats large and small. The Coast Guard station next to the boatyard was similarly unsporting about the nocturnal use of its pier.

So it was to the Boatslip beach that Joe walked, lured by passion, horny, to put it plainly. He walked along the beach from the wharf at the center of town. It was now 3:00 a.m. If the police came, he would say that he couldn't sleep and was taking a walk. He brought no identification, but pocketed a ten, a five and five ones, for what purpose he didn't know, but it gave him some security to have money.

There was no moon, but there were lights from the buildings he passed, Whalers' Wharf, the Marine Supply, Seamens' Bank, and the Post Office. As he got closer to the Boatslip he heard faint noises like the movement of sand and a whole variety of suction noises as well as murmurs and groans but he couldn't see anyone until he stuck his head under the deck. There must have been forty men there, in all sorts of combinations. One guy was completely naked getting fucked just to Joe's left. *Where did he leave his clothes,* Joe wondered? Another man was on his knees shirtless sucking off three men, two of whom were also naked. There were at least four circle jerks.

There didn't seem to be anyone near Joe's age. These were the studs and gym boys Joe had seen strutting down Commercial Street with their shirts off in the heat of the day. There were a couple of thin bald men with glasses looking on and a fat guy with tattoos wanking it all by himself in a corner, groaning quite effectively, almost as a chant to urge the others on.

Although, after he stopped worrying about the logistics, Joe became turned on, he was about to leave, thinking that he would not be anyone's desire in this crowd. All of a sudden he felt a hand on his chest from the right. "Ooh Daddy, am I glad you're here. Don't leave now; you have fans here. I saw you on the street with those beautiful French girls today. You can be my polar bear. What does Daddy want?"

All this came from a very solid young man, about 5´10", 180 pounds, round head, short hair, a wrestler Joe decided, who was himself being embraced by a taller, also well-built, black man. Joe's admirer continued rubbing Joe's chest with his one free hand, sneaking his hand under Joe's white Brooks Brothers' button down shirt, finding chest hair and moaning pleasurably. He pinched Joe's nipple, moaned "Fuzzy white daddy, let me at you," as he pulled away from the black man, who refused to be dropped. The black man opened up and moved forward, embracing Joe with his well-toned left arm. The wrestler smiled at this grace, kissed the black man and then Joe. Joe yielded. Joe rubbed the wrestler's hard chest, snuck his hand under the tank top and felt stubble from the stomach up. Joe pulled his hand back in unthinking revulsion.

The wrestler leaned into Joe's ear, alternately licking it and whispering into it, "I know. I'm sorry. I shaved for Drag Bingo. I was Carol Burnett."

Contrary to what Joe would have thought in more detached surroundings, like his study or his office, that revelation did not stop Joe. It did draw a smile and all three of them laughed before the wrestler put his hand down Joe's jeans and smiled at what he found. He and his dark mate then unbuckled Joe's belt, unbuttoned his pants, and zipped down Joe's fly. The wrestler dropped to his knees and put Joe's now erect dick in his mouth. He jumped up, leaned in Joe's ear and said, "I love uncut. Don't worry. Juan and I are safe. I hope you are."

That was more a question than an aspiration, so Joe, although unused to such verbal preliminaries, having cavorted in more tranquil days before the epidemic, replied, "I am too, thank God."

The wrestler returned to his knees and went at Joe as Juan unbuttoned Joe's shirt, rubbed his chest, squeezed his ass and kissed him. Joe soon came close to coming; he throbbed a bit and pulled out. The wrestler leaned back on his knees, smiled and pulled up his wife beater to take the load on his big, clipped, chest. Joe obliged and Juan rubbed it all over the wrestler's upper torso and then on his own chocolate pudding hairless chest.

The wrestler got up, smiled again and leaned into Joe's ear. Juan went cheek to cheek with Joe, on the other side, as if to listen. The wrestler said, "You're what we dream about all day."

Joe, ever the gent, replied, "Thank you very much and not just for the compliment. As I'm sure you know, 'It takes two to tango'—or in this case, three." He then smiled at Juan, who had been hitherto silent. Juan said into Joe's left ear, "*Hombre guapo, Muchas gracias, quiero besarte por toda la noche, Papi.*" "Handsome man, many thanks. I want to kiss you all night, Papi."

Joe buttoned up as the men watched. He turned to leave and they patted him on the back. "*Que tu suenas con los angelitos,*" "That you dream with the angels," Juan said.

Joe went home to bed. He walked Commercial Street on the way back. Joe vowed to get up early the next morning. He knew that he would awaken to take his first pill just before the last pee at sunrise and he could look again out the window at the sleeping Lorenzo, who lay in the hammock sprawled out like Rubens' *Dying Adonis*, but with body hair. That image and hope sent him to sleep with a smile. Joe never heard Peter come back. Maybe he had persuaded Jill to finish the job at her house. Joe hoped so. *Someone I know ought to be getting it tonight in this town full of sex*, Joe thought. *If only there was some way to get to Lorenzo....Don't even go there; don't even think about it,* Joe said to himself. *Besides he goes for little, muscley twinks and you've never been that. Have some humility, man. Know your place. You got yours tonight.*

When he woke up he looked out the window. Lorenzo was gone. At least he wasn't in the hammock. Joe couldn't see the entire yard for the leaves on the trees. From the other window he could see that Lorenzo's car was still in one of the neighbor's parking spots. Joe put on his clothes and went downstairs. There was no one in Peter's room so he stopped tiptoeing.

Joe made a cup of tea and then went back upstairs for the portfolio. He looked through it once again, even restored the 100-pound note, tied it with the red ribbon and went to the kitchen. He found a shopping bag in one of the lower cabinets and left the house by the backdoor, hoping to find a relic from Lorenzo in the backyard, although he never would have admitted that, even to himself. Joe walked around to the front and glanced into Lorenzo's car as he passed it. There was Lorenzo, asleep in the back seat with a red, blue and gold Hermès beach towel covering his thighs and hips.

Joe wanted to linger, hoping for a turnover that would displace the towel but reason prevailed and Joe went down the hill to Gabriel's Guesthouse still carrying the portfolio. It was now 8:30 a.m.

Maeve was there, all dressed for a run. Grainne was sleeping still. Joe asked Maeve to go over to the Bas Relief Park. They sat on a bench well out of earshot of anyone who might sit down, even though the park was now empty.

"There was nothing in there. I couldn't find your 'One Eighth'. Could it be somewhere else in the box that Nora gave you? Is it still in Ireland? Or is it in Paris? Did you bring it with you?" Joe asked.

Maeve replied, "Of course, it's not there. Do you think I'm an eedjit? It's safe. Believe me. It's safe. I'll not tell you where it is right now, but you'll find out soon. I'll go wake Grainne, then take my run. We can have breakfast. Didn't I promise to meet Lorenzo at the Café Heaven? You go sit at the 'Meat Rack' in front of Town Hall and read the *Times*. You can get it and a cup of tea at Adams' pharmacy. The large tea is only 70 cents. Don't worry about anything. We'll pick you up at half nine," she said looking at her yellow sports watch. "Grainne may arrive earlier. Give me the portfolio."

Joe was beside himself. What did she mean? How could she be so blithe about the whole thing? He did go to Adams' Drug and bought a cup of tea, 70 cents, and the *New York Times* for a dollar, and he did sit on the 'Meat Rack' with the other old timers. An attractive couple, Latin looking, sat down to his left; the woman was closest to him. After a bit she said, "Well, it burnt off; the haze burnt off."

Joe looked over. She was smiling at him. The man she was with was smiling as well. He said, "My name is Angelo; this is my wife Dina. Are you in town for long?"

"I'm not sure. I came to do an errand and it seems to be more complicated than I anticipated," Joe said, smiling weakly.

"Well, you just sit here and everything will resolve itself. The whole world goes by these benches," the kindly man said.

"This is where I met Angelo twenty years ago. I haven't been the same since. Neither has he," she added and they both laughed.

Joe decided that he had more than a half hour to kill and that the newspaper probably wouldn't interest him. He wouldn't be able to concentrate. So he might as well chat. These seemed like the first normal people he'd encountered in a few days. And more than that, they seemed kindly. He appreciated that they didn't probe, although they seemed to think that his was a romantic problem. Of course, at bottom, it was. Had he not been looking for love, or at least an assuagement of his loneliness, a while ago, his life would be different today. That much he realized. As he dwelt on this, he decided that Angelo was a bit of a looker, although a little older than Joe usually liked. But it was clear that Angelo was straight, and happy with his mate—just the way they behaved with each other told Joe that. They still laughed at each other's remarks. He finished her stories and *vice versa*. And they let each other do that.

Although Dina and Angelo didn't pry, they did manage to find out that Joe was a judge, that he was from Boston and that he was visiting a college classmate, Harvard, for a few days. They also watched his eyes wander into the passing crowd. Separately they each realized that Joe was gay and probably liked men at least fifteen years younger than he was, preferably tawny. Angelo and Dina did not acknowledge that they had the latter information, but they did store it away to tell each other later. They prided themselves on their acuity. Of course, the heterosexual presumption did not exist in Provincetown, so the gay observation was not rocket science. However, Angelo wondered if Joe was "out." He always wanted to know that. He had been a school superintendent, supervising many teachers, some of whom were gay and closeted and unhappy, and he thought he knew how hard it was for people to be "out." Even though it wasn't his battle he encouraged people to be "out." Sometimes his gay friends wanted to say to him, "You try being gay in straight America and then come talk to me about being 'out.'"

Joe also learned about Angelo and Dina. Angelo had been married before. He had three kids, all adults now. Dina was younger. She had been born in Cuba, came here when she was 10, learned English and taught it to her brother and sisters. She was a teacher, presently getting a Ph.D. in Latin American Studies. This year she was finishing her dissertation. It was their mutual interest in Education that brought them together after the initial meeting. She had been visiting Provincetown for the day with her mother. Dina and her mother sat on a bench in front of Town Hall next to Angelo. Angelo heard Dina and her mother speaking Spanish. He heard the mother ask Dina where they should eat lunch. Angelo interrupted and in pretty good Spanish he recommended the *Lobster Pot*. He then took them there and bought the two of them lunch, talking in Spanish as best he could, which meant with a bit of Italian. Dina gave him her telephone number in Boston and after a discreet two days he called her. They were married within three months.

In the middle of all this sharing, at about 9:20 a.m., Grainne came by, dressed in chartreuse Capri pants, red espadrilles, a big white shirt and a big straw hat. She leaned down, kissed Joe and said, "Well darling, are you ready for breakfast yet?"

Grainne and her glamour confused Angelo and Dina but they knew that one could take nothing for granted in Provincetown. They kept their confusion to themselves. Joe introduced Grainne and they greeted her kindly.

"We'll see you again, I'm sure," Angelo said.

"So interesting to meet you," added Dina with a big smile.

Joe knew that Angelo and Dina loved the variety of people that living in Provincetown allowed them to meet. Joe saw nothing wrong with that, although he usually didn't like being classified and categorized easily. He liked his own mystery and after baring his soul slightly with his opening remarks he tried to take it back, which is one reason he had not told Angelo and Dina that Grainne was his cousin and that he was gay. Let them think what they wanted, Joe mused, as he and Grainne walked west to the Café Heaven arm in arm.

"Were you trying to pass with those people, Joe?"

"Do you mean I wanted them to think that I was Protestant?"

"You know what I mean, Joe. Don't be clever. You *are* an enigma. Here you are the first openly gay Judge in America—it was in all the newspapers, I heard—and you won't be gay in front of a couple of strangers on the meat rack in Provincetown! You're deep, Joe," Grainne said.

Joe replied, "I'm not the first openly gay judge in America. That honor goes to His Honor, the Honorable Stephen Lachs, a very nice man in Los Angeles, California. And there were many after him in other states, particularly New York and California. I am the first openly gay judge, man or woman, in Massachusetts, the state we are in right now. Sometimes I get tired of wearing that badge. As far as I can see, being gay has little to do with my work. There are some uniquely gay situations that come up, but not frequently." Joe continued on this pedantic roll, like he had been saving this speech up for an occasion, which had never happened. So he was going to give it to this small audience, whether they liked it or not.

"And maybe there is a gay sensibility, a sideways way of looking at 'regular life,' as an observer watching the natives perhaps. I don't know. We humans are much more alike than we are different. Look how we seek respectability. Whoever would have thought of gay marriage ten years ago? It was important that 'being gay' no longer was a barrier to being appointed a judge and I'm proud that

I knocked down that wall. A lot of people followed me, mostly women. They were even sought by Governor Weld, who was determined to be a social liberal, although a Republican. I got a call asking for names of lesbians he could appoint. He did appoint one of them from Boston. She slipped right in. The funny thing is that another woman from the western part of the state, not known as a lesbian to the Judicial Nominating Committee but quite 'out' in Northampton, was appointed at the same time. So, he got two lesbians, maybe more than he wanted for his first appointments. Maybe not.

"Is all this too much information and too earnest for you on this beautiful sunny day in Provincetown as we plot how to outwit a family of beautiful, crazed Randozzas, now allied with Holy Mother, the Church?" Joe gratuitously added just as they reached the door of the Café Heaven. Grainne didn't answer, probably because she had stopped listening a few blocks back.

Maeve was inside the Café, looking like a picture in a fashion magazine wearing a spaghetti strapped, pink sundress. *These girls are too chic to be lesbians in Provincetown*, Joe thought. *There's not a bit of androgyny to them.* The usual lesbian look in Provincetown was the girl/boy, khaki pants and tee-shirt look.

Joe had little experience with Irish lesbians, or French ones either. Paris was probably the greater influence on Grainne and Maeve, he figured. On his last trip to Paris he had seen some very elegant tailored lesbians at Angelina's, the tearoom on the Rue de Rivoli, sipping *Chocolate Africaine* and eating *Pamplemousse sorbet* but they weren't as feminine looking as these girls.

"How did you get this way?" Joe asked as they sat down.

"What?!!" they both exclaimed.

"Just what way are you talking about?" asked Maeve. "Do you mean how did we become lesbians? That was easy. We've loved each other forever. From First Communion on we've been inseparable. In those days there were separate schools for boys and girls which helped. And as you know, for some Irish families marriage is an unnatural act." Maeve continued.

"As for the way we look, in Paris I worked for Valentino. Giancarlo Giammetti, his partner, liked my Irish white and pink complexion and my Dublin English. Grainne worked there too during showings to Americans and other English-speaking women. We Irish girls were trained to be polite, you know. Even the boys were. That training may be what's behind the Celtic Tiger. We still have civility as a virtue and we speak English—a strange but powerful combination in this nasty Anglophone world. Surely, these are unintended consequences of colonialism and oppression."

Grainne said, "If you're talking about our clothes, we really had no idea what to bring here. We knew that the summers were warmer in Boston and that Boston was a city, so we brought warm weather city clothes. We didn't expect to come to Provincetown; that was kind of last minute. Maeve thought that her classes started earlier than they did. Besides, we grew out of the tomboy look when we got to Paris. The women there, even the lesbians, just weren't interested in looking like that. Dressing well becomes second nature. It's not political surrender for me to look like a woman. The real butches in Paris wear men's clothes, but good men's clothes—like well-dressed men. Perhaps New York is more like Paris than here, no? Does our *chic* embarrass you, Joe?"

"No, *au contraire*," Joe laughed. "I love the way you look. I also like that it confuses people here. I'm sure that the couple I was just talking to when Grainne, looking so glamorous, arrived to take me away, now think that I'm at least bisexual, if not totally straight."

They all laughed at that and Joe explained his meeting with Dina and Angelo.

"I've seen that couple all over town, ever since we arrived," Maeve said. "They look very interesting. They were talking to Lorenzo the other day as we came to meet him at that same spot, the meat rack. I hope they're not part of the Randozza mob. The husband, Angelo you say, is Italian, you know."

"Not all Italians are in the mob, sweetheart," Grainne said.

"I know that, darling. I can't imagine Valentino as a Mafioso. He wouldn't wear their clothes, for one thing. I was just speculating."

"Now tell me about your 'One Eighth,'" Joe asked in a low voice, leaning across the table to Maeve.

"I mailed it," Maeve said, with a self satisfied grin.

"You what?" Joe asked. Grainne, sitting beside him, shared his surprise. "Maeve, what did you do?" she said.

"I mailed it to Tim Ronayne. Isn't that where it was going to end up? Why bother with all this middleman, heebie jeebie, mystery stuff! I just mailed it direct to Tim. I enclosed a lovely card of the sunset reflecting off the lighthouse out there," and Maeve looked to her right, where indeed the light house was, on the other side of the back wall of the restaurant. "This morning, after you left, I put it in an envelope with a card and as I ran by the Post Office I went in and mailed it. I had them weigh the envelope and bought the postage, two dollars and 40 cents, I think, to Ireland. There was a wonderful woman behind the counter. She wore an American Indian headdress, beautiful feathers and beads. She looked more African than Indian, but nevertheless. When she saw the Irish address she started to sing *The Wild Colonial Boy*. Very international, you Americans, even the earliest ones, it seems. As I left, she said, 'Goodbye, my dark Rosaleen! We'll get the *billet doux* to your sweetheart....' Then she looked down at the address and added, 'lucky Timmy Ronayne!' and looked up at me and winked. Whoever would think mailing a parcel could be such an adventure. And we don't have to worry about those dreadful people getting it now. It was not at all like visiting grumpy Mrs. Cadogan at the Post Office back home. She reads all the postcards, yet you're lucky if she says 'Hello.' Isn't that right, Grainne?"

Grainne just stared at Maeve, her jaw dropped. Joe looked the same. Then they looked at each other. Soon they began to laugh. Maeve joined in. People at other tables stared. They were causing a scene; Joe just knew it. The waiter came over to their table.

"Hi, my name is Brendan. I'll be your waiter today. Would you like coffee to start?" He never looked up from his order book.

They looked up at him, however, and began to laugh louder.

He was their messenger, Hermès, the angel, the man/boy who had warned them about Lorenzo the night before.

Brendan Pastorelli then lifted his beautiful head with his double eyelashed, chalcedony blue eyes, saw them and said, "Hey! How ya doin? Good to see ya! You guys!! You havin' a good time, I guess. Talk to me in Irish. Come on! I need an up this morning."

"*Póg mo thion*!" said Maeve and they all laughed harder, even Brendan. Who didn't know about the Irish band whose name that was? The Irish in England delighted whenever the BBC broadcast the band and announced the name in fruity, high Brit tones. Finally somebody told the BBC that the name meant "Kiss my ass!" and the band was forced to cut off its name to just "The Pogues," which it remains.

"I would, if you were a guy. Do you have a brother, who looks just like you, preferably about 28?" Brendan said. "What's so funny over here anyway?"

Joe, Maeve and Grainne looked at each other. Then Joe said, "We've just been relieved of a heavy burden. The laughter was relief. It's a long story, not over yet but certainly lightened. Pardon me if I'm being cryptic. I have to be. But we're so glad to see you. What's the best breakfast you have?"

"Would you believe it! The cook worked in Ireland. I'm sure that he could make an Irish breakfast. We don't have Irish bacon. Would Canadian do? It's either that or the fairy's native dish, Eggs Benedict. Them's the best breakfasts. I'd get the Irish; the hollandaise is sometimes too bland for me."

"I'll have the Irish," said Grainne.

"Me too," said Joe, "without the blood pudding, please."

"I've always been fond of the fairies; the Eggs Benedict, please. Just bring a little lemon and black pepper, if you will. Maybe I can chooch it up," Maeve said.

"Thanks guys. It's great to see you. You've made my day! I'll bring both coffee and tea." With that Brendan returned to the opening to the kitchen. Joe checked Brendan's now red Nike shod feet. There were no wings at the heels today.

"Well, what do we do now? The mystery is gone. I have no more tasks. I'll wait to hear from Tim Ronayne. I'll call him to tell him what's coming. He'll be glad for that. I'm still not sure what he's going to do with the complete page. He never really told me that," Joe said.

"Well, he could publish a picture of it and hold it hostage." Grainne said.

"For what? He could just as easily sell it at Christies or Sotheby's or the Irish equivalent and make the money at auction. Why the hostage stuff?" said Joe.

"Because there has to be a political statement. We're still rebels even though there's little left to fight these days. Ideally, he'd like the once Protestant Trinity to pay—reparations or something like that. However, everybody goes to Trinity now, Protestants, Catholics, Egyptians even," Grainne said.

"He could buy a lovely frame for it and put it in the parlor," said Maeve. "Of course, he'd have to have guards 24 hours a day. He could charge admission. It'd be almost as good as if the Blessed Mother landed in the rose bushes. They'd come from all over. Wasn't there a sighting over here last year? Breda Mulligan's aunt flew over and came back with lots of rosary beads and holy pictures."

Joe said, "That was a double-plated window in Braintree at a hospital. The seal broke and the moisture crept in. It did look like the Blessed Mother. One of my secretaries lived nearby. She rented her lawn for parking. It was tough getting decisions typed until her son took over the parking lot. Then, of course, some killjoy monsignor put in a new window."

"Ah, they're like that. That monsignor will never make bishop. You've got to play to their superstitions. Keep it ambiguous until it either fades away or catches on," Maeve said.

"Maybe he was afraid the moisture would evaporate and then

they'd all look foolish," said Grainne. "He was right to shut it down right then and there. 'Not all piety is well placed.' We learned that in school, Maeve. Do you remember when Ruth Healy claimed that she saw Joan of Arc in the copper beech tree at Dunbukulla? She took us all there and we didn't see a thing. Even the nuns went and they didn't see anything either. Monsignor Phelan shut it down. He almost made the owners of Dunbukulla cut down the tree just to get Ruthie sane. She never was right after that."

"Well, he didn't like Joan of Arc. She was too butch for him and she was foreign. If it had been one of the femmie Irish saints Ruthie saw, Dunbukulla would be the new Knock," Maeve replied. "The only foreign holy image that caught on in Ireland is the Infant of Prague, who wasn't an infant at all. He looks to me to be about eleven years old. 'What's up with that?' As you Americans say," Maeve said, looking at Joe.

Joe said wistfully, "I loved the Infant of Prague. I always wanted one. It would've been a legitimate way to play with dolls. He came with a set of dresses and capes that you could change with the calendar. My mother wouldn't permit him in the house, however. I think that she knew the real reason for my devotion."

"Mothers know these things," said Maeve. "They know them long before they will admit them to themselves or to others, least of all to their husbands."

Grainne said, "My mother saw me trying on my brother's trousers. She gave me a slap and said, 'Never let me see you do that again.' Maybe she meant that it was o.k. to do it in secret. That never occurred to me until now," Grainne added. "Which, of course, is exactly what I did do. I even called myself 'Danny' when I had his pants on, and his shirt."

Maeve said, "That explains your ratty underwear."

"And what explains your frilly bloomers? You're butcher than I am but you dress like a tart," Grainne asked, not entirely humorously.

"I like to keep them guessing," Maeve said. "Then I turn them over and give them a big surprise. Don't you remember, my sweet one?"

"I'm not sure I want to hear what the surprise is," said Joe. "What are we going to do with Lorenzo? He's going to be looking for your 'One Eighth'. His uncle sent him for it and he's so speeded up, he won't be satisfied 'til he finds it."

Maeve said, "You know that I made a Xerox of it."

"No, I didn't know that. How would I know that?" Joe said.

"Neither did I," added Grainne. "When did you do that?"

"I did it at the airport in Paris while you were having one last coffee. Remember we had a long wait for the plane; I was bored. I'd already exhausted the lingerie shops. So I went to the Internet café and made a Xerox. It's pretty good—color and everything."

"That's not going to fool Lorenzo, no matter how high he is. A Xerox won't do it." Joe said.

"I know. But, later on the plane I copied it on a piece of vellum."

"Where did you get a piece of Vellum, for Jesus sweet sake?" said Grainne. "I didn't see you do that," she added.

"Of course you didn't, darling. We didn't have adjacent seats. I was way up back and whenever I got up to visit you you were sound asleep."

"And the vellum?" Joe asked.

"I had it. I'd had it for years. In Art class with the Ursulines in Dundalk we had an assignment to do a piece of calligraphy—something pious. It didn't interest me. I never did it, but I kept the vellum. I had a mind to copy the 'One Eighth' ever since I got it from the family's bag that Nora gave me. About the same time that Nora gave me the bag I found the vellum in a box with some old oil paints from school. I took all of it, the family's bag, the vellum and the oil paints from Ireland to Paris and then to Boston. I'd been quite facile with oil paints in my day. I'd also done some *faux* finishing when I first came to Paris. It was easy money. I became quite good at reproduction—marble, *faux bois* and other stuff, even birch bark.

"I knew that I could reproduce the 'One Eighth's colors. I kept the paints in Nora's bag with some black ink, actually Sumi ink,

Japanese calligraphy ink. I thought that it would be interesting to use Japanese ink for an Irish manuscript—both islands on either side of the world, you know. I copied it on the plane. It was a smooth flight. I felt like a monk in a scriptorium. You know that all they did was copy. Sometimes they secretly made their own little additions—like an animal or a note in a margin. 'Marginalia' is what they call it. Scholarly tomes have been written about the marginalia in *The Book of Kells*. I didn't do any stuff in the margin; I copied just what was before me; I was a very good scribe, very serious," Maeve said, with a smile. "There was no one next to me and the flight attendants were fascinated. I had to convince them that the turpentine was not dangerous—that it was less toxic than the nail polish remover that the fat lady two rows over was using, and that it was much healthier because it came from pine trees."

"Maeve has always been good with stewardesses," Grainne interjected. "Once, on a trip from Paris to Dublin she brought seven large bags on as carry on. She told the stewardesses that the bags held her just deceased mother's precious china, and that she was bringing the china back to Ireland to distribute to her nine, now orphaned, younger brothers and sisters; that it was all their poor mother had been able to leave them, having been swindled by a no good French second husband. We were on an Aer Lingus flight and they loved the part about the no good second husband—French. Of course the bags were full of clothes."

Maeve smiled at this dubious praise and added, "So I copied the fragment right there on the plane. I did it. I still have it. I can show it to you—that and the Xerox of the original. They're in my bag. You can compare. I may have to age it a bit—rub some tea on the vellum—or perhaps coffee would be better. It still looks a little too new. Have you finished your cappuccino, Joe?"

Joe had given up being surprised by Maeve. But his face still showed astonishment. Grainne, of course, was used to such surprises and merely looked at her nails as if all this was everyday stuff.

Maeve reached into her big pink and green see-through Kelly

bag and pulled out something wrapped in a blue, white and gold Hermès scarf. There were lots of anchors and scallop shells on the scarf. She brushed aside an area on the butcher block table, even wiped the section clean with a napkin she wet from Grainne's water glass, dried the place with the other corner of the napkin and slowly lay the silken packet down.

She then looked at Grainne and Joe and said, "Should I open it?"

"Of course," both Joe and Grainne said in unison.

Maeve slowly untied the scarf. The fragment appeared. On one side it read "*Exeuntes emamu*" and then on the next line, "*nes etdabimuseis.*" There was an elaborate crouched cat at the 'E' of "*Exeuntes*" and a fish at the 'X.'

Joe knew that the page was complete. He spoke the Latin quietly.

This time it was Maeve who was struck dumb. She quickly recovered, however, pulled the Xerox and her copy of the original away from the now open scarf, and held both of them up. Maeve said, "What do you think? Does it need aging? I can use tea, coffee or burnt umber with just a little linseed oil. I think the black is too bold for what it's supposed to be—an ancient text. I'm not sure that I should have used the Sumi ink; it's almost too black. What do you think, Joe? Your eye is as good as Lorenzo's drugged eye will ever be."

"It's very beautiful. I want it. That's my first response," Joe said. "After that I think that you're correct. It looks too new, absolutely beautiful but new, almost as if Columkille's monks had written it yesterday. How did you learn the insular majuscule script?"

"Oh that! We had to practice that as an exercise every day in Irish Art class for Sister Dolores Veronique. She was French but had become a real Hibernophile. I loved that course. The lettering was easy to do after having done it 200 times before. 'Girls, we will now write as the holy monks did in Kells and on the lonely island of Iona, praising God with each stroke. Begin the alphabet, please. Then we will draw in praise of the holy virgin, Ursula.' That was the way she began each class. The lettering was the easy part.

It was the cat that was difficult," Maeve said. "I think you're right. Grainne, did you bring hair spray? I have to fix the paper before I distress it. Hair spray is good as *Fixatif*. That's a little artist's secret. The Sumi ink will run if it gets wet without being fixed and may even run if I wet it too much with the fix. This will be tricky but I think that I can do it. Just enough to hold the set against the wind; no lacquered look."

Grainne, who wore her brown hair naturally, or so it appeared, reached deep into her canvas, leather-edged, Coach bag and pulled out a small can of something labeled "Avalon Hair Mist."

Maeve took it, the manuscript, Joe's almost empty coffee cup, the scarf and her bag, stood up and said, "I'll be right back. This has to be done outside. The hairspray is toxic, you know." She hustled out the front door and turned left to go to the solitude behind the building. Joe and Grainne waited.

For some reason that she did not entirely understand, Grainne put the Xerox copy of Maeve's "One Eighth" into her own tote.

Good thing that! In came Lorenzo, all in white, like he'd fallen off a fashion shoot in Sardinia. He looked quite under the weather but he mustered his bravado, "Ah, my darling Grainne, you look beautiful today. Are we in Portofino in those beautiful green pants? And Joe, how do you keep your judicial dignity in this heat. You Northerners! Where is the lovely Maeve? I looked for her at that Amazon fortress you are staying in but they told me only that she'd gone to breakfast. I told them my name and they said there was no message. It's a good thing that I remembered that she liked it here."

"She told you to meet her here last night—just before you ran into Officer Krupke's daughter," Joe said, buttering his whole wheat toast. "Don't you remember?"

Lorenzo colored a little and then said, "Oh yes, I remember now. That is why I must have had it in my mind. Last night was so…how do you say, so distracting."

Maeve came through the front door with a big smile. She spotted Lorenzo, who had his back to her, and headed to the unisexual bathroom on the left. She had the scarf and something under it in her left hand and the hairspray and her Kelly bag in the right.

Grainne asked, "Lorenzo, my pet, are you alright this morning. You smell a bit peculiar. You Italians have some musky scents; very sensual, earthy, I'm sure. You were very odd last night and very agitated. You seemed troubled. Are you o.k.? Did you run into that imp of a boyfriend who treated you so badly? Was that what upset you so?" Grainne knew a hangover when she saw one and she also knew not to call it by name.

"Yes, Grainne, I saw him, I saw Brendan. He wouldn't talk and walked away from me. I went out. I need a cup of coffee—and a bloody Mary. Is there a waiter for this table," Lorenzo said as he twisted his head looking around the room.

Luckily, Brendan Pastorelli was in the kitchen and did not come out until Lorenzo had picked up Joe's coffee cup and began drinking from it. Brendan saw Lorenzo from the left side and darted back into the kitchen. Maeve exited the bathroom at the same time, sized up the situation and rushed over to Lorenzo. The scarf was now around her waist. The vellum was nowhere to be seen, nor was the hairspray or her expensive big bag.

"Darling Lorenzo, you poor thing! I hope that you are better today; you were so distressed last night. You'd think that you had too much to drink—like one of my brothers on a Saturday night. I hope that *bruta* of a peeler didn't harm you. The service here is terrible. We had some fop of a waiter—very cute, but irresponsible. Would you like to go next door to Bubala's? You can get a bit of 'the hair of the dog that bit you,' if you know what I mean. They don't serve alcohol here. It was a mistake to come here today. It'd been so nice two days ago," Maeve said, as she practically picked Lorenzo up and led him towards the door.

"*Scuzi un momento*, I'll be right back," and Lorenzo tried to pull away from Maeve towards the bathroom.

"Oh, Grainne, will you go to the loo and get my bag, please?" Maeve said. "I think that I left it under the sink.

Grainne complied. Grainne always complied. That is why their relationship worked. Even though some of the requests had been quite bizarre, Maeve had never asked Grainne to do anything unreasonable. Grainne knew why she had to get into the biffy before Lorenzo. Fortunately, Lorenzo was sometimes a gentleman and today he let Grainne precede him to the facility. He also knew that it wouldn't take her long to pick up a bag; that made chivalry easier.

Grainne returned with the big green and pink bag. Lorenzo lurched towards the bathroom. Maeve took the scarf from around her waist and covered the top of the bag's contents. "Time enough for him to discover the 'One Eighth'. It shouldn't be so easy; he should have to steal it. And I haven't completed the aging yet," Maeve muttered to herself.

Maeve stood just inside the screened front door with Grainne and Joe. Brendan stuck his beautiful head outside of the kitchen, blew them a kiss and retreated back into the kitchen. Maeve, Grainne and Joe went outside to wait for Lorenzo. He soon returned, looking remarkably more alert.

"Tina, crystal meth," they each thought to themselves. He went to do more crystal meth; that's what the trip to the john was about and that was the reason for his impatience.

They went over to Bubala's, Lorenzo with a girl on each arm and Joe straggling behind. The man at the gate, whose job it was to let people in, had a French accent; his name was Guy. He made them wait a little too long for Lorenzo. "We need a table now, Guy. I'm dying for a cup of coffee and a bloody and the ladies are Irish and can't take the sun."

"Ah, *cheri*, we have no tables right now. You can get a bloody at the bar inside the door. I'll take care of the Irish girls. Come in under my umbrella, darlings. And I'll give their granddaddy a chair," the *maitre d'* added, looking at Joe.

Lorenzo took him up on it and went to the bar.

"He's not a very nice man. What are you beautiful girls doing with that worm? Do you want a table or do you want to escape? I can delay him until the boat leaves or you can take a cab to the airport. That guy is, *comme se dit* in the States, 'bad news,'" Guy said.

"Thanks for your concern, but we'll take a table," Joe said.

Guy's eyebrows lifted as if to say, "O.K. if you want to be stupid," and he led them to a table in the shade, with an umbrella nevertheless. A waitress appeared promptly and they ordered breakfast with tea all around.

"Could you please put the tea in teapot and throw in two extra teabags, dear one?" Maeve asked with her best pleading smile. Then when the waitress left she said, "Americans drink such weak tea. Does it have something to do with that 'Boston Tea Party,' Joe?"

"No, Maeve, there is no political significance to our weak tea or our weak coffee, for that matter. The Boston Tea Party was about the British taxes on the tea. I think that the weakness of the tea may be a part of the Puritan legacy of avoiding stimulants. Mormons avoid them entirely; the rest of us just drink them weaker, although that's not the case for alcohol, except in lousy bars."

"And you don't drink. Why is that?' Maeve asked.

"I do drink occasionally but I don't do it well, so I avoid it. My family, like many Irish families, has more than enough alcoholics. It's been the cause of a lot of heartache. I have uncles who haven't been out of their pajamas in years. They stay at home behind the curtains and my aunts, their wives, either drink with them or cover for them. I don't have a wife to do either."

"Oh, we all have uncles like that," Maeve said. "In Ireland it's part of life. My father stayed home and drank. As a child I used to have to go get him his pints. It was dreadful," Maeve said. "We lost the farm to drink. I seem to be able to handle the stuff, but I'm careful. Grainne doesn't drink at all."

"Why not, Grainne?" Joe asked.

Before she could answer Lorenzo appeared in the doorway, with a big smile, carrying a tray with four bloody Marys.

"I think the best thing is just to humor him until we get to Boston and he finds the phony," whispered Joe, leaning down to pick up the napkin he had thrown to the ground. "He'll leave you alone after he gets what he wants."

"Greetings! I come bearing gifts. The bloodies are particularly good here. I think it's the celery salt."

Joe decided to just let his sit, but Grainne declined, "Darling, thank you very much but I am allergic to…tomato juice."

"Oh good, another one for me," Lorenzo said.

The conversation soon turned to their departure. They decided to leave at 4:00 p.m. Someone had told Joe that was the best time to leave. Joe tried to persuade the girls to come with him. Lorenzo was insistent that they ride with him. Lorenzo even offered to pick up their bags after they ate. "My Saab is very comfortable. I'll be lonely all alone. I'll just take a little nap after brunch and I'll be set to go. Joe, my friend, I'm so sorry you'll have to drive alone. You can think jurisprudential thoughts. Maybe you'll meet someone between now and four to help you with the ride. I am sure that lots of young men have to return to the city to turn the wheels of Commerce."

Return to Boston 26

While waiting for four o'clock Maeve aged her fragment with burnt umber, linseed oil, ashes and coffee grounds, then some more hair spray.

Joe walked around town trying to decide what would be the best place for Maeve to hide the "One Eighth" so it could be found.

Grainne took a nap at Gabriel's while Lorenzo passed out at the fashionably spare Young's Court condominum he had rented for the season. However, he eventually came to and a few minutes after four he appeared in his black Saab at Gabriel's Guest House. He rang the bell and the girls came down in linen dresses, Maeve in lime green and Grainne in raspberry. They each were carrying Pashmina shawls in complementary colors—in case the air conditioning in the car was too much. That was Grainne's caution, "We'll freeze in that beautiful car, Maeve darling. You know these Americans. They prefer air conditioning to God's good air," she said.

Joe told Maeve where to hide the fragment, which hadn't dried fast enough until Maeve put the hair dryer to it. He approved of the patina. "Maeve, put it in the pocket inside your suitcase where you keep your dirty lingerie. Make him work for it. Wrap it in your laciest panties. He'll find it, but he won't be happy about it. And Grainne, give me the Xerox, please. Maeve, you must promise to paint me a copy. I will give you back the Xerox in a few days so you can copy it. I don't want to make Lorenzo suspicious if he finds it."

They all were interested to see how Lorenzo was going to search the bags without them knowing it.

They didn't have long to wait. Lorenzo's car was stopped in Truro, just over the line from Provincetown at High Head by the same cop who had stopped him the night before, Clemmy Souza's daughter, the not so lovely Officer "Meany" Souza, she of the unibrow, sideburns, and not so faint mustache.

Meany said, "Oh, you again! I've followed you since Snail Road. You were going fifty in a forty mile per hour zone. License and registration and get out of the car." She led Lorenzo to the back of the car and then said, "Open the trunk." Once the trunk was open she said, "Open the bags." Lorenzo did. She then took off her black leather gloves and rummaged around in them. Finally she got to Maeve's lingerie pocket, which was probably all she really wanted to put her hands on in the first place. She felt around amongst the silk with pleasure until she hit something hard and pulled it out. "What's this?" she cried as she unwrapped its lacey wrapper. Not waiting for an answer, she handed the "One Eighth" to Lorenzo for identification.

He thought fast. "It's, uh…it's part of a relic that the Irish girls have brought from Ireland as a gift to His Eminence, the Cardinal Archbishop of Boston. It's…it's…from a holy book—very old and very sacred. It's being protected by the soft silk, as you can see. I can carry it now. Thank you very much." He was telling the truth as he thought it was, and would be if his people prevailed.

Lorenzo didn't protest the illegal stop, but he just had to let Officer Souza know that he knew what the rules were and that he thought she was breaking them. He puffed himself up and said, "I'm sure that you believed that this automobile stop and resultant exigent search were necessary, but, as you can see, we have no contraband and we are anxious to get to Boston before the traffic becomes too heavy."

"O.K. Go ahead but don't speed no more," Officer "Meany" Souza said reluctantly, a little intimidated by Lorenzo's knowledge of the buzzwords regarding legal automobile searches.

Lorenzo smiled in triumph. He didn't know how much of this conversation Grainne and Maeve had heard or what they had seen. He didn't care. What were they going to say? "Give me back my fragment from *The Book of Kells*! The piece that my great great grandfather stole as he torched the Big House!" Not likely. Lorenzo had the "One Eighth" tucked tightly in the left side pocket of his Hugo Boss black slacks; those which wrapped his bum so well and practically made his privates public. Better yet, he hadn't had to do anything sneaky to get it. "Thank you, Meany!"

The girls had heard. At least Maeve had, and she quickly told Grainne. "He's got it," she whispered. "The butchy cop found it for him. I hope he doesn't make us walk home now."

Joe passed by and saw Lorenzo outside his car with Meany. He drove a little further and then turned around in case Lorenzo was locked up and unable to get the girls to Boston. Not to worry, Lorenzo passed him before Joe got back to the sight of the stop. Joe did another U-turn and followed at a great distance. Lorenzo was at risk for getting stopped again, especially if he was hungover and panting for another tweek, Joe decided. *These girls might need me*, he thought.

The girls didn't need Joe. Lorenzo drove very carefully for the rest of the trip and delivered the girls right to the door of the Nurses' Residence on Charles Street. He even carried their bags into the lobby. They all kissed goodbye with great effusion and promised to call each other soon. Lorenzo then headed for the North End.

Shortly thereafter, Joe parked his old station wagon in the Underground Garage of the Boston Common and walked over to the Nurses' Residence.

Lorenzo meanwhile, a few miles away, was proudly unwrapping

his find in front of Uncle Dino on Charter Street in the North End.

Dino said, "Well Lorenzo, you did a good job. Now we have to get the other seven pieces. I'm sure that they're in Louth. Tim Ronayne hasn't been out of the county in months. Of course, he knows the terrain much better than we do. And those bastards have been hiding guns in the Mourne Mountains for years. Hiding seven of these pieces would be easy. Your aunt isn't going to be any help. She knows that we're not helping the Fireboys anymore. Those fucken Irish talk. Young Maureen, her daughter, won't even talk to me now. I like that kid too. She used to live here with me, for Christ's sake. But I guess we know where her loyalty is.

"Maureen did tell me about you, however," Dino added, leaning towards and close into Lorenzo. "You're using again, huh? This time you're going out west. We're sending you to Minnesota, and not to that queer joint. You'll go to Hazelden. They just started a special unit for guys like you. Crystal meth! We don't even sell that shit! Who's going to take over this family? You're on drugs; your cousins think they're debutantes, and that's just the men, and the half Irish ones hate me. His Excellency, Bishop Rocco, can't run the enterprise from Hartford, even if he wanted to. What's the point? The Irish Monsignor wants me to go to Rome and live with him. I can get an apartment near my mother's and he can slip in and out. I go for him, but living like that is not the life for me. I need some action. And we can't just give up our businesses here. I had hopes for you—in spite of your high rolling bullshit. I thought that little cutie pie Brendan Pastorelli would straighten you out. Instead you fucked that up too. We hear about everything, Lorenzo. There's no place to hide."

Lorenzo knew better than to interrupt his Uncle Dino, even if Dino had gotten religion and was no longer so threatening.

"There's a bag packed for you. Anthony will take you to the airport. He's going to Minnesota too. After he leaves you at Hazelden he'll stay there. I got him a nice place and a big-boobed, blonde Norwegian girl for the six weeks you'll be there. And Lorenzo, we have friends there too. So, don't even think of using. No fucking around! You did a good job here, with this 'One Eighth' piece, but you were sloppy and we can't afford that. So get clean and stay clean. There's a future for you if you do, I can tell you. We're going to turn this operation around. We're going legit. We can afford to."

◊ ◊ ◊

Back on Charles Street, Joe and the girls were having tea in the Beacon Hill Bistro. The girls were laughing about Meany Silva and her moustache. "I guess that means that we aren't P.C.," said Grainne. "You Americans are so worried about that stuff."

"Well, a lot of people have suffered from being made fun of," Joe explained. "Even your Irish cousins when they came here were ridiculed. We have to learn to tolerate each other over here, accept each other even. After the Famine, when the poor Irish were pouring into Boston they were caricatured as apes and monkeys—just like the South portrayed blacks, interestingly enough. Sometimes the very people who were trying to free the Negro slaves were trying to keep the Irish out of the country and they used any means to do it, even, if not especially, ridicule. And for too many of their descendants it's not much different. At Harvard, just across the Charles River, in the Hasty Pudding Club, the year after I graduated, I was in the company of the scion of one of Boston's best families, a descendant of the man who led the 'colored' troops in the Civil War, the Colonel who is riding the horse on the beautiful St. Gaudens monument across from the State House up the street— and you know what he said?" Joe was really on a roll now. It was obvious he was very aroused—and conflicted by this incident. "I heard that bastard make a slurring remark about the Irish waitress. What I'm ashamed about is that I didn't throw my drink in his face. I was the guest of a friend who was a member of the club, but that's no excuse, I realize now. My friend should have said or done something but he's a Yank too, a Catholic Yank, but a Yank, nevertheless. I should've thrown the drink and walked out. It was, and is, even worse for the Blacks or the Latinos, even the Chinese. You girls didn't come from a multiethnic community. You don't understand."

Maeve jumped in, "Lighten up, Joe. What do you mean we didn't come from a multee-ethnic community? There was that Eyetalian, Vittorio, who ran the restaurant in Dundalk. Half the girls in town wanted to bop him. I think he was gay, but nobody believes me. They say he had a wife back in Abruzzi, but I always doubted it. And the Chineee had two restaurants and a laundry; there was an Indian restaurant too. Nobody wanted to bop them, however, except Kathy Mahoney did get up the pole by Jawarahl, the Indian's son, who was gorgeous, and she has a lovely little brown baby now. Of course, they sent Jawarahl back to Jaipur and let Kathy keep the baby. The priest would have killed them if they hadn't. 'It's better than buying a Mission Baby,' somebody told Kathy. I'm not sure she thinks so. But, you're right we weren't big on the mixing—especially with the Protestants ready to shoot us for all these centuries."

"But let's have a few laughs, even if it's at the expense of our sister Meany," Grainne added. "You must admit she's not going to be winning this year's Rose of Tralee contest."

"And if Meany didn't want the moustache, she could do something about it. This is the twenty-first century, for Jesus' sweet sake," Maeve jumped in. "She could borrow some depilatory from those boys down there who are dehairing their tits and be done with it. She could shave it off! It's not that she has to have a moustache. Nobody does," Maeve added.

"I saw at least one electrolysis joint in Provincetown. From the looks of the men I saw bare chested in Provincetown, you'd think they sprang from boyhood to 35 without a pubic hair. It's not natural!" Grainne said. And they all laughed.

Joe said, "They all look alike with their shaved chests. They ought to keep the shirts on and take their pants off. Then you really could tell the difference."

They laughed again. "I guess that we just have to wait to hear from Tim Ronayne then. How long does it take for mail to get to Dundalk from here?" Joe asked.

Revelations at the Dolmen

Three days later, on Saturday, in Dundalk, Tim Ronayne went to the Post Office in response to a notice that there was a special delivery package waiting for him. Grainne had sent the package to Dundalk because they weren't quite as nosy in Dundalk as they are in Ballyfirglin. Dundalk is almost a city rather than a hamlet. Nevertheless the postmistress in Dundalk didn't have any compunction about inquiring, "Is it a packet from the girls you're getting, Tim?"

Of course she knew it was. The return address was "Grainne Lavin, 24 Charles Street, Boston, MA, 02110, U.S.A." and any fool, including the postmistress could read it, as she had. She had even shaken the packet. But it was too well wrapped to rattle. Maeve was no fool. Following Joe's advice about how to conceal the fake "One Eighth" she had also wrapped the real "One Eighth" in silk panties, green, white and a pale orange, like the Irish flag, and then tied a scarf around the whole thing before putting it in the padded envelope and marking it "Please do not fold or bend." It was the same scarf Maeve had worn in Provincetown, the nautical one—with anchors for faith and scallop shells for the pilgrims to *Santiago de*

Compostella. It didn't matter to her that such piety may not have been what *M'sieur Hermès* had in mind when he designed it. Perversely, its religious symbolism came to Maeve's mind after she'd "borrowed" the scarf during a photo shoot in Paris.

Tim took the package without answering the postmistress—giving her the old Irish chill. Ignore the nosy bitch. Pretend you never heard her. She doesn't really exist. He walked over to the Courthouse and sat on its steps. He thought a bit. His heart was racing. Although he had a plan, he hadn't told the other Fireboys. He had to execute the plan.

Some minutes later he got up, passed the rebel statue, turned right and went into Kelly's shoe store at the corner. He asked Mrs. Kelly inside for an empty shoe box.

"Of course, Tim. Didn't you just buy those lovely ECCO shoes here last month. I hope they're serving you well. They look handsome on you. Do you care which brand shoebox? We've got some very elegant ones back here," Mrs. Kelly said from the backroom.

Young Kelly, her grandson, who looked about 16, leaned on the cash register while his grandmother moved around out back. He just stared out the window, probably wondering why the fuck he was in this musty old shop on such a fine day and not out shagging his girlfriend.

Finally Mrs. Kelly came out. She bumped the young one out of his inertia as he leaned on the cash register and said, "James, go get Mr. Ronayne a bag for his shoebox."

The young one came back with a bag too small. Tim whispered, "Don't worry, Jim. All I need is the box." The young one smiled gratefully. "We'll see you, Mrs. Kelly. The shoes are just fine," Tim said as he went out the door.

Tim put the package in the box as he walked up Market Street to the Sports Store, which was all modernized up. Tim selected two things, a jockstrap and a pair of athletic shorts. The jockstrap was one of the modern ones, not one of those made of string that got abrasive on your balls when you sweated. This one was made of very soft cotton and it hugged you "as if your privates were resting on a cloud." At least, that's what the box said it would do.

He left there, returned to his car and drove to the Leisure Center at the Dunbukulla Hotel. It was also a health club for the locals, and many of Tim's pals, many Fireboys, were members. Tim took the shoebox with the package into the locker room as well as his gym bag. He locked both of them in his locker after he changed into the new jockstrap and new shorts. The box was right about the jock; it did feel like his balls were resting in a cloud.

Tim knew that if he sat in the Jacuzzi soon enough one or more of the Fireboys would come in.

Sure enough, Sean Murphy, a fisherman from Carlingford and young Peter Lavin, from the Ballyfirglin Marsh farm across the road came by. Peter was Maeve's first cousin and a cousin of Joe Lyons as well. From the looks of him Peter had been working out. He was 35 years old, about 5′9″, 160lbs, pale white skin, short black hair thinning in front and beautiful green eyes. He worked out almost every day and ran three times a week. It showed. His snowy puffed chest was covered with silky black hair, which shot down in a line to his narrow waist and navel and then spread out a bit as it went under the shorts. His legs were also covered with black hair. Tim had seen him naked. His bum was as white as milk and he had a nice, proportional uncut dick. Interestingly, Tim had noticed, Peter shaved his balls, which was not yet the fashion in County Louth.

Tim was glad that Peter was with Sean because he would be tongue-tied alone with Peter in the Jacuzzi. Legs would touch underwater and eyes meet across the tub and Tim wouldn't know what any of it meant, if anything. Tim had hopes but Peter had given him no reason for them, except a lot of easy, noncommittal smiles. The story was that Peter had had a girlfriend for years, a model, but she worked in Dublin. Supposedly Peter went down every weekend to visit her. She rarely came up to Louth. Actually, nobody had ever seen her. Not much else was said about them— not even the color of her hair. Peter lived at home with his father, also named Peter, his mother and two his sisters at a house on the farm on the Marsh that his grandmother had let his father build. Peter's uncle and two aunts also had houses on the farm. It was like the Kennedy compound, on a smaller, less grand scale.

Sean Murphy was big, husky, garrulous and frizzy. He was strong as an ox, and almost as unattractive—at least to Tim. He had bad skin, a big nose and always looked untidy. Sean had a wife and six kids. That was why he went to sea and came to the Jacuzzi. He needed peace away from them and he loved being with the boys, his mates. Everyone in the Club liked him. He was everyone's best friend. If anyone new came in, Sean was on him like a sauce and he found all about the newcomer. Why, last week he had even introduced Peter to one of Peter's American cousins who Sean met and chatted up in the Jacuzzi.

After the obligatory manly greetings and after the new arrivals adjusted themselves in the tub Tim whispered, "It's arrived; the last piece is here."

There was a silence. Then Sean said, "What the fuck do we do now?"

Peter said nothing. Peter always said nothing.

Tim said, "You both have cellphones. Call the boys. We'll meet at the Dolmen in a half hour. Have some of them pretend to be golfing and meet us at the third tee, which is right next to the Dolmen. We have some important decisions and I can't make them alone."

◊ ◊ ◊

There was an informer, Tim thought. There's always an informer in Ireland. The young Kelly Boy, James, who Tim had just seen in his grandmother's shoe store, was up at the Dolmen when Tim and Sean and Peter arrived.

Sean chatted the boy up as if all four of them were tourists who'd just found their way to Diarmuid's Dolmen.

"Grand day! No?" Sean said as he nodded to young Kelly, who nodded back wordlessly in agreement.

"Have you been here before?" Sean asked.

The boy nodded affirmatively, but still spoke nothing.

There was silence for a bit. More of the Fireboys arrived. The three plasterers in their white encrusted overalls came up the path next to the golf course. They all looked at the boy like "Who the hell is this kid?" as the Kelly boy remained silent and motionless.

"Are you waiting for something, James, for Christ's sake?" Sean said finally.

The boy blushed. He said, "I'm waiting for my friend. He's supposed to be here at five o'clock. He's late, I guess. I hope I'm not intruding or anything."

More Fireboys appeared at the third tee, some carrying golf clubs. Still the Kelly boy stayed, looking at Sean's watch every once in a while.

"And who's your friend?" Sean asked.

"His name is Peter."

"And what does he look like?"

"I'm not exactly sure. I think he's average height, well-made and has green eyes and black hair. He said he'd be here at 5 o'clock."

"What do you mean you're not sure? He's your friend, right?"

"We've never really met. We've talked on the computer. He said that he'd be here. We've been chatting for about a month, now."

"Oh, that computer stuff," Sean said. "My oldest has been looking at porno. We had to unplug the goddamn thing. How old are you, anyway?"

"I'm eighteen. I'm eighteen. I'm legal. I turned eighteen two months ago."

Finally Sean realized what Tim and some of the others had picked up earlier. This was a date—an assignation. And the poor lad had been stood up.

Sean said, "Well it's now 5:30 and we're up here to reset the second hole on the golf course. You're welcome to help us. We have to begin soon before it get's dark. If you want to run along, that's o.k. too and we'll tell 'Peter' if he comes by. Something must have happened to delay him. Did he have your phone number?"

"No, I never gave him that. My granny is always answering the phone."

The boy walked sadly back down the path.

When James Kelly was out of earshot Tim began, "We have the last 'One Eighth'. It's in the package in this box, which came from that lad's granny's shoe store, by the way. He's young Jim Kelly from Dundalk. His father, God rest his soul, was a Fireboy, some of you will remember. The boy was in the shop today when I got the box. I think it's just coincidence that he's here, but if anyone has a problem, let's hear about it. Otherwise I'll unwrap the last 'One Eighth' and show it to you all. I also brought the other pieces. We can put them all together."

"Open the fucken package, Tim! Put them all together," Sean Murphy said. "We've only been waiting for this day 150 years and more. We can't let the serendipitous presence of that poor wee lad stop us now."

Sean looked around at the others. They too were eager. There must have been a dozen of them there now. Peter Lavin looked pale, but that may have been his way of looking excited.

Tim spread his jacket on the ground, inside out. He put the box next to it. He then opened the box and took out the packet. He handed it to Sean. "Sean, you open it. I shouldn't be doing everything here."

Sean leaned down, then went to his knees. He picked up the package, squeezed it and said, "I hope that what you say is in here is in here, Tim. This could be a bomb, a gelignite bomb! Okay, okay. I'll open it, but if it's a fucken bomb, Tim, I'll kill you."

Everybody laughed nervously.

Sean proceeded slowly. He pulled the string as indicated but, of course, it broke halfway around. He then separated the package delicately, as if he were opening a fig. Finally the top came off and Sean reached in. He pulled out the package with the scarf. He put it to his nose. "It smells fine, like a rich woman."

The other men smiled. Sean lay the folded scarf on Tim's jacket.

He began to open the folded scarf when he said, "Peter, I'll let you do the honors."

Peter, still pale as a ghost, knelt down beside Sean. He looked around, hesitated and then reached over to pull off the scarf.

Just then someone came running up the path, hidden by the evergreens. "Jimmy, Jimmy Kelly! Are you still here? My sister took the car. She said it was an emergency and I had to ride my bike. I hope you're still here." He passed the tall evergreens that had blocked his view of the dolmen and the view of the men at the dolmen from him. He was a well-made young man with black hair and green eyes. He looked at the men, stopped short and ran back down the path.

Sean Murphy ran after him. "Peter, Peter," he called, and Sean could be heard all the way back to the hotel.

"What's all that about?" said one of the plasterers.

"I think that the lad is his son Peter," Peter Lavin said quietly.

"Well, are we going to see this thing or not?" said another of the plasterers.

"Tim, you do it," said Peter Lavin, rising to his feet.

"Sure," said Tim, knowing the fright that Peter Lavin just went through. He shook open the scarf and the tricolored panties scattered all over the jacket, even onto the ground. The men roared, even Peter Lavin, now off the hook.

"I should've known that Maeve Sand would do something like this, turning our sacred moment into a strip show. She's some girl. Maybe you should marry her," Tim said to Liam, the biggest of the plasterers.

"And maybe I should jump off the Needle on O'Connell Street. She's a tough woman and it's a stronger one than me that's going to tame her," Liam said.

In all the banter and excitement everyone forgot why they were there. It was just laid out before them, on Tim's jacket in an envelope from Gabriel's Guest House in Provincetown, Massachusetts, the United States of America. Tim picked it up and opened it. There it was—the last "One Eighth." It read, "*Exeuntes emamu,*" then the next line, "*nes etdabimusei*s." And there was an elaborate striped cat at the 'E' of "*Exeuntes*" and a fish in the 'X' heading to the cat's mouth.

Tim knew just where the piece fit. He opened his gym bag and then a manila envelope. He put its contents down on his jacket very carefully and pieced the whole thing together. This "One Eighth" was the next to last eighth on the left column of the page. Tim knew it and Tim put all the pieces in order.

There was a silence among the men. About this time it began to get dark.

"Well, men, what do we do now?" Tim asked softly in the setting sun.

"We take the bloody parchment to Trinity College and make the fucken Protestant bastards give us 10,000,000 punts," Jimmy O'Connor, an old timer, shouted.

"There aint 'punts' anymore; It's euros we got now. And the Protestants don't run Trinity anymore, Jimmy," Liam, the plasterer, said. "My own nephew, Alan Moran, studied there, and he's a Catholic farmer's boy like most of us."

"Well, we'll let him show us the way to the money then and whatever snots are in charge!" Jimmy O'Connor roared. And they all laughed.

When the laughter quieted down Tim quietly said "I have a suggestion."

"And what's that Tim?" more than one of the men shouted.

"That we take pictures of 'The Page', very good photos like Larry, the photographer, takes at weddings; that we put 'The Page' in a safe place, a very safe place; and then we call a press conference and announce that we are going to sell it for the benefit of the people of the area to the highest bidder. It'll be a coup, a veritable coup. We'll let 'The Market' decide. That's the Irish way these days of the 'Celtic Tiger.'"

"And what's the 'safe place,' Tim? Your Swiss bank?"

Laughs again, but not so hearty.

"Maybe," Tim responded with a sly grin. "First, we have to get some expert to authenticate the thing. We know what we have, but if we're going to go on the world market, we have to get an expert and have him write up his opinion. And it probably should not be someone from here."

"Who else knows Irish Manuscripts but Irish scholars?" said Liam.

"There are Irish Scholars everywhere now—even in Japan," Tim said. "Well, the best manuscript people are in Rome, because they have the best ones, short of ours."

"Not Rome. They're our rival and much too crafty. Rome has rarely been our friend. Remember Dermot McMurrough."

"Who the fuck can remember Dermot McMurrough? He was around in 1138, for Jesus sweet sake!"

"He got Rome to let him bring the English in. And the English Pope couldn't wait to turn on us."

"Well, it won't be a Roman then, even though they're good scholars in this field. And it won't be an Englishman either, even though they have a few manuscripts themselves," Tim said, smiling knowingly, letting the process send the decision where he wanted it to go.

"Yeah, the Brits stole them from us."

"And we don't know the Japanese guy. Or is it a girl, Tim? I've always liked those little China dolls myself, Tim."

"So what are you thinking, Tim?"

"Yeah, what's up your sleeve?"

"Share it with us," Paddy said sarcastically. He'd been watching American talk shows.

"At Boston College, in the States, there's an Irish Studies Department. They've got a whole mansion to themselves and there's a man there, who studied in Ireland at University College, Dublin. His name is Padraig Barmerian. He was the assistant curator of *The Book of Kells* at Trinity a few years ago. His mother is from Donegal and his father was Armenian."

"Armenian? How did that happen?"

"An affair of the heart, Jimmy! An affair of the heart! There's no explaining those things. They happen all the time in America."

"Christ, I've never seen an Armenian. What do they look like, Tim?"

"They look fiercer than they are—dark and swarthy, burning black eyes."

"Like the 'Pakis' in London, or the Patels at *The Punjab Restaurant* in Dundalk?"

"They're tougher looking than that. They've suffered, like us. The Turks massacred a lot of them in the early 1900s. Many escaped to America, like us. Some of them are Catholics but more are Orthodox. This one is Orthodox so he has no truck with Rome."

"It sounds like you've talked to him Tim," Liam said suspiciously.

"I haven't and I wouldn't until you men tell me to. I did do some research on him on the Internet, however. It's grand what you can find out about people without them knowing it. After I went through a list of Irish manuscript scholars I 'googled' him."

"You'd better not tell your mother that," teased Sean. "It'd turn her gray. That sounds like a confessable sin. Did it feel good—the googling?"

More laughs. Half of these guys had never touched a computer. The other half were on it all the time, and not 'googling' Irish scholars, at least not with their other hand.

"I'll take some pictures, Tim, and you go see this man. Check him out and we'll go from there," said Larry the photographer.

"Is that a motion?" said Liam. "If so, I second it." Liam looked around the group quickly for a protest: then said, "All 'ayes!'"

Liam was the most skeptical of the lot, so it was good that he was pushing the motion. His support added credibility to Tim's suggestion. He'd be Tim's rival but he knew that Tim was smarter.

There were all 'ayes.' That's how much the men trusted Tim—and Liam.

Sergeant Detective Shaughnessy Does Extra Duty 28

A few days later, in Boston, Joe sat at his desk in his office in the recently renovated Old Courthouse, now called *The John Adams Courthouse*, in Pemberton Square, trying to draft an opinion which would rule that the suspicion that you'd been given a blow job while in a drunken stupor because your dick was hanging out of your pants when you came to, and it was wet, is not sufficient provocation to kill the guy lying on the floor across from you.

Why did I ever take this job, Joe thought, not for the first time in his 15 year judicial career.

There was a knock on the door. It was after work hours and Joe thought that he was alone. Joe was about to call Tommy Murphy to tell him that he'd be late for supper. The knocker was a law clerk, Allesandro Pantaleone.

"Judge, there was a call for you at the Receptionist's desk, Ms Pomeroy's desk, the front desk. I was walking by so I picked up the instrument. Everyone has departed the premises except you and me. Or is it 'you and I?' I thought you'd retired for the evening as well. The caller said he was Sergeant Detective Shaughnessy.

He didn't give a first name. Hmmm? There can't be more than one. Anyway, he'd like you to telephone him at his office. I took the privilege of checking the Police Internal Directory. There is a number for a Sergeant Detective William Shaughnessy. It is 617, of course, that dreary prefix, then COPley 4231."

"Thank you very much, Mr. Pantaleone. I am surprised that you know the old Boston telephone exchanges. You seem much too young."

"I am, Judge, but I've been well taught in the ancient ways of the City. Thank you, Judge. Good evening."

Joe wondered if Pantaleone ever got laid. That wasn't a very judicial thought for Joe to have in his historic chambers, one floor up from Oliver Wendell Holmes' office, above the august Massachusetts Supreme Judicial Court, Joe also wondered what Pantaleone looked like naked. Pantaleone was short and appeared to be very skinny. It was very hard to tell under the baggy suits if there was any body there at all. Pantaleone never took his jacket off. Allesandro did have a wonderful head of black curls which, Joe hoped foretold a fine Italian distribution of body hair. *Maybe he was related to the Randozzas and blessed with their pelt*, Joe mused before picking up the phone to call Sgt. Det. Shaughnessy back. All these North End families had intermarried, at least those who came from Avellino, near Naples. He could ask Shaughnessy, who knew the strangest things about a lot of Bostonians.

Sergeant Detective Shaughnessy picked right up. "Is that Pantaleone kid who answered the phone from Emerald Court, in the North End?"

"I have no idea. Why?"

"If he is, your opinions are being published in the North End first and probably your drafts as well. Probably even your secret deliberations! Those Bastards!" Shaughnessy did not share Joe's appreciation of the Latin races, and that included the Italian popes, with the possible exception of Giusseppe Roncalli, John XXIII. "Watch him and don't leave anything hanging around. Of course, you guys only get the boring shit like land easements and environmental shit; maybe an occasional motion to suppress. But that's not why I'm calling. We're going to Ireland, you, me and some Armenian professor, Padraig Barmerian, whose mother was from Letterkenny in Donegal. We leave on Thursday at 6:00 p.m., so have your bag packed. We'll be staying at Dunbukulla and I'm your roommate, unless you want the rug merchant."

"Maybe, how old is he?" Joe asked, much to the surprise of Shaughnessy, who never understood Joe's attraction to the tawny. Shaughnessy had a bit of a shine for Joe himself, nurtured by their Venetian bang, which he, Shaughnessy, didn't understand either. Shaughnessy's usual taste was for white, blond or redheaded, Southie or Charlestown Irish *boyos* in their late twenties or early thirties, who wore workout pants and athletic gear. Shaughnessy spent a lot of time in the locker rooms and showers at the L Street Bathhouse in South Boston, the Boston Athletic Club on the Waterfront and the World Gym in Somerville, the hangouts for these darlings. He rarely scored but he had a great fantasy life. And the requisite working out and swimming kept him in very good shape.

"How the fuck would I know? He teaches at NYU. Wait a minute. I got his *Curriculum Vitae* right here. He's 38. Is that O.K. with you?"

"Hhmmm? Sounds interesting. Do you have a picture?" Joe asked as he called up Google to look up Professor Barmerian himself. *Oh, the wonders of the 21st century*, Joe said to himself as he typed away—B-A-R-M-E-R-I-A-N.

"Fuck you, your honor," Shaughnessy said. "I'll pick you up at 7:00 tonight. Meet me in front of One Beacon Street. We have to make plans. I'll fill you in on the rest of this caper. Don't bring Pantaleone. I know you go for his kind, but he could be trouble. He's probably listening in on this call."

He was.

◊ ◊ ◊

Joe was in front of One Beacon at 7:00 p.m. From his office he'd called Tom Murphy's office and left a message that he couldn't have dinner with Tom tonight. He said no more, or less. Shaughnessy was waiting in the mandatory Boston detective issue navy blue Crown Victoria, "an unmarked car," known to every criminal from Roxbury to the North End.

"Where are we going?" Joe asked.

"We're going to your place so you can change your clothes. Then we'll go to Amhreins in South Boston for a bit to eat," Shaughnessy said as he took the turn onto Somerset Street to skirt the State House to get to Joe's place on the top of Beacon Street. Shaughnessy parked in one of the spots reserved for the Legislature. *Those fakers never work anyway. They aren't going to be here tonight*, Shaughnessy said to himself.

Joe and Shaughnessy walked a third of the way down the hill to Joe's apartment. The doorman let them in, opening the door while saying, "Good evening, Your Honor." It was the same man, Larry, who had been on duty the night Joe came off the elevator into the lobby on his hands and knees wearing nothing but a couple of neckties. Joe tried hard not to remember, but just the sight of Larry in the lobby always reminded him. It was their little secret, except Shaughnessy also knew because he had checked out Larry to see if he was part of that theft, if it was an inside job. It wasn't; in fact Larry was an Irishman from Cork, a musician. He played the pennywhistle on Sunday nights at a *seisun* in a bar in Brighton. For Joe, the additional presence of Sergeant Detective Shaughnessy, his interrogator later that same night, only sharpened the painful memory.

They took the elevator to the fourth floor.

"Why are you coming up too, Sergeant?" Joe asked belatedly. By this time they were in front of the door of Joe's apartment.

"Ooh, should I wait in the car, like your chauffeur, your honor? It's cold outside. Where's the tea? I'll make a pot while you change. Dress down. Look like you just left the American Legion—or the Knights of Columbus. We want to fit in."

When Joe opened the door and turned on the light he saw on the skinny Parson's table that held the phone a teddy bear demurely sitting on the edge of the table, its legs crossed hanging over the edge. The bear was holding a bouquet of tiny pink roses wrapped in a paper lace doily. Its felt mouth was smiling and its eyes looked up imploringly.

Joe looked back at Shaughnessy, who said, "Don't touch it. We'll get it checked for fingerprints. Leave it alone. I'll call for someone to pick it up. Just do your business, take a shower, pack your bag and we'll get out of here. I'll take care of it. You have nothing to fear. Our information is that the Tiger has lost his claws. The North End mob doesn't know what to do anymore. He's just stopped doing anything. There's no boss. One of them's going to bump the other off to see who'll become top dog."

Joe wasn't so convinced but he dutifully went into his bedroom and took off his clothes. While Joe was in the shower he wondered why Shaughnessy had come to pick him up and drive him home. He could have walked home in the same amount of time—out the back door of the Adams Courthouse, under the arch of the statehouse and down the front side of Beacon Hill.

Joe also speculated about Professor Padraig Barmerian, Ph.D. Even though his hairline was receding in the academic, black and white photo Joe had googled, the professor had a heavy beard and a tuft of dark hair appearing above the shirtline. He seemed a little stockier than Joe was usually fond of. However his light, possibly blue, eyes next to his big Levantine nose were what captured Joe most. He was dressed in standard Ivy League attire, a striped tie, pointed collar shirt and a dark, tweed jacket. Could it be Donegal tweed? Joe speculated. Why not? That's where his mother is from.

Of course, unlike *Gray & Gay* ads, there were no measurements accompanying the photo, just academic accomplishments—A.B. Harvard College, M.A., Notre Dame, Ph.D. Trinity College, Dublin. Then his numerous scholarly articles and lectures; the most interesting for Joe was a paper presented to the American Irish Scholarship committee two years before entitled, "The Missing and Duplicate Pages of *The Book of Kells*."

Joe's mind wandered from attraction, to lust, to scholarship, to the four Evangelists as he toweled off and ran the electric shaver over his face. He rejected the idea of a fresh application of the Old Spice stick deodorant but did put some Kiehls Men's Moisturizer on his face. It was his one concession to male cosmetics.

Joe went into his bedroom to change into somebody who had just come from the American Legion or the Knights of Columbus. He really didn't have a clue what that would be, but the idea of a disguise amused him, and there was a little grin on his face as he entered the bedroom.

"What are you smiling about? Did you have dirty thoughts in the shower? I hope you didn't wank it in there. You took long enough. Now drop the towel and come into bed and have a cup of tea—milk, no sugar, as I remember."

Shaughnessy was naked in Joe's bed, like he owned it, like a pasha, or a courtesan about to be waited on by the black maidservant *a la* Manet's *Olympia*.

Joe dutifully climbed in the bed. He had heated himself up with thoughts of the hirsute half-Armenian Professor. And something, in this case Shaughnessy, was better than nothing. That was an old legal principle. It went along with that other one, "Take the money and run."

Joe didn't run. He just laid back, his arms over his head as Shaughnessy kicked off the bed covers and went at him. Joe liked looking at Shaughnessy's bobbing head, and his strong swimmer's shoulders and back. Occasionally Shaughnessy's lily white, Irish farmer's bum would bob into view and that brought it all home for Joe.

When Joe was done, and after Shaughnessy wiped him off, Shaughnessy stood by the side of the bed and said, "I bet that Turk Professor can't do that." Then he smiled and came over to the edge of the bed offering himself to Joe, who was no longer in the mood.

It hadn't been my idea in the first place, Joe thought. *Why do I have to do this? Doesn't he know that* post coitum omni animales tristi sunt. Joe wasn't exactly sad, but he hadn't really been into the whole thing to begin with. Joe excused himself to pee, hoping that Shaughnessy would lose interest while he was gone.

No such luck for Joe, who did everything but take another shower before returning. He brushed his teeth, washed around, applied the deodorant, remoisturized, peed twice, and blew his nose. When he returned to the bedroom there was Shaughnessy lying on his back sporting a big smile and an alabaster rod.

On the other side of the bed Shaughnessy had neatly piled his clothes on a chair. His gun was on top. It was in its holster, but the butt made it clearly visible that this was a gun. Joe wasn't usually into kink, but something about the gun, maybe that it gave Shaughnessy the ability to force Joe to have sex, excited Joe. And he smiled back at Shaughnessy. "Turn about, fair play," Joe said to himself as he leaned over onto Sergeant Detective Shaughnessy.

Shaughnessy was a moaner, which Joe liked only if the moans indicated appreciation. Joe didn't go for the "Suck it, cocksucker! Suck that big cock!" kind of talk. He wasn't into that kind of dominance, but some well placed, "Ooh yeah, oh yeah, that's great!"s were appreciated and kept the business going for Joe, who was good, but lacked endurance. Joe added his hand to the play to speed things up. Shaughnessy had enough to accommodate Joe's hand, mouth and more.

Soon it was all over for the Sergeant Detective, much to Joe's relief.

"Jesus Joe, that was great. Thanks a lot. I haven't had a good blowjob in a long time. These young, townie *boyos* just want to get done. Either that or they want to get stuffed—with no face stuff. It's nice to be with someone who knows what he's doing. I forgot how good you are."

"Think nothing of it," Joe said. "Now can we get something to eat? I didn't have any lunch."

"Not until you pack your bag. I told you we're going to Ireland."

"You didn't say tonight."

"But it is tonight and the tawny professor is going with us. It seems that he's up here at a conference at that Boston College Irish Center and they are going to deliver him to the airport."

"I didn't tell my Chief Justice that I'd be going away."

"I checked your schedule; you don't sit again for three weeks. Your Chief Justice will never know you've gone. What with home computers, half your colleagues have never seen their offices. We don't want to keep the Armenian shepherd boy waiting."

"You're being hostile to the good professor even before you've met him. What's that about?"

"Maybe I'm jealous. A twirl is a twirl, but I know what you really like. Your heart, or whatever it is that engages two people, wasn't into that little diversion we just had."

Return to Ireland

The Professor was at the airport, and to Joe, he was even better looking in color. Joe recognized him from the *Google* black and white academic photo, which didn't do him justice. He was at least six feet two, his eyes were a grey green and there was a roseate flush across the tawny cheeks above his wild beard. He laughed a lot, even at Shaughnessy's grumpiness. His *bonhomie* was infectious. Soon Shaughnessy got over being a grouch and started to tell the professor Boston cop stories.

Nobody mentioned why they were taking this trip. They just pretended that it was a trip to the "Old Sod." Shaughnessy sat next to the professor on the plane. They talked and laughed all the way; Joe tried to listen in from the seat behind, but it was too difficult to hear, so he eventually just spread himself across the empty seat next to him and fell asleep. Joe did hear Shaughnessy recite the Last Gospel in Latin, telling the Professor that he had learned that in the Seminary along with the Nicene Creed in Latin as well.

Tim Ronayne was at the Dublin Airport to meet them. His eyes lit up when he saw Joe, but really got excited when Shaughnessy introduced him to the professor, Doctor Padraig Barmerian,

Shaughnessy's new best friend.

"Now tell me how you like to be called? Should I call you 'Professor' or 'Doctor' or will just 'Paddy' be alright?"

"My mother calls me 'Paddo.'"

"Well that solves that. If that's your mother's name for you, it'll be ours. We'll be your mothers here. Boys, the Professor is to be called 'Paddo' by all who wish him well."

Tim drove them to Dunbukulla. All three were in a two bedroom suite with a common living room, near the "Leisure Center" and pool. But for the row of trees lining the path up to it you could almost see Diarmuid's Dolmen from the windows. Paddo, who had done some research on the area, was anxious to see the dolmen. He had three willing guides. And it was still light.

There was no mention of "The Page"—none at all, at least not in front of Joe and Shaughnessy. Each knew Tim would get to it, when and how he wanted to. Ever the detective, Shaughnessy hoped that they hadn't been followed. Like Dino Randozza, Shaughnessy also presumed that the reconstructed Page was in Ireland. Shaughnessy had walked around on the plane a couple of times, chatting up the visiting Hibernians, a surprising number of whom he knew. He didn't see anyone on the plane from the mug shot book he carried around in his head of Boston bad boys, however. It could be that Dino went out of town to find someone for this part of *his* mission, but Shaughnessy didn't think that Dino trusted anyone enough to let him make the grab of "The Page." It didn't even look like there were any Italians on the plane, except for the retired fire captain, Mike Flynn's wife and mother-in-law, who were sitting on the other side of the plane five seats up.

Tim left Joe, Shaughnessy and Paddo in the room to get comfortable, but ten minutes later he came back and said, "Paddo, there's someone in the bar I want you to meet. He's a local historian and has read your work. Can you come down to see him before he leaves? And, boys, if it's okay with you, we'll meet for dinner in the dining room in a half hour. Will that be enough time for you? "

Shaughnessy looked at Joe and Joe looked back. They knew when they weren't invited. Joe resented what appeared to be his loss of most favored status in Tim's eyes, but he knew that this was now Tim's show and that the Professor had skills and knowledge that Joe couldn't duplicate.

Joe lay down on one of the two beds in the bedroom that he and Shaughnessy seem to have landed. Shaughnesssy lay down on his bed as well. Soon Shaughnessy got up and said, "I'd better take a shower. I don't want to be smelly for the Professor's debut." As he walked to the shower he looked out the window and then turned to Joe.

"Well, it looks like Tim is going to initiate Paddo into some pagan rites. They're heading to the Dolmen."

Joe got up to look. *He* had wanted to show the Dolmen to Paddo, as did Shaughnessy. The view to the dolmen was clear except for the rocks themselves. Joe too saw Tim and Paddo walking up the path almost to the point where one turned left at the end of the row of evergreens, just before reaching the ancient stones themselves, right next to the third tee of the golf course.

"Should we follow them?" Joe asked.

"No, Tim has his reasons. I know you have a shine for the Professor but I never went in for the tawnies myself. Give me a milk white bum anytime," Shaughnessy said with his back to the window as he took off his shorts in preparation for the shower and flicked it across Joe's rear.

"Well, they won't be alone. There are two ladies about fifty yards behind them. Serves them right," Joe said, still looking out the window.

Shaughnessy turned to look. "Why that's Mike Flynn's wife and mother-in-law. They were on the plane."

"Mike Flynn the fire captain?" Joe said.

"Retired," Shaughnessy added.

"I once worked on a case where he'd testified. He'd given a certificate to a joint in the North End, which was clearly a firetrap, and then he had the gall to testify that it was a perfectly safe place. The insurance company smelt a rat and wasn't paying. So the owner and his lawyer sued for unfair settlement practices, triple damages plus attorney's fees. Somehow the owner got Flynn to testify; it was bad enough that he certified the rathole. I had the case on appeal and read the transcript. Ronan Ladd, the lawyer for the insurance company, destroyed Flynn on cross examination. They lost the case and then had the balls to appeal. What do they think? That we judges live under a rock? Somebody paid Flynn off or had something on him. I remember the name of the owner of the building. He was Sal Gritti, like the Gritti Palace in Venice. It developed that Sal Gritti was Flynn's brother-in-law. How stupid can you get? I was tempted to send the transcript to the Mayor. Somebody else must have—it was probably my colleague Firrfield. He was always doing stuff like that. A few weeks after our decision I read in the *Herald* that Mike Flynn had resigned. I wouldn't know him if I saw him. Do you know him?"

"Of course I do. That's my job and all of us uniformed guys know each other. I thought he resigned because of his ticker. He drinks a little."

Joe was on a roll. "He's lucky that he wasn't indicted. Then he'd have reason to have a bad ticker. Did you know the brother-in-law?"

"Yes," said Shaughnessy, "and those dames are following Tim and Paddo for a reason—even the mother-in-law in her black dress and the braids tied up around her ears. She's got a pretty good stride, probably from herding goats in the mountains in her bare feet. The old witch! She'll probably give them the evil eye. Oh Christ, and just when I thought we were home safe! The other team is sending in the girls. Tim won't do anything with them around and I'm not just talking about "The Page." Do you want to shower first? I'll keep an eye on the back yard. Maybe I'll see a little action." Shaughnessy laughed.

◊ ◊ ◊

Tim and Paddo were walking around, looking at the Dolmen from all sides. Tim was holding a piece of paper and pointing out things on it to Paddo. It was a print of a digital photo of the complete Page. Paddo was reaching for a closer look when Tim pulled it back and began to fold it up again. He gave a warning toss of the head to Paddo, who went and stood under the 30-ton capstone and pretended to be Hercules or Samson tied to the pillars. Tim had hoped to put him there later for other purposes but this would do for now. Just as Tim got the paper all folded and into his jacket pocket the women appeared around the edge of the tall evergreens lining the path.

"Good afternoon, ladies!" Tim began. "Don't you love our long Irish evenings at this time of year! Welcome to Diarmuid's Dolmen. It is one of many in Ireland—a nice manageable size. Just a little over our heads. A man or two could take shelter under it. Oh, the Irish rains aren't always so soft as they are today. Are you Italian? There are a few dolmens in Italy too. In Mont Albano, Fassaro, Scusi and Bari most notably. They say that they are burial places. I'm not so sure. Perhaps our ancestors weren't so obsessed with death as we allegedly modern Irish are. I'm Tim Ronayne, this is a visiting professor from America, and what are your names, ladies?"

"I am Mrs. Michael Flynn, Laura Flynn, and this is my mother, Lena Pantaleone Gritti, Signora Gritti. We're from Boston. My husband is Irish—Irish American."

"Aahh, a grand combination! An Italian woman and an Irishman! It's not always so good the other way around. For one thing, Irish women cannot cook like Italian mothers. And for another, they are not always so beautiful. Translate please, for your mother," Tim ordered, surprisingly.

Tim was really turning it on. Paddo, who had been a little embarrassed to have been come upon so suddenly as he was about to go under the capstone, was smiling in admiration. He had Irish uncles who could shovel it like Tim Ronayne. Courtly hyperbole was not new to him

Mrs. Flynn did translate, into Neapolitan, for her mother, who gave a big smile to Tim. Tim knew Neapolitan when he heard it; he'd had a tryst a few years ago with a Neapolitan hairdresser working in Drogheda.

Laura Flynn had been listening to Irish bullshit for the 30 years of her marriage to Captain Michael Flynn of the Boston Fire Department and she knew it for what it was. She was not going to be deterred. "And Professor, just what do you profess?"

Tim suspected where the truth would lead so he jumped in, "You're a geologist, aren't you Professor. At least that's what the Email ordering your room said."

"I am a geologist of sorts. Yes, I am. That's why we came to look at these rocks. Aren't they marvelous? Kind of cozy, actually, human scale. One wants to set up house under here. Come in, Mrs. Flynn," he added as he stepped out from under the capstone.

"Perhaps the homey coziness is why people throw rocks on top," Tim said. "If the rock stays, then you'll be married within the year."

"What if you're married already? Do you get a new husband if your rock stays?" Laura Flynn asked.

"Ah now, that's a mystery, Mrs. Flynn. And we don't know the answer right off. Let me think if I've known of a married woman who threw a pebble up and it stayed," Tim said pondering. "There was a woman who was married, who threw a pebble up, which landed, and her husband returned from America where he'd been for 12 years and they had six children right in a row. That was my grandmother. She later said, with Saint Teresa of Avila, 'Be careful what you pray for. More tears are shed over answered prayers.' Would it be something like that you're looking for, Mrs. Flynn?"

Laura Flynn decided to retreat and try another tack. Rome wasn't built in a day. She'd do a little intelligence. "It's getting dark. Would you kind men walk my mother and I back to the hotel?" And she grabbed Paddo's arm before an answer could be given.

Tim smelled a rat. This dame was up to something. Tim knew that his rivals for the Page were Italians from Boston and she was Italian from Boston. That completed the syllogism for him for now, until something convinced him otherwise. He knew that she was from Boston because he had processed the reservation. There was no hint of Italian in that request. It simply asked for two rooms one for Mr. and Mrs. Michael Flynn from West Roxbury, Massachusetts, and the other for Mrs. Flynn's mother.

Tim needed to do a little intelligence himself but how was he going to find anything out with the *Signora*, who didn't appear to speak any English. He hoped that Paddo wouldn't be gabby as well. The less the Professor said about himself to Laura Flynn the better.

Tim could hear conversation up ahead of him. He just couldn't hear what was being said. Laura Flynn still had Paddo's arm. Tim was not so gallant; the *Signora* walked in silence next to him, but not on his arm. Just as they turned left to get back onto the hotel grounds she said, "Have your people always lived here, Mr. Ronayne?" in perfect Boston Irish English. Her voice sounded like too much scotch and too many cigarettes, kind of like Elaine Stritch.

Tim jumped. Why did he assume she spoke only Italian? Was it the black dress, the braids tied around the ears? However, he made a quick recovery. The truth was always the best defense, "Forgive me, *Signora*. I just assumed that you spoke only Italian. I don't speak Italian. I didn't intend to neglect you. I could've explained the terrain. Yes, my people have lived here for generations, on both sides."

"Then you know the story of the missing page of *The Book of Kells*. I heard about it…in my childhood. I was born in the United States, then taken to Naples with my father when I was four. He brought me back to Providence, Rhode Island, when I began my teens. All my friends were Irish. There was a teacher whose family was from here, Miss Lavin. And I heard the story of the wicked landlord and 'The Page' over and over. Where was the Big House that was burnt?"

Tim was completely taken off guard. The teacher in Providence must have been Joe's Aunt Josie Lavin. How did Josie know about the Page in those days? Joe had never told Tim that Josie knew anything—ever. As a matter of fact, Joe and Tim tried to keep her away from the secret when she was here with Joe. Could it have been someone else? What other Lavins were there from here? Families became so split up that it was impossible to tell.

Whatever the case, Tim was on his toes, thinking of how to say enough without revealing too much. He couldn't deny that he knew something about 'The Page.'

He had a brainstorm. "Ma'am, we are very careful talking about that over here. It was not so long ago and the trees have ears. Surely, you understand a community's secrets, being Neapolitan. Memories are still fresh. Most of us pretend it never happened. That way we're all safe." For the *Signora*'s benefit Tim created an Irish *omerta*, a code of silence, something she should understand and respect—if she was who she said she was.

At the hotel door they were greeted by one of Tim's many red-headed nieces, who whispered something in his ear. Tim said to the *Signora*, "Excuse me, we are late for a meeting. Come along Paddo. The 'dingitary' has arrived and needs to see us posthaste. It was a pleasure to meet you ladies. Enjoy your stay in Ballyfirglin. If you need anything at the hotel, talk to my niece Breda here. Breda, this is Mrs. Flynn and her mother, *Signora* Pantaleone. They are in suite 336. Captain Flynn is resting there right now. Help them any way you can. Please excuse us," as he now took Paddo's well-muscled (and hairy underneath the cloth, as Tim well realized) arm.

He took Paddo to the Leisure Center, to the Men's locker room. Paddo said, "But my gym stuff is upstairs."

"Don't worry. Don't be a'scared. Just take off your clothes. You won't need anything else to wear. We're going in the steam and have a talk."

While he got out of his own clothes Tim turned around once for what he hoped would be a surreptitious peek at Paddo. Paddo was pulling off a *V*-necked tee shirt. He was hairy, like a bear, even on the cordlike, well-muscled upper back. The hair on Paddo's arms stopped mid-bicep but resumed like a bear skin across his chest. And it was black, jet black and curly leading down the treasure trail below his belt. Paddo had a sturdy stomach covered with hair patterned like a butterfly, revealing, however, bronze flesh around it, the same as wrapped his ham-like shoulders. For all the hair there was nothing grotesque about Paddo; his body was just the least bit frightening, but in a very desirable way.

Paddo didn't see Tim looking at him so he went on unbelting his pants; he pulled them and his jockey shorts down with a tug of his right hand and then a push from his right foot on the descending pants. Surprisingly, although Tim didn't make note of it at the time, Paddo's big halfback's bum was hairless.

Paddo turned around to catch Tim looking at him in awe.

Paddo just laughed. "I guess the dominant genes outside were Armenian, but the soul is Irish, Tim. Don't worry, I won't bite," and with that Paddo threw himself at Tim, laughing, wrapping Tim in, what else, none other than a bear hug.

Tim hadn't got his pants off before being distracted by Paddo, his size and his pelt, but he rushed to do so within the furry wrap. Paddo backed off a little to let him and said, "For Christ's sake, take your pants off man! The steam's awaiting."

Tim led Paddo to the steam room, which had a glass door and two rows of benches on either side of the door inside. It was steamy upon entrance and Tim sat himself on the upper bench on the left. Paddo went to the other side. As he was putting his backside down he felt a body beneath him, already on the bench. The big black bear sat on the Polar bear.

"I think that it would be nicer the other way around, Professor Barmerian," the Polar bear said as he slid to the side. "How are you Tim? How was your walk, your *passagiatta*? Shaughnessy and I are both here, although he remains unusually silent in the corner on your side, Tim. Otherwise, we're alone and at our last reconnoiter no one was about." The speaker was Joe Lyons, the Polar bear, fuzzy, pink and white.

"Joe, tell me. Did your aunt know about 'The Page' before the recent past?" Tim asked.

Joe said, "Not that I know of. I didn't know that she now knows.

If so, her knowledge is recent. It's the kind of thing she would have loved to tell me as a kid. She gave me every tidbit she had about our Irish past. I was to be the keeper of the legends. She told me that."

"So she couldn't have told a Providence schoolgirl about 'The Page' years ago?" Tim said.

"No, why are you asking?"

"Because it turns out that in spite of looking like an old *strega*, the widow, *Signora* Pantaleone Gritti, the mother-in-law of Captain Michael Quinn, speaks perfect English and claims that she heard about the 'Rescue of The Page' from your aunt years ago in Providence, Rhode Island, when she was but a schoolgirl."

"That's unlikely. Did you say Pantaleone?"

"I did."

"Shaughnessy, you were right. The old dame is a Pantaleone," Joe said.

"They're on to us," Tim said. "I suppose I should have expected it. And Paddo, did Mrs. Laura Flynn get anything out of you on your walk back?"

"She wanted to talk about me, but I insisted that she tell me about her children and their academics. Mothers always like to talk about their kids. That's why I am a popular professor. I praise the kids to their mothers. She may know who I am, even why I'm here, but I told her nothing—not even my last name. She thinks that I am a Calabrese. Apparently, she once knew a Calabrese who looked like I do. She even said she should have married him."

"Well, we can't trust either of them," Joe said. "The Pantaleones are not our pals. What do you plan to do, Tim? Don't tell me where 'The Page' is, but what do you plan to do with it now that they are on its trail?"

"The esteemed Calabrese Professor and I are going to work on that as soon as we get out of this steam. I'll ask you and Shaughnessy to keep the Italian ladies busy until we get back, which won't be tomorrow but may be the next day. Professor, your bags are packed and along with mine they're sitting in the golf cart just outside the Men's dressing room. There's a fire door there and we'll slip out unseen, God willing. We'll take a little ride in the cart and then onto our next destination. Be of good cheer, boys. I'll take care of the Professor. You just enjoy yourselves. And Joe, should you feel frisky, Sean Murphy, the fisherman from the Carlingford has been asking after you. So has your shy, handsome cousin, Peter. They tend to work out in the late afternoon, spend a while in the Jacuzzi for the *craic* and then they take the steam."

Joe was not comfortable with the idea of being cooped up at Dunbukulla with the Pantaleones, not even with Shaughnessy to keep him company and protect him. So after Tim and Paddo left he said through the steam, "Listen, Shaughnessy, we have to get away from here. Why don't we take a trip? Lets go to the desk and ask one of the Ronayne redheads where we can go for a daytrip. Maybe they have an excursion or something. If Lucrezia Borgia and her mother and her rum-dum husband want to come too, all the better. They can keep an eye on us and we on them."

"I was thinking that I'd like to get one of the redheads here in the steam for a bit. They're good looking boys, as handsome as the townies I usually chase, and much less surly," Shaughnessy said.

Joe replied, "Well, that's not going to happen, and if we stay here any longer we'll look like prunes. I'm going to see about a daytrip for tomorrow."

As soon as Joe stepped out of the men's locker room into the main pool area the Pantaleone women were on him like sauce. The two of them were in the pool; Laura in a blue-flowered one-piece bathing suit without straps that showed off her trim figure at its best, and the *Signora* in a black, long skirted, full-fitting ensemble with a black bathing cap! That seemed a little too much. Who died that merited such a display of grief? Joe hadn't seen a widow's weeds bathing costume since 1951 when his cousin Julia sat on Second Beach in Middletown dishing with her bachelor sons and the McCarthy girls after her husband Con died. He couldn't help but stare at the widow's strange weeds.

"Weren't you on the plane with us from Boston yesterday? You look so familiar," said Laura smiling at the edge of the pool while her mother treaded water nearby.

"Well, yes, I did just arrive from Boston, very nice to see you," Joe said with his best chill.

"Was Mr. Ronayne in the men's locker room? We need to talk to him. He's been so accommodating but we have one more, tiny request."

"I didn't see him. There didn't appear to be anyone else in there but…and here he comes now."

Shaughnessy pushed through the swinging door from the men's locker room, combing his hair back into place with his fingers.

"Oh, Sergeant Detective Shaughnessy. How are you? We have to get some Alka Seltzer for poor Mike. Have you seen Mr. Ronayne? Mike seems to have an upset stomach. We thought that we saw Tim Ronayne come in here."

"I haven't seen the man myself," which was true because he hadn't been able to see through the steam. Witness the collision of the bears that had just occurred. "I think he moves around this place quickly—always on the go. I'm going to the front desk. Would you like me to order some Alka Seltzer, or the local equivalent, to be sent up to poor Mike?"

"Oh, that would be so kind," said Laura.

Although Joe had stopped for this interchange, he had pointedly not introduced himself and he didn't want Shaughnessy to introduce him either. He was sure the ladies knew who he was, but he wanted to let the mystery or its illusion last as long as he could keep it going.

James Ronayne Ferrick was at the desk in the old part of the hotel, the original, or second original (after the first was burnt to the ground by the Fireboys) Dunbukulla House. He was 19, tall and thin. Like almost all the Ronayne progeny (most of them with different last names because they were the children of Tim's sisters) he had red hair, pale skin and green eyes. And like most of them he was unfailingly polite, although he was innately shy. He had to be socialized for this job. His uncle Tim had taught him that it was not impolite to speak first from behind the desk, that usually someone in front of him wanted something and that people appreciated being coddled.

"May I help you, sirs?" he said to Shaughnessy and Joe standing before him.

Oh if you only knew, thought Shaughnessy.

"Yes, thank you," Joe said. "We want to take an excursion, some kind of day trip tomorrow. What do you recommend?"

"There are trips to the North, to Belfast and I myself lead a trip to Newgrange, a neolithic ruin, just south of here. We also stop at Mellifont, the 12th-century Cistercian Abbey in Meath."

"We'll take that," Shaughnessy said before James or Joe could go on any further. "What time does it leave?"

"A van will leave at 9:30 in the morning. We'll have a driver and up to six guests. If no one else signs up, it'll be just the three of us and the driver. I studied at the site last summer and I'm studying anthropology at University College Dublin. I think you'll enjoy the trip. Bring some rain gear. It may be a bit wet, but you won't melt." And he smiled at Shaughnessy.

Shaughnessy just had.

30
Meanwhile, on Madison Avenue

Tim and Paddo jumped into a cab at Kennedy Airport. "The Whitney Museum, please, on Madison at 65th. Thank you," Tim said.

Paddo just smiled. He knew when he took this assignment that there was going to be some intrigue, but he had no idea how it would manifest itself. All the way back across the Atlantic, Tim regaled him with stories about Ballyfirglin and the lousy Tilton family, the local Protestants, former landowners and land agents for absentee landlords. Some of them, dried up and cranky, still lived in an old house off the Newry Road and objected to Catholic boys wandering across their land, like the Rebellion had never happened.

Tim was no more forthcoming about the real purpose of the trip in the cab. All he said was, "We're going to see a pal of ours. You'll like him. He's a professor too." Like professorhood was a Masonic rite, guaranteeing friendship no matter where you went.

Paddo said nothing. He was being paid for his time. He had been given another peek at the digital photo of the Page, both sides, when Tim slipped it under the separator of a stall in a mens' room at the Dublin Airport before they got on the plane. He told

Tim that it looked real to him but one had to see the real thing.

The cabbie talked on his cellphone in Russian, interrupting only to ask, "You wanna take the Drive. Foreigners always wanna take the Drive."

Tim said, "Yes, thank you. That would be very nice and nostalgic."

The cabbie let them out right at the door of the museum. Paddo started to walk into the museum over the concrete bridge. Tim grabbed him saying, "No, boy, over here," while heading to the right. They went into the little doorway of the brownstone building immediately to the right of the museum. Tim pressed a buzzer that said "Callahan." The location rang a bell with Paddo. Déjà vu *all over again*, he thought. *Why is all this so familiar?*

"Hello, my pets. Come on up, third floor. You know the way."

Tim bounded up the stairs and Paddo followed behind. A tall, gangly man with dark curly hair stood leaning against the doorframe in a bold patterned, black and white Japanese *yukata* down to his ankles, belted by a yellow silk *obi*, smoking a cigarette.

"Timmy darling, I won't even ask what this is about. Just don't store bombs in my apartment. The landlady, Madame Whitney next door, wouldn't like that at all. She's already trying to evict me so she can tear this place down. I'm happy to help the cause, but I stop at bombs. And who is this big smiling brute you bring me? A visitor from the East?"

"Donal, this is Padraig. Padraig this is Donal. Donal's a Kerry lad, we met years ago. He's in the Professor business too. I'll keep it vague."

"In case they come and torture me, Tim darling? Tear out my fingernails? Attach electrodes to my genitalia? I'll never tell. You know me, Tim. Loyal to the end, which may be sooner than we all think." Donal muttered that last phrase almost, but not quite, under his breath. "Would you rebel boys like a drink?"

"It's a little early for that, Donal, but we would like a shower."

"Of course, darling. Just push the stockings and delicates to one side." Then he sang, "*Mama said there'd be days like this, Mama said*. I was out dancing all night and just took a cat nap when I got the call that you'd be coming. How is darling Joe Lyons? Do you see him? He's become so reclusive since he took the silks. He used to be quite the looker, you know. Has he told you of our trip to Ireland in 1970? He almost became the Duchess of Donegal. He would've been if he wasn't so hot for that fickle Fionna, who ditched him for that uppity dago. It's all in the book. All we have left is our memories. Memories and dancing. Thank Jesus that dancing is back. *I got two lovers, and I love them both the same.* That's what Fionna sang when she dated Joe and Lucrezia Borgia at the same time. Lucrezia and her family moved from Brooklyn to Westchester in the fifties. I saw her once at a fancy cocktail party and asked her, 'What did you do with the pigeons when you moved?' She was a pretentious one, that Lucrezia."

Donal added, "Who's going first? Or are you a pair? Do you bathe together? Joe Lavin usually likes the Levantines, and he used to take the steam," Donal said giving Paddo the old up and down. "I don't recall that being your interest, Tim."

Paddo was good-natured, but he wanted a shower badly. He hadn't even gotten rid of the sweat from the steam at Dunbukulla; "I'll go first. Can I put my things here?" he said stripping down without getting an answer, dropping his clothes in a pile on the pale Tibetan rug in the center of the floor.

"That'll be nice," said Donal admiringly from one of the two brown leather and chrome Breuer chairs in the fashionably pale yellow living room, which was at the front, the Madison Avenue end, of the apartment. Tim had already brought their overnight bags into Donal's bedroom and was laying out a blue suit, a shirt and a tie for himself and a dark charcoal suit for Paddo.

"We're going to visit gentry," Tim announced from the bedroom as Donal stared in awe at the back of Paddo marching to the bathroom. The awe had arisen at the sight of the front of him, but was not dissipated by a rear view of the boulder like, tawny cheeks of Paddo's butt rolling up the hall. In other company, in other days and at other places, perhaps even last night, Donal would have dropped to his knees. Today he just picked up Paddo's clothes and draped them neatly across the other Breuer chair, like a dutiful mother. Donal did take a sniff of the boxer shorts, and was not disappointed. "Like the Cedars of Lebanon, with a touch of jock after a Rugby game, and just a speck of frankincense and myrrh," Donal whispered *sotto voce* in the Irish fashion.

"What's that?" Tim asked, coming out of the bedroom, naked himself.

"And you. You always smelt like a spring day—with a little bleach. Your mother was fond of that bleach. That's why you're so white. It's not fair for you two to parade around here starkers, and it's cruel of you to bring this colossus and have him bound naked down my hall—and my heart. Are you bumpin' that child of God, Tim Ronayne?"

Tim was not used to such direct talk about sex, but he could handle it, and Donal. Tim said, "Oh Donal, you city boys think of only one thing...."

Before he could finish, Donal interjected, "Don't give me that bumpkin business. I lived on your father's farm. I spent so much time in the barn your mother was going to rent my room. I haven't had that much sex since. Talk to me not about urban vice!" He took a long drag on the cigarette.

"We're here on very serious business. You got my message. We need a place to stay for a couple of days. There's no room here, obviously."

"Oh, I could make room," Donal said coquettishly. "Particularly for the Sheik of Araby. You probably have him all to yourself and I'd never be a bird dogger, never—maybe a voyeur. *No muscle bound man can take the hand of my guy*," Donal sang. "I have a friend, who is away, in Italy. We'll call him 'Fionna', the same Fionna I was talking about, who went to Ireland with Judge Lyons and myself, in our joyous youth—in 1970. He was courting Joe Lyons. Fionna lives on East 51st Street, next to Saint Patricks. I have the keys."

"Next to Saint Patrick's? That couldn't be better! Couldn't be better. When can we go there? Can you get us some cassocks and Roman collars. You know the size of us." Tim said, his mind going a hundred miles an hour.

"I do. I know the size of you, but I might have to measure the big guy—particularly his inseam. Cassocks? What do you think I am? 'Toomey's Religious Apparel'? I know that I'm not supposed to ask any questions but what are you going to do, blow up Saint Patrick's? You're not going to have one of those sacrilegious 'Act Up' demonstrations, are you? Bedfellows do make strange politics. What are you up to? Never mind! Don't tell me."

"If things go as planned, it will all be revealed in a couple of days. I have to get a lot of people together and get things straightened out. It should be a good thing," Tim said.

"You're not going to let them sell us short, like they did to poor Michael Collins in 1921?" Donal asked.

"Don't worry about that. The people of Ballyfirglin will be well satisfied and so will everyone else, well, almost everyone else," Tim said. "Joe Lyons will be over in a couple of days and we'll have an announcement, if all goes well. May I please have the keys?"

Donal went into his bedroom and came back with some keys. He handed them to Tim. "It's the fourth-floor apartment front. There's an elevator in case your dogs are aching. Don't make a mess, although it would be hard not to with that gorilla throwing you around. I'm not the maid. I'll leave the cassocks there. Do you need Roman collars as well? They'll be there first thing in the morning. Would you like a little touch of purple for yours? You'd make a cute monsignor. I'll see if I can get birettas. They don't wear them much these days, but I always liked them. I'll call Mr. John."

Donal leaned back, gave Tim the full teacup, one hand on the hip and the other waving in front. He looked down at Tim's feet. "And don't wear your cow shit-kickin' Irish farmer's boots with the clericals. You'll be a disgrace to us all."

Joe's Escape from Ireland

Tim and Paddo caught a cab in front of the Whitney. They were all dressed up in their suits. Paddo's hair and beard were still wet and shiny in the daylight. "The Cloisters, please," said Tim.

Meanwhile, it was morning in Ireland, and Joe and Shaughnessy were in the van heading off for Newgrange with the Italian ladies and Captain Flynn, who had passed out in his seat. An academic looking Irish man, kinch-like, narrow like a razorblade, with little rimless glasses, in an old tweed jacket joined them in the van. He said nothing to any of them, not even "Hello." Joe hadn't seen him at the hotel.

He must be the sixth person for the tour, Joe thought. Maybe some high school teacher on holiday. He'll probably take notes.

Joe was still trying to make excuses for Tim Ronayne's absence to the Italian ladies. Apparently, they had done a room to room search for Tim at the hotel—at least of the public rooms and the kitchen and maintenance staff rooms, and the loos. Shaughnessy saw the mother-in-law in the men's room next to the bar at midnight pushing a mop, like she was there to clean it.

"Maybe he had an emergency," Joe said. "Doesn't his nephew know where he went? I have no idea. Shaughnessy, you haven't heard anything, have you? Why don't you just enjoy yourselves, ladies? This is a very important Irish site we are going to. I'm sure you'll enjoy it."

In Laura Flynn's mind, after 30 years living with Captain Flynn, the Irish hadn't improved much, not even when they crossed the water. She was never going to fit in at Holy Name Parish in West Roxbury. She spent her time in the North End—with Mama. Mama never had much truck with the Irish to begin with. Look at the food they ate! Why hadn't Laura married one of the Randozza boys? She could be living in a big house in Revere by now, Point of Pines. Dino Randozza was a nice boy.

At Newgrange the van parked at the bottom of a hill and they marched up the path to a mound at the top of the hill. The mound had a small opening. There were lots of other tourists there, standing on the rocks which barred entry and on the two wooden stairways flanking and allowing entrance over the rocks. There already was a group inside so they had to wait. A plain but lovely young woman in a royal blue jacket with lettering on it began to tell them the history of the site. She began with the Boyne River below.

Finally they entered the narrow passageway, all eight of them. Joe kept hitting his head on the low ceiling. Captain Flynn panicked about a third of the way in. He pushed his way out past Joe and James Ronayne Ferrick, the redheaded nephew, and Shaughnessy who took up the rear. The guide was followed by Laura Flynn, her mother, and the high school teacher. The guide had a big but not always helpful flashlight. She didn't speak another word until all were gathered in a cramped chamber at the end of the tunnel, about a quarter of the way across the inside of the mound.

"The Neolithic Irish were shorter than we are today," she deadpanned and they laughed nervously. "The sunlight shines in directly at the Winter Solstice. The Neolithic people were sun followers if not sun worshippers. They had to be in order to plot the year and plant their crops."

A few minutes into the guide's talk the flashlight, which she had put up on a rock above her, fell to the ground twisting the light crazily; then it went out.

The mother-in-law screamed, fainted and fell to the ground at the feet of the skinny schoolteacher. He reached down to assist her. Laura Flynn dove to the ground and screamed, "Don't you touch her, you Irish bastard."

Joe and Shaughnessy and James Ronayne Ferrick, the redheaded nephew, were on the other side, on the right. Young James panicked and tried to go back but Shaughnessy grabbed him and held him close. "Now, now James, don't worry. Everything will be all right," Shaughnessy said softly into young James' ear. He then put his face into the soft red hair. "I've got a match," said the schoolteacher, with a thick brogue. "Just let me find it now."

"You'd better not," Shaughnessy said, raising his handsome head. "There may be methane in here and we'll all be done for." Shaughnessy still held young James in front of him and leaned down to smell his copper hair.

"They'll come for us," the guide said. "These tours are all timed and they'll know that if I am not out soon, something went wrong. Besides they'll perceive that the light went out. Let me continue with my remarks."

"Just get us the fuck out!" screamed Laura Flynn. If the people outside hadn't noticed the absence of light down the tunnel, they would surely have heard her fishwife voice.

Joe felt somebody patting him down. He thought it was Shaughnessy, having a cheap feel, so he said nothing. Shaughnessy felt the same and thought it was Joe, although he hoped it was James Ronayne Ferrick, appreciating his savior at last. It was a professional cop's patdown, Shaughnessy noted.

Suddenly the light went back on. Sergeant Detective Shaughnessy let young James go before anyone noticed that he had clutched him. At least Shaughnessy hoped that was so.

"I think that we ought to leave slowly. For those of you still interested I can finish my remarks outside," the charming and sensible guide said.

Once outside the cave the two Italian ladies ran down the hill. The kinch went off in the other direction. Joe, Shaughnessy and James Ronayne Ferrick were left with the guide.

"Thank you Kitty," said James. "No comment on your tour, but I think we're too excited and distracted to concentrate now. I'll give the guests the guide book."

In spite of the aborted tour, Joe gave Kitty a ten euro tip. Shaughnessy, who, it seems, had made the best use of the darkness, followed suit, but only with five euros.

"We probably should go back to the van," James said.

"But the schoolteacher went the other way," Joe said.

"What schoolteacher? Oh, that was 'Skinnzie' Mulligan. He just came along for the ride. His daughter lives over here. He's a gardener at Dunbukulla, especially for the roses. You'll often find him at the cutting garden in back of the house. He also loves this tour to Newgrange, and if there's room he always climbs in the van. He does look like a schoolteacher, doesn't he? How astute, Judge Lyons."

Joe hadn't told James that he was a judge. But it didn't surprise him that young James knew. There are very few secrets in Ireland, and fewer in Ballyfirglin, particularly when dealing with one of their own, which Joe Lavin Lyons was, whether he wanted to be or not. There wasn't a lot of excitement in the village and the revisit of a cousin who was a judge in America was news.

For the first time in his career, however, Joe decided to ask how he'd been found out. Previously, in Boston, he'd wonder but just nod judiciously at the recognition, as if it wasn't a surprise that he'd be recognized.

"How do you know that I'm a judge, James? Who told you?"

"Ooh, everyone knows, milord. We remember you from your last visit, of course. Then those ladies asked for "the Judge's room number," and then my Uncle Tim called you that. Finally, your cousin Peter Lavin came by and asked if you were in residence."

"Why wasn't I told about Peter's inquiry?" Joe asked, remembering well Peter's smooth white skin, silky dark hair and creamy butt. He was thrilled that Peter would be looking for him.

"Ooh, Peter's the shy one. He told us not to bother you, that he'd probably see you in the health club, maybe the steam." With that, young James smiled and blushed. "Peter was with another man, a dark, foreign man about his same age. I think that Peter called him 'Lorenzo.'"

Joe was going to get all the news. He was kind of family, at least a villager, after all, and entitled to it even if he thought he belonged nowhere—an Irish American Catholic at Saint George's and Harvard, a Rhode Islander in Boston, a gay man in a straight world. That was just his self pity and it didn't pop up often. Joe liked being a loner.

"Lorenzo?!" Joe said.

"And what did Lorenzo look like?" Sergeant Detective Shaughnessy asked, reverting to his occupation.

"He was handsome, dark and handsome. Italian, I suspect. At least he looked like the Italians who come to the hotel, beautiful clothes. A little too much black for Ireland, but they like that these days, the Italians, and they look good in it—a little too mysterious for me, but it suits them. And the shirt wasn't really black, just a very dark green. He had a beautiful car too, a black Saab convertible. Is there something wrong? Peter always travels in fancy company. Peter's a good looking lad and his girlfriend is a model in Dublin. She flies around the world modeling, you know. My sisters point her out in the magazines. Is there something wrong? Should I tell you of every inquiry, Judge Lyons?"

Shaughnessy said to Joe, within hearing of James, who sensing the change in tone had moved away from Shaughnessy, "Jesus, they're everywhere. They don't give up. I thought that it was just the ladies, but here's Lorenzo again. Joe, you'd know him if you saw him? Wouldn't you? You'd better get to the gym as soon as we get

Lyons and Tigers and Bears   337

back. I'll go with you."

"What do we say to the ladies in the van?" Joe asked as they walked down the hill; young James now well in front and out of hearing.

"Not a word. We'll continue to pretend. By the way, why did you frisk me in there when the light went out, Joe?"

"I didn't frisk you. You frisked me," Joe replied.

"It was a setup, then. Somehow Laura Flynn knocked down the light and then she or the old dame patted us down. What do they think? That we're walking around with 'The Page' in our pants? I'll show her what I've got in my pants. It was a professional frisk, however. Do you think one of them was a cop in another life?"

"I have no idea. I have no idea about any of this. What is my cousin doing with that louse Lorenzo? I hope he hasn't turned." Joe said weariedly. Joe had only met Peter Lavin once, but blood is thick, particularly when engorging.

"Maybe Peter's just turning a trick," Shaughnessy said. "Or maybe they're in love," he added cynically. "'An affair of the heart,' as Tim Ronayne would say. There have been stranger couplings. Look at Professor Paddo Barmerian's mother and father! Look at Paddo and Tim! I wonder what they're doing now. And where and how?"

◊ ◊ ◊

"I'm fucken tired of this place," Sergeant Detective Shaugnessy said. "It gives me the creeps. First we get felt up by some Italian hag in a cave, and now that crystal meth no good is sniffing around. I'm going back to Boston. It's nuts here. They're crazier than we are. No wonder we left. There's no reason for us to stay. I feel abandoned. Tim's gone with the goods. Why do we have to stay? What are we waiting for?"

Joe said, "Well then, there's no reason for me to stay either. Should I get young James to book us a flight?"

"No!" Shaughnessy said emphatically. "I'll do it myself. The less anybody knows about what we're doing the better. Everybody's into intrigue here. If we go up to the room together, they'll think we're up to something. And, of course, we are. I'll make the calls; you go to the gym. Excuse me, 'The Leisure Center.' Maybe you can find some action in the sauna. Ha! I'll make the calls. When can you leave?"

"Anytime. In 10 minutes, if that's necessary. You pick the time."

"We'll get the desk to call a car to take us to the airport. Dublin Airport or Belfast Airport, it won't matter. We're about the same distance from either. I'll meet you in the gym."

Joe went to the gym and Shaughnessy went up to the room. The attendant gave Joe a pair of shorts and a tee-shirt that said 'Dunbukulla Leisure Center,' which had a rough drawing of the dolmen on it. Joe went into the locker room to change. He kept his shoes on. He looked a little foolish by American gym standards, but what did these greenhorns know, he thought.

He first did a few turns on a Nautilus machine. He used to pride himself on his chest. So he worked on the wing-like machine that expanded the chest. Three sets were what he remembered he used to do. Seventy pounds seemed reasonable, and it was. Shaughnessy still hadn't come, so Joe got on the bike to pedal off some weight. He'd do that until Shaughnessy came for him, he thought. After a half hour Shaughnessy still hadn't arrived. Joe went to the locker room and took off his gym clothes. Then, wrapped in a towel, he entered the steam room. It was not a sauna; it was steamy in there. He could see nothing.

However, he sensed that he was not alone. After a bit, after he'd relaxed, he felt a hand on his left leg and heard a cough from across the room.

What's this, an orgy? I'm game, he thought. He put his hand over the hand on his thigh and turned toward its owner.

"Dino is here. He wants to see you," Lorenzo whispered softly.

Just then Shaughnessy opened the door to the steam room. "Joe, are you in there? Come out!"

Joe did come out, even though he both did and didn't want to hear more. He also wanted to feel more or be felt more. He followed Shaughnessy into the locker room and began to change his clothes.

"Are you o.k? You look like you just saw a ghost. Did I break something up in the vapors? Were you about to get lucky? You can go back if you want, but we have a plane in an hour and a half from Dublin. It stops in New York and we have to change to a shuttle for Boston. We'll be home at eight thirty tomorrow. I packed your bag. You can check the room if you like. Maybe I left some of your lingerie."

Joe wondered if he should tell Shaughnessy what just happened in the steam. *No, it can wait. I'll tell him on the way to the airport. I'm too flustered now. And we have to leave. We're getting out of here, thank God.*

"Did you arrange for a car? Joe asked.

"Young James himself is going to drive us. I gave him a hundred Euros and he gets to stop in Dublin on the way back. He's eighteen; he knows a good time when he sees it," Shaughnessy said with a leer. "That Tim Ronayne is very resourceful. Not only does he run this place but also he owns the local livery service. All the good-looking local boys are drivers. I saw the photos. You get your pick. It's like a hooker service."

"Is that what took you so long to come get me?" Joe asked.

"No, I was busy," Shaughnessy replied. "There was another Lorenzo Randozza and Peter Lavin sighting. I had to check that out. I saw them on their way to the Dolmen from the room. I followed but couldn't find them and we don't have time for a search. When I came back to the hotel the Flynns were checking out. The poor Captain had a bun on, but the mother-in-law was holding him up as Laura paid the bill. They didn't even acknowledge me—after all we've been through."

Joe went up to the room. Lying on his bed were two teddy bears. They were face to face, as if kissing. The darker bear had its arms wrapped around a white Polar bear, his right hand on the bum of the white bear while the white bear held the dark one's face.

Joe smiled and nodded his head slowly, as if to say, "Dino, you're too much." He leaned over the bed and placed the Polar bear so that it sat on the dark bear, which was lying on its back.

Joe then sat down at the little desk and wrote something on hotel stationery. He put it in an envelope, also hotel stationery, wrote on the envelope, sealed it, put the whole thing in another envelope, wrote on that and sealed the second envelope. He put the packet in his inside jacket pocket. Then Joe got up walked to the door, looked back at the two bears with a smile, closed the door and walked down the corridor.

When he returned to the front hall Joe left the packet with the two envelopes at the front desk. It was addressed to Peter Lavin.

"What's that you're leaving at the desk?" asked Shaughnessy, who was waiting with the bags.

"It's a tip for the maids," Joe lied.

32 An Impromptu Vestry

Paddo and Tim stood before Professor Reouven Seder, who was seated behind a small, carved desk in his dark, book-lined office at a corner of the Cloisters, just below the Langon Chapel and the West Terrace, overlooking the Hudson. Professor Seder was the world's leading authority on Illuminated Manuscripts. Born in Berlin and trained in Paris, he had spent a lot of time at Trinity College in Dublin with *The Book of Kells* and *The Book of Durham*. He'd also been in residence at Cambridge and was familiar with the *Lindisfarne Gospels* and *The Book of Durrow*, and other early illuminated manuscripts. He'd examined each of the great Irish books and published many treatises and articles about them.

In 1940 he left Paris, just before the Nazi invasion, for Dublin. He alternated between Trinity and Cambridge for many years thereafter. More recently, in the late sixties, the Cloisters had given him an office in return for his curating its manuscripts while he taught in the Curatorship program at N.Y.U. Professor Seder was Paddo Barmerian's mentor; he was the one person whose judgment Paddo trusted more than his own. That wasn't vanity; it was good judgment.

Professor Seder was bald with a healthy rim of white hair and a kindly face. His eyebrows were bushy and his eyes sky blue, over which he was wearing half glasses, reading glasses. He almost looked Irish.

"How can I help you, Padraig?" Professor Seder asked. The Professor loved Paddo's Irish name and always called him by it.

"My friend Tim Ronayne has something to show you," Paddo said.

Tim nodded in a bow of sorts.

"We would like you to verify it, if you can," Paddo continued. "I think that it's the most important discovery in our field in our time, but of course, I wouldn't dare to presume on your judgment."

"You're a good boy, Padraig, and a fine scholar. You're probably correct. Let me see what you have."

Tim took off the jacket of his navy suit, turned it inside out and began to unzip the silk linings. First the right sleeve, then the left and finally the two sides of the back on either side of the vent. The zippers were tiny, like those used in a lady's evening bag.

The eight pieces of 'The Page' fell on the desk. Tim arranged them in the order he presumed was correct. He had studied one year of Latin before having to leave the Christian Brothers in Dundalk to go to work in the pre-Celtic Tiger Dublin of 1968.

The Professor said nothing, but stood up, all five feet four inches of him, came over to Tim and Paddo's side of the desk, and leaned over the puzzle Tim had put together. After a minute or so he looked up at Tim, smiled mischievously and then turned over the third piece down on the right. After a few more minutes he turned over the whole thing, piece by piece, beginning on the top left, speaking softly the text he was reading. When he came to the end of the page on the *recto* side he fell back into a chair and rubbed his eyes, but said nothing. He returned to his side of the desk, pulled open a side drawer and took out a tape measure that measured both inches and centimeters. He readjusted the page and measured it, the width first and then the length. He sat down again, this time in his own chair.

Finally he said, "As you probably know, this is a missing page of *The Book of Kells*, the Gospel of Mark, Chapter Six, lines 34 through 47, pages 148 *recto* and 148 *verso* specifically. The pages you have pre-date the gift of the Book to Trinity College by Henry Jones, the Bishop of Meath in 1665. Your page is a duplicate of a page that is in the Trinity Kells. There is at least one other duplicate page in the Trinity Book. Your page looks more like it was written by one of the original scriveners than does the page at Trinity. I've always had vague doubts about the Trinity page 148. Your page looks more like Hand B than the Trinity page. That's the name we've given to one of the scriveners of this beautiful book," the Professor said as he nodded to Tim Ronayne, as if Tim were a new student.

"What a shame that we can't give them a better name than letters of the alphabet. But they're in heaven, I'm sure and they know their own worth. This page has not been mutilated; it was not cut to a uniform size and gilded at the edges as was done to the Trinity pages in the mid-nineteenth century in preparation for the visit of Queen Victoria and Prince Albert. Your page also does not have the numbering that was added to the Trinity copy and does not have any of the marginalia of the Second Millenium. Gerald Plunkett, that peculiar annotator, never put his hand to this page. The page is probably the original size. The writing is on vellum that the monks of Iona prepared in the eighth century. They then took the book to Kells in 807 A.D. You are right, my good and faithful student, Padraig. It is a very important discovery, maybe the most important since the discovery of the pages now at Trinity.

"Of course, we should do chemical tests on it, on the inks, paints and vellum, but I have no doubts as to its validity. I regret that it is in so many pieces, but that is not fatal. As you know there are a lot of patches in *The Book of Kells* and perhaps the reason for its present condition justifies the cutting.

"Will you tell me how you obtained it, Mister Timothy Ronayne."

Tim very beautifully told the story of the Fireboys and the burning of the Big House at Dunbukulla as well as the reasons for 'The Page's' seizure. Tim ended by saying, "I'm sorry we cut it up, but that was the only way we had to preserve it. If any one person had the whole page, he probably would have been found out. As it was, we all were lucky and nobody else captured any of it—for long."

Tim said "we," but of course Tim himself hadn't cut up the Page. However, his identification, and the identification of today's Fireboys with their great grandfathers who did, was so strong that you would think that these contemporary Fireboys had cut it up themselves.

Professor Seder understood that and said with a kindly smile, "The division of 'The Page,' under the circumstances you describe, adds patina, Mister Ronayne, the patina of the Irish suffering during the Famine." Professor Seder understood the legacy of history. "'The Page's' scars are well earned. Thank you for giving me the privilege of examining this treasure. I don't know your intentions for it and I'm not a lawyer, but I would say that no one else has a better claim to 'The Page,' as you call it, than you and your people. What are your intentions for it?"

Tim replied, "We don't want 'The Page' to go to Trinity College. We want it to stay in America. And we don't want it to go to the Church. I'll be candid with you, Professor Seder, it's a dangerous game we're playing. There are people trying to get it for the Vatican Library—specifically the Randozza family of Boston.

Tim went on, "Who is entitled to the national treasure of a country? Trinity can keep its pages. This piece never belonged to Trinity or anybody else, we would maintain. It didn't belong to the Tiltons just because they had their hands on it in 1846. Someone of their bleeding ancestors probably stole it from Kells itself or else they bought it from a traitorous profiteer."

"Or maybe a poor starving farmer, who found it in a bog," interjected Paddo Barmerian.

Tim continued, ignoring Paddo, "It is now ours and we want to use it for the betterment of our people—the people of Ballyfirglin and Dundalk. As I understand the law, it's contraband—like flotsam and jetsam, things that float up on the beach—and nobody can claim ownership of it. Because it's contraband if those who are pursuing us on behalf of the Vatican Library get their hands on it, they're entitled to it more than we are. In this case possession is not just 90%, but 100%, of the Law. So we have to be very careful and can't let it out of our sight. I don't think that we can leave it with you for analysis at this time."

"Ah, that explains my next appointment. A Bishop Rocco Randozza and his mother wish my opinion on a manuscript fragment." Professor Seder then pulled an ebony box about 6"x12" out of his desk drawer, the same drawer that contained the tape measure. "They even told me that they want to donate it to the Vatican Library. Because of their noble purpose I agreed to see them. Besides, who turns down a bishop? They're supposed to arrive soon; they may even be here. Do you know them?"

"Yes, I know them. I am related to them in fact. My sister Fionna, God rest her soul, was married to Vito Randozza, another son of Mrs. Randozza, a brother of the bishop. And more important, they know me," Tim said, scooping the fragments up off the table and reinserting them into his jacket linings. "We hoped to have 'The Page' authenticated and then to sell it to a group of Irish Americans. I've already talked to people here and in Boston and Chicago. There's an awful lot of Irish American money around. Why, look at your New York Irish History Roundtable and the Irish Institute. Then there is the Ireland Fund and the Eire Society; to say nothing of The Charitable Irish in Boston. There's more money in the West and lots of interest. Now how can I get out of here without being seen by His Excellency, Rocco, the Bishop of Hartford and his sainted mother, Giuseppina?"

"They sent me this," the Professor said, opening the box revealing Maeve's fake in all its glory. "At first I thought it was the real thing, actually the third piece down that I just turned over on your page. However, it soon became apparent that it was a fake. The fish appears to be painted with blue and green eye shadow, good French eye shadow, and the black ink runs underneath the cheap fixative. It looks like Sumi ink to me and to Professor Karamitsu, who teaches Japanese Art with me at N.Y.U. Do you know anything about this, Mr. Timothy Ronayne? And what will I tell them when they arrive in this office at 11:30?"

"Stall them! Tell them you have to do more tests! Anything! Just give us a chance to get 'The Page' sold. I'm going to see a lawyer called John Quinn right now. He's helped a lot of Irish artists and writers. His mother was a cousin of my grandmother's. He says that he can meet our price if we have your validation. He's very connected. Can I tell him that you vouch for 'The Page'?"

"All of us who are interested in things Irish are indebted to Mr. John Quinn. He is the greatest patron of the Arts Ireland has seen since Columkille himself. You can tell him that I believe 'The Page' is part of the original *Book of Kells*. I will call him today and tell him myself, cryptically of course, so as not to reveal your secrets."

Paddo Barmerian had remained silent, but now he spoke up. "I'll go with you, Tim. I'll talk to this lawyer. This office is on the first floor and we can go out the side window into the gardens and then around to the garage. Is Hanrahan still with you, Professor Seder?"

"Yes, Hanrahan is still here, although the silly United States government wants to deport him back to Monserrat. You will find him in the garage. My car is there as well. He now drives me everywhere. He will take you back downtown to Mr. Quinn. You will enjoy Hanrahan, Mr. Timothy Ronayne. He talks just like you. If I closed my eyes while listening to you I would think the speaker is Hanrahan."

"My Aunt Rose was a sister of Mercy on Monserrat," Tim said. "She taught there for fifty years. I know about the Irish connection. She would weep at their suffering these days. Thank God, there are no volcanoes in Ireland." Tim added, "Be careful with the Bishop and especially with the mother. Giuseppina is smarter than all of them—and more ambitious. She wants to make Rocco a cardinal, and probably the Pope. Thank you for your kindness and your wisdom. Although I was certain we had a treasure, my heart leapt at your opinion. We are very grateful." And then, quite uncharacteristically for an Irish man, Tim embraced Professor Seder.

"I know how to dissemble when I have to. I wouldn't have lived this long on either side of the Atlantic without some dissembling," Professor Seder said with a conspiratorial smile. "I'm an old man and can't give an opinion yet. I can't work as fast as I used to. I'll tell them that. Before I see them, I'll call John Quinn."

◊ ◊ ◊

Paddo introduced Tim to Michael Hanrahan. Professor Seder was right. They sounded like brothers, albeit Hanrahan was black as coal and Tim as pale as milk. "Can you take us to Saint Patrick's Cathedral, Mr. Hanrahan?" Tim asked.

Paddo looked inquisitive, but said nothing. He thought they were going to Wall Street; that's where the lawyers were. The ride downtown was mostly small talk between Paddo and Hanrahan until Tim mentioned his Aunt Rose, Sister Mary Aquinas, in religious life.

"She was my third grade teacher, the dearest woman in the world. I never learned arithmetic because she let me read *The Lives of the Irish Saints* instead of learning multiplication. To this day I remember Saint Brigid walking across the Irish Sea in a long white nightgown. There was a photograph of her in the book. I remember she had black hair in a Dutch cut. I dream about her and hope she will come back and restore Monserrat—or let me stay here," Hanrahan said.

Hanrahan let them off at Saint Patrick's on Fifth Avenue, right at the steps leading up to the front doors, where the Cardinal and his crew stood watching the Parade every Saint Patrick's Day. There was no cardinal today and Tim was glad for that. But there was

Dino Randozza leaning against the left side of the middle door frame, smoking a cigarette, like a character in an Italian movie waiting for his long suffering *signora* to come out of Mass, so that she could go home and cook for him. Dino was looking up Fifth Avenue, in the opposite direction, but Tim could not be sure that Dino hadn't seen them.

Tim grabbed Paddo, put him on his right, between himself and Dino 30 feet away, and then walked briskly to 51st Street. At the corner of the Olympic Towers on the other side of 51st, Tim muttered, "Those bastards are everywhere." He then pulled Paddo down East 51st. Tim looked back occasionally. Although there were a lot of people on the street in the middle of the day, nobody seemed to be following them.

For a big guy, Paddo was light on his feet. He responded to Tim's tuggings and pullings gracefully and appropriately, even though he had no specific idea why they were occurring. He presumed, correctly, that the "bastards" were the Randozzas, or their coterie.

On East 51st Street, Tim pulled Paddo into a doorway just before Hamburger Heaven. Tim put his head out, looked up and down the street, and then stuck a key in the door to open it. At the elevator Tim looked back to the door to the street. No one had come through the door—*yet*, he thought. They went up to the fifth floor. Tim searched around, returned and said, "We have the wrong floor. They walked down a flight. Tim opened what looked like a service door and then walked to another door of what appeared to be the front apartment and opened that with two keys.

The door opened into a bright living room with a built-in banquette on the far wall. On the right were French doors and a protective grate leading to a terrace that looked across to the side of the beautiful 19th-century Gothic Saint Patrick's, Archbishop Hughes' triumph.

"It's like a living Monet," Paddo said breathlessly, walking across the terrace to the edge nearest the street.

Tim grabbed him, pulled him back and said, "Come back here,

you big lug. They can see you from the street. Ph.D or not, don't be so thick."

Of course, Tim then went to the edge of the terrace himself. After a few seconds Paddo joined him and they leaned on the wall overlooking the street, elbows touching.

The phone rang. Tim jumped. "Don't answer it," he said needlessly to Paddo. They waited for the message. A man's voice said, "Hello, darlings. This is Sheila, your New York concierge. Is everything in order? There's orange juice and milk in the fridge and coffee in the freezer. The tea, Bewleys of course, is in a canister next to the stove. Your dresses are on the bed. Tim, I also brought you shoes. Your bags are on the other side of the bed. Don't do anything naughty in the shadow of the Cathedral. *Ciao*! Oh, am I allowed to talk Italian? Bye, bye. Love, Ms Sheila Callahan." There was an emphasis on the 'Ms.'

Tim relaxed and Paddo smiled. Paddo wondered when he should tell Tim that he wasn't gay. He liked the attention these guys were giving him but he wasn't keen on satisfying their expectation. He'd better tell Tim sooner rather than later if they were going to sleep here because there was only one bed in this place.

While Paddo was in the living room pondering this delicate diplomatic problem the phone rang again. Tim was in the tiny kitchen nearby. They both stopped dead waiting for the message.

"I received a call from our mutual friend, the colorful professor on Madison Avenue, and another from the more scholarly Professor further uptown. In a half hour I'll meet you in the third confessional box on the left—the one that says 'Armenian and Greek.' I'll be on your right side. Dress accordingly and bring the paper. The purple stole will be on a hook inside the box."

Neither of them recognized the rich deep voice, but Tim knew who it was and smiled. It was John Quinn making the call Tim had been waiting for since they started this adventure.

"We'd better get dressed now, Paddo," Tim said quietly.

There were indeed two cassocks on the bed and the smaller one did have purple piping, with a purple sash, denoting its wearer as a monsignor, a papal chaplain. They were good cassocks, too, from two different Roman shops near the Pantheon. One was from the Fratri Fucini and the other, the monsignor's, from Gammarelli, the ecclesiastical tailors to the popes. Donal must be well connected. There were Roman collars too, and birettas. The monsignor's biretta had a purple pompom. The cassocks fit perfectly. Donal had worked at Brooks Brothers while going to graduate school and often identified men by their size. He would say, "John Schmitt, 48 long, and proportional—if you know what I mean," for example. He could pick a man's suit size from 20 feet and was proud of this gift.

Paddo put his cassock on first; he looked very somber, like a Patriarch of the Eastern Rite, which he could have been if things had gone differently. Tim on the other hand looked like he should be in a Bing Crosby movie, the benevolent pastor of a rich, suburban parish—in Weston, Massachusetts, perhaps. The purple piping brought up his color. "We should leave the birettas. No one wears them these days. And we shouldn't go across until the last minute. You've got it, the third confessional box down. Would you like a cup of tea?"

"No thanks, it'll just make me pee." Paddo said.

They both laughed. "What do you think this guy does—the guy who has this apartment?" Tim said, looking around the bedroom.

"I think he teaches Geography of the Mediterranean," Paddo said.

"Why do you think that?" Tim asked, leaning down to look at the photos taped to the side of the file cabinet. "Holy Jesus, there's Joe Lyons, in the seventies, about the time I met him. And he's on Inishmora. I recognize Dun Aengus. And there's another lad here, my cousin Neil. This looks like a fancy business photo. Neil's been quite successful. What the hell are they doing here?"

"Well, whatever he does for a living he gets around," Paddo said. "We may never know. Donal calls him 'Fionna.' We could snoop, but the less we know the better. We'll ask Joe when we see him next. We'd better get going, Tim. It's been about 25 minutes since the call."

Tim took one last look over the terrace wall down to the street. "We'll cross right here on 51st and walk up to the first open door in front of the church. I'll go in the third box and you wait in the pew outside. Watch out for any strange stuff. The man who's meeting us is tall, Irish looking and bald with a rim of black hair, probably dyed these days. He's getting old but still handsome. He'll be dressed like an old-fashioned lawyer, maybe even a velvet collar on the coat. Let him in the box on the right side. If anyone else tries to get in, cut him or her off and come in on the right side yourself. O.K.? Knock four times and I'll know that it's you."

Tim then unzipped the linings of his jacket and stuffed the eight eighths into his cassock pockets.

"Let's go, lad" he said. "Look priestly—whatever that means these days."

33 Bumpy Business at Saint Patrick's

Their route was clear until they got to the front steps. A group of what appeared to be Mexican pilgrims was climbing the stairs on their knees blocking a quick entry into the Cathedral. From the first step up the stairs Tim saw Dino again, this time on the side of the main doorway opposite where he'd been before, looking searchingly in the other direction, uptown. Tim tried to slip by the penitents with his head down so that Dino wouldn't see him; Paddo followed behind. Just as Dino, who had a thing for the Celtic Monsignori, you may recall, began to turn his head towards Tim, a very large nun, in the old habit of the Sisters of Notre Dame de Namur, stepped alongside Tim blocking Dino's view. *The Grace of God*, Tim thought.

The nun said loudly in her best Boston accent, "Do they think they're at Guadalupe, Monsignor? They should get up off their knees. This is the United States of America. There's no need for that stuff here. Jesus will love them on their feet. Don't you agree, Monsignor?"

By this time Tim was inside the door and Paddo right behind. The nun nodded to Tim, then turned right to march proudly down the center aisle, as befit a woman of her dignity and station. "Monsignor" Tim Ronayne and "Father" Padraig Barmerian proceeded down the left side aisle to the third confessional box. It had a sign above that said, "Armenian and Greek" in English and presumably the same thing below in the languages themselves. It was a handsome sign but looked rather new for all its ancient references.

Tim opened the screened and curtained door and went into the center section of the confessional, like he owned it, like he was indeed a priest multilingual in ancient tongues. As he entered he thought *what will I do if a Greek or Armenian comes in? I could call for Paddo to absolve the Armenian, I suppose.* Tim put on the purple stole which was hanging on a hook to the right of the door and checked his watch. Just as he sat down he heard Paddo speaking loudly in a foreign language. A woman talked back, also in a foreign language. She was not happy; that was clear. Silence. Then there were four knocks on the left hand side of the box.

Tim opened the screen and said, "Yes, my son."

"Some old Armenian lady in a mantilla worn like a veil tried to get in this side. I held her back. She called me a few bad names in Armenian—something to do with sheep. She's outside waiting now. I'm trying to save this side for our guest."

"Good job Paddo, but the right side from my, the priest's, point of view, is the other side. That's the side we have to keep clear. She may just slip in there. She may be there now. I don't know a word of Armenian. What should I do?" Tim asked.

"Punt, Tim!"

"What?"

"Punt! It's an American football expression. Do whatever comes up. If there's a real serious problem, fall out the door. Open the other screen now. Maybe our man is there."

Tim paused and thought for a bit before doing so. But at last he did.

A man's voice said in Irish, "It's a good thing you know your right from your left." Then in English, "That bruiser almost took the head off the poor old lady. This screen lifts up, and I'll take the prize. There are four of New York's finest nearby waiting to escort me out, and an armored limo outside waiting for the treasure. We will meet your price and have the money in your account at the Hibernian Bank in two days. Here's a box. I'm taking 'The Page' to the New York Public Library. It'll be safe there. We'll make the announcement tomorrow at 11:00 a.m. You should be there."

Tim lifted the screen. He recognized John Quinn from his pictures. Quinn was wearing a black Chesterfield coat with a velvet collar. The box was wooden, about 9"x12". It was lined in green velvet. There were initials on the top, "J.L.L."

Tim reached in his pockets and took out the pieces. He counted them and began to put them in the box. He stopped *en route* and kissed the pile of pieces; then he put all eight of them in the box. He'd thought about keeping one or two, but he realized that he now had to let go, to have faith in other people. There were tears in his eyes. So much suffering was written on those eight scraps of vellum.

John Quinn got up from his knees and pulled the screen down from the penitent's side of the confessional. As he did so he said, "Leave with me, Tim Ronayne. You'll see me safely to the car."

Tim did leave the center of the confessional after hanging the purple stole back on its hook near the door.

There was a lot going on in Saint Patrick's that afternoon—not only the Mexican penitents and this Irish intrigue. A wedding had ended at the main altar in the front of the church; the bride and groom were leaving the church down the center aisle followed by the guests. It was a small wedding. The bride did not wear white, although she did have a little chiffon veil on her hat covering her eyes. The groom appeared older. He had silver hair, Tim could see from behind. *Probably a second marriage*, thought Tim, without paying too much attention. The bride was in a beautiful royal blue dress. That much Tim could discern as he adjusted his eyes to the dim light of the Cathedral from the dark of the box and tried to follow John Quinn's lead.

Four burly men, two of them in dark suits, the other two in cassocks and Roman collars, moved in around John Quinn as he crossed the Cathedral halfway. Tim couldn't figure out where they came from. *I hope they're on our side,* Tim thought.

John Quinn crossed over to the center aisle just as the newlyweds and their party approached the juncture. He waited for them to proceed, giving a courtly half bow. Tim was behind. Paddo was still in his pew. The old Armenian lady was still berating Paddo, tugging at his cassock and muttering at him in Armenian, presumably. Paddo tried to ignore her. Finally, he got up and followed Tim.

The wedding party included a mitered bishop in a white roman chasuble and the big nun who had engaged Tim outside on the steps. She winked at Tim as she passed by.

It looked like there was going to be a collision. The Mexican penitents were moving very slowly down the center aisle, still on their knees.

The big nun stepped around the newlyweds and cleared a path—with her right foot—through the penitents. The wedding party bridged the gap. Tim kept his eyes on John Quinn and the box in John Quinn's arms.

All of a sudden he heard a woman's voice, "Timmy Ronayne, what are you doing here? And what are you doing in that getup?"

Josie Lavin, in a bright green silk suit, got right up next to him and whispered not so softly, "This isn't some IRA rebel thing, is it? I shouldn't ask. Forget that I did. We're here for Giuseppina's wedding to the Count. Bishop Rocco married them. Isn't it wonderful! She's now a countess. And I was one of the witnesses. She bought me this beautiful, green suit for the occasion. Your neice Maureen was another witness. Here she is. We finally got her out of black. Isn't that Cerulean blue dress lovely on her? Say hello to your Uncle Tim, Maureen." And then in an Irish whisper she added, "And don't ask about his dress. It's some IRA thing, I'm sure."

"Hello, Uncle Tim. You're handsome in your cassock. Is it a delayed vocation you've had? Judging from the purple piping and sash, you've certainly moved quickly up the ranks," Maureen said, just barely concealing a smile.

Tim and John Quinn's retinue were processing up the center aisle right behind the wedding party, the penitents having retreated into side pews at the urging of Sister Mary Turpentine's foot.

"Isn't that John Quinn, Esquire, you're following, Tim?" Josie said. "He's very handsome. I've only seen him in pictures. He's been such a benefactor to the Irish, and a patron of the Arts, and not just Irish Art. God bless him! Will you introduce me to him, please, Tim? He's so good looking! Why hasn't he ever married?"

"I'll try to, Josie. I'll try," Tim replied, trying to keep an eye on the box John Quinn, Esquire, held tight to his chest.

Maureen wore a big grin. What with her mob uncles, her memories of her father, and her grandmother Giuseppina, she was well accustomed to intrigue, even intrigue she would never discover the purpose of. It was unusual to see it on the Irish side, however, and that amused her, that and Josie's husband hunting in the middle of it all.

From the door of the Catheral, after a look back at Tim, who was captured by Josie, John Quinn and his bruisers went to the left, to 52d Street, and jumped into a long, black limousine which promptly took off.

Josie said, "The wedding party is at the Plaza. Please come. You're part of the family. But you better get out of that cassock and collar. You'll look ridiculous. I have to go now. Toodle loo."

Tim said to Paddo, who had ditched the old Armenian lady by sending her into the Haitian confessional, "She's right. Let's go change at least." And they headed to the apartment on 51st Street to change their clothes. Tim noticed that Dino was no longer lurking at the doorway of Saint Patrick's. Perhaps he'd gone off to his mother's wedding party, Tim conjectured.

Tim and Paddo returned to the terrace apartment on East 51st Street. This time they got off on the right floor—the fourth—and went through the unmarked door to their right. At the apartment door Tim reached into the soutane and retrieved his keys. There was loud classical music coming from within. Tim opened the door.

"Sweeet Jesus! What's this?" Tim shouted. The place was a mess. Somebody had ripped it apart. *They're too late to find "The Page,"* thought Tim as he stepped further into the living room.

The French doors to the terrace, and to Saint Patrick's Cathedral beyond, were wide open. The wind blew the sheer curtains into the apartment. The music was Beethoven's Ninth, Leonard Bernstein's Berlin recording. It blasted out onto the terrace, bounced across to the crenellated wall of St. Patrick's, and echoed back to this apartment and the street below.

Then there was the real surprise. In the bedroom, to the left off the livingroom, Joe Lyons and Dino Randozza were lying naked in the bed. Their hairy chests exposed above the duvet. Joe's right hand and Dino's left hand were handcuffed to each other on top of the blanket. Each had a big smile on his face.

"Did you make the delivery, Timmy?" Joe shouted over the music.

After turning down the CD player Tim Ronayne said that he did.

Joe Lyons said, "I ditched Sergeant Detective Shaughnessy at Kennedy Airport this morning; I stole his handcuffs. I've kept Dino distracted for the last half hour. Ha! It's the least I could do for 'The Page.' Dino made the mess. He was convinced 'The Page' was still here. I told him it was long gone. I guess he finally believed me." Joe smiled contentedly.

Joe added wistfully, "You know. I've been here before—a long time ago. Some things never change. Your real clothes are on the other side of the bed. If you find the key to these cuffs, don't tell anyone—at least not for a couple of hours. We won! Dino won't do us any harm now. Isn't that right Dino?"

Dino Randozza, with a small smile, nodded assent and then said, "Timmy, I've always liked the Irish monsignori. Keep the cassock on. Do you have another one for Joe?"

About the Author

Dermot Meagher comes from a very proud Irish American family. Most of his ancestors came over as a result of the terrible famines in Ireland in 1846, 1847 and 1848. His ancestors on his father's side were Fenians, opposing the British occupation of Ireland.

Unlike "Joe Lyons," the hero of this book, Dermot is one of six children. He was raised in Worcester, Massachusetts, although his family has strong Newport and Jamestown, Rhode Island, connections.

For seventeen years Dermot Meagher was a judge of the Boston Municipal Court, the oldest trial court in Massachusetts. Before that he was an assistant district attorney, a bail reformer, a court reformer and he taught Criminal Law and Procedure to police officers. He also had a private law practice at various times. When he was appointed in 1989 he was the first openly gay judge in Massachusetts. He has been active in a number of gay political and social organizations, including the Gay and Lesbian Advocates and Defenders (GLAD), the Massachusetts Lesbian and Gay Bar Association and the Aids Action Committee.

He is the author of *Judge Sentences: Tales from the Bench* and co-author with Robert Coles, M.D. and Joseph Brenner M.D. of *Drugs and Youth*.

Dermot Meagher graduated from Harvard College, Boston College Law School, The Kennedy School of Government and was a Fellow at the Harvard Law School Center for Criminal Justice.

He is also an artist and shows his drawings, paintings and prints at the Schoolhouse Gallery in Provincetown as well as other venues in New England and Florida.

Praise for Dermot Meagher's
Judge Sentences: Tales from the Bench

Dermot Meagher has given us a great read. The Daumier-like scenes he paints in his courtroom are fabulous, rendered with wit and compassion. Like Doritos, you can't consume just one. Nothing feels forced in this book. The man writes like a dream.
Sam Allis, *Boston Globe*

Meagher's writing is insightful and compassionate; the muscular prose laced with an attractive self-deprecatory wit. Keenly and sympathetically observed, the characters and their stories, like life in the courts, are never tidy, frequently carrying a disquieting, thought-provoking edge. An excellent, absorbing read.
Lavanya Sankaran, author of *The Red Carpet*

Irish wit and a painter's eye for the human comedy (of every social class) that washes up in the lower courts of Boston. This is what it feels like to be a judge—this judge, Dermot Meagher, who ends up being the best character in a book filled with people you won't forget. Hilarious, one-of-a-kind and deeply intelligent.
  Andrew Holleran, author of *Dancer from the Dancer, Nights in Aruba* and *Grief*

The stories in *Judge Sentences* are short, each involving a case or character, observed from the point of view of the judge; not the cartoon version of judges seen on daytime television and crime shows but a workaday judge in the daily grind of a big urban court system. Again and again in these stories one gets the sense of a deeply humane man trying to thread the law through the needle of human misery. The judge is empathic but not naïve. He is worldly but he is never cynical—he is what used to be called *civilized*. I loved the stories and I am inspired by Judge Meagher, as a lawyer and as a human being.
  Michael Nava, novelist and attorney

Made in the USA
Charleston, SC
21 January 2012